Until You

JEANNIE MOON

Teresa!
Love is the
answer!
xo
Jeannie
Moon

TULE
PUBLISHING

DEDICATION

This book is dedicated to all the moms out there who love unconditionally, sacrifice endlessly, and risk everything for their children.

ACKNOWLEDGEMENTS

Until You is a book that's been a long time in the making. I began writing it over ten years ago as a flash fiction challenge. The scene I wrote initially evolved into a very complex and beautiful love story between two people who didn't know how much they needed each other.

And isn't that often the way?

I didn't know what my story needed until it landed in the very capable hands of Kelly Hunter and Jane Porter at Tule Publishing. Jane has created a haven for writers at Tule; a place where we can stretch our wings, and try new things. I will be forever grateful that she welcomed me into this community of artists, believed in my vision for this book, and gave it a home.

My editor, Kelly Hunter, has a gift for finding the heart of a book and helping a writer exploit all that is pure and beautiful in the story. Kate and David's journey became something truly special under Kelly's guiding hand. It's a wonderful feeling for an author when her editor truly "gets" a book. Thank you, Kelly, for all you've given *Until You*, and to me in the process.

So, it takes a village, right?

Many thanks to my writing sisters at Tule for all your wisdom, and special thanks to my #Fab4 girls, Jennifer Gracen, Patty Blount and Jolyse Barnett. May we have long careers and continue to talk each other off those ledges. To my plotting buddies, Myra Platt, Liz Slawinski, Lisa Guilfoil, and Maggie Van Well—thank you, girls. Love you tons.

Big hugs to CTRWA, you rock; extra love to some of the best beta readers ever, Donna DeLuca, Danielle Giambrone, Jennifer Carberry and Clara Antunes.

Thank you to everyone at Tule, especially Meghan Farrell and Lindsey Stover, who make everything right in this writer's world. Lee Hyat designs the most beautiful covers and she outdid herself with the one for this book. Endless thanks go out to BookSparks PR for getting the word out, and to my agent Stephany Evans for her friendship and guidance.

My street team, The Moonpies, are the absolute best people in Romancelandia. You have no idea how much I appreciate each and every one of you. Thank you, ladies.

Last but not least, I couldn't do this job, and love it the way I do, without the support of my family. I'm truly blessed.

And to you, my dear reader friends, you make this fun. Thank you for joining me on this journey and I hope you enjoyed *Until You*. I'd love to hear what you think, so feel free to drop me a line through my website,

www.jeanniemoon.com.

Chapter 1

October

KATE SPENT HER fortieth birthday in a hotel bar overlooking the Pacific Ocean, celebrating the milestone with a bottle of red wine and her divorce papers. Fiddling with the stem of the wine glass, she stared at the bulky package. The documents had arrived right before she'd left on her trip to California, and for the life of her, Kate didn't know why she'd brought them with her. Maybe she needed a dose of reality. Maybe she needed to work up a good mad. Maybe she was using them as an excuse to feel sorry for herself. It really didn't matter.

Her life was changing faster than she could keep up.

The events of the past ten months were a blur. Her ex-husband was going on a trip as well, taking his fiancée to Europe. Richard's paramour was a thirty-five-year-old adjunct English professor and sometimes writer who sprinkled her casual conversations liberally with academic drivel and spouted pretense wherever she went.

The woman pushed every one of Kate's buttons. Tall and

exotic looking, Marie professed to be a literary novelist. What bullshit. Kate was the novelist. Kate was the one who, surprisingly, had over two hundred and fifty people show up for her last book signing. Though Marie what's-her-name did do the whole intellectual artist thing well. Always in black and unimpressed by the world around her, the woman was a cliché. She walked the walk and talked the talk, but who the hell read her books?

Kate swirled the last of the wine in her glass and took a deep breath. Cliché or not, the "other woman" had forced Kate to see what a mess she'd allowed her life to become. A million best sellers wouldn't fix that.

Biting her fingernail, Kate poured the last few drops of wine into her glass. *Where did the bottle go?* An expensive bottle of Shiraz was gone and she didn't even feel like she had a good buzz. Boy, that sucked. She wanted to get drunk on her birthday and couldn't even do that right.

Glancing at her watch, she saw she'd been sitting on the deck, outside the bar, for over four hours. That would explain why the wine hadn't done any good. If she'd stayed inside the bar, she would have downed the bottle more quickly, but instead she lost herself in the seventy-five degree sunshine and the cool breeze off the ocean. There were people walking on the beach and a few wet-suit clad surfers in the grey-green water, and she let the scene play around in her mind. There were stories here, but then again, there were stories every-where.

Opening her bag, she placed the leather-bound journal on the table and started to jot down ideas. She wrote notes about what she experienced, taking in the sights and sounds and smells. This would be a great place to set down one of her characters.

Characters. Her editor had been calling, her agent had been calling, and both were asking for chapters from her latest work in progress. Unfortunately, over the last few months, when the divorce started to get ugly, Kate couldn't think about her writing. She couldn't think of anything except how stupid she'd been.

Her recent attempts to get any words down were a joke. The plot was weak. Her research was shoddy. And the honorable, brave heroine, whom she'd written over the course of the series, became a vengeful shrew, hell-bent on punishing everyone in her path. Oh yeah, her readers would love that. But regardless of the problems Kate was facing, she had to get back to her writing. She had a contract and a career and a reputation to consider.

A lone teardrop blurred the ink on the journal page. It spoke volumes. Professionally, Kate would get a handle on things, but personally, her life was a disaster.

DAVID HAD BEEN watching the woman on the deck for almost half an hour.

Three times he'd started over to talk to her. Once he chickened out, reminding himself he was past the point in his life of having to find a woman in a bar. The second time, he was halfway to her when her cell phone rang. The third time, he'd gone through the open door and was about to take the final few steps toward her when she pulled a book out of her bag and started writing. It was the last time, when he was just a few feet from her, that he caught a whiff of her perfume and got a look at her up close. Brown hair, smooth skin, and she didn't wear much makeup. Not that she needed it. She wasn't flashy, but quietly sexy; from her tailored slacks to the soft blue sweater that allowed just a hint of cleavage to peek out, she was a refined package. Women like her never went for guys like him.

This, of course, was why his buddies had issued the challenge. *Assholes.*

He was about to walk out of the bar and forget the whole shittin' bet when he saw her draw a deep breath, push her sunglasses up onto her head, and wipe at her eyes. She was crying. In most cases that would have been enough to scare him off, but the fact she might need someone changed everything. David went to her, because if nothing else, he saw an opening he could use to his advantage. *Game on.*

Circling her table, he saw an empty bottle and a wine glass. The woman didn't look drunk, but he proceeded cautiously, just in case.

Still moving slowly, David took her in. *Damn, she was pretty.* For the first time he could see her eyes. They were hazel—not quite green, not quite brown, large and surrounded by dark, spiky lashes. She placed her book in her bag and let out a shaky breath. Her hands were steady, her demeanor calm. Obviously upset, but definitely not drunk. When she looked up and caught his gaze, David felt a whole new kind of kick in his chest. Something about this woman, about the way she looked at him, stopped him cold. When she finally broke eye contact, David regained his senses.

"Hi," he said, willing himself to say something. *What the hell was he doing?* "Are you all right?"

Gazing up, her lower lip quivered, but before speaking she

sucked it in and composed herself. "Yes, thank you. I'm fine."

"You don't seem fine." He moved around the table in her direction. *End this. End this.* David's conscience screamed at him. *This is a dick move. Leave her alone.*

"I am. Really." She stood and he saw she was a tiny thing, petite, but with curves in all the right places.

When she started to leave, he almost let her, but his competitive streak got the better of him and he touched her arm. The woman jerked back and David pulled his hand away, realizing he'd crossed a line.

Again, those eyes drilled into him, flustering him, so before he could stop himself, the first thing that came into his head flew out of his mouth. It wasn't clever. It wasn't witty.

He simply got to the point. "Please don't go."

"Who are you?" she asked.

Her voice was clear and soft; she wasn't afraid, but confused. Hell, he was confused. He needed a line. But instead of something smooth and charming, he was bumbling.

"David. David Burke. I've been watching you for a while and I just got up the nerve to talk to you."

The woman stared blankly. David couldn't tell if she was annoyed or disgusted. It didn't matter; neither would get him what he wanted. "You looked upset a few minutes ago. Can I help?"

"I don't need your help." Her jaw was set, her gaze steady. Initially, this woman may have seemed vulnerable, but it was obvious she was no pushover.

"What's your name?" he asked. "There's no harm in telling me that." *Please tell me. Or I'm out a few thousand bucks without even getting up to bat.*

Her mouth curved into half a smile. "Kate Nicholls." She

paused and chewed on her lower lip. "Thanks for your concern, but I'm fine." When she started to walk away again, David took his last shot.

"Would you have dinner with me?" The question shot out before he could stop himself. He wanted a drink and some sex. Dinner would mean he'd have to have a conversation, but he was desperate.

"Oh, I don't think—" A loud crash inside the bar provoked a roar of laughter, and a huge male body stumbled outside and landed on his hands and knees. Her scowl was unmistakable. "I'll be so happy to go home tomorrow."

"Why is that?" He tried to ask the question as innocently as possible, but based on her reaction, he pretty much knew the answer.

"With all the idiot hockey players in and out of this hotel, it's been like living in a frat house."

No surprise there. The guy who'd almost face-planted on the deck was one of his teammates. Kate snarled as the kid belched with enthusiasm. Perfect. Hopefully, the rookie wouldn't talk to him.

"Hey, Padre." *So much for luck.* "How's it goin', man?"

Graves was an asshole. Talk about getting hosed. David was thinking he could toss the son of a bitch into the cold ocean as revenge, but the idiot was so drunk he'd sink like a stone. He turned his attention back to Kate, who nailed him with those gorgeous eyes of hers.

"*Padre?*" she inquired. "You're a priest?"

"No." His answer came out on a growl. "Padre is a nickname."

"Nickname? Let me guess. *You're* a hockey player?"

His eyes settled on his teammate, who was examining the

deck closely for some reason, and then David looked back at Kate. He had nothing to lose at this point. "Will you have dinner with me anyway?"

"You're very nice to ask, but no."

"Please?" He smiled. "I promise I'll be on my best behavior."

"I don't even know you." A grin teased the corners of her mouth and she nodded toward his teammate who was easing his way off the deck. "You could be insane, like your friend over there."

He laughed. "We'll tell the desk clerk that we're leaving together. If they're worried about you, they'll know to find me."

She glanced away, but he waited patiently and almost willed her to look at him. David wanted her to believe he wasn't like his teammates, so he asked again. "Don't make me hang out with that bunch. I'll be scarred for life."

A smile played on her lips and in her eyes. "Okay, dinner." Pausing for a moment to consider him, she took out the notebook and wrote something down.

"What was that?" he asked.

Kate grinned again and looked at him. "A note," she began. "So I remember to find myself a good psychiatrist."

THEY ENDED UP on Highway 1, heading toward Santa Monica. There might have been quicker ways to get there, but the winding drive along the ocean was, by far, the prettiest. Kate had rented a sporty convertible to help her deal with her birthday blues, but she handed the keys over to David. She didn't feel drunk, but she'd consumed an entire bottle of wine by herself, and she was fairly sure she shouldn't get behind the wheel.

Then again, the alcohol must have done something, because she was sitting in a car with a strange man heading to points unknown. It wasn't like her in the least. And it felt great.

Apparently they were headed to a great restaurant he knew on the beach, and after an initial burst of small talk, they settled in for the drive. That gave Kate the opportunity to take him in and convince herself she hadn't fallen into some alcohol induced, midlife delusion. This was too good. She was depressed and alone on her fortieth birthday, a landmark in any woman's life, and out of nowhere came a gorgeous man to whisk her away for dinner on the beach. If she'd written a story like this, her editor would tell her the scenario was just too perfect and readers wouldn't buy it. She would have been right. Kate wasn't sure she bought it herself, but for now, she was going to slip happily into the delusion and enjoy it.

David concentrated on the road, keeping one hand on the wheel and the other hand on the stick shift between them. He looked so *young*. Damn. Couldn't she focus on something else? She turned a little in the bucket seat and gazed at him. His hair was dark brown, almost black, and wavy, the ends of it curling over the collar of his shirt. His eyes, which were now covered by a pair of Ray-Ban aviators, were the same deep brown. At first glance, he looked like someone in town for business, but then Kate noticed the remnants of battle. His nose had a bump, probably from being broken, and his face was etched with tiny scars. One long, thin scar ran from his ear to his chin along his jaw line. She hadn't noticed earlier, but his cheek sported a bruise. This man, who could have passed for an executive, was, in fact, a warrior, and it surprised Kate that the fact thrilled her more than a little.

He glanced at her and smiled when he caught her staring. "What are you looking at?"

She felt the heat rise in her face. "Just enjoying the view."

That was a lie; she was trying to figure out why he looked so familiar. Although, there was no denying he was nice to look at.

He grinned and reddened. She'd embarrassed him? That was unexpected. She'd never have pegged him as the humble type.

"Why were you crying earlier?"

The question took her by surprise and she struggled to think of an answer, even a meaningless one. "It was nothing."

"It must have been something," he said.

She hated when her emotions got the better of her. It had been happening way too often lately.

David must have seen how deeply she had fallen into her own thoughts, because he cleared his throat before speaking again. "Want to talk about it? I'm the perfect person. Who am I gonna tell?"

"Are you sure you want to hear it?"

He nodded. "Why the tears?"

She drew a deep breath, preparing herself to face the truth she tried to drown in the red wine. "Today's my birthday, and it's a little depressing because five days ago my divorce became final and tomorrow my ex-husband leaves for Europe with his fiancée."

"Oh, man—" He reached over and took her hand with

the one he'd had on the shifter. "I'm sorry, Kate."

"He left me ten months ago, and it was bad long before that." She shrugged. "You'd think I'd have adjusted by now."

"Were you married long?"

"Since I was twenty. Too young."

He didn't say anything, but let the silence between them comfort her. She appreciated he didn't offer any trite platitudes or silly advice about 'moving on'. She'd had enough of that from almost everyone she knew.

"It's your birthday?"

"Yes," she said. "But I'd rather not discuss it."

"Aren't you going to tell me which one it is?"

"It's not polite to ask a lady her age." Kate felt the smile pull across her face and she hoped no new wrinkles popped up.

"Sorry. I'll assume it's a crisis birthday then."

"A crisis birthday?"

"Yeah, you know, a big one. Twenty-five or thirty. A birthday that confirms you're not a kid anymore."

"Well, I'll give you that. I'm no kid." *That's for sure.* She wondered if he really thought she was that young. "How old are you?"

Why did she ask that? She didn't want to know.

"I'll be thirty in December." He said it proudly, as if he were trying to make a point to her that age was no big deal. Kate felt a little twinge of guilt for not coming clean about her age, but why? They had no relationship. She'd never see him again, and lots of women lied about their age. He'd picked her up in a bar, what did he expect?

Kate sucked in a breath.

Oh. God. She'd never been picked up in a bar and she had

no idea what he expected. He'd been a gentleman so far, but a wave of panic washed through her. She was totally une-quipped for an encounter like this.

Her eyes went back to David. So taken with his face, she hadn't really paid attention to anything else. She knew he was tall, probably about six-three, and taking a good look she could see every inch of him was lean muscle. Her eyes were drawn to the hand that held hers. His fingers were long and tapered and the skin was roughened from constant battering and use. But there was a gentleness in the way he touched her, in the way his thumb played lightly over her knuckles. Kate felt a curl of heat in her abdomen as she started to imagine how it would feel to have him touch her in more intimate places. When he moved his hand to change gears, she snapped back to reality. This was bad.

Very bad.

DAVID SLOWED THE car as he turned off the freeway, finding a place to park near the pier. Kate was fidgeting in her seat as he threw the car into gear, pressed the brake, and turned off the engine. What was she thinking about? He'd certainly gotten points with the sensitive male routine in the car, but he was having an attack of conscience. He felt bad. She was a nice woman, and times had been tough. But then he thought maybe what she needed was a night out and some great sex. It was her birthday; he'd take her out for a nice evening, get her in bed, and she'd feel like a million bucks in the morning. The rationale made perfect sense to him... and then Kate made him feel like a total shit.

"I really want to see the carousel," she said with a smile. "It's supposed to be beautiful. I've made so many trips to California, and I've never been here."

He smiled in response. It was easy because she was the most sincere person he'd ever met. Her joy was completely genuine, and David felt like the scum of the earth. Once upon a time, he'd been a nice guy. Life intruded, things changed, and he'd lost track of that person somewhere along the road. But watching the happiness spread across her face, knowing he was responsible for it, was a sort of personal epiphany. The bet no longer mattered. Kate offered him redemption, even if it was temporary.

Looking at her again, there was no indication her birthday made her feel older; she was a big kid, eager and enthusiastic. "Let's eat first, and then we'll walk around and check things out."

She agreed and they made a short walk to the restaurant. It was an informal place, almost a shack, and not much to look at. But even the rough tables, the votive candles held in shot glasses, and the paper placemats couldn't take away from the romantic evening that was developing. The soft piano music playing in the background gave the place a hip ambiance that David liked. Kate took her menu, asked him if he knew what was good, and he marveled that it never occurred to her to snub her nose at the place.

She ordered Pellegrino with lime, folded her arms on the table, and grinned, her eyes sparking with life. *God, she was adorable.*

"Do you want wine with dinner?"

Kate shook her head. "I've had more than enough today."

"Drank the whole bottle, eh?" He had to tease her a little.

He couldn't help himself.

"I never do that," she chuckled. "But it was over several hours and it *is* my birthday, after all."

"True enough." She may have been feeling a little beat up over her divorce, but David liked the sweet, sassy personality he saw emerging.

"Okay, David, I bared my soul. Now it's your turn."

"What do you want to know?" He tore off a piece of bread and dipped it in olive oil.

"Tell me about hockey. How long have you been playing?"

"Professionally? This is my eighth season."

"And before that?"

"I played at Boston College, which is where I picked up my nickname." She leveled her gaze and leaned in. That little bit of info wasn't going to satisfy her—she wanted details. "My freshman year I kind of kept to myself, didn't go out much, and my teammates teased me for acting like a priest."

Kate smiled, and nodded her understanding. "My dad went to B-C," she said. "It's where I should have gone."

"Where did you go?"

"Harvard." She smirked and broke off a piece of bread for herself. "Dad wasn't happy."

He chuckled. Only a person who went to school in Boston, and who understood the rivalries, could comprehend why a parent would be disappointed his child had chosen Harvard. "My father didn't want me to go at all. He wanted me to play in Juniors in Canada. If I'd gone that route, I'd have jumped to the NHL two seasons sooner, but my mother wanted me to get an education."

"She must be proud of you."

"I hope so. She died when I was sixteen." Why had he said that? He never talked about his mother, ever. But something about Kate, about the sudden softness in her expression, told him she'd understand.

"That had to be difficult for you."

"It was. We were close and she was sick for a long time."

"Did you get your looks from your mother?"

"I did." He narrowed his eyes. "Why do you ask?"

"Burke is an Irish name, and you don't look Irish."

He felt a little twitch around his heart—it was new and unexpected. Those little details would have been lost on most women. "Her people were Italian."

"Where did you grow up?" She stared at him with those amazing cat eyes. He was convinced she could probably see in the dark.

"A town outside Calgary." He took a sip of his beer. "You never told me what you do."

"I'm a teacher and… a writer." She fiddled with her fork, almost as if she were embarrassed by the fact.

"What do you teach?" he asked.

"High school English. I'm here for a conference."

"And what do you write?"

She paused, considering the question. "Um… I guess you could call them crime novels, suspense."

She surprised him. She seemed so down to earth, and he always thought of novelists as having an air of mystery, or pretense, around them. "Would I have read anything you've written?"

"Maybe." She shrugged and her tongue played over her lips, spreading a stray drop of olive oil.

"I am literate," he teased.

Her eyes twinkled and she nodded. "I know."

David tapped his finger on the edge of his glass. Maybe she did fit the bill. She sure wasn't giving up much. David wanted to know what was cooking underneath Kate's cool exterior—he had a feeling he'd find a lot of heat. "How many have you written?"

"A few, but you changed the subject. I want to know about the NHL."

Again, David felt warmth spread through his chest. It was a nice change to be with a woman who wasn't talking about the best personal trainer or the newest, hottest club. Kate was genuinely interested in him—in who he was and how he lived his life. So, he told her about his games and what it was like playing pro. He explained how the travel got to him, about his teammates and their antics, and about the injuries. He hadn't opened up like this to anyone in a while, but Kate made it easy. She asked him questions, but her undemanding manner made him comfortable, and David was never comfortable. Something wiggled inside him, something that told him this was the way it was supposed to be with a woman.

They ordered different pasta dishes and he fed her a bite of his. She closed her eyes, savoring the taste. Then she looked in his eyes, not a coy glance—she went deep, probing. Unexpectedly, her hand came up and grazed over the bruise on his face. David felt a rush go through his body. The touch was innocent, but it upset his balance; the part of him that kept his emotions in check and his actions controlled spun and collided with a physical response that was so sudden, he felt weak.

David grasped her fingers. "Jesus," he whispered, unable

to say any more than that.

"What happened?" she asked.

Realizing she was talking about the bruise, he answered, "High stick last night in San Jose."

"Does it hurt?"

"Not really." He laced his fingers with hers and drew a deep, painful breath. The air felt thick in his lungs. "Are you finished? We could take that walk now."

She acknowledged him without a word. David paid the check and led her out toward the beach.

Chapter 2

A LIGHT BREEZE blew in from the ocean and Kate rubbed her arms. Without hesitation, David handed her the jacket he'd brought with him from the car. He didn't ask if she was cold, he just saw her response and acted, never thinking of his own comfort.

"Won't you be cold?" she asked.

"Nah." He grinned. "Where I come from, this is balmy."

She pushed up the too-long sleeves and caught his warm, musky scent as she drew the jacket around her. Kate welcomed the way she felt. It had been a long time since she'd been so content.

As David promised, they checked out the pier, which was like a year round carnival. They went to the arcade first, where Kate learned she was a pretty good air hockey player. David dropped at least fifty dollars on games trying to win her a cheap prize. Then he took her on the Ferris wheel, which appeared to grow right out of the ocean. And while they sat in the gondola at the top of the world, he pulled her close. She snuggled into the crook of his arm, telling herself it was to get away from the chill, but actually she loved feeling his body next to hers.

After the rides, he bought ice cream cones and they ate them while strolling on a path by the beach, sometimes talking, sometimes just enjoying the shared silence. Music floated out of a bar they passed, and the notes of an old ballad hung in the air while couples slow-danced on the outdoor deck.

He licked the vanilla ice cream right where it met the cone. "I can't believe I picked you up in a bar."

Kate laughed. "Have you ever done that before?"

"A bar pick-up? Too many. You?"

"Never. You're my first."

"Rookie," he said playfully. "But to tell you the truth, this is more like a first date."

"A really good first date," she added.

"Have you dated at all since you and your husband separated?"

"Nope, another first." She felt her heart speed up just a little as she thought about how the night was unfolding. This was turning out to be her best birthday yet.

His mouth curled up at the corners. He was obviously pleased that he was the one reinitiating her to the single life. What was it with guys and being first?

"Long time since you've been on a first date," he said.

The statement was the perfect opening, but again she decided to keep her age to herself. Why spoil a perfect evening with a bit of worthless information? People were right, age was just a number. "The last time I was on a first date I was eighteen." That was the truth. Then she screwed up her face. "I married him."

He chuckled. "You're good at it. First dates, I mean."

"So are you."

"Not usually. It's always a production. I never really feel like I'm getting to know the women I'm with."

"How is that possible? You're so nice."

He groaned. "Being with you is easy. I mean, look at that place where we had dinner. Most women would flip if I brought them there."

"Because you're David Burke?" Just saying his name made her feel like she was missing something. That she should know more about him.

He glanced at her out of the corner of his eye, then took a bite of the crunchy sugar cone. "The women I date know who I am. It's all about being *seen*. It was different with you."

"I didn't have expectations."

He tossed his napkin in a trashcan and stuffed his hands in his pockets. "Are you offended? I should have taken you someplace nicer."

"Don't be ridiculous. The restaurant was perfect and I'm having the best time." She lightly rubbed his bicep.

"Me too," he said quietly.

They found a bench and sat, and Kate knew she might have to make a decision about how far this evening was going to go. Three hours ago, all she wanted was for David to leave her alone; now she didn't want the night to end. She genuinely liked him, and unless she was completely clueless, he liked her, too. But it was the chemistry between them, the honest-to-goodness chemistry, which made her wonder what was going to happen next. When she looked in his eyes, touched his hand, felt the warmth of his skin, Kate's heart beat faster.

She wanted him to touch her.

It terrified her and it thrilled her, and she wasn't at all sure letting herself go would be the right thing. But Kate had done the right thing all her life. She'd never slept around or done drugs. She had always been a good girl, doing whatever she was told, working hard and pushing herself. Where did it get her? Women who took control of their decisions seemed more content when they got to be her age.

This had been a most unusual evening. She was with a man she'd met only a few hours ago, yet she felt completely at ease. It was like being with someone she'd known for years. It was the comfortable, connected feeling she always wished she'd had with her husband.

There was a subtle shift in his position, and Kate found herself gazing into David's eyes. Eyes as deep and beautiful as the darkening sky.

David gently cradled her face in his hands and his gaze settled on her lips. He waited, possibly expecting her to pull back, but when she didn't, David closed the space between them.

She held her breath, waiting what seemed like forever for the first touch. When his lips brushed hers, soft and inviting, her eyes drifted closed and she was lost. She didn't feel anything but heat as his fingers combed through her hair and his mouth played with hers. She felt the ridges of muscle as her hands drifted along his sides and to his back. Kate had never touched a man like him in all her life—one who was hard as steel, a man with enough physical power to crush her, and yet so gentle, so aware of his own strength that he tempered it for her. His arms came around her and enveloped her in a tender embrace as he continued to kiss her, urging her lips apart, dipping his tongue into her mouth until he finally pulled away. Both of them were breathing hard and Kate collapsed onto his chest, drawing in the scent of the ocean and his cologne.

He nuzzled her hair and Kate heard his breathing steady while he maneuvered her onto his lap and started kissing her again—gentle, probing kisses. Kisses that were meant to make her drunk, lose her mind, and surrender.

"David?" He moved to her jaw and neck nipping as he explored.

"Kate." He whispered in her ear. "We should stop."

"I don't want to stop." She ran her hands up and down his spine. With each stroke, he shuddered. It was crazy wanting him like this, unbelievable that the feeling was mutual.

"Are you sure?"

"Very sure. We should go back to the hotel." Her lips touched his Adam's apple and he swallowed hard. She smiled, loving the flash of power she felt.

"Your room," he said. "I have a roommate."

"Uh huh." Her fingers ran through his hair and she took tiny sips of his lips. "I don't care where we go."

He drew in an unsteady breath, moved her off his lap, and pulled her behind him on a mad dash to the car. They didn't touch during the entire ride from Santa Monica to the hotel. Kate sat pressed against the passenger door, afraid to get too close. If they had any physical contact, they wouldn't make it to her suite. They glanced at each other occasionally, and she knew if David was feeling half of what she was, he was in pain.

They made it as far as the door of her room when he spun her around and pressed her against the wall, kissing her until she could barely stand. His lips were soft, his tongue probing, and he took possession of her mouth in a way no one else ever had. When he steadied himself and stepped back from her, there was still heat—unbelievable heat—between them. Kate didn't know how she found the plastic room key in her bag, and she couldn't hold it still enough to insert it and open the door.

"My hands are shaking."

"Give it to me." He took the key, slid it in, and as soon as the light turned green, he opened the door. They didn't get two steps into the room before they were on each other.

His mouth was magic, and when he kissed her again Kate couldn't do anything but hold on. She loved how he felt, loved that this powerful man would be inside her. And then her brain took over.

Suddenly, the thought of being with him terrified her. Not because she felt she would be condemned for all eternity for sleeping with him, but because she felt so inexperienced. Richard had been her only lover, and he wasn't patient, gentle, or particularly innovative. For five years before her divorce, Kate's sex life had been reduced to the missionary position once a week.

Before that it was the missionary position twice a week.

How could she be with him? It wasn't that she didn't try with her husband. She coaxed and teased, never refusing him. She did research, for God's sake, to try and spice things up, but that had been a complete disaster. Now, here she was with David, who was probably used to women who knew their way around a man's body.

Kate needed a map.

To her horror, instead of pulling away from him and

putting an end to the encounter, she burrowed into his broad chest and he pulled her close.

"What is it?"

"David, I can't."

"You don't want to make love?"

She looked in his eyes and felt a little dizzy. "I do. But I'm afraid I won't know what I'm doing."

He grinned softly. "What?"

"My experience is fairly limited. My husband used all his best moves with his mistress."

The back of his hand grazed over her cheek and he smiled. "I guess I'll have to use all *my* best moves then."

His words touched her on so many levels. He was trying to ease her mind, make her feel desired, make her smile. And as nervous as she was, if she turned him away she would have another regret to add to the list that was already too long. She couldn't do that. She wanted him; and more, she needed him. She needed the freedom he represented.

Staring at the buttons on his shirt, Kate ran her palms over the hard muscle hiding beneath. Then, she did something she would never forget. She started to undo the buttons. The progress was painfully slow. David watched her; she could feel his eyes. When the shirt was open Kate ran her hands under the soft fabric and pushed it off his shoulders. A gasp escaped her lips.

He was a sculpture, a classical painting, a vision all rolled into one. Every muscle of his torso was defined, like it had been cut from a slab of marble. *"Oh... God..."*

She didn't recognize her own voice as it came out on a breath. He was *David*—as imposing and as perfectly formed as the statue by Michelangelo. She pressed her lips to his chest and he groaned. Still holding the remnants of a summer tan, his skin was slightly gold, and dusted with dark hair. She looked up when he held her away from his body.

"My turn," he said, and he tugged at the bottom of her sweater.

Kate's mind strayed to thoughts of the stretch marks he might see, of the ripples and sags that came from mileage. "I'm not like you," she whispered.

He grinned. "I hope not." Her sweater fell to the floor and David's hands traveled over her shoulders and down her back. She trembled at the gentle movement of his fingers. He had the most amazing hands. Her bra was gone before she knew what was happening.

"You're beautiful." He unbuttoned her trousers and eased them over her hips and thighs.

Kate stepped out of her shoes and then out of the pants, letting them puddle at her feet. He stroked her everywhere, and while she should have felt exposed, standing nearly naked in front of a man she'd known less than six hours, she didn't. Kate felt no embarrassment with David, no shame, just desire. It balled in her belly, waiting to explode.

When their bodies finally made contact, Kate's skin burned and her bones melted. David kissed her neck and shoulder, and without any warning he lifted her into his arms. *This is a dream. It can't be real.* She wrote things like this, scenes where passion fueled every action. But David wasn't a character in a book, he was real, and she looped her arms around his neck and kissed his face as he carried her toward the bedroom.

A lamp on the bedside table was on. The maid had turned down the bed and David set her down gently. He took a condom from his wallet, placed it on the table, and then made short work of his remaining garments. Fully naked, he was glorious and terrifying. He stretched out next to her and must have sensed her apprehension, because his touch was so very gentle.

"Don't be afraid."

"I'm not afraid," she lied.

"Yes, you are. You're shaking." His lips dropped to her breast and drew on one nipple. She arched and moaned as the pleasure shot through her. He partially covered her body with his own, gazed at her, and brushed the hair from her face. "I'm going to make love to you, Kate. Forget about everything else. Forget what you know about sex, this will be different."

How did he know? How did he know that in twenty years of marriage her husband had had sex with her but had never made love to her? The emotions that welled up inside her, emotions she'd locked up for so long, started to break through. Her arms found him and clung as if he were the only anchor she had. But then David started to touch her, stroke her, and give her such pleasure that she let go and allowed herself to drown.

DAVID AWOKE ON his back. Without thinking, he leaned over and pulled Kate against him. She curled in, half asleep. Logic told him he should leave, but everything about her flew in the face of logic. She was a contradiction, a puzzle, and David was in way over his head. What had started out as a bet, and was supposed to be a simple one-night stand, had become much more. This woman could matter to him. At some point, David had stopped thinking about himself and started thinking about her. Her vulnerability, her openness, her intelligence were at the heart of what he felt, but there was more. It was the way they connected.

They understood each other.

He and Kate were emotional train wrecks—victims of their broken lives. She hadn't told him much, but once he knew her husband had cheated on her, he could fill in the blanks. His fingers played with the ends of her hair; her breathing was soft and steady. This woman was supposed to be just another notch on his belt, a quick lay. Instead, David was faced with the sad prospect of leaving and never seeing her again.

Easing away from her, he rose, and pulled on his boxers before walking to the French doors that led to the balcony. The sky was turning grey, and beyond the pool deck, the Pacific stretched on forever. He felt off-balance, unsteady, like he might have actually faced something life changing. The feelings were new and scared the crap out of him. He had to get control of himself.

But when she stirred, David looked back, and immediately wanted to make love to her again. *So much for leaving.* Kate smiled and sat up; the sheet bunched at her waist. David wondered if she realized how magnificent she looked with her tousled hair, her flushed cheeks, and her body begging for attention.

She tugged at the sheet in silent invitation. David's brain screamed at him to go, even as his heart and libido were leading him back to bed.

"You okay?" he asked, looking down at her.

"Never better," she said.

"I checked out your view—very nice." He motioned to the door that led to a small balcony just before he climbed back into bed.

"Yeah, it's something. My publisher booked the hotel."

"Your publisher? I thought you were here for a teachers' conference?"

"Kind of double duty. While I was here for the conference, I did some book promotion, too. I took advantage. I should have left yesterday, but I couldn't face being home on my birthday."

"I'm glad you stayed." He kissed her nose and let his hands play with her hair. "So, mystery writers do okay, I guess?"

"Yeah. I've done alright."

"What kind of book promotion?"

"This and that. A-a-bookstore visit. Some media stuff." She was stuttering, fidgeting, and that made David curious. Obviously, there was more to Kate and her career than met the eye.

"So you never told me, how many books have you written?"

"A few." She looked back at him and fiddled with her necklace before answering. "Six have been published."

She might not have appreciated all the questions, but he was having a hell of a time teasing her. "How many times have you been on the bestseller list?"

She nibbled on her thumbnail. "Which one?"

He grinned. "The Times."

She cleared her throat and looked at him. "Five times."

"Five times, including this book?" He didn't expect her to

say that. Even he knew five bestsellers was serious business.

The oath she uttered was nothing more than a mumble as she rolled away from him. David watched her wrap herself in a plush terrycloth robe and walk into the parlor of the suite. She returned with a hardcover book and held it out for his inspection.

The imprint of a major publisher graced the spine and as he examined the thick volume, he made his discovery. "Katherine Adams?"

Holy shit.

"Uh-huh."

He examined the cover. Oh yeah, he'd heard of her. Mystery writer, his ass. She wrote political thrillers. Her lead character was a sexy, kick-ass, female FBI agent named Elliott Hunter, and he'd read every one of her books except this one.

Damn.

"I can't believe it." He was still holding her book. "I'm a huge fan."

Her eyes widened. "You are?"

"Yeah." David couldn't stop grinning. Inside he wondered if this made him a groupie. "You're a teacher, too?"

"I love teaching and I don't like change. Publishing can turn on a dime. I could never sell another book." She tugged the robe where it was falling open, giving him another delicious peek at her breasts. "David, look... I know we'll probably never see each other again, but..."

He put the book aside, grasped her hands, and pulled her onto the bed. "I've been thinking about that." His brain was telling him to agree with her and move on, but he was saying something totally different. "Maybe we could get together when I'm on the road... or you could come and see me in

Philly."

All the color drained from her face, and for a second David thought she might pass out. Something had spooked her.

"Philly?" she said softly.

"Yeah, why?"

"I live in Pennsylvania. In Bryn Mawr," she answered, and as she did, awareness sparked in her eyes. "I knew you looked familiar. I just couldn't place you. You play for the Flyers," she stated.

David's smile broadened as he nodded.

In one motion, he pushed her book to the floor and had her under him. "So much for a one night stand." *So much for the nice, safe personal life he'd modeled for himself.*

"Yeah," she said.

They'd gotten along great, and David thought she'd be happy, but instead Kate bit her lip and looked away. "Kate? You do want to see me again, don't you?"

She looked back and her eyes brightened, showing him a lightening in her mood, and betraying her desire. She wanted him. That had to be a good sign. Her hands held his head and she kissed him on the mouth—once, twice, three times. The fourth kiss almost made him forget his own name.

"I want to see you again, but things could be complicated," she whispered.

"Whatever, we'll talk about it later." His mouth covered hers and they started all over.

LYING ON THE bed where she and David had made love an

hour before, Kate clutched the pillow where his head had been and snuggled in. He'd taken her number, given her his, and promised she'd hear from him in a few days.

Kate giggled. Talk about a great birthday present. She'd had more orgasms in one night than she'd had in twenty years with her ex. God, she missed David already. But thinking about it, it was more than the sex—it was the ease of the whole night. From dinner to the bedroom, being with him was relaxed and fun. Kate had no idea what she'd been missing until last night. Rolling on her back and taking his pillow with her, she thought about it. She missed his laughter, the deep timbre of his voice—she missed his touch. Breathing deep, she caught a whiff of his scent. God, she hoped she saw him again.

And if she did, she'd tell him.

Not that her age was a big deal. It shouldn't be, but it could be uncomfortable for him. And there was her daughter to consider. Even if David was all right with the age thing, he may not be able to cope with the fact that Kate had a seventeen-year-old daughter.

For that matter, Kate wondered how her daughter would deal with the fact that her mother had slept with David Burke, the man whose poster hung on her bedroom wall.

DAVID SETTLED INTO the wide seat on the team's charter. The guys were tired so the lights were dim, and a just smattering of conversation could be heard in the cabin. Players were either reading, listening to music, or settling in to get some sleep. But not him. His shoulder and knee ached, and his mind kept drifting back to Kate. And how after only twenty-four hours, he missed her.

He rubbed his eyes and tried to get her face out of his head. When one image of her faded, another one took its place. He saw her on the deck wiping at her eyes, at dinner listening to him like he really mattered, talking about her work, sleeping after they'd made love. He was trying to remember the last time a woman got inside his head like this. The answer: *Never*.

He was almost thirty and wondered if it was possible that "the right girl" had finally crossed his path. He looked around the cabin. Most of the guys his age were married, or at least serious about someone. Here he was, still bouncing from one girl to another and winding up in the local gossip pages as often as he was in the sports pages. It sucked.

He'd taken a lot of shit from his teammates when he wouldn't give up any details of his time with Kate, forcing him to accept losing the bet. He looked to his right. His teammate, Cam Roth, had a smug grin on his face and David knew he was in for it again. He didn't care.

"What?"

"I owe you this." Cam extended a folded hundred dollar bill and David waved it off.

"Keep it," he said.

"Seriously? We all know you won." Cam tucked the cash back into his wallet. "Did you grow a conscience or something?"

"I don't feel right about the bet. She's nice. I like her."

"I cannot believe you got her in bed. She looked a little on the cool side."

Chuckling under his breath, David knew Kate was anything but. "Not cool at all. We clicked. But that's all I'm saying."

"Come on!" Cam pleaded.

David shook his head and Cam nodded, resigned, as he leaned back into his seat. David thought about where his friend's life was going. At thirty-seven, his career was winding down. He'd given up his "C" this season, and David had assumed the responsibilities of captain, but his old friend and mentor still drove hard every time he was on the ice. He did the same with women. David wondered if that's where he was going to be in seven years. Could he ever settle down?

"You okay, Padre?"

"Yeah. She's just in my head, that's all."

"Mind blowing, eh?"

David thought about that. Kate was mind blowing, but not in the way Cam meant it. It was something else. Something intangible. It was in the way she looked at him. The way he felt when he touched her, kissed her. He liked being with her, and it wasn't just about the sex. He could lose himself in her—in her softness, in her intelligence, in her genuine sweetness. But it was the strength he saw along with the vulnerability, something so powerful it was scaring him shitless, that made David realize this woman, if he let the relationship go any further, would completely own him.

And then there was the book thing.

"Yeah, mind blowing… on a lot of levels."

Cam raised an eyebrow. "Levels?"

He wasn't surprised his friend asked the question, but he didn't know how much he wanted to give up. So, David looked around the cabin for the part of the explanation he could share without sounding like a candy ass. "Hold on," he said before he called out, "Yo, Graves. Toss me that book."

Tyler Graves looked at David for a second, then lobbed the book that had been in his lap across the aisle and back a few rows. David grabbed it cleanly from the air and showed it to Cam.

"She wrote this." David flipped the paperback over and the entire back cover was imprinted with Kate's gorgeous face.

Cam grabbed the book and looked at the image, then at the cover. "Ho-ly shit. I actually read this." He looked David square in the eyes. "She's fuckin' famous."

"I know."

Cam laughed out loud. "Did you get her to autograph your ass, man?"

"You are such a dumb shit." David grabbed the book and looked at the picture again.

"Hey, chicks ask me to autograph body parts all the time!"

David heard the growl come deep from his throat. This could get complicated, and her fame was only part of it.

And that was what unnerved him; he didn't need the complications a woman like Kate would bring. She'd want a real relationship. He didn't need a relationship. He hadn't been turned down for a date or sex for as long as he could remember—usually he didn't even have to ask. Most women were more than willing and eager to keep things casual. They'd put on the act, play the games, but they were always available. The current woman in his life made it very clear she was going to sleep with him, and did him following their first dinner together. She was the gorgeous, blonde, twenty-three-year-old daughter of a surgeon. The difference with her was that since he'd been seeing her, and sleeping with her, more regularly than the others, she'd started hinting at making things permanent, and at that moment David realized he had to let her know it wasn't going to happen.

No doubt, Chelsea would be the perfect trophy wife; she was a hot piece of ass and possessed the common sense of a breast implant. But David didn't want a trophy. Until Kate, he didn't think he wanted anything but a warm body. The whole situation made him realize just how far he'd dropped on the personal relationship scale. There had always been plenty of women, lots of great sex, but no one who actually cared about him.

Kate would care. He had no doubt about that. What he didn't know is if he was up to it. Or if she was interested.

David took his phone from his pocket and typed a quick text. What the hell. He hit send. *Home day after tomorrow. Dinner Wed? Piccolo's in Ardmore. Do you know it?*

Within a minute, an answer came back. *Yes. Talking to a book group at the library in Haverford. Will be done around 9. Can meet you after.*

David smiled. *"I'll be there. Get there when you can."*

Just as they were starting to taxi, he got her response. *Can't wait.*

The plane was picking up speed and soon they were airborne. David focused on the lightness he felt as they left the ground. Piccolo's was BYOB, so that meant he had to get a good bottle of wine. He'd probably get two, a red and a white. *Crap.* What was happening? He was actually planning a date, and doing more than making reservations, or counting on his fame to get him in someplace. Sticking his phone back in his pocket, he acknowledged Kate was different, and she was going to require some effort.

KATE DROPPED HER bags when she entered the laundry room and flipped on the lights. There had been a little blast of cold weather while she'd been away and the house was chilly. She took a quick glance at the basket of mail on the counter to her left, checked to see if the plants needed water… and it was then, when she looked around, that Kate felt the loneliness wash over her.

But it wasn't the usual loneliness, the kind that screamed at her that she'd been left. This was a new feeling, one that left her more resigned than miserable. One that reminded her it was time to move on.

Right next to the laundry room was the kitchen. Kate took another look at her bags, deciding to leave the largest one in the laundry room since most of the clothes had to be washed anyway. She grabbed the carry-on and headed upstairs. When she reached the first landing, she turned and went to Laura's room. Opening the door, her daughter's essence reached out. It was the smell of a seventeen-year-old: denim and deodorant, makeup and perfume. Stepping into the room, Kate reached down and turned on the bedside lamp. There, right in front of her, was David. A large poster hung at the head of Laura's bed. He was in full hockey gear, a helmet covering his dark hair, but the intensity in his eyes held her. The pads and jersey weren't there for Kate. All she saw was the man beneath. And as the smells of her daughter faded, the musky, warm scent of David flooded Kate's mind.

It came over her like a wave, and she felt the happiness stir deep within her. All at once, she started reliving last night. She kept replaying the moment he approached her in the bar, worried she would forget the instant when their eyes first made contact. Kate tried to pretend there was nothing between them. But as he stood before her on that sunny deck, being genuinely concerned and perfectly gorgeous, Kate melted. Talking with him was like being with an old friend; making love with him was like finding her other half.

And she was going to see him again.

As a writer, she lived by her ability to make people feel things, but over the years Kate had grown numb. The years with Richard, the fight for her daughter, had forced the life out of her. But one night with David helped Kate realize her heart was still beating.

She reached out and touched the picture and smiled. He'd given her the most remarkable gift... hope. Something she hadn't had in the longest time.

Forgetting about the fatigue and her carry-on, Kate climbed another set of stairs. At the top was her office, the place where she went to let her imagination take hold and create her stories.

When she touched the switch on the wall, just inside the door, the overhead light came on. The fixture was a beautiful conglomeration of twisted vines she'd found in a decorating catalog, and the final touch to the space she'd been planning since the sale of her first book. Two years ago, when book three was optioned for a movie, Kate took the money and hired a contractor. Richard had been furious, but she didn't care. The third floor needed work, and she laid claim to one of the old, run-down bedrooms.

The whole floor had been gutted and transformed, but her office was special. With wide-plank wood floors, built-in shelving, and a custom made desk, this was her space. *Hers.*

Looking up at the light shining from the chandelier, Kate stepped into the room.

She hadn't come up here very much since Richard had climbed the same stairs, told her he had someone else, and left her. She wrote on her laptop instead, avoiding the memories of this place, but that was going to change. Looking at the bag hanging from her shoulder, Kate decided she was done. Done mourning, done feeling sorry for herself. *No more escaping.* Reclaiming this room was the smallest of gestures, but it was important nonetheless. Her life had become a series of turning points. Some were big, some were small. This was a small one. Stepping toward her desk, Kate put down the bag and turned on her computer.

She felt like writing.

Chapter 3

PICCOLO'S ITALIAN CAFÉ had been housed for the last fifteen years in a pretty house in historic Ardmore. The owners, Albie LoScala, and his partner and chef, Vinnie Abruzzo, had never bothered to get a liquor license, so patrons who brought their own wine were given a corkscrew and glasses to go along with the best Italian food anywhere in or out of Philly. Kate loved the restaurant, but hadn't been there in over a year, since well before Richard left. She'd heard from friends that he and Marie went from time to time; she couldn't imagine it being a very pleasant experience for them since Albie and Vinnie never liked her ex-husband. Ever.

Cars were scattered around the street, but being it was late, the town was quiet. After finding a parking spot a few doors away, Kate thought it was ironic David picked this restaurant. It was possible, over the years, they were here at the same time, having dinner, and never taking notice of each other.

She checked her makeup and reapplied her lipstick, looking carefully at her reflection in the visor mirror. Breathing out, Kate knew she should find a way to drop her age into the conversation, if only to see his reaction. Then she'd know if this was going to go anywhere, or if the whirlwind would stop.

He'd called her yesterday. Just to talk. He asked how school was going and how she was doing… specifically, David wanted to know if she had any regrets about the night they spent together. Hearing from him caught her a little off guard. God, did she want to tell him the truth—any regret she felt lasted a total of twelve seconds. After that it was lost in a wash of hot, sweaty, very satisfying memories. He made her feel so good, so *wanted.* Kate could never feel sorry for making love with him. She assured him she had no regrets. *Hell, no.* Kate had to pinch herself so she remembered it wasn't going to last. This was a rebound. It was fun.

It was dangerous.

The alarm tweeted and she started toward the restaurant. Her heels clicked on the pavement, and when she looked down, Kate wondered if all the cleavage she was showing was too much. The sweater was tight and plunging, and not something she'd usually wear, but the whole evening was taking her out of her comfort zone.

Pausing on the restaurant's porch for a second, Kate took a deep breath. Then another. The butterflies in her stomach now felt more like bats; she figured she'd better walk in before she lost her nerve. The door squeaked when she pulled it open and Albie looked up. The butterflies, the bats, everything faded when she saw the smile on her old friend's face.

"I'm back," she said quietly.

He came from around the maître'd's podium and pulled her into a hug that crushed the wind out of her. Then he stepped back, looked at her face, and hugged her again. "I am so happy to see you!" he finally said. "We've missed you terribly!"

"I've missed you, too."

"Your louse of an ex has been in with the crazy one. I had to stop Vinnie from spitting into their dinners, although the last time I was tempted to let him."

Kate chuckled. She was amused, but she was also annoyed for letting Richard drive her away from people who cared about her. She'd known Albie for better than a dozen years. They'd had book launch parties at this restaurant, birthday dinners—every special night out had been spent here. There were also many nights she spent alone. Both men had called after the separation, but Kate, reeling from the hurt and the humiliation, pulled back from all but a few people. She regretted it now. Albie and Vinnie were like family. Family she hadn't seen in almost a year because of Richard.

"What brings you in? A late dinner? VINNIE! Come out here!" Albie was talking a mile a minute. "He'll want to see you. You look fantastic, by the way. Love the hair. It's shorter? I'll join you so you don't have to sit alone."

Kate smiled but she held up her hand to stop the stream of words. "No, it's fine." She paused, focusing on each breath. "I'm meeting someone."

Albie stopped dead in his tracks. "What?" His eyes went wide and hopeful, but then a shadow crossed over them, right before another booming voice joined the conversation.

"Oh, my God! Where have you been?" Vinnie rushed forward and pulled Kate into a hug. "Crap, you look amazing. I wish the shithead was here so he could see how amazing you look. Too bad you don't have a date."

Albie folded his arms and stared at Kate, waiting for her

to come clean. Vinnie picked up on the vibe right away and raised an eyebrow. Perfect. They were going to want details.

The giggle escaped before Kate actually said anything. "I... ah... I do have a date."

"Okay," Albie said. "Spill. Because the only person in the dining room, who's alone, is one of my other regulars, and he's meeting someone."

"*Who?*" Vinnie asked.

"Fellas, are you trying to hijack my date?"

All three turned toward the voice, and when she laid eyes on David, Kate's heart flipped around in her chest. He stood, hip shot into the doorframe, hands stuffed in his pockets, looking so gorgeous she tingled from head to toe. Then, he met her eyes and smiled, and she melted from the inside out. Yup. She was done.

Albie leaned in, whispering in her ear. "You're blushing."

"I know. It's sad." Kate actually loved the nerves. She loved the flutter she felt when David was close.

"It's about time."

He settled his hand between her shoulder blades and gave her a nudge—a push towards the change David represented. Kate didn't have any delusions about David, at least she didn't think she did, but he was a step forward... a risk.

David reached out a hand; it was large, rough, and warm, and as his fingers curled around hers, he leaned in to plant a gentle kiss on her cheek. It was just a brush, the faintest of contact, and her knees nearly buckled as his clean scent surrounded her. Had this ever happened with Richard? Even when they were first together, when Kate believed she was so in love with him—did he ever make her feel this much? Was she ever this aware of him? She didn't think so.

Vaguely conscious they'd passed into the dining room, Kate felt suspended in the moment. Everything stopped, and all that was left was awareness—awareness of her own heart beating, of the blood racing in her head, of the heat churning from the center on out.

The room was practically empty, understandable since it was after nine on a weeknight. There were two other couples and a table of men who looked like they'd had a business dinner. An aria from *La Traviata* played in the background. It was beautiful and romantic. The table was tucked into a corner near the fireplace, and once she settled into the large wing chair, and David was safely on the other side, Kate allowed herself to breathe.

Albie brought over a basket of fresh bread and leaned toward David. "Your taste has improved."

"I'm trying to take your advice," David responded.

Albie gave him advice?

"So, an appetizer to start? We have a fabulous special— squash blossoms stuffed with an herbed mixture of goat cheese and ricotta, and then fried."

"Mmmm, that sounds good." Kate was eager to try, but David didn't look convinced. "Doesn't it?" she asked.

"It's a stuffed flower."

"A *fried*, stuffed flower," Albie said. "That should appeal to your inner Neanderthal."

"Hey!" David feigned offense and Kate hid her smile behind the menu. The banter between him and Albie was such fun. She composed herself, finally, to come to his defense.

"I don't think he's a Neanderthal," she whispered to Albie.

Albie rolled his eyes. "Oh, honey, of course he is. It's not a bad thing, but he totally is."

With a wink and a smile, Albie left to put in the order.

"I guess I'm trying the stuffed flower."

"I guess you are, but you didn't put up much of a fight."

"Not worth it, and it *is* fried."

She giggled again, loving how things were so easy between them—how was this possible? "I can't believe you invited me here."

"It's a strange coincidence, but it's a good thing to have in common."

Nodding, Kate focused on her twisting fingers, then looked into David's warm eyes. His smile was sweet, gentle, but she knew, after watching him in his previous night's game, he was anything but gentle. Kate wondered if she could handle being with someone so physical.

"Red or white?"

"What?"

"Wine? Would you like red or white?"

Thank God. She could use some wine. Actually she could use lots of wine. "Hmm. What are you having?"

"The red. It's a good Chianti. Want to try it?"

The cork was out in one smooth motion and Kate marveled at how easily he moved. Everything about David was fluid and relaxed, while she was being revisited by those bats.

"I was so glad you had time to see me."

That shocked her. Did he think she wouldn't meet him? Seriously? "I was surprised to get the text so soon."

"You shouldn't have been."

He poured the wine and raised his glass, tapping it gently against hers. Glancing around the dining room, Kate allowed herself to get used to the surroundings again. "I love this restaurant."

"Me too. Do you come here a lot?"

"I used to. Before the divorce. I've missed it."

He nodded. "Did you grow up around here?"

"Me? No. I'm a Long Island girl. I grew up in a small town called Holly Point."

"There are small towns on Long Island?"

She grinned, thinking the only impressions David had of her home was a slab of concrete on Hempstead Turnpike where the Islanders played, or maybe the Hamptons. "Yes. They're not small in comparison to other places, but they dot the coast, have all the small town gossip you'd expect. Some families have lived in those towns for generations."

"I guess I bought into the stereotype."

"Most people do. Aren't you going to ask about the lack of accent and big hair?"

He laughed and shook his head. "No, as long as you don't tease me when I say things like '*aboot*'."

"Deal."

"What brought you to Philly?"

"My husband's work." She stopped and bit her lip. "Sorry. *Ex-husband*." Taking a breath as she adjusted to the term, Kate continued. "I'll move home someday, but not until Laura's out of school."

"Laura's your daughter?"

Kate nodded and hoped he didn't want to know about her. She wasn't quite ready to share, so when he didn't press her for more, she was relieved. The explanations could wait until later.

"How did your talk go? You said it was a book group?"

Kate took a sip of her wine and nodded. "Yup. It was fun."

"I can't imagine writing a whole book, let alone six. It kind of blows my mind."

Kate let the words roll around in her brain a little. She savored them, let them sink in. He was... well... he was impressed. And interested. Another little miracle.

"What do you talk about with groups?"

"Ah, usually it's question and answer. Sometimes I get a lot of craft questions, you know, how I write, how I get my ideas... things like that. And people always want to talk about what's coming next. I try not to give too much away."

David smiled. "Tease."

"I know. But if I said too much, what would be the point of reading the next book?"

"Lots. Your story, the little things that happen to the characters. The way you describe action and the setting. There's no way you could give all that away."

"I guess not." She ran her fingers up and down the stem of the wine glass and while the compliments made her a little uncomfortable, she loved that he appreciated her work. Loved it. "How did the rest of the road trip go? I saw you won last night."

"Not bad. Some of the new guys need to learn the system, but it'll be fine. Do you follow hockey at all?"

"No, not really." She had a feeling she'd be following a lot more if anything came of this.

"Not into sports?"

Kate hesitated. She had the perfect response to that question, but decided some things shouldn't be shared just yet. "I wouldn't say that. I used to be a big hockey fan. I don't have a lot of time to keep up."

"We should go skating sometime."

She could feel the grin pull across her face. "I haven't been on skates in years."

"You know how?"

Her eyes met his and she fell right into their dark depths. "I do."

"Damn," he said, leaning in. "I wanted to teach you."

A cover of a popular love song, sung in Italian, was in the background, and Kate shifted the music from the restaurant to her imagination. She could feel the fluidity of their movements on the ice, his powerful stride, her graceful one— the contrast mirrored everything about them. And in response there was a squeeze in her core and every part of her from the waist down tingled. *Great.* Way to stay in control.

Albie delivered the appetizer, doing his best not to interrupt, but Kate knew he was reporting back to Vinnie. She didn't wait and dug right into the food. If she ate, maybe she'd stop having dirty daydreams about David. As she chewed, Kate looked up to see the two men watching her and grinning stupidly.

"She's very flushed," Albie said to David.

"She is." David said. "Is it too warm near the fireplace? I'll change seats with you?" Still sporting a crooked smile, Kate wasn't sure what to make of David's teasing. Was he able to see how easily he'd gotten to her? Was he that tuned in already?

He and Albie were still chuckling quietly at her expense. "You know," she said, while looking back and forth between them, "I think I hate you both, just a little."

That did it. The two men burst out laughing and Albie

headed back to the kitchen, while David took her hand and gently kissed her knuckles. "You don't hate me—even a little. I think you like me just as much as I like you." Another kiss, but this time he'd turned her hand over and touched his lips to her palm. "Don't you?"

Kate's hand went from David's lips, to the side of his face, resting on the warm skin of his cheek. No answer was necessary, but once she steadied her shaky breath the words came out easily. "Oh, yeah."

DAVID WONDERED WHAT he was going to have to do to make this thing between him and Kate work. He'd have to keep himself away from the women who made themselves readily available. Her husband had cheated on her and there was no way he would put himself in the same category as that asshole. So, even while they were feeling this out between them, he had to make sure it was known he was no longer available.

He held her hand as they walked down the street. She was amazing—funny, smart, and not impressed with him at all. She liked him, there was no doubt about that, but for the first time in a long time, David felt like a woman really wanted to know him. Kate asked him about college and his family, and the hockey talk was more about how it affected his life. She knew what it was like to be in a fishbowl and didn't care for the superficiality that came with celebrity. David came to the realization that he didn't like it either. This quiet dinner with her was better than any ostentatious restaurant in the city.

Her car was classy. Understated. A silver Volvo that identified her as a suburban mom. The alarm chirped and the interior lights went on, backlighting her as she leaned against the door.

"I had fun," she said right before she bit down on her lower lip, setting off his libido like a rocket.

"Me too," David said, stepping closer and eliminating the space between them.

He brushed a strand of hair away from her face, and bent toward her, getting a whiff of her sweet breath. He had to get close, kiss her. She was everything. At first, his lips just teased hers. His one hand continued to caress her face and the other slipped under her light coat and around her waist. The sweater she wore was soft under his hand, and her body felt warm and supple pressed into his. His lips tormented and tasted until she let out one of those little sighs that brought him to his knees. Then he just dove in, letting her take over his brain. Fighting against what she did to him was useless.

She was perfect for him. Her small frame fit against his like they were made for each other. Their scents mingled together and their mouths meshed in a hot dance. He couldn't get enough of her—of the feel of her. He wanted to make her sigh again, for his name to be carried on that sigh.

"Oh, David," she said.

There it was. He didn't want this to end. He wanted her. It seemed whenever he touched her, he wanted her. Then just as quickly as it began, the moment ended.

"Kate? Kate Nicholls, is that you?"

Kate's eyes squeezed shut. "Damn."

She peered around the wall of his body and her eyes fixed on a pair of women who were walking right toward them.

She looked up. "Neighbors."

He nodded, stepping out of her space, but still staying

close. "Do you want me to leave?"

She shook her head and trained her eyes on the women who had finished their trek across the street. "Carla, Noreen... good to see you."

"You too!" Carla leaned in and pecked Kate on the cheek. Noreen was too busy checking him out to acknowledge Kate.

"What brings you out?" Carla asked. Now she was checking him out.

"Dinner." Touching his bicep, Kate said, "This is David."

He received polite acknowledgement from both women, but what they were really doing was filing away information. He could see clearly that Kate being on a date was going to be gossiped about within the hour. Knowing what that was like, David felt bad that someone had seen them, but he was happy Kate hadn't told him to go. The three women exchanged small talk that he was tuning out, until one of them said something really odd.

"Have you started thinking about college visits yet?"

David didn't know who said it, but he did feel Kate's muscles bunch under his hand. "Nothing specific, yet."

"Don't wait too long," Carla said. "The whole process creeps up on you. I think the junior counselors are having a parents' meeting next week."

"I saw that," Kate said.

David was doing math in his head. *College Counselors? Campus visits?* What the hell had he stepped into? He was relieved when the women finally left, because now he could get some answers.

When he looked down, Kate was chewing on her thumbnail, which seemed to be what she did when she was nervous about something. "Sorry about that," she said.

"It's fine." David turned and leaned his shoulder into the car. "You have to take your daughter on college visits?"

Kate looked up. Her eyes wide. "Yes, later in the year."

"How old is she?"

Kate looked off in the distance and straightened before answering. "She just turned seventeen."

Whoa. Changing position, David moved and turned his back into the car. He took Kate's hand and held tight, but he didn't say anything. There were so many possibilities—how did he get the facts? Finally, he heard her draw in a breath.

"Remember in California when you said something about my birthday being a 'crisis birthday'?"

"Yeah."

"It was a crisis," she whispered. "I turned forty."

Time passed. It felt like minutes, but it was only seconds. "You're forty." He didn't say it as a question. He didn't move and didn't utter another word. Her hand was still in his, but again, he could feel she'd tensed up.

"You're in shock. I should have known." Kate wiggled her fingers, trying to get out of his grip, but David didn't release her. Shock or not, he didn't want to let go.

"I'm just trying to get my head around this. You aren't what I think a forty-year-old woman is going to be like."

"I don't know if I should be insulted by that."

"Don't be. It came out wrong."

"I understand if you have a problem with it. I mean, you're twenty-nine and I'm... well... I'm not."

"No, you're not." David kept holding on, he couldn't let her go, but he shifted position again and looked out across the town square. "Do *you* have a problem with it?

"The age difference?" She shrugged and there was a little

flicker in her eyes. It was entirely possible she'd be the one who put a stop to the relationship. Forget the age thing, his reputation alone might send her running. "I should have said something to you sooner," she said.

"Why didn't you?"

"Honestly?" Looking up, her eyes looked sad, and David felt a tightness around his heart that he'd never felt before. "I never thought I'd see you again," she said. "Considering who you are, I was shocked you asked me to dinner."

Did she really think he wasn't interested? Leaning in, David absorbed the sweet smell of her hair before dropping a kiss on her forehead. He liked her, probably too much for his own good, but he couldn't help but think the years between them might be too much.

"I should let you go, I guess." She was running. Her voice was small and he could tell she was upset. There had to be something he could say to reassure her, but his mind blanked.

"I'll talk to you," he said. Then, not being able to stop himself, David kissed her once more. And then again. "Night."

"Bye."

Kate got in her car without looking at him and he turned and went toward his. *Forty?* Was he supposed to be attracted to a forty-year-old woman? Usually the girls he saw hovered around twenty-three, maybe twenty-five. They were beautiful and entertaining. But they were girls. Self-centered, unre-markable, unimpressive girls.

For the first time in his dating life, David had gotten involved with a woman. And the woman was way out of his league.

THE RIDE HOME wasn't bad. Maybe fifteen minutes, and it gave Kate time to adjust to the fact that while marriage to Richard Nicholls could probably be termed a nightmare, being single and forty was going to suck in its own way.

There were so many things wrong with a relationship with David. Unfortunately, the fact that Kate liked him, really liked him, was getting in the way of reason. He was funny and he was so smart. That was something she never expected. He was educated and well read. He knew about politics and world affairs. He was big, athletic, gorgeous, and brilliant. What a way to blow the stereotype.

But he was too young for her… or rather, she was too old for him, and the look on his face when she told him how old she was really hurt. He did a good job hiding his discomfort, and when he said he'd talk to her, she almost called him a liar. She wouldn't hear from him. In all honesty, she didn't know if she wanted to. He'd never stay interested.

The bitter pill she had to swallow was that it wouldn't just be David. She'd pretty much figured this would be her life.

Young, old—it didn't really matter. Richard, the dirty bastard, hadn't just cheated on her. He'd condemned Kate to the life of many women her age whose husbands had found other women. She wasn't the type to try to find dates online, and in truth, she led a pretty solitary life. She had a few friends, and even though her family didn't live nearby, she was close to them.

But even knowing that, she'd never felt more alone. She would face the loneliness, the pitying looks, the rejection, and Richard would have his new wife until he got tired of her and found someone else. Kate, on the other hand, would have experiences like the one tonight. Nice man, lovely evening, but nothing would come of it. Everyone kept saying forty was the new thirty. She had a feeling those people weren't divorced and alone.

Kate swallowed hard. Bitterness wasn't becoming, and it wasn't something she was comfortable with, so she tamped it down as she pulled in her driveway.

After she threw the car into park, Kate stared at her house. It was beautiful, but she wondered if she should sell it and make a fresh start somewhere else.

Maybe when Laura went away to college she'd think about it.

Maybe by then she'd find the nerve.

Chapter 4

H IS DOORBELL RANG for what felt like the thousandth
     time that night, but he didn't mind.

David was glad he was home this year. He hated when
they had a game on Halloween and no one was there to
answer the door for the kids. Twelve bags of candy later,
things seemed to be slowing down.

He liked kids. They were honest—no bullshit. Someday
he'd like to have a few of his own, but the way things were
going, it was a long way off. He certainly wasn't going to give
any of the usual women in his life a baby. They were so
wrapped up in themselves he doubted they'd have time to be
mothers. Of course, he wasn't exactly model father material
either.

Over the past few weeks, ever since he had dinner with
Kate, David had been questioning everything in his life. He
didn't know if he wanted to settle down or even if he could,
but he wasn't happy with his partying bachelor existence
either. Granted, the sex was great, or it used to be. Lately, he
wasn't interested in seeing anyone. He just didn't care. Dating
the kind of girls he did was pointless. They were shallow and

self-absorbed, and what David had talked about with Kate was true—no one ever really cared about anything but appearances. He took his dates to the right restaurants, the right clubs. They were seen with the right people, but nothing felt *right*. Nothing felt right since he'd been with Kate.

He'd messed up bad when he ran scared because of her age, but what really finished it off was running into her in New York last weekend.

The city had fucking nine million people and they'd managed to end up in the same restaurant last Sunday morning. She was with an older woman; he was with Chelsea and two of their friends. He would never forget the look on Kate's face when she saw them. How she tried to slip out unnoticed and how he felt like the biggest shit on the planet.

David looked at the clock. His friends were out at a bar someplace, but lately he'd been stalked by a couple of overly ambitious photographers. He'd been trying to get them off his back, but he wasn't having any luck. For some reason, he was news, and he couldn't figure out why. Going out would just give them something to sell, so he decided to stay in rather than risk it.

Irritated that his movements were being controlled by other people, he grabbed his jacket and keys and headed out for a walk. He was restless, and he kept dwelling on the fact that even though his professional life was great, on the personal front it was anything but. The season seemed to start well, but he didn't seem to be helping the team. Nothing was more frustrating than feeling like he made absolutely no difference.

It was after nine and the street was still busy, but it was more adults than kids who were crowding the sidewalks and coming out of restaurants and bars. Some wore costumes and some just enjoyed the cool fall evening. He decided to get himself a cup of coffee and took a short walk to the local bookstore. He hadn't gotten ten feet in the door when he faced a huge display of Kate's books and a poster announcing when she would be making a visit.

Bestselling author Katherine Adams will be signing and talking about her newest book, Past Lives, on Sunday, November...

The rest didn't matter. David picked up a copy of the book, the same one she'd showed him in her suite. It was a thick volume. He flipped it over in his hands a few times, absorbing its weight and texture. He wondered what it took to write something like this. He read the synopsis on the inside flap and then the short biography in the back.

'Katherine Adams is the author of six novels in the best-selling Elliot Hunter series, including Fleeting Glance, Give Back, and Playing the Game. She lives in Pennsylvania with her husband and daughter.'

Her daughter. Her seventeen-year-old daughter. *Christ.* David focused on the picture on the book jacket. Kate was beautiful. Her face glowed, her eyes sparkled, and he thought about her after they'd made love. He could still feel her hands, her lips—he could feel everything, and he got crazy just thinking about her. He remembered the entire night with perfect clarity... and he'd been a dick and wrecked it.

David tucked the book under his arm and went to the café.

Never had he felt quite so empty. He wondered if they could have been something to each other, but just like always, he made sure he would never find out. There had been times in his life he'd been disappointed because something didn't work out the way he expected. He'd suffered personal and professional losses. But this was different. Rather than feeling that life had blindsided him, David knew he had no one to blame but himself. And looking once again at Kate's picture, he knew he was the only one who could fix the mess he'd made.

THREE WEEKS.

Kate sat at the desk in her classroom staring at the playing fields in the distance. It was getting colder, and pretty soon she wouldn't be able to look outside and see the activity, see the kids playing football or field hockey. Soon all she'd see would be a barren winter landscape.

It had been three weeks since she'd been in New York City and had seen David having brunch at Sarabeth's. Kate wasn't surprised she hadn't heard from him, especially since he wasn't alone in New York. She'd been working up the courage to actually call him, to take control of the situation. Now she was glad she'd never found the nerve. She'd watched his game on TV the night before, and a photograph of David, crushing an opposing player into the boards, dominated the back page of the newspaper she'd borrowed from the library. She stared at the picture and remembered the man who'd made love to her in California. The picture and the reality she'd experienced were in direct conflict. Did she want to take a risk on him?

Oh, yeah. She wanted him bad.

"Hey."

Kate's head shot up and she glanced toward the door where she saw her closest friend, Julie Higgins. Blonde and stunning, Julie was a French teacher and a few years younger than Kate. As silly as Kate was serious, as adventurous as Kate was cautious, Julie still didn't know about David.

"Hi," Kate said.

Julie walked in and glanced at the newspaper. "Following hockey?"

"A little."

"Laura's a big fan, isn't she?"

"Yeah. Maybe it'll give us something to talk about."

"Maybe." Julie sat in a student desk facing Kate. "One of the chaperones for the Honor Society trip backed out. I could use a hand. Are you available Friday night?"

"Sure." Laura was with her father this weekend, going to his house right after school on Friday. Kate stood and walked toward the windowsill with a stack of papers. "Where are we going?"

"The Flyers game."

Julie flinched as Kate spun toward her. "Flyers game?"

"Uh huh. The kids were invited because they adopted one of the team's charities."

Kate took three deep breaths to calm her racing heart before she spoke. "You know, I won't be much fun. I'm not a big fan."

A crease formed between Julie's drawn brows. "You just said you want to learn about the team. This is the perfect opportunity."

No, not perfect. She wanted to forget about David, not throw herself into his path. It was bad enough she was obsessing, watching his games on TV, reading about him in the newspaper, and staring at the poster on Laura's wall. She couldn't show up at one of his games. She drew in a deep breath and walked back to her desk.

"Kate, you've been acting weird since you got back from that conference. You want to tell me what's going on?"

"There's nothing going on," she said quietly.

Julie looked away and Kate wondered what she should do. Her friend knew her better than almost anyone, so telling her nothing was wrong was insulting. And in reality, Kate hated keeping secrets. Maybe if she told her she'd feel better. Confession was good for the soul—right?

Walking to the classroom door and closing it, Kate faced Julie. "You really want to know?"

"I want to help if I can."

"If I tell you, do you promise not to tell a soul? *I mean no one.*"

"Absolutely." Julie leaned forward and folded her arms on the desktop. "This must be a pretty big deal. You've never sworn me to secrecy before."

Bracing her hands on a desk behind her for support, Kate licked her lips. "I don't know how to say this," she began. "I had a—well, I sort of had a—fling when I was in California."

Julie's mouth hung open and then broke into a huge smile. "You did? Oh. My. God!"

"On my birthday, no less."

"Happy Birthday to you! Was he amazing?"

"He was a god. Younger than me."

"Really?" Julie squeaked. "How much younger?"

"Twenty-nine."

Julie let out a long breath. "You're killin' me. What did he look like?"

Reaching out, Kate turned the newspaper and tapped the picture of David. "Like that."

"Like David Burke! No way!"

Kate glanced at the picture, and the corner of her mouth twitched. "He didn't just look like David Burke." She bit her lip and blurted out the truth she still barely believed. "It *was* David Burke."

Nothing.

There wasn't a squeal, a gasp, nothing. Just a blank stare. Kate wasn't sure, but she was afraid her friend was in shock. "Julie? Are you going to say anything?"

Julie blinked once, looked away and then looked at Kate straight on. "You are my hero," she said quietly. "David Burke. *Mon dieu.*" Julie patted the desk next to the one she was sitting in and Kate obliged. "I want the whole story, and if you leave anything out I'll never speak to you again."

Thank God.

Kate drew a breath, smiled, and gave up her secret.

A LITTLE LESS than an hour later, Kate finished her tale, and this time, it was Julie who drew the breath and crossed her hands over her heart. "How did you keep it to yourself for so long?"

"I don't know. I didn't even tell my sister, and you know I tell her everything."

Julie nodded. "That is, without a doubt, the most romantic story I've ever heard."

"Yeah, well, it doesn't mean much. I haven't heard from him since I told him how old I am."

"No?" she asked.

"I should have known. I mean, why would he want to be with someone my age?" Kate folded her arms on the desk and dropped her head.

"You liked him, didn't you?"

Kate nodded. "It's sad. The first man who pays attention to me after Richard and I'm like a lovesick fifteen-year-old. Deep down, I'm still hoping for something—a call, a text. Every time my phone so much as chirps, I hope it's him."

Julie reached over and patted her shoulder. "Maybe it will be."

Kate shook her head and grabbed for the newspaper. "Want to see the other picture of him in this issue of the paper?" She flipped to the gossip page and there was David attached to a very attractive, very *young*, woman.

Julie scowled when she took in the picture. "Yeah, well, maybe he took a hit to the head that night. I mean she's beautiful, but she has nothing on you."

"Are you kidding? The only thing I have on her is about twenty years."

"Maybe it was a previous commitment?"

"Maybe, but it gets worse." Kate paused because this part of the story was humiliating—there was no other way to think about it. "Last weekend, I met my agent for brunch, remember?"

Julie nodded, remembering Kate's trip to New York. "You took her out for her birthday."

"Right. There I am, on a gorgeous Sunday morning,

enjoying my French toast and berries, and who walks into the café? David, with a gorgeous blonde on his arm."

"Shit. You have the worst luck."

"Tell me about it. The blonde was Chelsea Connor."

Julie gasped and Kate nodded. Chelsea was one of St. Andrew's most well-known alumni. Unfortunately, she was well known for being a society party-girl and a spoiled brat. Kate always thought if the faculty could give senior superlative awards, Chelsea would be voted *Most Likely to Marry for Money*. "I could see them the whole time. They were there with another couple and I felt like I was going to die. I had to go right past them when I left. I actually tried to cover my face with a coat. It was like a perp walk."

"Did they see you?"

"He did, she didn't. He looked terrified, like I was going to start a scene or something." Kate shook her head and glanced at his picture again. He was so gorgeous it hurt to look at him. "I'm pathetic." Kate dropped her head into her folded arms once again. "I actually thought there might be something between us. How could I think that? Am I stupid?"

"You aren't stupid, he is." Julie rubbed Kate's shoulder. "So, he's why you don't want to chaperone?"

"Uh huh." She lifted her head and sat up. "I know there will be thousands of people there, but I'll feel like such a stalker. What if he sees me?"

"You're going to let the possibility of seeing this man run your life? Are you going to stop going to the city because you might run into him?"

Kate stood and started putting papers into her briefcase. Julie was right—her life couldn't just stop. Kate was in the city a few times a month, at least. Damn. She hated it when people made sense.

"Our seats are somewhere up in the stratosphere," Julie added. "It's not like you're going to be rink-side."

Kate nodded. "Fine, I'll go. How many kids and how many of us?"

"Thirty kids, three adults. One bus. Not so bad."

"No," Kate said on a sigh. "Not so bad."

KATE RIFLED THROUGH her drawers, wondering aloud why she cared about what she wore to chaperone a field trip. "What's the big deal? I'll wear jeans and a sweatshirt."

"What are you doing, Mom?"

Kate turned when she heard her daughter's voice. "Good, you can help me."

"What's up?" Laura stepped into the room and her presence overwhelmed Kate.

She still didn't know when her little girl had grown into a goddess. Long limbed with dark hair and eyes, her daughter was a stunner. She didn't know why there weren't more boys calling.

Of course, there could have been boys calling and Kate didn't know. A lot could have been happening at Richard's and she wouldn't have a clue. Laura didn't tell her much. Things between them were uneasy, because even when the family had been intact, Laura favored her father. Each and every day, Kate mentally slapped herself for letting the creep drive a wedge between her and her daughter.

"I'm chaperoning a trip tomorrow night to the Flyers game and I don't know how to dress. It's my first time to a hockey game since I went to The Beanpot in college."

"The Beanpot?" Laura raised an eyebrow.

"The most intense college hockey tournament ever. B-C, B-U, Harvard, and Northeastern. You'll probably hear about it when I take you to visit schools in Boston. It's all about bragging rights."

"Cool, I didn't know you were into hockey."

"I used to be. Although, hockey players annoyed the crap out of me when I was younger. But it was a social thing in college. Everyone went. I remember the arena was freezing."

"How did you get roped into chaperoning tomorrow?" Laura sat on the bed and fiddled with a pink pullover Kate had tossed on the bed.

"Julie. Someone backed out." Kate shrugged, wondering herself how she managed to get into such awkward situations. But at least Laura was in a good mood. This was the most civil collection of sentences she'd shared with her daughter in a month. "So, what do you think?" Kate looked at the clothes on the bed.

"I could loan you my jersey," Laura offered.

"No, thanks. It would probably hang to my ankles." Even Laura had to chuckle at the image of Kate, nearly a full head shorter, in Laura's beloved jersey. Of course, Kate thought about the name emblazoned on the back—*Burke*. No. Absolutely no way she was wearing that.

"Jeans and a sweater should be fine. Where are your seats?"

"We're in the upper level."

"Nah, then don't worry about it. Dress like you're going to the mall." Laura seemed nervous, quieter than usual.

"How was your lesson?" This was an easy subject.

Kate loved talking to Laura about her piano classes and Laura loved telling her about it. Her daughter was truly talented, and Kate enjoyed every note she ever heard Laura play.

"I have a new piece for a recital in January. It's different. I think you'll really like it. It's a variation on the Canon in D."

"I can't wait." Kate sat next to her, loving the flow of the conversation. "And school?"

"Not bad. I got a ninety-four on my chemistry exam." Laura played with her hands, twisting and turning her long, slender fingers like Play-Doh. She stopped to tuck a lock of dark hair behind her ear.

"That's great. It's a good thing you have your dad's talent for science." Laura's nervousness was becoming a distraction, and Kate was curious about the real reason Laura wanted to talk. Something told her it wouldn't be good. "Is something bothering you, honey?"

Laura took a breath and then spoke slowly. "I have a favor to ask you."

"What?"

Laura's back stiffened and Kate braced herself. The conversation had been pleasant, but the sudden change in posture made Kate wonder how long it would take for things to turn sour. Every once in a while, they had moments that told Kate their relationship had the potential to be better, but she was always ready for Laura to turn into her father's daughter.

"I talked to Dad today. He and Marie are going to the Bahamas over Thanksgiving, and they asked if I could go with them."

She drew an audible breath. She had a special Thanksgiving planned for them, and now Richard and Marie were going to ruin it. "Didn't they just get home two hours ago?"

"Marie wants to do the beach for a few days. I'd like to go. It will only cost a thousand dollars."

Kate stood and forced the bile down. She was expected to pay, too? Give up her daughter and pay for it. *Turn this around.* "Well, since you're changing plans, I guess I can expect you for Christmas then. Grandma and Grandpa will be thrilled to see you."

Laura bowed her head and stayed quiet.

"Still planning the ski trip for Christmas?" Kate asked.

Her daughter's head bobbed up and down.

Once again Richard struck and used Laura to do it. It was underhanded and cruel, but she had to give him credit for being effective. No matter what she did, she found herself competing for her own daughter and losing.

"I see." Kate rose slowly, stood for a minute, and then excused herself to the bathroom because the burn behind her eyes signaled the inevitable loss of control. Crying would give Richard the upper hand. Again. Looking in the mirror, she rubbed her eyes and wondered what she'd ever done to deserve this treatment. Her husband rejected her, now her daughter. Even a dumb jock didn't want her.

Perfect.

She threw some water on her face and, trying to appear unaffected, reentered the bedroom. Laura was gone, probably growing impatient while she waited for an answer. Just like her father in that sense. Richard always wanted everything yesterday, doing whatever was necessary to get his way. How did this happen? They had an agreement about holidays, a plan that lawyers had hashed out over the previous months.

However, an agreement meant playing by the rules, and

Richard never played by the rules.

"Reality check, Kate," she mumbled. "Why did you think the divorce would be any different than the marriage?"

Seeing no way around the situation, Kate had to let Laura go, but decided she'd pay for half the trip. She found her purse, dug through and scribbled a check. If Richard wanted to play games, he could pay for half or Laura could use some of her savings for part of the ticket.

When Kate arrived at Laura's room, her daughter was lying on her bed with the cell phone pressed to her ear.

"She's not going to let me go." Kate stood quietly and listened to Laura's half of the conversation. "I asked, but then she wanted to know about Christmas... yeah, I told her I was still going skiing... I don't know... my dad said she would give in, but... yeah... I know... God, why can't she be easier? Marie would be totally cool about it."

Kate rubbed her hand over her heart. God, this sucked. Logically, Kate knew Marie could afford to be the 'good guy'. She was an outsider and she didn't have to make the tough decisions. But hearing Laura say things like that still hurt. Kate hadn't realized she'd made a sound until Laura turned sharply and swallowed.

"I'll call you back... uh huh... bye."

Kate held out the check and cleared her throat. "I decided to give you half. Dad can take care of the other half or... a... um..." It was hard to breathe. "I'll cosign for you to take the rest out of your savings account. Okay?"

"Half?" Laura's face twisted. "Um, but Dad was kind of thinking you could pay all of it."

"He'll have to rethink that." Kate rubbed her temple. She felt a headache coming on and she was so damned tired, she spoke without thinking. "If he wants you to go that badly, he can pay for it, or maybe *Marie* will give you the rest." It was a petty comment and Kate regretted it the minute it came out of her mouth. Laura went from defensive to angry and neither of them needed a confrontation. Kate took a step away from the door hoping to make a clean getaway. "I'll see you in the morning."

"I can't fucking believe this." The words were said under Laura's breath, but she fully intended Kate to hear them.

Kate turned and stared at Laura, who was now standing in her doorway with her arms folded and her face stone cold. Usually, Laura was more mature than most teens, but at that moment, she was pure attitude. She was a seventeen-year-old girl through and through—part woman, part child. Steeling herself, Kate was determined to maintain some shred of dignity. She took one step toward her daughter and then found herself getting irritated.

The girl was pushing every one of Kate's buttons. "Excuse me? What did you say?"

Laura tried to backpedal at first, stuttering, but then attacked. "That I can't believe you won't give me the money." Laura paused before she snarled and shot back. "You can afford it."

"It's not about the money, Laura. The simple fact is I don't see why I should have to pay for your father's whims."

"He wants me to go on a nice vacation! That's more than you're doing."

Now Kate was pissed. She'd told Richard all about the resort on St. Bart's. He'd done this—pitted them against each other—on purpose. "Really? Is that what you think?"

"What I think is that you are freaking useless. I need the

money, Mom."

Kate's blood started to roll. Mostly, she was angry at Richard, but Laura was giving a whole new meaning to the words 'spoiled brat'. No. She was not going to back down; for the first time, she didn't recoil at the attack but pressed toward her daughter. Kate was done being a doormat. "The only thing I've done that's 'useless' is give in to you at every turn. I shouldn't even give you half."

"Oh, my God! Why are you doing this to me?"

"I'm not doing this to you. This is not a punishment. But I have some real issues with the trip."

"Issues? What issues? It will be fun, and that's not in your vocabulary? You need to get a life." Laura snipped. "And to stay out of mine."

Watching her baby retreat behind the wall she'd built between them, Kate took a deep breath so she wouldn't lose it. She was fed up with worrying about everyone else, and what people around her, would think.

"You know what?" Kate felt the bile burn her throat. "Maybe you're right. Now that I'm free, maybe I'll do just that."

Kate did her own storming off. Leaving Laura with her mouth hanging open was the best thing she'd done all day.

JULIE HOPPED IN the Volvo as soon as Kate put the car in park. "What's going on? What's the emergency?"

Throwing the car in reverse, Kate backed out of the driveway, shifted hard again, and drove down the street. "My daughter is going to the Bahamas for Thanksgiving."

"What about the spa trip you planned?"

"I never got to tell her about it."

"Oh, Kate…"

"After I heard her say she wished I could be more like Marie, I got pretty upset. Then Laura told me I'm useless and I needed to get a life."

Julie reached out and touched Kate's arm.

"Screw them all," Kate murmured.

"Okay… so, why did you pick me up?"

"I need moral support." Julie braced her hand on the dash as Kate took a turn. "I'm going to do something crazy."

Julie reached out and gripped Kate's arm. "What are you going to do?"

"You'll see."

FIVE MINUTES LATER, when Julie froze at the door of Dragon's Tattoo Parlor, Kate grabbed her hand and pulled her through.

"Kate, are you sure you want to do this?" Julie whispered.

Kate nodded and smiled as she looked at the multiple-pierced, young man who approached them. "Positive."

Chapter 5

KATE SHIFTED UNCOMFORTABLY in the bus seat. She wasn't sorry she'd gone through with it, but getting a tattoo the day before she had to ride in a bumpy school bus wasn't her best idea. Julie saw her twisting and smiled.

"Does it hurt?"

"A little. Achy. Like a bad bruise."

"You look fabulous." Julie scanned her friend.

Kate looked down. Her jeans and white top were hardly anything special. "Whatever." *He isn't even going to know I'm there.* Which was what she wanted. Wasn't it?

"Whatever?"

"I'm not allowed to look nice?"

"Kate, you look more than nice."

Kate glanced at herself again, thought about the past day and a half, and had to acknowledge she'd prepped for this. She'd spent too much time putting together the 'perfect' outfit, right down to the jewelry, and spent an equal number of hours at the salon today having her hair and nails done.

Julie smirked, waiting for her to say something, but Kate wasn't going to admit to anything out loud. Okay, maybe she dressed thinking *if* he saw her, and *if* was the operative word, he'd notice—maybe. But why would he? She was a blip on the screen of David Burke's life. He was too busy being seen with local socialites. But earlier, as she stood before the full-length mirror in her bedroom, Kate knew exactly what she saw when she looked at her reflection. She couldn't help it. As she pulled on the high-heeled black booties and sponged on her lip gloss, the person staring back from the mirror wanted to be noticed; she wanted David to suffer. But it was only in her twisted imagination that something like that would actually happen.

The bus pulled into the parking lot at the arena and Kate's stomach lurched. It might have been up in her throat, it might have been in her chest—she wasn't sure. Doing a quick head count after disembarking, they followed the kids into the arena. Kate wondered if it was too late to get the bus to take her home.

The place was packed. People moved along the concourse, stopping at concession stands for food or souvenirs. The kids bolted into the rink and headed toward the boards to watch the Flyers and that night's opponents from Buffalo, during the pre-game skate.

Kate had forgotten about hockey arenas and was unprepared for the rush of testosterone that hit her as she walked down the steps. Rock music blared from the speakers and the players moved with a combination of brute force and poetic grace. The cutting sound of their skates, the click-clacking sound of the pucks hitting sticks, the entire scene assaulted every sense. She heard, she smelled, she felt…

Then she saw David, and her hormones headed south.

Julie gave her a nudge and Kate took another step, watching his movements with intensity. If she'd never seen this man before, she still would have wanted him. He didn't wear a helmet during the warm up and his hair caught the breeze as he skated. He was enormous, fully padded, and so handsome she had to remember to breathe. Part of the thrill for her was knowing what was beneath the equipment, and knowing what David was like when he was off the ice. It took her a moment to absorb the rest of her surroundings. Women lined the boards, many of them wearing David's jersey, and reality slapped Kate right in the face just like it did the day she saw him in New York.

He could have any one of them.

They were young and beautiful, with perfect bodies and flawless skin. His time with her was an aberration. She took a last look and just as she was about to turn away, David glanced in her direction and saw her. He froze. His eyes connected with hers and then a smile broke across his face. Part of Kate wanted to smile back, wave, something, but she held her enthusiasm and didn't respond in kind. She saw no reason to give his ego the boost.

"He is so *hot*," Julie said, tugging her sleeve. "And he's looking right at you."

"Don't read too much into it." Kate focused on the students because it was better than focusing on David and his phony flirtation. He was used to affecting women, and Kate had no intention of being affected. She called to the third chaperone who was at the boards with the kids and told him she and Julie were headed to the seats. A few of the kids waved and Kate turned to leave, never giving David an inch.

She glanced at Julie. "Where are we sitting?

"Kate, he's still staring at you."

"So?" Kate glanced back and saw the smile gone from his face.

David didn't look angry, but confused. *Confused? Really?* She started up the steps. *Well, good.* After the way he treated her, he needed to feel like crap, even if it was only for twelve seconds.

NORMALLY, DAVID NEVER looked at the crowd. It was an unwritten rule: the only fans who got his attention during warm-ups were the kids. He'd always toss a few pucks over the glass to the little guys, but everyone else didn't exist. The signs, the women gawking and flirting, broke his concentration. And on a game day, from the minute he walked into the arena, the thing he focused on was the game at hand. Nothing else. He couldn't afford distractions. But tonight, something made him look into the seats.

There she was. Her fitted jeans accented every curve and her shirt was cut just low enough for David to notice a bit of lace peeking from behind. When she moved her head, her hair softly swept her shoulders. Kate raked him with her hazel eyes, and even though she was staring at him like he was the lowest form of life on planet Earth, he couldn't do anything but smile. Like a fucking idiot, he stood there and smiled.

Kate, on the other hand, didn't smile at all. There wasn't even the slightest twitch at her mouth. He thought she might soften, might give him some encouragement, but after a minute of making him feel like a complete shit, she looked at a group of teenagers near the boards, said something, and then turned on a very high heel and walked up the stairs.

Cam skated up next to him and fixed his eyes on the stands where Kate had been standing. "Was that the chick from California?"

David nodded.

"She looked pissed. Didn't you take her out to dinner?"

David tapped his stick on the ice. "Yeah, I haven't talked to her since, though."

Cam shook his head. "Okay, so? You didn't click."

David focused on the blue line embedded in the ice. The problem was they had clicked. He liked her a lot and then he put her off, lapsing into his old routine.

It seemed impossible, but as David watched her retreating form, he felt a chill. Maybe it was a good thing he'd put the brakes on the relationship. Granted she was great in bed, but knowing how old she was, and all the baggage she brought to the table...

He stopped and used his gloved hand to push the hair back from his forehead. *Jesus Christ. When did I become such a dick?*

Kate wasn't like any girl he'd ever known. She was sincere and sweet and totally unprepared for what happened between them. She didn't expect anything. She'd been minding her own business and he took advantage. On top of that, *he* was the one who invited her out to dinner when they got home. David thought about how happy she looked in California, when he'd left her in that big bed with a light kiss and a promise to call. How she looked when she first saw him at Piccolo's. Thinking about her made his heart tighten and his stomach jump, and David blew out a long breath. She mattered to him, regardless of how much he fought it. After just a couple of times together, Kate mattered.

Then he remembered the look on her face when he saw her at that restaurant in New York a week ago. She looked— then it dawned on him that the look on her face a few minutes ago was the same one he had seen last Sunday morning. He thought she was angry, but that wasn't it—it was hurt. He'd hurt her. He'd said he wanted to see her again and then she saw him with Chelsea, and that made him a slimy cheat—just like her ex. Kate didn't know how he felt about Chelsea, that what she saw that morning wasn't a date. No, it was the perfect storm of misunderstandings. Except for the part where he avoided Kate when he found out her age. That was totally on him. He didn't even want to think about it because basically it made him a first-class asshole. He may not be a cheater, but he was definitely a coward. *A real fucking prize.* Turning away from her retreating form, he skated toward the tunnel.

Shit. This game was too important for him to think about anything else. A win against a team like Buffalo early in the season would set a tone, but how was he supposed to get her out of his head? David leaned against the wall next to the dressing room door and cursed. She was up there someplace. He wanted to get a message to her. Maybe she could meet him after the game and he could explain what she saw last week.

She's not important to me. I haven't been with anyone since I met you.

Like she'd believe that. Trying to see Kate was probably not the best idea he ever had, but hey, what was life if he couldn't live dangerously?

So where was she? When he last looked, she was on her way to the mezzanine with a tall blonde. He needed to see her. David didn't know where the attack of conscience was coming from and why this woman was giving it to him, but something told him he should listen to himself. If he let Kate get away, he had a feeling it was going to be one of the worst mistakes of his life.

"YOU REALLY FROZE him out," Julie said. "No pun intended, of course."

Kate finished the head count and sat down in her seat. "How is it you're the advisor of this group, but I'm doing all the work?"

"You're better at it, and the kids expect you to be in charge." Julie handed her a bottle of water and pressed on, even though Kate had ignored everything she'd said about David so far. "I think he likes you."

"I don't think so," Kate said. She shook her head and looked at Julie. "You know, I almost folded. I almost acknowledged him."

"He's so good looking. How did you breathe?"

"I don't recall." That was a lie. Kate remembered every second of their night, before and after they made love. The things they'd talked about. The easiness of it all. But she wasn't going to be that kind of fool again. David may have been sweet when they spent time together, but that man was a broken heart waiting to happen. She must have been crazy, going out with him after California. Between Richard and Laura, Kate had more than enough to deal with.

She felt her phone buzz in her pocket. Taking it out, she saw the text. Damn him.

Meet me after the game. We need to talk.

"I can't believe him." Kate didn't think she said it out loud, until she noticed Julie looking over her shoulder at her iPhone.

"He wants to see you?"

Kate was going to ignore the message, but instead she opened a reply and keyed in one word. *No.*

She sent it and then looked at Julie, who raised an eyebrow and shook her head.

"What?"

"Kate, you could see him if you wanted. Al and I can handle the trip back."

"And what am I going to do? Wait around the locker room door like some desperate puck bunny?"

"I'm sure if you told him you were willing to meet him, he'd make sure that didn't happen."

For a split second Kate considered it. Part of her, the weak part, the part that let her ex-husband control her for twenty years, almost took out the phone and sent him another text. Then she thought about what would happen. He'd take her out. He'd make excuses. He'd seduce her. Make more promises. And then he'd vanish from her life.

"No. He's a mistake. I don't know what would make him think I'd actually go out with him after what he did."

Julie laughed. "Uh, he's David Burke. I'm guessing he doesn't get turned down a lot." She paused. "I mean if it was that number twenty-two guy, Tricarico, I could understand. That boy looks like he walked into a light post."

"You're a big help. I'd like to think I have some pride."

"Pride isn't going to keep you warm tonight," Julie said.

"No," Kate began, "but it could keep me from being hurt

again."

DAVID CURSED AS he walked through the tunnel. The other team was up by two goals and had held them to six shots on goal. Of course, he and his teammates were acting more like prom queens than pro athletes, so it was no wonder they were getting their asses kicked. He got snagged for an interview, since he'd actually managed to score a goal, along with his three penalties, but he really just wanted to tell their media guy to shove it. What was he going to say? He was going to shovel clichés at the interviewer about teamwork and coming out and working hard the last two periods. Blah, blah, blah. It was all bullshit.

But bullshit or not, he had to do it, so he turned on the charm and gave them what they wanted. When he entered the dressing room, the coach was already screaming at the defense.

"...we'll be lucky if the fans don't start throwing shit at your sorry asses." Coach spun at David. "And you—what was your fucking problem? We don't pay you to sit in the penalty box, Burke."

David almost responded, but didn't. As captain, he had to set a good example for the younger players, and with the coach being in such a shit-ass mood, anything David said would likely earn him a fine.

The tirade went on for several minutes, and David tuned it out. He kept thinking about Kate and how she looked at him. Why did he feel so guilty? He'd ditched women before. But his mind couldn't let go of how she felt in his arms, and how she kissed him, and more than anything, how what he did for a living didn't matter. She'd gone out with him in spite of his playing hockey for a living, not because of it. Finally when the coach slammed his office door, David refocused and checked his messages.

She'd responded with one word. "*No.*" She didn't clarify it, didn't rip his head off, she just said no. He wiped his face with a towel, glanced to his right, and saw Jay Hemmings with his head down. He was a perennial forty-goal scorer and one of David's best friends, but tonight Jay hadn't been able to get close to the net. "You okay, Hemmy?"

"I had a fight with Annie before I left."

David slapped his friend on the back. Jay was so in love with his wife, it was almost scary. "Call her. You're no good to us if you're worried about where you're sleeping when you get home."

"Yeah." Jay looked over. "What's up with you?"

"I'll tell you about it later."

"It? Or her?" Jay asked. "Your face says you're having woman problems."

David grimaced. Jay knew him too well. Realizing he'd pretty well blown it with Kate, David looked across the dressing room toward Cam and nodded. They'd talked briefly about going out after the game, but he'd held off answering until he heard from Kate. Now that he had, David was going to his back-up plan, to get drunk and laid.

Sticking his phone back in his pocket, he thought about that for a second, and it helped him understand yet another reason why Kate probably didn't want to see him.

Chapter 6

LAURA WALKED TO the bus stop, fully intending to go to school. But when her friend Tracy pulled up in the shiny red Mustang she'd received as a seventeenth birthday present, Laura hopped in. The two girls looked at each other, smiled, and knew they weren't going to school that day. Who the hell needed school, anyway?

"Breakfast first?" Tracy asked.

"Let's go to the city. There's more around, and then we can go shopping," Laura said. She scooted into the seat, and rummaged through her purse for a pair of sunglasses. "I hate my mother."

Tracy looked over and rolled her eyes. "I don't know what your problem is. Your mom is like the nicest person on the planet."

"She's such a pain in the ass. I swear she has no clue what it's like to live with her, with her questions and prying and always wanting to get into my life. She won't give me the money for the Bahamas, which totally pissed off my dad, and, get this, I think there might be a guy in the picture."

"That's awesome! Who? Is he nice?"

"I have no idea. She and her friend were talking. I think it might be over, though. I dunno. I hope it is."

"Why? Your dad has a girlfriend," Tracy responded.

"That's different. Marie is, well you know, she's cool."

"Marie is weird."

"Whose side are you on, anyway?" Laura asked.

"Lor, I love you, but your mom got treated shitty by your dad. He talked to her like she was dirt and cheated on her. And Marie is creepy."

"Dad said she deserved it." Laura did *not* want to talk about this.

"No one deserves that. I hope she found some hot guy to date."

"Not likely."

"Why do you say that? Laura, your mother is gorgeous and famous. She could probably have any guy she wanted."

Everything Tracy had said was true. Her mother was all those things and more, and Marie *was* a little off, but Laura still didn't know what to believe. Who was telling her the truth? Maybe that was the problem. Her mother never told her anything.

"I don't want to talk about her anymore. Can we go eat?"

Tracy shook her head and drove toward Philadelphia. There was a little café near Rittenhouse where they could eat, and hopefully Laura would cool off and relax.

THEY ENTERED THE café and were seated at a booth near the counter. No one questioned their presence. They didn't look like two high school girls cutting school; they looked like two college girls out for a bite to eat, and they knew it.

They'd been there close to half an hour when Laura watched Tracy's eyes go wide as she stared at the door. "Ohmigod, ohmigod, ohmigod!" Half whisper, half scream, her friend was barely breathing as spoke.

"What?"

"Tyler Graves and Jack Nelson just walked in."

Laura turned in her seat and her own mouth dropped open. It was true. Coming toward them were two gorgeous hockey players. And the guys were looking right at her. *Holy crap.*

Tyler Graves was huge and good looking in tough kind of way, but Jack Nelson was so… he was just perfect.

"I think I'm dreaming." Tall and buff, with light brown hair and amazing eyes, the twenty-one-year-old center was a vision. She always thought David Burke was the best-looking guy on the team, until she saw Jack in person.

"They are *so* hot," Tracy whispered.

Laura could only nod. Jack smiled at Laura and Tracy as he walked past and sat in the next booth. Tyler Graves sat directly behind Tracy and she just about fainted. But Jack slid into the other side of the booth and before he looked at his menu, he grinned at her again and winked. Was she awake? He just winked at her?

Laura drew a deep breath and forced herself to calm down. She went back to her breakfast, but looked up from time to time to see the hockey player was still staring at her. She almost died in her seat when he broke into a wide smile. He was flirting with her. Honest to God flirting, like he was interested in her or something. She couldn't help it; she bit her lip and blushed.

"You are bright red," Tracy told her.

"I know—I can feel it. He keeps staring at me." She glanced up again. Yup. Still watching.

"So what? You could do worse."

That was the truth, but since when did this happen to her? He was the hottest guy she had ever seen. She was only seventeen, a music nerd, and other than one guy last year, who was so shy he could barely talk to her, boys were not interested in her. Not that Jack Nelson was a boy. He was a man, which made the situation even more unnerving. Running away seemed like a good idea. "Let's go. It's making me uncomfortable."

She grabbed her jacket and purse, and just as she was about to slide out of the booth, Jack slid in next to her.

"Hi," he said. "Okay if I sit down for a minute?"

"Uh, sure." Laura moved in, toward the window, and glanced at Tracy, who was completely dumbstruck. Tyler Graves walked by the table, patted Jack on the shoulder and nodded at them. "See you later, Nelly."

"Later, man." Once Tyler had left, he turned his attention to her. "I'm Jack."

Laura blinked her eyes, but didn't speak. She couldn't. *Oh, God. Holy crap. Say something. Something!*

"I figured I should talk to you rather than just stare." He grinned, more than likely realizing he'd sent them both into shock, but he was sweet. Kind. In fact, he almost seemed a little nervous. *No way.* "Do you have a name?"

Finding her voice wasn't easy, but finally she managed to squeak out a response. "Laura." She could play coy or dumb, but decided not to. "You play for the Flyers, right?"

"A lady who knows her hockey."

Sipping what was left of her tea to give herself a few seconds to regroup, she nodded. "Mm hmm."

He started talking and Laura responded, but the words were bouncing around her brain. She took in the whole package, while Tracy tried to keep from fainting. He seemed genuinely nice, very down to earth, and he could form complete sentences, which was always a plus. He kept his hair short, but it was thick and gleamed with gold flecks. Laura marveled at the length of his eyelashes, which framed eyes that were such a deep blue she could swim in them. What made him even more beautiful was his smile. He was one of those people who smiled with his eyes. That was all it took. Laura melted and just barely heard herself say yes when he asked for her number.

She keyed it into his phone for him and only started breathing again when he'd left the diner.

Laura dropped her head on the table. "Tell me that really happened."

"It happened."

"Holy shit," she squeaked.

"Holy shit is right," Tracy said. "If he wants to see you, how are you going to get out?"

"I'll figure it out. How old did I tell him I was?"

"You didn't, but he thinks you go to Penn."

Laura nodded. When Jack asked if she was a student at the Ivy League university, she said yes. "I did take a class there." A little lie.

Tracy raised her eyebrows. "How are you going to get out?"

"I'll make sure I'm at my dad's. Marie believes in giving me my freedom. You know, the ability to take charge of my life."

"Your mom would flip."

This was how Laura was going to deal with her screwed up life. What was that old saying about lemons and making lemonade? The upside to her father having custody was that he and Marie wouldn't be paying attention. Her mom would be, and that would make seeing Jack impossible. Not that he was going to call her. She didn't believe for one second that she would actually hear from him, but if she did...

"My dad keeps talking about petitioning for sole custody. Chances are I'll be with him fulltime anyway. They're so wrapped up in each other they won't even notice."

Tracy stood and grabbed her coat. A small redhead with a riot of freckles across her nose, she spoke her mind. "That sucks."

"Maybe," Laura said. "But he could make it feel better."

KATE RAN THE brush through her hair, pulled it neatly into a clip, and mentally prepared for her day. She didn't have to keep teaching, but she really enjoyed the time away from the house. When her last book was sold, quitting crossed her mind, but then Richard left and the thought of being isolated in her office with only her characters to keep her company was too frightening. Her work at school, her friends, kept her sane through the divorce.

It was three classes at a very wealthy private school, hardly a tough schedule, and the headmaster gave her whatever time she needed to tend to business about her books. But ultimately it was about the kids. She enjoyed being with them, teaching them, watching them develop a love for the written word. Kate knew this was good work, not lucrative, but good work nonetheless, and she was happy she didn't have to worry about money.

"Kate?" The deep voice carried effortlessly through the old house. "Where are you?"

Kate's stomach churned. *Richard.* Why was he there? How did he get in the house? Eight-thirty in the morning and she had to deal with this aggravation. What a way to start the day. She slipped into her shoes, adjusted her plaid skirt and looked in the mirror one more time. Evaluating how she looked, Kate opened one more button on her sweater, and then headed downstairs. She met Richard in the hallway, getting ready to come up.

"Oh, good. I want to talk to you," he said.

"How did you get in?"

"Laura gave me her code to the garage door." He grinned sheepishly, hoping to use the charm that always made Kate bend to his will. She knew his pattern. Unfortunately, if his charm didn't work, he'd resort to using something else to get his way. She steeled herself and walked past him toward the kitchen.

"I'd appreciate, since you no longer live here, that you don't come in without an invitation."

He followed her, tossing his blazer over the back of a chair. Kate checked over her shoulder during a prolonged silence and saw her ex-husband staring at her ass. *Great.*

Mentally counting to ten, Kate filled her thermal mug with coffee, added a packet of sweetener, a little milk, and then turned to face him. "What do you want, Richard?"

"About Laura's trip," he started. "You only gave her half."

"That's right. I figured that was fair. You can pay the other half."

"I'm not as well set as you are."

"What do you mean, 'well set'?"

"Your book is doing very well. And I know your agent is negotiating a new contract for you. Something quite lucrative."

"How do you…" Kate's stomach turned at the amount of information he had. Her agent had spoken to her a few days ago about the *possibility* of a multi-book deal and Richard already knew about it. How? And why didn't her lawyers have information about him? It was making her crazy. He cleared his throat and that forced her to focus her attention back to the matter at hand.

Laura.

"Richard, according to the joint custody agreement, she was supposed to spend Thanksgiving with me. I had a trip planned for us that I may now have to cancel. We shouldn't even be having this conversation."

"So this is your way of forcing her to spend time with you?" He folded his arms and leaned against the counter.

"No, I thought she wanted to spend time with me. I guess I was wrong. She can go, but I'm not footing the whole bill." Kate moved away from him again, going into the back foyer, putting on her coat and picking up her messenger bag. Trying to maintain her composure in the face of her ex-husband's assault wasn't easy. "If you don't want to pay the other half, she has plenty of money in her savings account. I told her I'd co-sign the withdrawal."

"You are one selfish bitch." Richard had perfected the disdainful sneer he cast in her direction, but Kate felt her heart chill down ten degrees when he started to approach. "That bag you just tossed over your shoulder cost nearly as much as what Laura needs. You'll spend money so you can have your little toys and luxuries, but your daughter can go to hell." He trapped her against a wall with one hand on each side of her and pressed his hips against hers. Kate could feel he was aroused and she looked away. Once upon a time she would have been happy to know she could excite him, now she was disgusted. It wasn't about attraction, but about power. He had it, she didn't, but she had to find a way to get it away from him. Finally, when she made eye contact, when she didn't fall apart, Richard stepped away.

It was a small victory, but Kate would take it. Drawing a breath, she centered herself and thought about getting a restraining order.

"Richard, I know it's a novelty for *you*, but *I* have to go to work." At this point all she wanted was to get away from him. The comments about her supposed selfishness were the most ridiculous things she ever heard. Talk about the pot calling the kettle black, jeez! Richard and Marie had turned materialism into an art form. Kate pulled open the back door and held it for him.

"You aren't going to change your mind?" he asked.

"Why should I? It's bad enough I have to bear the indignity of my daughter choosing you and your mistress over me. You want me to pay for it, too?"

"Face facts, Laura doesn't want to be with you." Richard crossed the room again and stood over her. He was close, threatening, but he didn't do anything. He didn't even make a move with his hand. He just talked. "She wants to live with Marie and me. Every minute she's here, she's miserable."

Kate drew a long breath as her heart collapsed. It was an old dig. She knew Laura was unhappy, but hearing Richard use it yet again, hurt. Another minute and Kate would lose it.

"You know I've been trying to avoid this," he began, "but Laura's been begging me to call the attorney. I think I might." He turned away from her and walked toward his car.

"Richard!" she called.

"We'll be in touch."

He didn't turn back, didn't give her an inch. Having joint custody was all Kate had to keep her relationship with Laura from completely falling apart. If she went to Richard permanently, she'd lose her daughter altogether. Climbing into her car, she slammed her fist on the steering wheel. Life just sucked.

THE CHOCOLATE ICE cream slid down her throat and Kate thought that some days seriously needed to be do-overs. Hers had started with Richard being a disgusting pig and was ending with her tearing apart her den.

Kate thought she'd left the folder with all her old rejection letters in the desk in the den. Setting aside the now empty ice cream bowl, she rifled through the drawers, found nothing, and moved her search to the large bookcase. The doors on the bottom half concealed more papers than Kate wanted to see at that point, but finding the letters was important. She wanted to show her creative writing class how many rejections she received on her first book.

The saying went that most writers could wallpaper a bathroom with all the rejections they received; Kate could wallpaper several.

It had been an interesting journey. She sat down to write her first book when Laura started school. She was working part time, just as she was now, and needed something else to fill her days while her daughter was at school and evenings while Richard climbed the academic ladder. There were always late meetings and drinks with colleagues. He made sure he was home for Laura, always eager to hear about her day and take her to whatever activity she may have had. Kate loved his devotion to their child and admired that he took care of business after she had gone to bed for the night. It was then that Kate worked on her stories, sometimes late into the night, following a childhood dream of writing wonderful books. Her first two books were horrible, and were still tucked in a drawer in her desk, never to be seen by another soul. She was struggling with the third one, and then everything changed.

She always envisioned herself writing romances, because that was who Kate was, that was what she believed in. But one day, she put a gun and a badge in the hands of her heroine and Special Agent Elliot Hunter was born.

The character took her places she never imagined. Elliot was strong, smart, and could put a bullet between a bad guy's eyes without even trying too hard. She was also soft as goo on the inside, having fallen hard for a gorgeous, and often absent, Navy commander. Kate loved her, because as Richard became more controlling, and more abusive, Elliot became tougher, more capable, and less likely to take anyone's shit.

It took her a year to finish her first book in the series and get up enough nerve to start querying agents and editors. The rejections came fast and furious. Finally, she found an agent who believed in her and started her on the right path. It took another full year to sell it.

It was a paperback and did better than anyone expected. The book that followed sold even more, and it mushroomed from there. The most recent book, *Past Lives*, was her fourth hardcover and a bestseller from day one. Kate never imagined people would actually want her autograph.

Pulling out a stack of papers, Kate smiled as she went through the memories. Most of what she found were remnants of Laura's childhood, old schoolwork or drawings. There were some announcements from school, and finally the file she was looking for. She had no idea how it had gotten here, except that since Richard didn't think it was terribly important, he probably shoved it in there to get it out of the way. When she tugged on it, a manila envelope came out as well. Never being one to squelch her curiosity, Kate bent the metal clasp and emptied the contents into her lap.

It was a record of betrayal. The envelope was filled with pictures of Richard and Marie. Kate guessed Richard had forgotten it even existed. Most of the photos were taken at social functions Kate could only assume were all the "faculty" meetings he attended over the years. Not being able to help herself, she kept looking and the tears flowed. She wiped at her eyes with the sleeve of her sweatshirt and felt the full weight of her divorce come crashing down. *How could she have been so blind?* Based on one picture alone, the affair must have been going on for at least seven years. She figured the time based on a shirt Richard wore in one of the pictures. A shirt she'd picked out for him.

Marie hadn't changed that much. Her hair might have been a little longer, but her ultra-thin frame was highlighted by the fitted black clothing she wore. In every picture, she was hanging on Richard. Kate's husband. The man Kate wanted to love her more than anything, and now she knew she never had a chance. Richard's affection was always with Marie and Kate was just there to keep the house—and, for the last few years, pay the bills.

At least the money problems were starting to make sense. If Richard was keeping a mistress for all that time, she understood why money was tight a lot longer than it should have been. Kate gazed at one picture of Richard and Marie at the beach. It looked tropical, like they'd taken a vacation together. Kate had wanted a vacation like that, someplace warm and romantic. They never went. He was always too busy.

Kate wanted to be in love, but more than that, she wanted someone to love her back. She wanted someone to hold her, touch her, protect her. Even though they hadn't had a marriage in years, she missed the feel of Richard's body in their bed. How he would unconsciously wrap himself around her during the night and tell her she was beautiful. Kate understood, after he'd asked for the divorce, that he was talking to someone else when he uttered the words in the dark, but she missed them anyway. Even though they belonged to another woman, those words were all she had, and at the time, they gave her hope.

Well, now the photos gave her hope. And leverage. Glancing again at the pictures in her lap, and thinking about her ex-husband's latest threat, Kate tucked everything back in the envelope and marked it for her lawyer.

Chapter 7

"GODDAMN! WOULD YOU be careful? My arm hurts like a son of a bitch." David spat the words at the trainer who was strapping a huge ice pack to the upper part of his right arm.

The trainer grinned and continued applying the ice. David was sure the guy was a closet sadist. How else could anyone get pleasure out of a job like his? He was suffering in silence when one of the media assistants poked her head into the trainer's room and asked him about doing an interview.

"I'm not doing any fucking interviews."

"But, Dave, John said—"

He turned on the assistant, who might have been twenty-three. "I don't give a shit what John said. No interviews!"

The young woman scurried off and the trainer clucked his tongue. "A little hard on her, don't you think?"

David heard his own low grumble. He had been too hard on her. It would cost him. Any minute their communications director would be reaming his ass for the venom he spewed. He'd have to buy flowers or something to make it up to her.

For the past eight years, his life in the NHL had been

enough for him. The games, his teammates, and the women who were always available for company were enough. But now there was a hole inside him, something vacant. He hadn't ever felt the need to settle down. But since he met Kate, everything had changed. None of it made any sense. For the first time in a long time, David felt like he was missing out on something.

Jay came in and lay on the training table next to David's. "Rough night?" he asked.

"Fuck off," David responded.

It had been a bad night, and if he was lucky he'd get away with a slap on the wrist from the NHL. But holy shit, it wasn't his fault that the Canucks leading scorer liked to admire his own passes instead of watching for other players. So, David hit the kid hard in open ice. It was a clean hit, but it was ugly. After that, their enforcer dropped his gloves and David had his first serious fight in two seasons.

Jay propped himself up on his elbows. "Still thinking about the teacher?"

David draped his unwrapped forearm over his eyes. "Shit."

"You wanna tell me about it?"

His best friend knew him better than he knew himself. They'd been teammates for seven years, a lifetime in this league. "I can't get her out of my head."

"What is it about this one?"

David growled.

"Look," Jay clapped his hands together and rubbed them quickly, like he was trying to start some internal fire. "Let's get the hell away from here and go to my house. We'll pick up some beer and pizza and watch your fight on Sports Center."

David glanced at the ice pack resting on the knuckles of his right hand. He'd be remembering the fight for a few days. "Annie won't mind?"

Jay grinned and shook his head. "Nah, I'll call her."

David flexed his fingers and rolled his shoulders when the trainer took the ice off his arm and hand. He stood and thought about his friend. Jay had the best marriage of anyone he knew, and his wife was something special. She was practical and down to earth, and she had a job. She worked part-time as an ER nurse at the university hospital. That was how she and Jay met. Annie was on duty when Jay was rolled in with a dislocated shoulder and a concussion. He said he fell in love with her when she told him to stop screaming like a baby and threatened him with restraining straps. For six months, he pursued her with a passion until she finally agreed to marry him.

David sat on the bench in the dressing room and pulled one of Kate's books out of his bag. This was a problem. He was obsessing over a woman he'd gone out with *twice*. Jesus. If he wasn't the captain of this team, he would have been the subject of every joke and jab for the rest of the season. He flipped it to back cover and gazed at the picture. Every inch of him responded to the image. He had to find a way to see her again. For some reason it was important to him that she know he wasn't a total idiot.

DAVID SWUNG HIS car into a parking space and felt intimidated before he even opened the door. The ivy covered walls and quiet elegance of the old private school screamed money. The students here had made a huge contribution to the team's annual food drive and had earned an appearance from a member of the team. Originally, one of the rookies was supposed to come, but the kid separated his shoulder in last night's game and David volunteered. Being a veteran meant he could pick and choose the charities he supported, and he usually represented the team at more high-profile events. This was a simple photo op at a small school, but being the team captain, he had a responsibility to go above and beyond. That, and he owed the community relations director a favor since he bit the head off one of his little minions the other night.

The school was incredible. There were three old, brick buildings, one with a large tower, facing a grassy common. Students walked past him in small groups. If ever there was a perfect image of a prep school, St. Andrew's was it.

It was foreign to David. Even with his top flight education, he never really felt like he completely fit in at a place like this. At B-C he stayed with his own kind, jocks mostly, kids who were there to learn and play hockey. He partied, he broke heads on the ice, and he pulled good grades.

He looked at the slip of paper, and after a survey of the grounds, still had no idea where he was supposed to be. Normally, he'd have one of the community relations people with him, but no one was available, and, initially, David didn't see the big deal in taking a ride by himself. Until now. He didn't know where the hell to go.

He walked over to a group of students and cleared his throat. They turned to him and he noticed they were perfect, all the same... not even a zit.

"Can one of you tell me how to get to Larchmont Hall?"

One of the girls cocked her little blonde head to the side

and spoke, although it seemed her mouth barely moved and her words came out with a nasally cadence. She didn't make eye contact, and once she'd pointed out the building, David ceased to exist. Oh yeah, this was going to be a rip-roarin' good time.

DAVID FOUND THE headmaster's office without too much trouble and the photo session was relatively painless. The headmaster, the teacher, and kids who attended the reception were very pleasant, and he guessed that was why they were involved with the charity. Unlike the kids he met outside, this group seemed to care about something other than themselves.

He signed some autographs and made small talk with everyone about the team and how the season was going. It was standard stuff, and David had to admit he rarely minded these personal appearances. He made a lot of money playing a game for a living. The least he could do was give a little time to the people who supported him and the team.

However, he had no intention of staying forever. The clock on the wall and the lull in the conversation told him it was time to craft his exit. This was a twenty minute visit and he'd already been there for twenty-five. He'd moved away from the group to put on his jacket when something he heard brought him back into the conversation.

"It was a great game."

"Buffalo was ruthless."

The Buffalo game. He was going to say something but didn't. David had tried to block that one out for so many reasons.

"I don't recall that outing," the headmaster said stiffly. "Refresh my memory."

"Honor Society," the teacher said. "Julie, Kate, and I chaperoned."

"Ah, yes. Now I remember." He nodded thoughtfully and turned to David. "Thank you so much for coming. The students were very excited to meet you."

David barely heard him. All he could think about was the fact that he was at Kate's school. It had to be her school—either that or he'd stumbled on the coincidence of the century.

"Mr. Burke?" the headmaster said.

"Oh, sorry." He grasped the elderly gentleman's extended hand. "It was my pleasure to come. Thank you for your support."

A genteel nod was the only acknowledgement, and as the headmaster started to retreat into his office, David spoke. "Excuse me, sir? I believe an acquaintance of mine is a teacher here, and I wanted to say hello." The old man turned and gazed at him over the top of his glasses. "Kate Nicholls?" he said. "Where would I find her?"

The headmaster considered him, and for a minute David wondered if he would get his answer.

He was more than relieved when the craggy voice said, "Room fifteen, across from the library."

"Thank you. Thank you very much." Stepping out of the office, David cleared his head just like he did before he stepped on the ice. He took a deep breath, and as he started down the hallway, he hoped she would forgive him.

Chapter 8

KATE CROUCHED DOWN and gripped the drawer handle with both hands. She braced one knee on the floor, squared her shoulders and pulled.

Nothing.

Biting her lip, she did it once again, throwing all she had against the recalcitrant drawer. With a final tug, the drawer flew open and tossed Kate right onto her backside.

"Damn it." She shook her head and vowed to ask the assistant headmaster, beg if necessary, for a new file cabinet.

The hand that settled under her elbow startled her, but not nearly so much as when she looked up and saw David Burke's face.

"Nice landing," he said.

Scrambling to her feet, Kate dusted off her skirt and stepped away from him. He filled up every inch of space in the room, took all the air. He was such a presence. Kate didn't know how she was still standing. "What are you doing here? How did you find me?"

"Which question do you want me to answer first?" he said.

"You know what? It doesn't matter." She waved toward the door. "Go away."

"I have a few things to say and then I'll go."

"The bad days always manage to get worse." Kate pressed her fingers to her temples and massaged, hoping to relieve the tension in her head.

"I'm sorry. I want to explain. When I saw you in New York—"

Kate put her hand up in a stopping motion. "Oh, God. Not New York. Please. I don't need placating."

"I'm not. Like I said, I'm explaining. I owe you an apology. I was meeting a friend and his fiancée asked Chelsea to join us without knowing we weren't seeing each other anymore."

"I wish you wouldn't."

"I wasn't playing you."

"Okay, so you've explained. Thanks. Bye."

He didn't move. He just stood there and stared at the floor, but he was a little too close for comfort. Her desk was an effective barrier, so Kate moved to the other side to put some distance between them.

"I think too much," he finally said.

What?

Kate raised her eyes and looked at him through the veil of her lashes and actually bit down on the inside of her cheek to keep from laughing at what he said. "You… excuse me? I find that hard to believe."

"I'm sure you do. Look, I'm not good at this relationship stuff, and I thought that since you were so fresh off your divorce, you needed time to readjust to being single. And then there's the age thing…"

Now she was interested. The idiot didn't even realize he was insulting her. She dropped her head and folded her arms. "There it is."

"Even you have to admit you were thrown by the age difference. You had to be."

He had a point, but still, the evidence told another story. "So it had nothing to do with the woman I saw you with, or the other women you've been photographed with, over the past month? You didn't call me because you were afraid I'd get—what—the *wrong idea*?"

He opened his mouth to speak, stopped himself and then started again. "I don't know."

She walked around the desk and faced him. "You thought what? That I was some sad, needy *cougar*?"

He kneaded the back of his neck, obviously frustrated. "I didn't mean it like that."

"*Really*?" She walked in a circle and clenched her fists. "I don't even know how to respond to such stupidity. If you recall, you were the one who invited me out."

"I know, but you wanted to see me. There's something special between us." She looked in his direction and saw the low-slung jeans, the polo shirt that spanned his chest and the leather jacket he hooked over one shoulder. His voice was low, husky, and he was so very handsome. "That's why you're upset. And I'm sorry."

She looked at his handsome face and into his eyes, and Kate felt herself soften. Damn. This was not fair.

"I'm not upset. I'm not…" Her eyes burned because he was right. "This can only end badly and—"

"Kate, please—"

"No." She stopped him. "You're right about one thing.

I'm not cut out for casual relationships. It's no one's fault, it's just me. We're too different."

"I don't think we are. We were great together."

"We were great in bed," she snapped. "It wouldn't work."

"It was more than bed and you know it. I like you," he argued. "Give me the chance to show you."

"Show me?"

He stuffed his free hand in the front pocket of his jeans and shrugged. "It's different with you. You make me feel like a... like I don't know... an adult."

"Well, see. There's that forty thing again. Remember?" Kate rubbed her hands over her face. Her midlife delusion, the one that started in California, was about to come crashing to a halt.

"That shouldn't be an issue," he said.

"I'm older than you, David. A lot."

"I know. And it's not that much."

"What! Not that much?" She turned. He met her gaze with eyes that possessed a strong sense of purpose and a grin that made her toes curl. "When I had my daughter, I'll bet you didn't even have a whisker on your chin."

He stared at her. His mouth didn't move. It seemed locked in that silly grin, while his eyes didn't stray from her face. He'd either gone deaf or gone into shock with the image she'd given him.

"Are you processing any of this?" He nodded and Kate threw up her hands and her voice shot up an octave. "Why are you smiling?"

"I'm trying to figure out why you're upset."

"Oh, my God! David, I'm ten years older than you. I have a seventeen-year-old daughter!"

He casually sat on the edge of a desk and put his jacket on the desk next to him.

"You don't want to date a younger man?"

"It doesn't bother you?"

"No. Not seeing you again bothers me a lot more." He closed the distance between them and his hands glided slowly up and down her arm.

Those amazing hands—big, strong, expressive. The warmth that shot through her made her muscles twitch, and David's eyes sparkled at the response.

"From the minute I met you, I knew something was different about you. It's the difference between a girl and a woman. It just took me a little while to get my head around it." The pad of his thumb brushed over her lips. "That's about you, not your age."

"I feel like a girl," she whispered. "I'm scared and confused… I'm not ready for you."

He dropped his head, resting his forehead on hers. "I shouldn't have blown you off—for any reason. I'm an idiot."

"Yeah, you are."

"Don't you believe in second chances?"

"Believing in people cost me everything." She turned away from him.

"I'm not going to give up." His voice was firm.

"David, I'm sure you thrive on challenge, I get that part of your personality. The competitive part of you wants to win." Kate swallowed hard and turned to face him. "But I'm not a game to be played. Go back to your girl of the day and leave me out of the mix."

He stared at her long and hard with his beautiful brown eyes. His expression turned stony, cold, determined. She'd seen the same look when she watched him on the ice. She'd hit a nerve with the "girl of the day" comment.

"Kate, I haven't been able to stop thinking about you. That's no game. I wanted to talk to you because I screwed up. When I'm wrong, I admit it." He stepped forward, took her face gently in his hands, and kissed her lips. It was feather light, a mere brush of his mouth on hers, but Kate felt a charge that made her head go fuzzy. He pulled back and gazed at her before picking up his jacket. "I hope you'll be able to do the same when you find out you're wrong about me."

Kate licked her lips and tried to maintain her composure as he backed out of the room. What in the world had just happened? Letting out a slow breath, she tried to shake the fog from her brain, but then went to the window and watched him walk across the lawn. The twilight made the whole scene surreal. The fading light on the colorful leaves and the sight of the big man turning and glancing up at her window had her heart pounding against her ribs. He waved; she stepped away, determined not to encourage him.

Encourage him? Not likely. It was over; David was never coming back. This was a pity trip, something to help him feel better. Kate shook it off and tried to forget how his lips felt against hers, how his hands felt warm on her skin. She had to forget it all.

RICHARD KEPT HIS fingers steepled so his attorney would know he was serious. Intimidation was one of Richard's most effective tools. As a rule, people didn't like him, and he never really thought about it. He used his arrogance to his advantage, bullying people to do what he wanted.

"I know what she's worth. I have no doubt that she can afford to pay the child support and a settlement."

"Richard, I understand the child support, but *two million dollars?* How do you justify asking for such an amount?"

"If I hadn't taken charge of raising Laura, Kate wouldn't have had time to write, much less promote her books. It's all she's ever really been interested in anyway, and I feel that the time I spent with our daughter should be recognized."

"Kate isn't exactly the picture of a literary diva or the neglectful mother. It's going to be difficult to convince a judge that you deserve two million on top of the support you're asking for."

"I want you to try. I heard there's a new contract in the works, her current book's been on the major bestseller lists since September, and negotiations are taking place with several film studios about turning her last book into a movie. The movie based on the first book is being cast as we speak. If I do get full custody of Laura, and I expect I will, I'll require the support to keep her in the style to which she's become accustomed."

"Okay, but during our last meeting her lawyers gagged when I mentioned the amount. One actually laughed."

Richard stood, pulled up to his full height, and ran a hand over his blond hair. "I suggest you start working on it. Please call me when you know about the hearing."

Richard shook the attorney's hand, stuffed a file in his briefcase, and left the office.

Once he was on the street, he thought about his ex-wife. Kate was on the verge of signing a four book contract worth five million dollars. She wouldn't see all that money at once, but Richard wanted to make sure he got a piece of it. Since getting his hands on her family's money hadn't worked, he figured he was entitled to it. He'd gotten over the fact that she wrote such crap when her books started to make them rich, but Kate herself was too much work.

However, marriage to her had been profitable.

DAVID DOUBTED IF anything was more relaxing than a Sunday afternoon watching football. It was too bad he wasn't relaxed. He sat on the couch in Jay's den watching the half-time report while Jay wrestled his twin toddlers down for their naps. It wouldn't be easy. They liked hanging out with Daddy and Uncle Dave and Uncle Cam too much to sleep.

He heard squealing coming from upstairs and he knew Jay would be playing with the kids for a while. Looking through the French doors, he saw Cam on his cell phone, probably dumping his latest girlfriend. The guy had two difficult ex-wives, so even if he met the right woman, she wouldn't have a chance, which made David think about his situation with Kate. He just didn't know what to do about it. It made his head hurt, so he refocused on the TV, and about thirty seconds into the scoring recap, Annie Hemmings sat next to him on the couch. He'd been waiting for this.

"So," she began. "Tell me about the teacher."

"I've been here two whole hours and you haven't said anything. You're losing your touch." David took a pull on his beer and accepted the fact he wasn't getting out of talking to her about Kate. And if he was honest with himself, he'd admit he needed her take on what had gone down.

"I figured if you had a beer or two I'd get more information. Jay said you're obsessed. That's new for you."

"Thanks." No surprise that his best friend's wife had something to say about his reputation.

"You can't possibly be offended, Dave." She picked up Jay's beer and took a sip. "You have no attention span when it comes to women." She poked his shoulder like an annoying little sister. "What's different about this one?"

What *wasn't* different about her? He leaned forward and propped his elbows on his knees and tried to grab onto the one thing that made her special. "She didn't care who I was."

Annie took another sip and considered what he said. "That makes no sense."

"I said that badly." He savored the taste and the chill of the liquid as another swallow of beer slid down his throat. "She wanted to know all about me, the person, not the hockey player. My career is just something I do. For her, it's not who I am."

Annie leaned back, sinking into the sofa and smirked. David could see she understood.

"So," she began, "You like her because she's not impressed?"

"Yeah, I guess that's part of it." David scrubbed his face with both hands, exasperated, trying to get a handle on what he wanted to do about it. "She's got this life that has nothing to do with me. She's successful, educated. She doesn't—"

"Ha!" Annie cut him off. "She doesn't need you." Pulling her legs under her, Annie leaned toward David. "You're attracted to a woman who doesn't need *you* to be somebody. That's freakin' awesome."

"How do you figure that?" It was the kind of revelation

that could change the way a person led his life and David felt his mood sink. Vulnerability was not something he was used to, but he'd known from the start that Kate could cause him a mountain of trouble if he let her in.

"What's her name?"

"Kate."

"She's a teacher?" Annie had officially launched into the third degree.

"And a writer."

"She's hot. That's what she is." Cam entered the room and flopped in the big arm chair.

"Shut up, Cam." Annie laughed as David scowled. "What has she written? Anything I'd know?"

David couldn't help himself, he smiled and took a sip from his beer. "Uh huh. Her new book is called *Past Lives*."

"What?" Annie drew in a deep breath. "You're talking about *Katherine Adams*?"

David nodded and rolled the beer between his palms, knowing he'd blown her mind sufficiently.

Annie was actually a little star struck. "I can understand why she intimidates you."

David never thought of himself as intimidated, but maybe he was… a little.

Jay walked in the room and leaned on the arm of the sofa right near his wife. "So you figure out what's wrong with our boy?"

Annie smiled and patted David's leg. "Yup. He's scared, and it's almost understandable."

Jay laughed. "That's pretty much what I figured."

"You're such a girl, Burke." Cam took a mouthful from the bottle and shook his head. "Man up and go after her."

They were having a lot of fun at his expense and he'd have been pissed off if Annie was wrong, but she wasn't. On some level, he was afraid.

"I'm glad you three are enjoying this."

"David, you had to grow up sometime. You finally realized that the girls you've been dating aren't right for you." Annie leaned over and kissed his cheek. "I can't wait to meet her."

He'd love for Kate to meet Annie. But David had yet to show her he wasn't a complete ass. Another photo had made the newspaper; a picture of him and Chelsea that was taken months ago, and he kept wondering when he would get himself out of the gossip columnists' cross hairs. Each time he'd seen Kate since California, he'd managed to piss her off, upset her, or both. He needed time to figure this out, but if he waited too much longer he'd be out of the game—for good.

KATE, JULIE, AND three other teachers emerged from the theater chatting about the play and whether or not the lead had pulled it off. The banter went back and forth with all of them talking at once, hands going, voices rising. It was verbal chaos. Kate and her friends did that often. She didn't know how they actually had conversations with everyone talking over each other, but they seemed to manage every time they got together. They were all opinionated, as most teachers were, but Kate recognized it was these people, Julie especially, who had gotten her through the past year. Without them, she might not have made it.

"I don't know," Julie said. "I saw Angela Lansbury do the

part in New York and I think she ruined it for me."

The others agreed that a comparison with Angela Lansbury was unfair, but understood why Julie thought that way. Angela Lansbury was a theater goddess.

Kate loved these nights in the city. The Forrest Theater ran a wonderful schedule, and she appreciated she could see good theater without having to travel to New York. Several times a year Kate, Julie, and a few of their friends arranged to see a show and have dinner after. They made a quick dash between the theater and the nearby pub, and were lucky to get a table, considering it was a Saturday night and the bar was famous for its karaoke.

They settled in and ordered drinks and appetizers. Taking in her surroundings, Kate reveled in the atmosphere. Everyone was happy. A drunk bachelorette stood at the microphone being cheered on by her equally drunk friends. Men were surveying the crowd to see who was an easy target, and she and her friends were still arguing about the play. Looking down at her menu, Kate couldn't decide what to order. In England, she became a fan of good pub fare. One thing she was grateful to her parents for was the opportunity they gave her to study abroad before she married Richard. She spent a summer at Oxford and it was one of the best memories of her adult life. One year later she was married, and the nightmare was just beginning.

The first round came and Kate was the first to drain her wine. Great. That should be good for a buzz, especially when she was planning to follow it with another one, or two, or three...

She gazed around the bar and started cataloging ideas in her head. She never knew when she might need this image or one of these people to fill out a story. Looking toward the end of the bar, she thought she saw someone... no, it couldn't be him. Just her imagination. The wine and the heat in the bar had made her a little fuzzy in the head and that was just fine, but it bothered her she couldn't go anywhere without thinking David was there. He was always in her head and she wished he would just get the hell out.

When the waitress came by with their food, Kate ordered another glass of wine. She figured since she wasn't driving, she could indulge. She most definitely deserved it.

Chapter 9

KATE WAS ON her third glass of Merlot in less than an hour and that necessitated a trip to the ladies' room. Julie was putting her name on the list to sing, which Kate was almost tipsy enough to do herself, but right at that moment, as she made her way to the bathroom, all she could think about was relief.

That was when she saw David sitting at the end of the bar with another man she recognized as a teammate. He was hunched over a glass of beer and made eye contact with her as she got closer. It wasn't her imagination. He was actually there. Damn. He watched her walk past, raking her with his eyes, but he didn't speak to her—he didn't even nod in her direction, he just stared. *Asshole.* So much for being a nice guy.

But, oh boy, she really hated how she felt. Just seeing him made her insides warm up and go soft. He was wearing jeans and a soft, gray sweater that looked absolutely touchable. She wasn't sure if it was the wine she'd had or something else, but she wanted him. Even with all he'd done and the way he'd blown her off, the way he'd blindsided her in her classroom, she couldn't deny she was attracted to him. It was unfair that he could do this to her without even uttering a word. Where David was concerned, she was the easiest woman on the east coast. It was a good thing he didn't talk to her; if he did, she'd be a goner.

Her luck didn't hold out. As Kate was putting her lipstick in her bag, and not watching where she was going as she left the ladies' room, she ran smack into David. She stumbled and in a split second his arms were around her.

"Hey," he said gently. "You should watch where you're walking." Kate didn't answer him immediately.

Her words vanished and, apparently, so did all her common sense. Her body responded, warming from the center, tingling in all the right spots, and leaning into him. It was like she was hard-wired to respond to him—no one had this effect on her except David. The feel of his hands on her back and the press of his body against hers made her a little crazy. It was all she could do to say something, anything, which would get her out of this situation.

"You can let go now." Her voice was a whisper and she wondered if he heard her.

She placed her hands on his hard chest, and the truth of it, she didn't really want him to let her go. His arms were wrapped around her like bands of steel. Finally, Kate did what she had been avoiding. She tilted her head back and gazed up at him. She looked deep into his dark eyes and knew she was in big, big trouble.

"David, I need to get back to my friends." Okay that was good. Polite. Firm.

He ignored what she said.

"You look beautiful." He let his hands run up and down

her sides.

God, his hands were magic. The gentle force on her body where he touched her made her nearly delirious.

"This dress should be illegal."

"Thank you. I think." It was a simple black dress, and covered with a cardigan it was nothing special.

However, she'd shed the cardigan and David took advantage of the fact the dress fit her like a second skin. She should have been furious with him, but she wasn't, she was dying inside. She didn't want to feel this way. She wanted to be aloof and cool, but with David, Kate was powerless.

He released her for just a moment, took her hand, and led her to a more secluded corner of the bar. A hot light passed between them as he gently pushed her back into a wall. His fingers threaded through her hair and his thumb stroked her cheek. Kate shuddered when he pressed against her and she felt his erection. His other hand settled on the back of her thigh, and then he kissed her with an urgency that went right through her.

Her muscles quivered under his touch and Kate felt a smile tease his mouth. His lips were soft and warm, heaven. She was locked against him... like she was being held captive by a seductive force that was out of her control. His mouth consumed hers, coaxing and playing, while his hand had started to push up the bottom of her dress. His long fingers caressed her thigh and traveled north. His hands slid over her cheeks and fingered the edge of her panties, all while his mouth worked miracles with hers.

His tongue moved over her lips and then swept inside. Kate inhaled sharply, taking his essence into her lungs and losing any common sense the wine hadn't stolen from her.

Why did he do this to her? Why couldn't he see her for what she was—middle aged, past her prime? She worked hard to look respectable, but she'd never be twenty again.

"David, my friends…"

"Aren't invited." His lips grazed her neck and collarbone; his hands kneaded her bottom. "God," he said into her hair, "I haven't been able to get you out of my head, Kate. You're all I think about."

"David," she struggled for breath, "People are waiting for me. Oh… God… oh…" But at this point he was kissing her neck and touching her in places no one should be touched in public.

She had so lost control of the situation and she didn't care. He could have taken her right there against the wall and she wouldn't have stopped him. Instead, he moved his fingers and touched her center. She moaned, and then with some pressure and a little bit of movement, he brought her to climax. Kate arched and started to cry out, and everyone in the bar would have heard her if David hadn't pressed her face into his chest to muffle her cries. He held her tight, kept her safe, as the orgasm passed and she shook uncontrollably.

"Let's leave." His voice was throaty, raw. "Please."

"I can't…"

"Why not?"

"Because," she said, still gasping for breath, "I hate you."

He tilted his head back and when Kate looked up at him, she saw his mouth twitch into a grin. "I don't believe you."

He was so freaking smug. She looked away and cursed him under her breath. She did hate him, she did. He was shallow and arrogant and obnoxious and… and then Kate felt his lips brush against her temple and she sighed like a schoolgirl. Crap, even she didn't believe she hated him. Flushed and sweaty, her breasts were aching for him and her girly parts were warm and wet. The air around them smelled like sex. He'd gotten her to such a point that she couldn't go back to her friends and act like nothing had happened. There was a break in the karaoke and she heard music—Eric Clapton was wailing about not wanting to be lonely. Kate didn't want to be lonely either, so she gave in.

"Okay," she finally said meeting his gaze with her own. "Okay. Meet me outside."

He nodded and dropped one last bone-melting, sense-stealing kiss on her lips before he left her to pull herself together.

She watched him walk away and Kate took a minute to assess the situation as best she could. What the hell had happened? Since when was she the woman who let herself get felt up in a bar? Why didn't she just go back to her friends and leave him standing there? Kate ducked in the bathroom, breathed out, and touched her neck. She felt the heat and the racing pulse and she knew why. David made her made her feel sexy; he made her take risks, and do things she wouldn't have done before. After the emotional battering she suffered when she was married, Kate *wanted* to feel that way. She wanted someone to want her. And even though she knew this wasn't going to be her love story, David made her feel beautiful.

The next step was to get Julie's attention, but it was un-necessary since her friend came looking for her. When she walked in, Kate was leaning against the tile, fanning herself, and trying to cool off.

"Holy shit," Julie said. "What happened to you?"

"David happened."

"He's here?"

Kate placed her hands over her chest and tried to slow her racing heart. "He's waiting for me."

Julie smiled and leaned her hip into the sink. "Oh, really? Where are you going?"

"I don't know." Kate's words came out like a little song. "His place, I guess."

Julie didn't say much. She was obviously too stunned to come up with anything witty or even cautionary. But the faint giggle that escaped her throat told Kate she was amused.

"Stop laughing at me, Julie!" Kate stomped her high heel and didn't care that she probably looked like a spoiled brat.

"Oh, no. This is too much fun."

"You're a horrible friend."

Julie laughed again and nodded. "I can live with that. You're not too drunk? Should I get your things for you and make your excuses?"

Kate thought about David waiting for her and her heart started thumping in her chest like a drum. "Not too drunk. Just tell everyone I didn't feel well and that I'm taking a cab home. Okay?"

Julie was still giggling and Kate was too aroused to care. "You are too much." Taking her by the shoulders, Julie guided her out of the restroom and gave her a little push. "Go. Have fun."

DAVID LEANED AGAINST a lamp post and waited. God, what that woman did to him. When he touched her there was a roar in his head—he couldn't make sense out of his thoughts, she was everywhere. When she was close, Kate was all that mattered. No one challenged him like she did. No one made him think about being a better man the way Kate did. No one. And somehow, he had to make sure she knew that.

His eyes were fixed on the door of the restaurant and finally, she came out. She was pulling a soft wrap around her shoulders and her hair was lifted by a gentle breeze. Her cheeks were still flushed, her lips swollen and pink from him kissing her senseless. Kate walked to him and pressed her body into his without a second thought. David settled his hands on her hips and dropped a kiss on her forehead.

"Where do you want to go?" he asked.

"You live nearby?" Kate's eyes rose to meet his.

When David nodded, she did as well, giving him her answer. They walked to his car, hand-in-hand, and David's only thought was that if he did this right, Kate wouldn't want to leave him come morning.

His vehicle was right around the corner and it was a short ride to his house, but it felt like an eternity. When he got her past the door, he had to fight the urge to just pick up where they left off in the bar. He was pushing down his needs so he could focus on hers. Only hers.

Her hand trembled in his. If she knew how nervous he was, she would question whether he had enough testosterone to follow through. When he broke it down to basics, David was scared to death he was going to screw this up. They barely knew each other, but when he looked at her, he had the feeling he was messing with the rest of his life. He'd had a lot of women and never before had one made him feel like he had something to lose. He took her wrap and she turned into his arms. Kate rested her head on his chest and the sweet smell of her seeped into his blood. His hands came up and cupped her face, her beautiful face.

"Do you want to go upstairs?"

She nodded and he led her up the stairs and to his room. Once inside, he pulled her close and left kisses over her face and down her neck, while he unzipped the black dress and touched the bare skin on her back. She wiggled and the dress fell to the floor, and it was at that moment, when he stepped back and took her in, that he started to say prayers of thanks.

Kate stood next to his bed looking like every man's erotic fantasy. Her breasts were enveloped in a frothy bra; peeking over the tops of the lace he could see the shadow of her nipples. Moving down, she had on matching lace panties that were barely there at all, and finishing him off were the stockings and heels. Talk about a contradiction. The woman was a conservative, preppy mom one minute, and then underneath it all she dressed like a centerfold. Maybe that was the missing piece with her. Kate was an extremely controlled woman on the surface. Her wild child was hidden inside.

As he moved toward her, Kate's breathing grew heavier, and her hoarse whisper broke the silence. "I shouldn't be here."

David could see that as much as she had doubts, she wanted him. However, he had to give her the chance to stop it from going any further.

"Do you want me to take you home? I want you to stay, but if you don't, just say the word..." David stepped back and waited for her answer and once again he said a prayer, this time for her to stay. If she did, he was going to make sure she wouldn't regret it for one minute.

Her eyes met his and he could see the decision was hard for her. David was sure it was because she probably did dislike him on some level. Being here went against every safe, sensible thing she'd ever done. It took a minute, but her eyes changed, and he saw when she'd made her choice.

"I want to stay." She reached up and took his face in her hands before touching her lips to his. The kiss was gentle, barely there, but it shocked David's heart. "I want to be with you, even though I have no idea why you want to be with me."

He took her hands from his face and held them before she slipped them around his neck and continued kissing him. When they first came in, David was revved up enough to take her on the floor of the foyer. But something had changed and the tenderness, the sweetness that was coming from Kate, deserved no less from him.

When he laid her on the bed, she stretched and probably didn't realize she'd struck a pose that was worthy of a magazine spread. This woman had no idea how magnificent she was, how beautiful. Years didn't seem to affect her, and if there were any flaws, David didn't notice. What kind of idiot divorced her?

David was falling for her, and his biggest fear now wasn't that Kate would become too clingy, but that he wouldn't measure up. He had to make sure he did everything right. He had no room for error with a woman who'd been through so much.

He began undressing her. Slowly removing each item, touching every newly exposed jewel as he whispered how beautiful she was, how much he wanted her. The urgency was gone and it was replaced by soft warmth—something that was more enduring than the flash of heat—something that would last.

WITH EACH TOUCH, words flooded Kate's brain, but her reaction was to reach out and twine her arms around David's neck. He responded in kind, pulling her close.

She couldn't understand why she was there or why he even wanted her, but here she was, naked in his bed, and completely and totally happy.

And at that moment, losing herself in him was enough. She stopped trying to attach a reason to everything. The only thing left to do was kiss him. So she did. Her hands threaded through his hair and her mouth touched his. This was more than a physical kiss; it was a kiss of souls. It took seconds for his weight to settle on her and for his hands to start stroking. In California, David had been about wonderfully patient; now he was so tender she was close to crying.

"David," she whispered over and over, allowing herself the pleasure of feeling totally possessed.

He was strong and gentle, each touch made her burn. For the first time in a very long while, Kate trusted someone enough to be completely vulnerable. He entered her and each movement was a remedy to the problems of her life. Each time he said her name, Kate's world mended. Whether it was possible or logical or wise, she felt her heart crack and open and then fall. When he came, the warmth of him penetrated her core and touched her deep within. She held on and this time, when she cried, Kate was happy.

AT THREE-THIRTY IN the morning, Kate sat on a stool in

David's kitchen. Wrapped in his blue terrycloth bathrobe, the ends of her hair still wet from their shower, she watched as he made omelets. Sporting a pair of gray knit shorts and nothing else, David moved around the kitchen like he moved on the ice and in the bedroom—with total confidence. It was too bad her head was throbbing and she couldn't enjoy it.

"Feeling any better?" he asked.

"Eh." She took a sip of water and waited for the Advil to kick in. "I haven't had that much to drink, that quickly, in a long time."

"How many glasses of wine did you have?"

She held up three fingers. "And they were those oversized glasses, so that's more like five.

David laughed. "No wonder."

Taking another drink of water, she got her mind off her headache by watching him cook.

"You really know what you're doing." she said, astounded.

He was chopping vegetables so quickly she was afraid he'd take off a finger.

"I love to eat. And since I didn't want to condemn myself to a life of menus and take out, I learned to cook." He tossed the vegetables into a hot pan and threw on some seasoning.

"It's a kick watching you, but it's such a cliché."

"What? Cooking?"

"The omelet." He looked confused, so she explained. "Why is it in books or movies whenever the hero cooks for the heroine, he's always making an omelet?"

He continued to chop vegetables while he thought about what she said. "Well, things become clichés for a reason, but if I had to guess, it's probably because people almost always have eggs around. Add whatever you have in the fridge and bingo—omelet."

She considered him for a minute and nodded. "That makes sense."

"Hasn't anyone ever cooked for you in the middle of the night?" He grinned at her while he cracked eggs and Kate felt the warmth shoot right through her.

"If you're asking if Richard ever did, no. Richard had a clear idea of men's work and women's work. He never cooked."

"Neanderthal?"

"He doesn't seem to have a problem thinking like a modern man regarding divorce settlements," she murmured.

"At least you have a good career. You didn't need a settlement."

"I didn't get one, I had to buy him out of the house and now he's looking for money—a lot of it."

David stopped beating the eggs for a moment to consider what she said. Kate felt a little nauseous just thinking about the way Richard took advantage of her.

"What does he want?"

"Two million, plus child support when he gets custody," she croaked.

David's hands gripped the whisk more tightly. "Are you kidding? He cheats, he leaves you, and *he* wants a couple million bucks?"

Kate sat back. "The thing is, he could get it. If it's for Laura, I guess I couldn't really argue. I don't know where he thinks I have this money right now, but he could get the award based on my contracts."

Not missing a beat, David put the bowl aside, turned off

the burner and went around the counter. He wrapped his large hands around her tiny ones and crouched before her. "I just can't believe he'd take the money. No man with any self-respect would do that."

"Richard isn't just any man, and his self-respect is limited only by his greed. I don't care about the money for Laura's support, but I know I should fight the settlement. Unfortunately, I've never been very good at standing up for myself."

"What do you mean?"

Kate dropped her head and thought about the intimidation she suffered for years. Feeling she was never good enough, and believing, when she was young, it was his brilliance that made him act that way. She looked up and David was still there, gazing at her, waiting for an answer. Something about the way he held her gaze made her feel as if she could tell him anything.

"I was just twenty when Richard married me. He was twenty-nine, handsome, and intelligent. He'd come from San Francisco to Cambridge and was working on his PhD in Chemical Engineering at MIT. I was young and inexperienced and thought he was sophisticated. I let him run my life and he took away everything I was." She stopped.

David didn't say anything, but his eyes asked the questions. His hand came up and stroked her cheek and his silence encouraged her to go on.

"I went to Harvard with a history. I wasn't just a student, I was an elite athlete." She drew a deep breath and kept her eyes on him.

This part of herself was lost long ago, and she never talked about it. But if David was going to be with her, he had to know who she'd been and how she got here.

"What sport?" he finally asked.

The look in his eyes betrayed his surprise. Hearing Kate was a competitive athlete was the last thing anyone expected from her. The way her life evolved, she was anything but athletic. He held her hands, and from what she could see, he had no intention of letting go.

"I was a champion figure skater. I was one-one-hundredth of a point from making the Olympics."

David was just plain stunned at this point, but the look on his face also told her he knew why they understood each other so well. Figure skaters and hockey players were different breeds, but they both grew up on the ice, and that bound them to each other. "That's amazing. What happened?"

Kate shrugged. "Before I went to college, I crashed during Olympic trials. That's why I didn't make the team. I missed a jump I'd landed a thousand times. I should have been given a spot on the Olympic team regardless of the fall, because of my finish at worlds, but it didn't happen. I don't know why." Even now, the unfairness of it still burned. "All those years training and it was over. I walked away from the whole scene because I just couldn't do it anymore and went to college ready to reinvent myself."

"So you gave it up? All that work? How'd you do it?"

Kate had asked herself the same question over and over. She had thrown away fifteen years of hard work. Fifteen years of sacrifice. Fifteen years of her identity. But each of those things were part of the reason she quit. Kate wanted to be normal. She'd never had a boyfriend, had never had a normal social life, or a normal family life for that matter, because of skating. Walking away from it was easier than she'd imagined.

"After not making the team, I let the dream die."

David didn't say anything but kept hold of her hands. At one point he brought one to his lips for a kiss.

"I enjoyed school, made friends, but I was still pretty broken. I did everything possible to put the fall out of my head. And then one day Richard walked into my life. I was young and inexperienced and vulnerable. Easy picking for a guy like him. I became the center of his universe. Or so I thought."

"Why you?"

"My parents think money was the prime motivator. My family is very well off. But I don't know if that's the only reason he pursued me so relentlessly; there were a lot of girls on campus with more affluent families." She drew a deep breath. "I think it was about control. He gets off on it. Richard is very charming when he wants to be. He's also handsome and intelligent, and he read me like a book. I was smitten by our second cup of coffee.

"After a year or so, I started missing my skating, and I thought about going back—even contacted a coach. Richard discouraged me, saying I wouldn't have time for him, and by that time, he was involved in every part of my life. I did what he wanted. I've had skates on maybe a half dozen times since I was twenty."

"If you went back to skating, he'd lose control over you."

"I thought I'd made my own choice. He wanted me to believe that. It was his way. Insidious. Manipulative." She'd never told anyone as much as she was telling David, and as terrified as she was that he'd think she was too damaged, freedom came with every word. "But I loved him. And I wanted to make him happy, so I said yes when he proposed and then we eloped because my parents were so against it."

She chuckled at the irony. "I accused them of trying to control my life. I was so stupid."

"You were young, not stupid," David replied.

"No, I was stupid. He was so much older than me, and I figured he knew more about everything. But as time passed and I grew up, I felt caged. I should have seen the warning signs. Red flags should have been popping up when he wanted me to drop out of school and follow him to some job on the west coast. I didn't go, obviously, but whenever I did new things or tried to take control, Richard put me down. Once we were married, he went from subtle to straight out intimidation." Kate stopped to compose herself before continuing with the story.

"He landed a job at a college in upstate New York, teaching chemistry, and when I graduated I was admitted to the writing program at Cornell. God, I learned so much. But he taunted me, insulted me in front of his colleagues and friends, so I kept what I was doing to myself. I didn't finish the program. He got a job here and we moved. When Laura was born, he controlled her, too, getting me help because I was too 'incompetent' to care for my own child." Thinking about Laura brought the tears. "She got older and I was only working part time, so I wrote to give myself something else with meaning. I needed to feel, to have control over something." Kate looked at the hands that held hers and used the strength he gave her to continue. "I never expected my writing to take off like it did. Richard hated my books, calling what I wrote garbage, making me use my maiden name and swearing me to secrecy." Kate bit her lower lip. "He hated it until the money came in."

"And then you couldn't have done it without him, right?"

"Exactly. That's what he'll tell the court again. That I was too busy for Laura then, and that I'm too busy now. He came by the house a few weeks ago and that's basically what he said."

"He's a real son of a bitch," he said.

"I think that's too good for him. Do you know he's still never read one word of anything I've written?"

They paused, while the revelations of the past few moments swirled around them. "You know I'll never treat you like that, don't you?" he asked.

"It's so ironic." She looked in his eyes. "Richard poses as this suave intellectual, who's nothing more than a thug, and you're such a physical man, in a violent sport, but you're so gentle and..."

He didn't hesitate for a second, pulling her into his arms. She burrowed in, holding him tightly. David felt such contempt for Richard Nicholls he thought he might lose himself in it. Up until now, he'd kept the women in his life at arm's length, but not her. Kate, he wanted to draw in, keep close. He couldn't explain it, but as she held onto him, it was like she grabbed onto a piece of his heart and he knew he was never getting it back.

Chapter 10

KATE ROSE EARLY and looked out the window at the quiet city streets. They'd come back to bed after their late night meal and he'd made love to her again. Did real people live like this? Because Kate felt like she was caught up in a romance novel. David knew what she wanted, what she needed. Every time he touched her, it was like an electric charge going through her. But more than that, she had a feeling this relationship had the potential to be something life changing.

Looking at him, asleep in the big bed, Kate sighed. David's dark hair lay tousled across his forehead and his muscular frame was relaxed, but still exuded power. He had a large bruise on his right side that had just started to fade, and his breathing was slow and steady. It made Kate wonder if he could be like that with her—slow and steady. If he could, they might have a chance.

She'd told him everything. Told him about her past, and how she'd gotten to this place. Once upon a time she was confident, competitive, and even a little reckless. But Richard had broken her spirit on many levels, and it was only now that Kate understood not only how far she'd come, but how far she needed to go. Her writing was so much more than the hobby she'd made it out to be. It had saved her. It gave her something to be proud of and it gave her an identity. It gave her the ability to be independent. David, on the other hand, was something else. Talking about her past made her realize he was helping her rediscover the person she used to be.

If ever there was a contradiction, David was it. He presented a fierce and violent presence on the ice, but with her he was warm, caring, and understanding. He personified the dumb jock in interviews, giving short, clichéd answers, but in reality he was intelligent and articulate. The most remarkable thing was this man, who had the most beautiful young women ready to throw themselves at him, was with her—a middle-aged divorcée with custody problems and a pending nervous breakdown.

She glanced outside again and saw the newspaper on the front stoop. She figured a cup of coffee and the paper was a good way to pass the time while David slept. He had another game that night and had to be at the arena around ten for a morning skate, which meant he still had a couple of hours to sleep.

Grabbing his robe, Kate headed downstairs so he could rest.

IN THE DAYLIGHT, she could see that the kitchen opened onto a deck that led into a small yard. The house was the biggest surprise. She never expected him to have such a refined home. Everything was tasteful and classic. There were few frills, nothing trendy, and only one flat panel TV that she could see in the whole house.

His den gave her the clearest picture into his personality and his history. There were some pictures of his family, and one of him and some of his teammates when he played hockey for Canada in the last Olympics. But the most dramatic thing about the room was that it was filled, floor to ceiling, with books. All of her titles were there, which she found flattering, as well as volumes of history, philosophy, and literary fiction. He wrote notes in the margins; as she flipped through a copy of Thomas Paine's *The Rights of Man,* she marveled at his insights. His degree from Boston College hung proudly on the wall, from which she discovered that David earned a B.A., summa cum laude, in history. This man who cracked heads on a nightly basis was a deep thinker, a scholar, and most definitely an enigma.

Who knew?

She washed the dishes from the previous night, made herself a cup of coffee, and sat down with the paper. The news was depressing, as usual, and after getting her fill of national and international tragedies, she went to the local section. A little fashion, some gossip, and local news was how she normally offset the global problems in the main section.

This time, however, the gossip page made her feel like she'd been hit by a bus. A fairly good sized picture of David and her former student, Chelsea, was front and center. The image was disturbing enough. He had his arm around her as they walked along a city street. They looked like they were in a conversation—a perfect, happy, plastic couple. But what really had Kate ready to snap was the caption:

"Local celebutante Chelsea Connor may have snagged the ultimate prize in Philly's most eligible bachelor, David Burke. The word is a summer wedding is planned."

Kate closed her eyes and let it all sink in. It didn't make sense, but when did her life ever make sense? She gazed at the picture and felt a tightness around her heart, which made her run her hand across her chest. It physically hurt to look at the picture and think about what it might mean. It was the same feeling she had when she saw them together that morning in New York. It was humiliating, and while Kate knew she should talk to him about it—he'd probably be able to explain it—she just couldn't. Kate didn't want to have to ask questions; she didn't want to have to wonder about the people in her life. If David was engaged, everything she'd hoped for, everything he'd let her believe, meant nothing. Even if he wasn't engaged, he and Chelsea were obviously enough of a couple that such speculation wasn't a complete reach.

Which meant David would never really be hers.

Sobs caught in Kate's throat as flashes of last night played in her mind like a cruel movie. The way he touched her, the things he whispered to her in the dark, made her believe there might be a future. Now all she wanted to do was get away from the reality the picture in the paper forced her to accept. He was a ladies' man, a player, and expecting him to change was foolish. If it wasn't Chelsea on his arm, there would be someone else. This was who he was, and nothing short of a miracle would get him to change.

Young women, beautiful women, women without stretch marks, spider veins, and teenage children were the ones David would really want. Kate was never going to fit into his life and she had to get out now, before the damage to her heart was irreparable.

She tiptoed into the bedroom, gathered her clothes, and stopped to look at him sleep. The pain she felt, the feeling of inadequacy, was all too familiar. He hadn't been honest with her, and after what she'd gone through with Richard, that was something she couldn't forget. David was peacefully asleep, peacefully unaware, as Kate left the room and faced the fact she might never be able to fully trust anyone again.

DAVID AWOKE HOPING to wrap himself around Kate, maybe make love to her again before he had to be at the arena, but instead found he was alone in bed. It wasn't the way he wanted to wake up. Rolling onto his back, he thought about her, about how being with her had changed him.

They'd talked about everything. His family, his job, her job, her divorce, her daughter. They laughed, they made love, and a couple of times he'd held her while she cried. He knew more about her than he did about people he'd known for years. This was what people meant when they talked about soul mates—finally he understood.

He got up and when he looked around his room, he realized her things were gone. Her lingerie, dress, and shoes were no longer on the chair in the corner of the room. *Strange.* The house was eerily quiet, and David had the sense something had gone very wrong, very quickly.

The night before, he'd learned about her addiction to coffee, so he pulled on a pair of jeans and made his way to the kitchen, where he hoped he would find her. But the only thing he saw in the kitchen was the newspaper. The dishes they'd left in the sink were clean, but Kate wasn't around.

He didn't understand.

He couldn't believe she'd left without saying anything and he wondered what the hell he'd done. Shuffling the sections of paper around, he figured Kate must have been reading it before she decided to take off. Was this payback for the way he treated her?

He glanced at each section and felt the bile rise in his throat when his eyes fell on the old picture of him and Chelsea. *Mother of God.* This gossip shit was getting out of control. He glanced at the caption and the only word that jumped out at him was *wedding. Wedding?* According to the article, he was getting married.

"Fuck." The word came out on a breath of pure disbelief. Did these reporters just make this shit up? The more he thought about it, only one answer made sense—Chelsea.

Now he knew what made Kate bolt. He finally found a woman he was crazy about, someone who made him feel like a real relationship was possible, and that blonde bitch wrecked it. David didn't know how the information about the non-existent wedding had made it into the paper, but he was certain Chelsea was behind it.

The paper usually arrived on his doorstep around six in the morning. It was almost nine. She might have left thirty minutes or three hours ago… he had no way of knowing when or where Kate had gone. The worst part was he couldn't do anything except set the record straight. And maybe tell Chelsea exactly what he thought of her manipulative little games.

David let loose with a string of expletives and slapped the

sugar bowl that was on the table. It flew and exploded against the wall, raining down in hundreds of little pieces. It was exactly how he felt.

Everything was in pieces.

Chapter 11

H E FELT LIKE shit. Not knowing what he could do about it, David settled down at his kitchen counter with a cup of coffee, a bottle of pain reliever, and his tablet and thought about what had transpired over the past forty-eight hours.

Since yesterday morning, he'd called Kate three times and left as many voice mails. He didn't hear from her. In one of the messages, he damn near begged her to call him back and David never begged, but he was desperate. He should have ended everything cleanly with Chelsea, with everyone, before he took up with Kate, but he didn't think it mattered that much. He was wrong.

Chelsea met him after the game last night and tried to get him to take her home, but he told her in the clearest way he could that they were finished, that they were not getting married, and that he would *never* marry her. He'd done everything he was supposed to do, according to Dating 101. He did it calmly, in a public place, and he took all the blame, even though he knew, after her most recent stunt, she was one obsessed bitch. It didn't matter how he handled it. She freaked and made a scene. It took two security guards ten minutes to get her out of the arena and another fifteen minutes for him to calm down.

Had he really missed all the signals? Had he been that arrogant? Chelsea's mission was to use her face and body to snag a wealthy husband. And not just any husband, but one who fit her *profile*. She'd let that piece of information slip, how David was perfect for her and how he was exactly what she always planned for in a husband. *Planned for?* In her eyes, they were all but married. She never even considered what he wanted. Chelsea sure didn't fit into his ideal of a perfect mate. No matter what people thought, he wasn't that shallow. No matter how beautiful a woman was, no matter how good in bed, if their hearts couldn't find any common ground, there was no chance he'd want to be with her long term.

But that was what David would do—he'd find beautiful girls who'd do anything for him and then he moved on. He never treated women badly; in fact, he was known as charming and considerate. But when he was done, he was done.

No one ever held him accountable for his behavior. He went out with who he wanted and never thought about how it affected any of the women involved. Obviously Chelsea was a special kind of crazy, but he was sure there were other women he'd hurt or offended. Probably a lot of them.

Last night he was so pissed he wanted to hit something. Instead he got drunk. Jay and Cam got him home and poured him into his bed at three in the morning. Sleep was what he needed, but what he got were dreams. Erotic, sweaty dreams about Kate. He decided when he woke up he either had to try to see her or forget about her.

Normally, he'd check out all the local scores, but after last night, he didn't want to read even one account of the game. The media had been all over his lack of production, now they would start slamming him about bad penalties and selfish play. Of course, they were right, as were his teammates and coach. He took them right out of the game the night before with his stupid play. He got called for a 'delay of game' and the Pens had capitalized. He couldn't catch a break. Instead, he went directly to his e-mail and saw the usual crap from the team, but then his eyes fell on something from Annie Hemmings.

The link in the e-mail led him to a site for a local foundation, and when he read the blurb about their upcoming event, he wanted to give Annie the biggest hug ever.

Many of the city's most prominent will be gathering to raise money for the Children's Literacy Foundation of Greater Philadelphia. The foundation gets books into the hands of underprivileged children and helps support school library programs. One of the most notable in attendance will be bestselling author Katherine Adams, who has donated a percentage of the royalties from her latest book to the program.

A fancy fundraiser was the last thing David wanted to do with a rare Friday night off, but if it meant he could try to set things right with Kate, he was all for the effort.

He sat as his desk, picked up his cell, and called his agent. The secretary put him right through, which was the advantage to being one of the top clients, and he waited for Alan to pick up.

"Dave, how's it goin'?"

"Hey, I need you to do something for me."

"If it's legal, anything."

David wondered how he was going to ask for this. Alan would know immediately that something was up. "There's this organization, locally in Philly, they're doing good work with literacy in schools." That was all true, now came the hard part. "They're having a benefit next week and I'd like to show my support."

Alan didn't respond immediately, but when he did, he got to the point. "Why?"

"Why what?" David said.

"Literacy? You always do the kids' charities, but usually it's a sports thing."

"What are you saying? I can't support something academic?"

"No, you just aren't known as an academic kind of guy. You ready to let the world see you have a first-class brain?"

David didn't deliberately come across like a dumb jock in the press, but he didn't like interviews. If reporters thought all he'd spit at them were clichés, they'd leave him alone.

"I want to go to the benefit."

His agent groaned. "What's the charity?"

"Ah… The Children's Literacy Foundation of Greater Philadelphia," David read from the screen. "I'll e-mail you the website."

"Okay. I'll check into it and call you back in an hour or so."

It didn't take an hour.

"Dave, it's Alan." He paused. "I can get you into the cocktail party, but it's going to cost you."

David rolled his eyes. "How much?"

"Five grand."

"*What?*" David dropped the phone. "Are they fucking kidding? For watered down drinks and bad hors d'oeuvres?"

"They do a lot of fundraisers during the year. This one is the real society bash. University people, Main Line Philadelphia, politicians. Definitely not your scene. Very formal."

"Shit," he growled.

"Do you still want to go?

David thought about Kate and the way she looked at him with such contempt at the game, of how she pleaded with him to get out of her life when they stood alone in her classroom. After what had happened this past weekend, with the gossip about him and Chelsea, she'd probably tear him to shreds. He should stay away from her. That would definitely be the smart thing to do.

Screw it.

"Yeah, get me a ticket." So much for being smart. "See if you can get the team's community relations to put a spin on it and get the foundation a little more publicity, okay?"

Alan laughed. "You should give those society types an eyeful. I'll make some calls and get back to you later."

When he hung up, David grinned and then shook his head. This was the most desperate thing he'd ever done. He'd just been hosed for five thousand dollars to go to a cocktail party to impress a woman he had only seen a few times, a woman who was probably so pissed she wouldn't give him the time of day. But after playing around for all these years, David was pretty sure Kate was *the one*. He had to make it right with her.

He had to at least try.

⤫

"YOU'RE PACKING?"

It was Tuesday evening, eighteen hours before her flight was scheduled to leave, and Kate had walked out of her bathroom to find her daughter surveying the open suitcase on her bed. Closing a zipper bag full of toiletries, which she placed in a closed compartment of her bag, Kate thought carefully about what she was going to say when the questions started coming. This was going to end badly.

"Yes, I'm a little confused about what to take." Kate turned her attention to the bathing suits she'd taken from the drawer. "Are you packed, honey? I'm dropping your things at your dad's after I take you to school tomorrow."

Kate smiled as Laura walked over and picked up a black bikini that was a lot more revealing than any of her other bathing suits.

"This is new," Laura said, holding up the skimpy string bottom. "You didn't tell me you were going away."

"We talked about going away several times." Kate sat on the bed. "I planned this trip a while ago."

"You did? Oh. Well, the Bahamas is more my speed than an amusement park at this point." Laura was trying so hard to be cool, it broke Kate's heart. "But this bathing suit is a little much, isn't it Mom?"

"No amusement parks." Kate grabbed the suit and tossed it in the suitcase. "I'm going to the spa we talked about. You know, the one on St. Bart's."

There was an audible 'whoosh' as the air left Laura's lungs. "The last place you mentioned was Florida, not the spa on St. Bart's."

"I was going to surprise you, but you were set on going with Dad and Marie, so I didn't say anything. Dad knew."

Laura's eyes darted around and her face flushed. Laura was angry, but Kate found she didn't really care. After everything she'd been through over the past week, she was in no mood for anyone's crap, including Laura's.

"Are you going alone?" Laura asked.

"No, Julie took your ticket."

"I can't believe you're going without me."

"I was disappointed, but I didn't want to use a fancy trip like a bribe. I want to spend time with you, but I won't manipulate you like that." It was the truth, and it was time she leveled with Laura. "I'm sure you'll have a lovely time with your dad. Where are you staying?"

"No place as nice as you."

And isn't that too freaking bad, Kate thought.

Laura was trying to find words to make the situation Kate's fault, but she seemed to realize she had no argument. She was angry because she'd let herself be manipulated by her father and her future stepmother. Poor Laura was a mass of selfish confusion. She wanted all the things her mother brought to the family, but she didn't want her mother. Was she realizing her father was only a marginally successful academic who couldn't support them? Interesting. Being with Richard and Marie so much, Laura was absorbing their self-centered, materialistic values, and it upset Kate that her daughter was so easily manipulated by money. Kate could have called the airline and gotten Laura a ticket, upgraded their room, and never missed the money. She could have stolen Laura right out from under Richard and Marie, but she wouldn't play those games. Laura finally seemed to understand.

After a protracted silence, and no apology from Kate, her incensed seventeen-year-old stormed out and slammed her bedroom door.

Score one for the grown-up.

AFTER WHAT FELT like an endless day, Laura sat with her father and Marie in the lawyer's office. They were leaving for the Bahamas the next day and Dad said they had to get the meeting done before they left, so she was missing three tests to sit here and feed this guy information. He was shooting questions at her about her mother and taking notes on a large yellow pad. It didn't seem like she mattered at all, but Laura put up with it because once the hearing was over she would be with her dad full time and maybe he would stop talking to her about Mom. It was like he was obsessed that Laura like him better. Maybe if she lived with him full time, he'd believe she loved him.

The lawyer asked questions about what her mom did, who she saw, and how often she went out. The truth was, Laura didn't know too much about her mother's life because it was never important to her. Lately, the only thing she did know about was the trip she was taking with Julie to the Caribbean. They left this morning and were going to this awesome spa—a trip she should be on, but stupidly she blew off Mom for the Bahamas.

Mom always made dinner when she was there. She worked at night in her office. Her only friends were people from the school. That was about it.

"Oh, and there's some guy who's interested in her."

That got her dad's attention. "A man?"

"Yeah." She looked toward her dad. "I heard her and Julie talking about him. But I don't know if anything is going on. It may actually be over. I haven't met him or anything."

Marie looked at Richard and then the attorney. He nodded, knowing what they wanted him to do. "I'll have the detective look into it."

"Detective?" Laura asked. "You're going to spy on Mom?"

Marie smiled and shrugged. "How do you think we know so much about her? You can only tell us so much, and we need this information to protect you, dearest."

Her father leaned in and patted her shoulder. "I want to know who your mother is with to keep you safe. God knows who she's cavorting with."

Her relationship with her mom was far from perfect, but Laura doubted Mom would be with anyone dangerous. She hated all this legal shit. She just wanted a normal family, and at this point Dad and Marie were as close as she was going to get. God, that was pathetic.

Her phone buzzed and she glanced to the screen. It was a text from Jack. He wanted to see her that night, but she didn't know if she would be able to get out. They were going to be packing and her dad would be around... it probably wouldn't work. She really wanted to see him though. They'd been out twice and Laura really liked him. Based on the way he kissed her, she guessed he liked her, too.

"John, make sure the financials are part of the custody petition." Laura snapped back to the conversation when she heard Marie's voice.

"Financials?" Why were they talking about money? This

was about custody.

"Sweetheart," Marie said, "Any custody suit brings with it monetary issues. Your mother will have to pay us."

"Whoa. You're going to be *paid* to have me live with you?"

Her father was growing impatient and he shot Marie an annoyed look. "Laura, it's money to support you. Your mother has it, so she'll have to give it to us for you." Her dad leaned over and kissed the top of her head. "Try not to let it worry you. All you'll have to do is tell the judge where you want to live. The rest will take care of itself."

She slouched in her chair and kept quiet for the rest of the meeting. Even though the discussion centered around her and where she would live, Laura knew it wasn't about her at all.

Chapter 12

KATE SAT AT her vanity, brushed out her hair, and methodically checked for the dreaded gray. Her dark hair spilled over her shoulders and she thought maybe she should cut it. Change was good, and certainly a more stylish haircut would be a step in the right direction. She set the brush down on the table top. *Pathetic, Kate, truly pathetic. Just get a grip and accept who you are. Changing your hair isn't going to change your life.*

Her makeup applied, she went to her closet to get her dress. The Literacy Foundation Holiday Party was her event. She'd founded the organization several years ago, and she was extremely proud of what she'd accomplished. But she just wasn't looking forward to the evening. Her deadline was looming, and since she'd returned home from the Caribbean she hadn't gotten much work done. Waves of tiredness kept hitting her at unexpected times. No matter how much sleep she'd gotten the night before, any time became a good time for a nap.

"It's probably just old age," she muttered.

She went to the doctor that morning, but it would be a

few days before all her test results were back.

The trip to the spa had done her some good, aside from a minor meltdown the first day. Julie had been great. Instead of accepting a date from one of the many men who asked, Julie stuck to Kate, claiming a girls' weekend—no men welcome. Along with seeing a condo she might buy, they'd been massaged, buffed, facialed, manicured, pedicured, and toned. Her skin was tanned and glowing, her muscles were relaxed.

But no matter what she did, she kept thinking about David. Kate wondered if anything was more pitiable than a woman obsessed with a younger man. She supposed part of it was the sex. It was intense, passionate, and when she was with him she'd felt desired, and that was what she kept revisiting. Of course it was a lie. He called and tried to explain about the bit in the paper, but he didn't come after her. In fact, he'd given up pretty quickly. David didn't need her any more than her family did. He'd forget all about her, but at least with him it was understandable. He was a complete stranger.

She donned a simple midnight blue gown that was fitted tightly at the bodice and then flared out to sweep the floor. She added her grandmother's pearl necklace and examined herself in the mirror. She was probably showing off too much cleavage, especially for this crowd, but overall, she looked more than respectable. The perkier boobs were a nice surprise. She turned to the left and then the right, looking at her profile—the extra time at the gym was paying off. She left for the party, hoping the evening would go by quickly.

HARMON CASTLE GLOWED as people arrived for the benefit.

Pulling her car forward, Kate gave the keys to the parking attendant and happily greeted a few acquaintances as she walked up the grand steps. Friday night, a beautiful setting, a worthy cause, pleasant company—it was good to get out, away from her manuscript for a while. The entire week, when she wasn't at school, she was in her office, writing, or attempting to write. Laura was barely home, so Kate would hole herself up for hours, late into the night, when she could stay awake. She had to force herself to do the most basic or necessary things like eat or exercise. No, this was definitely the right thing to do; if she didn't get out, she'd become some weird old hermit.

There were quite a few familiar faces and she started to relax, plucking a glass of champagne from a tray as a waiter dashed by. Circling slowly, Kate took in the scene. The grand ballroom was beautiful. Decked in garlands of pine, gold, and silver, a massive Christmas tree adorned with Steuben and Swarovski ornaments towered over one end of the room. People who passed by glittered almost as much as the decorations. It was a large turnout, and she had no doubt the event would raise a fortune for the foundation. Then she choked on her Dom Perignon.

David was here.

There were four of them—tall, muscular men, all in formalwear. Two had blondes on their arms, another was escorting a lovely brunette, but David was alone.

She bolted to the other side of the room so she could strangle the foundation's director. "You didn't tell me the Flyers had taken an interest in the Foundation." She seethed. She'd asked about the guest list three times and hadn't received a straight answer.

"Why would it matter? Oh! Jay Hemmings is here. And Cameron Roth. Look at all of them, aren't they just delicious?"

Glancing in David's direction, she saw he was coming toward them. He was gorgeous and with each step he took, her heart slammed harder against her ribs.

"Oh God," she whispered, gulping down the remaining champagne in her glass. "Not again."

DAVID RAN THROUGH what he wanted to say in his head. *The picture was old. I'm not engaged.* He thought for a second, regrouping. *Chelsea means nothing to me…*

David cursed himself. The truth was, as much as Chelsea was responsible for planting the story about the non-existent engagement, David was responsible for the attitude that surrounded him. People expected him to be with women like Chelsea—to be more concerned with style than substance. Kate had never been anything but honest with him, and it was possible he might not have a chance to save what they started.

He'd messed up too many times, but now, seeing her, David knew he had to try. As he walked toward her, he enjoyed the view. She stood defensively with her arms folded and her head cocked arrogantly to the side. He watched her eyes for any emotion, and then saw something faint. She looked… nervous. That was an interesting development. He made her nervous. Thank God. There might be hope.

DIANA PUSHED RIGHT past Kate with a hand extended in greeting. "Hello, I'm Diana Micelli, director of the foundation. It's so nice to meet you."

He grinned and accepted her hand politely. "David Burke. Nice to meet you, too."

"We're so pleased the team has taken an interest in the work we're doing. Thank you for the very generous donation. Do you know—" Diana gestured toward Kate and started the introduction, but he cut her off.

"This is a nice surprise, Kate. I didn't get to say good-bye the last time I saw you." He wanted to add the word "naked" to the end, but that could end with him succumbing to a slow and painful death.

"David." Her posture went rigid. Yeah, she was plenty nervous. "What are you doing here?"

He smiled, looking around the room. He had to get her alone. He had no chance at all of breaking her down when she could run off into a sea of people. "This is a beautiful place," he said, ignoring her original question. "Have you been here before?"

"Yes," she said, "I have."

Handing him the perfect opening, David offered her his arm. "You know I love history. Would you give me a tour?"

He'd trapped her. Running in the opposite direction was out of the question—her manners wouldn't allow it. She had no choice but to go with him, and she was not happy.

"Of course," she said. Her words were clipped and formal, as she slipped her hand through the crook of his arm. "My pleasure."

THEY LEFT THE ballroom and ascended the main staircase to see the entry hall and the chandelier from above. Having spent almost eighteen years in the area, there had been many opportunities for her to make visits to the grand estate, so she gave him a mini-history lesson about Main Line Philadelphia as they walked.

"You look beautiful," he said. She had to give him credit; it was the safest opening, if not original.

"Thank you."

"Are you going to let me explain?" he asked quietly.

She was putting on her most professional face, her most formal tone. "Nothing to explain."

He laughed. "Oh, come on."

"I have no reason to be angry with you. Just myself. Fool me once, and all that." She wondered if he could tell how she felt about him. Her heart was firing rapidly just being near him. They hadn't known each other long, yet she had a sense he could almost read her mind.

"I'm not engaged. They used an old photo and bad information."

She stopped and looked away, then raised her face toward his and said what she felt. She had nothing to lose. "That doesn't change the fact you turned me into a conquest. You had no right making me one of the girls in your entourage."

He gave her a narrow, tentative glance and Kate had no clue what he would do next.

"I never meant for you to feel that way, and you know it."

"Whatever." Kate barely looked at him. Her body was tense, so tense. Could he read her feeling? Could he tell?

David shook his head slightly and cast another glance in her direction before turning his body and inching closer.

She prayed he wouldn't touch her because when he did, she'd lose all control.

"Kate." His finger slipped under her chin and he tilted her face toward his.

She blinked and focused on his eyes, which gave her a chance to see what might be going on in his head. There was something sincere in the dark depths and she wondered if her eyes betrayed her in the same way her heart did.

"I'm sorry," he said. His voice was soft, contrite.

"Alright," she whispered, looking away again.

His cologne mingled with the scent of pine and Christmas candles and made her feel a little lightheaded.

"Alright?" He turned her gently and took her face in his hands this time, pressing his lips to her temple. "You'll forget about it?"

Everything flooded to the surface. The betrayal, the distrust, the feelings of inadequacy, the hurt—she couldn't stop it, couldn't run from it. "Forgetting about it would be a good idea."

She was in her own personal nightmare. Kate was being as polite as possible, but she wasn't giving him an inch. She couldn't—he affected her so completely, she couldn't risk the loss of control. "I don't know what else to say."

Stepping away from him, Kate turned and grabbed tightly to the rail on the landing, fixing her gaze on the crystal chandelier. "Look, I obviously misconstrued what that night meant to you. I thought... I thought it meant *something.*"

"*It did.*" David stepped behind her and placed his hands gently on her waist.

His fingers caressed her through the silk of her dress and he pressed his body into her back, allowing his warmth to penetrate to her core. Just when she thought her senses were assaulted to the fullest, his lips touched her just behind her ear.

"You're perfect," he whispered. "And I'll try to deserve you."

That was it. She was melting.

"But everything you represent scares me."

So much for melting. She froze.

"*Scares* you?" she asked. *Shit. Even being perfect wasn't good enough.*

When a man was scared, it was fight or flight. He was still having doubts, and she wasn't about to set herself up for another fall. If it wasn't another woman causing a problem, it would be David's immaturity. Kate straightened her spine and tried to get out of the situation without letting him see what he'd done to her.

Plastering a polite smile on her face, she took a step away. "I should really get back."

"No, wait." Now he was confused, but he seemed to realize he'd done something wrong. "I didn't mean…"

"Have a lovely evening."

Turning on her heel, she left him.

WHEN SHE GOT to the bottom of the stairs, David saw her greet an older man with a kiss and a warm hug. She glanced up the staircase to where he was standing, their eyes met, and he could see she was distressed. But then she gave him her back and allowed the older man to escort her into the ballroom.

"Good job, Dave," he said.

Why was this so complicated? He got that he was totally out of his league with her, but he wasn't giving up. Not until there was no other option.

Kate was making him work for this relationship, and that hadn't ever happened to him. But he was ready for it now. David wanted a woman who was moody and difficult; one who thought too much, who wasn't interested in impressing him. He wanted a woman who would keep his interest, make him think, and make him look inside himself. David wanted Kate. She was all those things and more.

He went back to the ballroom and found his friends. It was a nice enough party and he was sure they would raise a ton of money for the charity. Kate stood with a group of very aristocratic looking women, drinking champagne, and carrying on a very dignified looking conversation. David wondered if those women had read any of Kate's books and what they might think about the love scenes she wrote. His body responded as he thought about those scenes, and pictured Kate in the various scenarios, instead of her heroine. It wasn't hard seeing her that way, all he had to do was let his mind slip back to the hotel in California or his bedroom two weeks ago. Sipping a beer, he kept his eyes on her. He caught her looking at him and he smiled. She blushed. Jay wandered over with Tyler Graves in tow, both of them looking bored.

"Fun group," Jay said before he saw David staring at Kate. "So tell me, did we drop five large so you could make goo-goo eyes at the teacher?"

"Yeah, basically." David nodded.

"You suck, Padre," Tyler said.

"Graves, you should be right at home here. Half of this

group consists of Ivy League professors." He was making a reference to Tyler's degree from Yale.

Jay surveyed the room. "Did you talk to her?"

"Yup." David took another drink and watched Kate get more and more agitated.

He hadn't taken his eyes off her. The band started playing a slow, jazzy version of *Teach Me Tonight* and he could only think of Kate, and how she would feel pressed against him.

"Did you apologize for being a dick?" asked his friend.

"I did, again, but I think I insulted her."

"Asshole." Jay shook his head and then let out a low whistle. "Will you look at that? Gramps just asked her to dance."

"Yeah, well…" David's reply was more a grumble than anything.

He hated the thought of anyone else touching her, even the senior citizen who'd just led her onto the dance floor. When he saw the old man glance down her dress, he burned. When the guy's hands started to wander, David's thoughts were nothing short of violent.

"Oh, she didn't like that." Jay laughed as David watched Kate push her partner's hand off her behind. "Although looks like Gramps is having a ball, eh? You going to do anything?"

David nodded, drained his beer and handed the glass to his friend. Gathering his nerve, he walked onto the dance floor and tapped her dancing partner on the shoulder.

The old man turned and raised an eyebrow.

"May I?" David asked.

When the man stepped away, reluctantly allowing him to cut in, David thanked him. Without hesitation, he took Kate's hand and slipped his arm around her tiny waist, pulling her closer than was appropriate. He spread his hand on the small of her back and allowed the feel of the silky dress to soak in.

"The gentleman was taking some unwelcome liberties."

Kate didn't respond, but her cheeks reddened before she changed the subject. "You can dance?" she asked.

"My mother taught me," he said.

"What do you want, David?" She sounded defeated, hopeless, and that made him feel guilty. He didn't want to be responsible for causing her pain.

"Please forgive me," he said.

"Okay."

"Kate. I know you left because of the picture in the paper. I don't blame you." As soon as the words left his mouth he wanted to kick himself. *You're an idiot, Burke.*

"How nice," she snipped. "It's quite gratifying to know I won't be blamed for something for which I bear no responsibility."

Grinning, he looked down at her. She was wonderful—proud, stubborn, and completely vulnerable. David pressed her body into his. Heat shot through him.

He leaned closer and whispered in her ear, "I love how you feel in my arms." All David heard in response was her sigh. That was his cue to push it a little farther. He rested his cheek on her hair as his breath played over her temple.

"You don't play fair, on or off the ice," she said.

"I can't play fair with you."

"You have plenty of women, why can't you just leave me alone?"

The words let him know she was hurt, and he felt responsible for every bit of what she was feeling. Kate drew a ragged breath and David saw she was fighting to maintain the last of her dignity.

"There's no one else. Not since I saw you that morning in New York and even then, Chelsea didn't stay with me. She only met me in the city. Ever since California, there's only you."

"No one?" she asked her voice soft and almost hopeful.

"No one. After the night we spent together, you have to know I only want you." She leaned into him and David thought this was too much to hope for.

People were watching them. As he glanced around the room, he could see the whispers and curious looks. No doubt the ladies in polite Philadelphia society were wondering what a caveman like him was doing with their Kate. He held her close and let his lips brush against her hair. When the music stopped, he cupped her cheek and dropped a kiss on Kate's mouth. He let his tongue play over her soft, sweet lips— nothing more—but his intention was clear.

Breathless and trembling, she could barely speak when she pulled away from him. "Why did you do that?"

He didn't answer, but watched helplessly as Kate touched her fingers to her lips and backed away, leaving him standing in the ballroom.

KATE LEFT THE dance floor as gracefully as possible, stopping when she entered the main foyer. What the hell had he done? Her heart was hammering in her chest and her lips were still warm. Everywhere he'd touched her was warm and tingly, and part of her wanted nothing more than to fall in his arms. But part of her, the sane part, had to get away.

She did exactly what he wanted. She went weak at the knees and then fell apart. And she should have expected it. David had that effect on her whenever their paths crossed. From the romantic evening in California to the near-sex experience in the bar to their night together a few weeks ago, Kate tended to lose her mind when he was in the vicinity.

Hiking up her dress so she wouldn't trip, she took off down the main hallway. What she wanted was to get good and pissed, so she could shake off the urge to go back to the ballroom and rip off his clothes. God, did she want to rip off his clothes. Thinking about him, thinking about touching him, and about how his body felt against her, was a heady thing. Pushing through a door at the end of the hallway was a mistake. It was the solarium and it was technically closed at this time of year for one reason—no heat. The windows were tall and frosty; as soon as Kate stopped to think, the cold hit her. Her arms came around her body and she quickly turned to leave. That was when she saw David had followed her into the room.

He took off his jacket and wrapped it around her bare shoulders. "Here, it's cold."

Seeing him brought the reaction Kate wanted and it came in a great rush. She was pissed. *Finally.* Even she didn't know what to think about it. This anger, this indignation, was all new—and she lashed out at him, spitting out the words like venom. "I should slap you."

David, who obviously thought he was going to charm her, stepped back, surprised at the attack. "Uhhh…"

"What were you thinking about in there? You humiliated me in front of three hundred people!"

"Humiliated? I kissed you!"

"In a room full of wealthy, connected people and photographers!"

"So what? I'm sure they've seen people kiss before!"

"What will they think?! I can't have gossip floating around about me! I have a reputation to protect."

"I have a reputation, too!"

"*Your* reputation is the problem." She moved toward him and waved her hand around his head. "Do you have hockey pucks for brains?"

He leaned into the edge of a wrought iron garden table and dropped his head. He couldn't argue with her about his reputation. "Apparently."

"Look at me." Kate brought her hands to her chest. David's expression stilled and grew serious, and his eyes met hers. "Do I look like one of your publicity hungry bimbos?"

He averted his gaze, shook his head.

"I'm in the throes of a custody battle, and my ex-husband's lawyer will do anything he can to paint me as a bad mother. That kiss will probably be exhibit number one."

"I'm sorry."

Kate paced in circles, not quite sure what to do with all the fury that was building inside her.

"Haven't you done enough?" The words came out on a trembling breath.

She wanted to throttle David, but she found more of her anger was because of Richard—Richard, that asshole and his stupid, manipulating games. Truth be told, she liked the kiss. She liked how David made her feel, but she couldn't take any chances, not where Laura was concerned.

Kate faced David directly and felt her body tremble. She

was on the verge of a breakdown and she couldn't hide it. "What possessed you to do that?"

"I don't know." He stood and ran his hands through his hair. "I thought a 'big gesture' would show you I'm serious about us."

"Big gesture?"

"Coming here, making a big donation, doing something romantic..." He straightened and took a step in her direction. "I'm sorry. I didn't intend to cause you problems."

Kate wrapped her arms around her middle and looked away. She couldn't face him, but he was so close, consuming all her space, all her conscious thought. The wash of emotions, the feeling she was falling and couldn't stop herself, was overwhelming. Where was this coming from? Why did he do this to her? Kate felt David's hand on her shoulder and she looked at his face. Everything he felt was right there, the sadness, the regret, all of it.

"I'm sorry," he whispered, and as he did, he pressed his lips against her forehead.

Kate couldn't help it. Her breath hitched, and she swallowed a great gulp of air before the sobs broke through the cold.

He took her in his arms, his hand pressing her head into his chest. His other arm was around her back, and Kate felt totally safe and completely defenseless at the same time. She was lost to him. Kate knew she had to put the brakes on this relationship before it destroyed her. But the tears wouldn't stop.

"Please don't cry, Kate. I'm sorry. I'm sorry for what happened. Please. Shh... shh."

"I can't... I can't... help it... I..." Kate was losing her

breath, and no matter how hard she tried, feeling David's warmth, feeling his heartbeat under her cheek, was allowing all the emotion that had been stored over the past year to break free in one giant wave.

"There's no one else. There will be no more pictures. I promise."

That didn't help, Kate just cried harder. David whispered to her, trying desperately to staunch the flow.

"I don't know what to do," she finally said.

"I'm not a good bet. I know that." He looked down into her face. "But I'm crazy about you."

He held her for a few more minutes, keeping her head pressed against him while he stroked her hair. His steady breathing calmed her and his strong arms were safe and secure. It allowed Kate to think about giving in and loving him. It wouldn't be a stretch, she was just about there, but the wall she'd built was hard to tear down. It was hard to forget how it felt to be left, and she knew that if she fell in love with David and then if he decided he didn't want her, she wouldn't survive it.

Finally, she felt strong enough to stand on her own. Her breath was still shaky and her heart was beating like a tom-tom. Kate's thoughts were scattered all over the place. But she got to the heart of the matter.

Stepping away, she pulled his jacket tight to ward off the cold, and then sat on a garden bench. "So, uh," she began, "you came here to impress me?"

Kate faced him and David stuffed his hands in his pockets, looking like a man facing the firing squad. "I wanted to show you I was serious."

"A ticket was five thousand dollars, David."

He rolled his eyes. "I know."

"Wow," she whispered. "You really don't get it."

He stepped toward her, almost desperate. She could see the sadness in his face, in his eyes. This was new for him. He was never at a disadvantage with women, and Kate could see he was frustrated. "Then explain it to me. Tell me what I have to do."

Kate rose and walked to him. Her heart hurt as she gazed up into his face. "Spending all that money just to impress me tells me you think I'm like all the other women in your life. I'm not." Her tone changed, leveled off. "You're telling me that it's a show; that it's about money. I don't want that." She locked eyes with him. "I want someone who can keep his promises. Someone who's honest."

They stood facing each other for what seemed like ages. Neither one of them moved, neither one of them spoke. Kate's response had effectively ended the conversation, and David, who was always quick with a comeback, was now without one. He looked up, and moved toward her, stopping only inches away. Kate was still amazed that a man like him didn't intimidate her, especially considering her past. He was so big and so strong, yet Kate knew, deep down, he would never, ever hurt her.

David's large hands reached out and cradled Kate's head. His fingers laced through her hair and his thumbs grazed over her cheeks. She looked into his molten, brown eyes and saw he was sad, truly sad and sorry, and her own eyes filled with tears again.

He leaned in and touched his lips to hers, first taking tiny sips, then drawing her mouth into a gentle dance. Her insides bubbled up and then melted away as David made her forget who she was, and everything she'd just said, as his mouth captured hers.

When he finally broke the kiss, David leaned back slightly and gazed at her. "I want to be with you. I messed up so bad, but I want to be with you."

"You may think I'm what you want, but I'm not." As much as it hurt, Kate shook her head.

It was over. Kate nodded and reached up, covering his hand with her own.

"Kate, please..."

"I can't do this with you," she whispered. "I just can't risk it."

The quiet that settled between them led to a feeling of resignation. They were over before either of them had a chance to make it matter. Kate looked in his eyes and saw everything she ever wanted. *Love.* She saw love there, but for some reason she couldn't trust it was only for her.

"I think it's a mistake," he said. "But I won't bother you anymore." He stroked her cheek again, still had his fingers tangled in her hair. "If you change your mind, you know where to find me."

She nodded, but she knew she would never be ready for him. She would never be able to meet his challenge. "Good-bye, David."

"Good-bye, Kate." He dropped one last soft kiss on her cheek and left.

Kate stood with David's jacket still draped over her shoulders. She pulled it around her to ward off the chill, but in doing so she caught a whiff of David's cologne. And it was the smell, the same one that lingered after they made love, which forced Kate to the conclusion that she wasn't getting over him anytime soon.

Chapter 13

December

KATE SLAPPED AT the screeching alarm clock and stretched her arms over her head as she sat up. Mornings were hard, especially after a night that brought on the story fast and furious. It happened in waves. For days she wouldn't write anything, and then inspiration would hit and words flowed like water. Last night had been one of those nights.

She threw the covers back, anxious to get back to her manuscript, but instead plopped her feet on the floor to get ready for work. It was seven and her first class was at ten. It was the first time in months that she really looked forward to her writing. The first time in months the day held promise, and Kate didn't think about how long it would be before she could crawl back into bed. Instead, she thought about running errands and teaching her classes and writing. Maybe seeing David at the benefit wasn't a bad thing. It allowed her to close the door on him and move on.

Even though it hurt like hell.

Kate's mood dropped by degrees as she thought about her real life. It got more complicated when she looked up and Laura stared at her from the door of her room. Tan from her time in the Caribbean, Laura's dark hair had picked up some subtle highlights and was pulled into a tight ponytail. Her jeans rode too low and her sweater rode too high. But it was her eyes, sharp, dark, and blazing, that were telling Kate this was not going to be an easy morning.

"You were up late," she said.

"I was working. I have some revisions to make on the new book."

Laura sauntered in. She was still angry about the vacation Kate took and had been shooting daggers at her mother for a week. "Still can't get it right?"

Kate was in no mood for this. Her stomach was a little jumpy, probably from lack of sleep, and she changed the subject to avoid a confrontation at the crack of dawn. "Aren't you going to miss your bus?"

Several inches taller, Laura stared down at her mother. "I'm going to Dad's after school and I won't be home till about nine. Marie is helping me with a writing assignment."

Kate had to admit Laura was getting good at cheap shots, but something about the argument felt contrived, like Laura had planned to pick a fight. She wondered if it helped Laura feel better, if it justified the bad feelings between them. Might as well give her what she wanted. Kate took the bait. "What's the assignment?"

"It's a creative piece." Laura stuck her nose in the air and tried to be indifferent. "Nothing you would understand."

"Well, that insult was quite predictable." Kate walked to her closet and picked up her robe. "Don't let Marie force you into using that bombastic prose she's so fond of. It'll weigh down your story."

"Marie is a brilliant writer," Laura declared.

"Really?" Kate tilted her head and decided to stoop to her daughter's level, just for fun. "Let me know when she's joining me on the bestseller list and I'll be the first to bow down to her talent." Her daughter's face twisted in anger.

"What do you know?" Laura snapped. "With the violence and the sex, your books are just... just... *trash*."

"Trash?" Kate's breath caught before she broke into a stunned smile. "Your father should be thanking his lucky stars for my *trash*." Richard was unbelievable, he'd brainwashed her. Her *trash* was paying for his life. He should shut the hell up. "My writing is light fare compared to what other people are doing and it's never going to win me a Pulitzer, but I'm very proud of my work."

"Someday Marie will win a Pulitzer," Laura said.

Kate sat at her dressing table and watched her daughter in the mirror. The girl was standing her ground. Her back was straight, her arms were folded. It hurt Kate that she was so protective of Marie, a woman who had been part of the destruction of their family. Kate met Laura's gaze and sent out her last shot.

"Someone would actually have to like one of her books for that to happen."

"People love her books."

"What?!" Now Kate was fighting back the laughter. "The reviews of her last book were scathing. One said it was a crime that trees were sacrificed for her 'incoherent nonsense'."

Laura's lips were pursed, her neck was tight, and the sheer frustration in her face told Kate that Laura was done being subtle.

"I'm going to live with Daddy. That's why you're seeing the lawyers today."

Well, there it was. It hurt Kate to think about losing her rights to see her daughter, but seeing Laura's face, she wondered if it hurt her, too. Something was not right about all of this, about the anger and the accusations. Laura seemed tired of the fight.

Kate turned and faced her beautiful daughter. How had things gotten this bad? "I know, but I don't want that. I don't want to lose you."

"Why should you care? You never wanted me." She spouted more of Richard's lies, but Laura's tears were real. She believed what she said; believed all the things her father told her.

"Laura, that is *not* true. I wanted you. I wanted you so much."

"Daddy said..."

Kate held up her hand. "I don't care what he said. He doesn't know my heart." Kate approached and laid a hand on Laura's face. "You are my child and I will always love you. On this point, your father has not told you the truth. Deep down, you know that."

Laura stared at Kate and swallowed hard. "I have to go to school."

"Have a good day. Let me know if you need to be picked up."

She shrugged. "I think Dad said he would bring me home."

"Fine."

The tightness in Laura's voice told Kate her girl was holding back. Kate had the feeling a reservoir of emotion was waiting to break through the cool exterior she'd fashioned, and a glimmer of warmth formed in the pit of Kate's stomach. Maybe her baby did feel something, maybe she wasn't as cold as her father tried to make her, but Kate wouldn't find out that morning as Laura turned on her heel and bolted down the stairs.

A few minutes later, the back door closed and Kate dropped to the bed, blowing out a breath. There was a point when she was sure she didn't have a chance in hell of having a relationship with Laura, but now... something about the way Laura looked at her, a split second softening, that told Kate it wasn't all bad between them, that maybe Laura missed having a mother. It was a mere kernel of hope, but Kate would take what she could get.

Chapter 14

I T WAS JUST a matter of time.

Kate had every intention of taking this to court, but she also knew her daughter had the final say. She was on the brink of adulthood and could articulate her wants clearly in any court. Sure, she wondered if Laura really wanted to leave her, but the truth was, Richard was a master intimidator and her daughter was 'daddy's girl'.

Kate had always held out hope Richard was bluffing and he wouldn't really want to take Laura completely, knowing how devastating that would be. But once again, she'd underestimated him. He didn't give a rat's ass about anything but hurting her. This was a power play, a way for him to get what he wanted. And it was working. Feeling a heaviness in her chest, Kate closed her eyes and tried to think of a way to fight back.

She was on her bed staring at the wall when the phone rang. A glance at the caller ID told her it was her doctor's office. Part of her just wanted to let it ring, but she knew they were calling with test results and she needed to answer.

"Hello?"

"Hi, Kate. It's Doctor Finn."

Kate pushed herself into a sitting position. She expected to hear from the office, but not the doctor. If she was making the call herself, there must be something wrong. *Great. Let's add a terminal illness to what could go wrong with her life.*

"Oh, God. What's wrong with me?"

"Calm down. Nothing's wrong. You're healthy."

"Then why are you calling?"

"Well, your test results did indicate something *new*."

Kate's stomach sank and she grabbed the glass of wine she'd placed on her night table. "New? New how? Oh, my God. I have a brain tumor, don't I?"

"Well, since we didn't examine your brain, I wouldn't know about that, but the truth is, you're pregnant."

Kate froze, the wine glass touching her lips. She stared at the golden liquid and put it back on her night table. Pregnant? The shock was working its way through her system and finally, her brain processed the information. "Pregnant?"

"Yup. Hard to say how far along you are. Do you remember when you had your last period?"

"I'm pregnant?! How?"

The doctor chuckled a little on the other end of the line. "The usual way, I'm guessing. You're seeing someone?"

"Yes. Well, not anymore."

"Did you have unprotected sex?"

"No! He used a condom!" Now she was trying to remember when she had her last period. Was it in September? Did she really not notice?

"No birth control is foolproof, Kate."

"That's why I've been tired and a little queasy from time to time."

"More than likely," her doctor said.

"I don't think I've had a period since September."

Her doctor went silent for a moment. Silence like that was never good. "So you're almost out of your first trimester then. Look, you need to see an obstetrician as soon as possible."

"The doctor that delivered Laura only does gynecology now."

"Okay. Your age makes you high risk, so let me give you the name of someone very good at University Hospital."

Kate grabbed her journal and a pen from her night table and started to write all the information. With her free hand she touched her belly, and couldn't believe how things could go from bad to nightmarish with a phone call.

LATER THAT NIGHT, Kate sat in her den, still in shock, watching the hockey game. It seemed only right she share this moment with her baby's father. Even if he had no clue what was going on. David was having a good game, brutalizing the New York's top scorer, as well as having a goal and an assist. Of course he didn't know their carelessness had produced a child.

When the panic set in, David was the first one she wanted to tell, and she'd made the mistake of dialing his cell phone. She hung up and didn't leave a message. Hopefully, he wouldn't see her number in the missed call log. It was too soon. She needed some time before putting herself in the position to be rejected by him.

Over the last three hours she'd made a list and gone to the

grocery store because Kate realized she had to adjust her diet. She stocked up on produce, milk, cereals, yogurt—lots of real food. While she was out, Laura called and told her she was staying at her father's house.

That left Kate alone in the house… just her and the baby in her belly. David's baby. What the hell was she going to do?

Kate picked up the phone and dialed the familiar series of digits. Her lifeline. Her sister.

"Hello!" The bright sunny voice that came from the other end of the line brought the tears.

"Trish?" Her voice cracked—the fear, the confusion, all flooding to the surface.

"Katie? What's wrong, honey?"

The tears choked her. "I-I need you to come here."

"Oh shit, Kate, what did Richard do now?"

"It's not Richard." Kate tried to compose herself, but watching David on TV and talking to her sister broke any control she had on her emotions. "I'm pregnant," she cried.

"What? Holy shit." Trish had no idea how to respond because Kate hadn't ever told her about David. "Kate… who…?"

"Can you come, Trish?"

"Absolutely. I can be there tomorrow."

"Thank you."

"Kate, are you all right?"

"Umm, other than being pregnant by a man who doesn't love me, yeah, I'm just peachy."

Trish drew in a deep breath. "Hang in there, honey. I'll be there in the morning."

"Thanks. I really just…" She started to cry again. "I need you."

"I know."

After she hung up with Trish, she focused on the TV and watched David in the postgame interview. It brought the tears harder than ever. She wanted to tell him about the baby so badly, but she couldn't bear the fact he didn't love her. Since the night they spent together three weeks ago, Kate was certain she loved David. The night had been her romantic fantasy come to life. He was gentle and kind and they emptied their hearts to each other. At least she had. She talked to him about things she hadn't even told her sister.

Then reality intruded in the form of Chelsea Connor. She didn't think David cared for her old student; Kate knew she had his heart, but for how long? The photo shook her out of her stupor and forced her to face the fact that while David could have been hers for the moment, it wouldn't last. How long would it be before David got tired of her and moved on to someone else? He was completely wrong for her, but she loved him anyway. She was adjusting to the fact she'd have to move on, and now this. His baby. Something that would always remind her of the man she couldn't have.

DAVID HELD THE phone and had his thumb on the button that would dial Kate's number. When he saw the missed call, hope shot right through him. Maybe, just maybe, she'd changed her mind about him. About them. Glancing at the time on the phone, he saw it was after eleven, and knowing she had to go to work in the morning stopped him from making the call. He'd have to wait until tomorrow to hear what she had to say.

KATE CALLED IN sick.

It wasn't a lie, really. She was an emotional wreck—exhausted, nauseous and in no shape to teach. Thank God her sister would be there soon.

Kate had been up half the night thinking about what she was going to do, and when she did sleep, she was restless, dreaming about her baby and David. Their baby.

She'd called the doctor and gotten an appointment for the following day. The fact she was so far along was probably what caused the concerned tone in the receptionist's voice. This was going to be very different from the last time.

Her pregnancy with Laura had been uneventful in the sense that Kate delivered a healthy girl. She had been twenty-three and the doctor had little doubt that all would be fine. Richard, however, became the Svengali of expectant fathers.

Being older and wiser in Kate's eyes, she did everything he said. He researched pregnancy and nutrition extensively. She ate a special diet that was meant to limit her weight gain and maximize the baby's health. He made her walk three miles a day regardless of the weather.

When she went into labor, he was a beast. She was miserable and having back labor. The baby wasn't breech, but was facing the wrong way, so Kate didn't dilate. The doctor offered an epidural to ease her pain, and Richard refused it, bullying Kate into going natural. It proved a problem when they decided to do a C-section and Richard fought that as well.

Kate had few memories of anything from that day, but she vividly remembered Richard telling her she was a failure as a woman, if she couldn't do something as natural as give birth. Her doctor finally threatened to remove him from the maternity ward if he didn't back off.

It turned out Kate and the baby would have died if they hadn't performed the Cesarean.

Richard would have been crushed if he'd lost the baby, but Kate doubted he would have cared at all if he lost her. A month after Laura had been born, he hit her for the first time. She kept hoping he would settle down and become the loving husband she needed, but he didn't, and no matter what she did, Kate ended up alone anyway.

Now she stood in the kitchen and looked out at her big backyard. She shook her head, wondering how this happened. She knew the biology, but how was it that shit just kept raining down on her? The abuse, the cheating and divorce, the custody problems, falling in love with a guy who was too young for her, and now getting pregnant—would it end?

Her biggest concern was the baby's health. If she got pregnant in California, she was an easy two months gone, and she'd been living it up. She'd had alcohol on multiple occasions, had been in a hot tub, exercised vigorously, and actually lost weight. She placed both hands on her abdomen.

"Sorry, honey. Mommy will feed you better from now on." She heard a car pull in the driveway and looked at the clock.

Eleven o'clock. Trish was right on time. Kate went to the side door and opened it just in time to launch herself into her big sister's arms.

Patricia Adams-Reed had a life most women would envy. The wife of a congressman from a district just north of Atlanta, she had a fulfilling career as a research scientist with the Centers for Disease Control, two great kids, and a husband who adored her. She was stunning to look at, defying her forty-eight years with incomparable grace. She was taller than Kate, but with the same large hazel eyes and dark hair. It was her irreverent sense of humor and "screw the world" attitude that made Trish exactly what Kate needed.

Kate fell apart as soon as they got into the kitchen.

"Shhh, now, shhh." Trish's voice was laced with just the slightest drawl, the result of over twenty years in the south. "Honey, tell me what happened." Kate stepped back, wiped her eyes on her sleeve and her sister placed a hand on her belly. "I'm going to be an auntie again?"

Kate nodded. "I-I can't believe this is happening." Her voice was hoarse, raw from the endless crying.

Trish took her arm and guided her to the couch in the den. The room was a mess, with tissues littering the floor and coffee table. "You need to tell me the whole story. First— who's the daddy?"

Kate pointed to the table. There sat her laptop, and on the screen was the team website, featuring a photo of last night's star of the game—David.

"What? Does he work for that hockey team?"

"Sort of." Kate took the clicked the link enlarging the photo and pointed again. "David Burke. The hockey player. He's the father."

Trish blinked. Looked carefully at the picture and then back at her sister. "You shagged a pro athlete?"

Kate nodded.

"*Goddamn.*" Trish leaned back and extended her long, slender arm across the back of the leather sofa. "We have some catching up to do."

Kate wiped her eyes with her sleeve, nodded, and launched into the story.

TRISH HUNG ON her every word, wiped every tear, and finally Kate got to the point she was at right now. Alone and pregnant. Kate was sniffling like a five-year-old with a runny nose. Trish walked into the kitchen and grabbed the box of tissues that was sitting on the counter. She wasn't falling all over herself, so Kate imagined her big sis was a little peeved.

"I have to give you credit… you do nothing small. It's like the old days."

"What's that supposed to mean?" Like Kate didn't feel shitty enough already? Trish was going to lecture her now? She remembered what it was like. Perfect Trish never made a wrong move and Kate, well, that was something else.

"Never mind." Trish sat on the coffee table and took her sisters hands in hers. "Have you made an appointment with the doctor?"

"I'm going tomorrow."

"Good. I'll go with you."

"Okay." Kate swallowed hard, relieved.

"You need anything from the store? Baby's gotta eat."

"I went grocery shopping. There's lots of healthy food in the house and I got rid of all the alcohol."

Trish shook her head, disapprovingly. "Oh, darlin', that's just a crying shame. After that story, I need a drink."

Kate chuckled, but just as quickly turned serious. "I think I love him, Trish, but it's not going anywhere."

Her sister wrapped her in a big hug and when the phone

rang, Kate picked up the cordless and froze. It was David.

"Please answer this." Kate thrust the phone at her sister.

"Why? Who is…"

"It's David."

"Why is he calling you?"

"Trish, please?!" Kate was frantic.

Trish didn't answer, the answering machine did, but her sister turned up the volume to hear David's message. "Hi Kate, it's David. I saw you called last night. I hope everything's okay. I'm going on a short road trip tomorrow, but if you need to talk to me, well, ah, call back. Thanks."

Trish listened to the click disconnecting the call and glared at Kate. "You called him?"

She nodded. "He didn't answer, so I hung up."

"He sounds worried, Kate. You should call him back."

She didn't say anything. Instead, Kate stood and walked to the kitchen to get some water.

Trish followed and leveled her gaze at Kate. Damn her sisterly instincts—she knew what Kate was thinking. "You *are* going to tell him, aren't you?"

"I don't know yet."

"Kate! You have to tell him."

"Why?" She was serious. Why did he have to know?

"Because he's the father?" Trish approached her. "Why *wouldn't* you?"

The knot in Kate's heart twisted again and she ran her hand over the plane of her stomach. "He'll try to do the 'right' thing."

"Is that a problem? There's nothing wrong with doing the right thing." Kate could see her sister didn't understand.

"I don't want to trap him," Kate said. "It would be a

disaster."

Trish wrapped an arm around her shoulder and Kate felt more raw sadness than she could ever remember. The only thing that would be worse than being rejected by David was if he was with her out of pity. She knew that kind of relationship wouldn't last. As much as she wanted to be with David, as much as she missed him, she couldn't risk her heart again.

Chapter 15

D RIVING INTO THE city was never easy during the week, but Kate wasn't going to take a train to see her obstetrician. Trish settled into the passenger seat of the Volvo, drank her coffee, and stayed quiet most of the ride. Her sister was never a morning person, and of course Kate had made an 8:30 appointment.

Kate's mind was a little quieter today. She'd stepped off the emotional roller coaster sometime yesterday and actually had time to adjust to the idea of having a baby. She sat in the guest bedroom that was on the second floor right next to her room. It was big, but not huge, had lots of great light and a window seat. The floors were already refinished, so all it needed was some paint and new furniture.

She still didn't know what to tell David, if anything. He may have cared for her, but as Kate told her sister, he wasn't ready for this kind of relationship. What was he going to do? Marry her? She was too old to trap a guy into marriage, and David would end up miserable.

Although, she did think he'd be a good dad. He loved kids, and he'd talked about the work he did with youth hockey programs and with Children's Hospital in the city. She also knew all there was to know about his nieces and nephew, whom he was seeing at Christmas. He was like a kid himself, describing the toys he bought for them.

Without a doubt, he'd be a wonderful father, and at that moment Kate felt a little guilty for not telling him.

"Thinking about Hockey Boy?" Trish was finally waking up.

Kate grinned. "How did you know?"

Trish laughed. "I've been here for less than twenty-four hours and every time you get that dopey look on your face, he's on your mind."

"Great." That was all Kate needed. She was hoping to be a little less transparent.

"Kate, are you sure you shouldn't tell him?"

"I don't think so. I don't want to saddle him with this. If I was worth it, he'd have fought a little harder for me."

"I don't think that's fair."

"I can do this on my own, Trish. Like I said, I don't want to trap him. And…" She hesitated, knowing this was the most important part. "I don't want to settle for someone who doesn't love me."

Kate glanced over when she slowed the car to a stop at a light. Trish was taking in all she said. Right or wrong, this was the most independent she had been in her entire life.

"I Googled him," her sister said. "I can see why you'd think that boy would be a heap of trouble."

"Yeah… and?" Kate was wondering what her sister had found out. The good and the bad, no doubt.

"Is he as good looking as his pictures?"

Kate smiled. "Better."

"Damn," Trish said. Kate laughed and Trish continued. "So, was it all the women?"

That question cut to the heart of it all. "Pretty much. I guess my own insecurity played a part in why I didn't want to pursue it."

"He wanted to pursue it?"

Kate nodded. "But it wouldn't last. How could it?"

"Oh, no, it couldn't possibly last." Trish's voice was laden with sarcasm. "You need to have more faith."

Kate was trying to process everything Trish said to her over the past day so, including her latest jab, so she could respond. Yes, she was insecure, and she'd been impulsive, but with the baby to consider, she had to pull back. Kate turned into the parking garage at the hospital and found a space.

Before they got out of the car, Kate turned and faced her sister. "Trish, I need you to understand where I'm coming from."

Trish nodded, ready to listen. "Shoot."

Kate was doing all she could to keep the tears from welling up. Whenever she talked about David she tended to cry, and she couldn't spend the rest of her life bawling every time his name was mentioned. "David is probably as perfect a man as you'd ever find. He's handsome, smart, gentle, a wonderful lover, and he's successful."

"I hear a big 'but' coming…"

Kate nodded. "Where women are concerned, he has the attention span of a Golden Retriever."

Trish laughed even though the whole situation was so sad. "Oh, Katie. I'm sorry."

"God help me, I'm in love with him. I can live with that. What I can't live with is the possibility of being left again."

"Why do you think he'd leave?"

Kate felt her lip tremble as the faced her fear straight on. "Why…" She took a breath, trying to stem the tears. "Why would he stay?"

It was Trish's turn to be thoughtful. She tilted her head and took hold of Kate's hand. "If I could castrate that stinking ex-husband of yours, I'd do it in a heartbeat. Not every man is Richard. From the sound of it, David may have real feelings for you."

Kate dropped her head and couldn't respond. It was too much to hope for.

"So the question, little sis, has nothing to do with Hockey Boy. It's whether or not you want that rat bastard ex of yours to have that much power over you. Are you going to allow him to keep taking up space in your head?" Trish opened the car door, and before climbing out she simply said, "Think about it."

Kate hesitated, then got out of the car herself. Trish might be right, but Kate already had too much to think about.

THE MATERNAL-FETAL HEALTH specialist worked out of a practice two blocks from the hospital and the waiting area was still quiet, which was why Kate picked an early appointment. She'd rather fight rush hour traffic than wait in a crowded doctor's office.

It was a little nerve wracking, actually, sitting there, filling out forms. Some of the questions should have had very simple answers, but of course, Kate's life made the answers more complicated. She answered the questions correctly, like a good girl, but God, did she want to tell the truth.

When was your last menstrual period? *Who knows, I've been too worried about my nervous breakdown.* Method of contraception? *The kind that failed?* STD screening? *Had one when I learned my rat bastard ex-husband was cheating.* She liked Trish's description of Richard. She'd use it again. Social history: Are you: Married? Single? Divorced? Engaged? *Divorced and alone.* She had space to write the name of her significant other, but Kate left it blank. There was a space for the name of the baby's father and Kate left that blank as well. She didn't want questions or complications. Finally, she had to answer a question about whether there had been abuse in the household at any point. Kate got brave on this one. She answered *Yes.* Admitting she was an abused woman was a step, wasn't it? Trish was looking over her shoulder and even she raised an eyebrow.

Kate brought the completed forms to the desk and sat down with her sister. She looked around. The waiting room was filling up, and she looked like all the other women there. For all her problems, no one could tell she was going to do this alone. Kate pulled her journal from her bag and jotted some thoughts. Her book was taking shape and she only had another hundred or so pages to write.

She glanced around the room and bit her lip. Sitting across from her was a woman reading *Past Lives.* Seeing people reading her books became a more common occurrence, and it made Kate feel good about her work and herself. She liked knowing she gave people a break from real life. That was what books were supposed to do, right? The woman had a beautiful blonde girl with her who might have been five years old. Kate remembered when Laura was that age, and it made her wonder how life would be with this baby.

"Mommy? Look."

Kate instinctively looked up and saw the little girl was staring at her, then examining the back cover of the book and pointing. Kate shook her head, not wanting to be recognized. Even a little attention embarrassed her.

"What is it, honey?" The woman smiled kindly at her child.

And of course, the little munchkin gave her up. "It's the lady on your book."

Her mother looked at the back of the book, looked at Kate, and smiled. "Oh! Oh, it is."

"Busted," Trish said.

The woman was grinning, dumbstruck, and so Kate smiled back and gave a little wave.

The woman gushed. "I just love your books. They keep me up at night."

"In a good way, I hope," Kate said. "You're enjoying the new one?"

She smiled and nodded. "It's amazing. But when are Elliot and Josh finally going to get together?"

Kate shrugged. It was a question she heard all the time. Women wanted to know when Elliot and her on-again/off-again boyfriend, Navy Commander Josh Gavin were going to make it permanent. It made her smile. Her readers loved the action in her books, the intrigue, but some people loved the love story.

The woman started fishing through her tote and Kate knew what was coming. "Would you mind signing... damn, you'd think I'd have a pen in this thing... would you...?"

Kate stood, walked over, and sat down next to the woman. "I have a pen."

Her fan passed her the book with an absolutely giddy expression on her face. Kate opened the front cover, careful to hold the woman's place. "What's your name?"

"Amanda," she said. "Thank you. This is so exciting."

Kate inscribed the book and handed it back to her very happy admirer. The reaction she received from people still surprised and embarrassed her. Maybe it was because Kate still heard Richard's voice when she thought about her work. She patted the child's hand. "Be extra nice to Mommy, okay?"

The little girl nodded. "Did you write all those words?" she asked.

"I did."

"*Jeez Louise!* I don't even know that many words."

Kate laughed, as did the munchkin's mom. "You will someday." Kate smiled again at Amanda and went back to her sister.

"Show off," Trish said.

"I do what I can. You still have me topped with that vaccine you worked on."

"Eh, I guess. But no one has ever asked me to autograph a syringe."

They both laughed.

IN THE EXAMINING room, Kate waited on the table, looking anxiously at the stirrups and all the instruments lying out on a silver tray. The room was comfortable and nicely appointed for what it was, but everything in there made her think about some dungeon where prisoners were tortured. And Kate was nervous.

An attractive woman with long, blonde hair and dark brown eyes entered the room. She wore a wide smile, a white coat, and extended her hand. "Katherine, I'm Michaela Emmanuel."

Taking the doctor's hand, she felt herself relax a little. "Call me Kate. This is my sister, Patricia Reed."

"Brought moral support? Perfect! So…" She pulled up a rolling stool and sat. "Let's chat. You're forty?" She had Kate's file in her hand and she started reading. "One child, uncomplicated pregnancy, but you had a section seventeen years ago. Placental abruption. Dr. Mariani delivered. Okay." She looked back at Kate. "Your daughter is fine, though?"

"Oh, yes. She's perfectly healthy, intelligent."

"Good." She stood and kept her eyes on the chart. "No father listed. Any reason for that?"

Kate drew a long breath. "We're not together and we won't be. I don't feel the need to involve him."

"Except that it's his child, too." Trish shot out the comment before Kate could stop her.

Dr. Emmanuel glanced over and grinned. "It's your decision, naturally, but if there are medical issues, it would help if we had his family history. Just having his blood type could give us an advantage."

"I'll think about it."

"You don't remember when your last period was?"

"I'm very irregular. It could have been September."

"Oy. Okay. Let's get you settled in. I'm going to do an exam and a sonogram to see how old your baby is."

During the sonogram, the doctor asked about medicines, alcohol, and stress. She also alluded to the abuse Kate acknowledged on her intake form. By the end of the exam, Kate had a prescription for prenatal vitamins and a picture of her child. She was eleven weeks pregnant. She made an appointment for a screening test the following week and she and Trish left the office.

"Eleven weeks," Trish said. "Plenty of time to break it to Mom before you start to show."

Kate felt sick. "Oh, good God."

"Forgot about her, huh?"

"She's going to go nuts. It's not like I haven't caused her enough grief."

Trish laughed. Their mother was the least of Kate's worries.

AFTER THE GAME, David walked into the hospitality room where he and Jay were meeting Annie. Even though David wasn't sure if it was a good idea, he'd agreed to go to dinner with them. Annie suggested she could invite a friend to come along, but David wasn't into to a fix up. And honestly, he didn't know when he'd be ready to date again. His friends were being as supportive as guys could be, but that usually meant they would drive him home if he got drunk. He didn't have anyone to confide in, and even if he did, he wouldn't be baring his soul any time soon. As much as Jay was his best friend, he didn't get it. If David was this miserable over Kate, he hoped Jay never had to find out what life would be like without his wife.

Playing in Washington was always a good time, especially when they won. The city had great restaurants, and for some reason this weekend a good number of the wives had decided to drive down and see the game. They were gathered in the room like a giggly pack, waiting for their husbands and boyfriends, gossiping, talking about the upcoming holidays and reveling in this very unusual life. He knew a good number of the women were different—mature and settled—especially the women the guys tended to marry, but some of them were just like Chelsea.

He heard a peal of laughter from one side of the room. Mark Blauvelt's wife was at the center of a small group, telling a story. He liked Amanda. He didn't know her well, but it seemed she was pretty level headed, and that was always a plus in his book. She and Mark were a nice couple, and when her husband came in the room Amanda's face lit up. The night David was with Kate, he thought maybe she looked at him like that, like he was everything. He was such a fucking goner it was pathetic. It was just like David thought when he first met her—Kate owned him.

"So," Amanda said, "I'm sitting in the O-B's office and Carissa goes, 'Mommy, there's the lady on your book.' Can you believe it? Katherine Adams was sitting right across from me. She was so gracious. She signed it without a problem."

Annie was standing with the women, a fake smile plastered on her face. She looked at David, who felt his legs turn to stone. He was stuck where he stood, trying to make sense of what he was hearing.

"So I guess I'll be seeing her because we use the same doctor. Maybe if we're pregnancy buddies, she'll tell me about her next book."

Annie piped up, hoping to get more information. "Are you sure she's pregnant, Mandy? Dr. Emmanuel sees women for a lot of reasons."

"She's pregnant. I overheard her make a screening appointment." A flutter of conversation rose from the assembled group and Amanda continued. "She must be older than I thought—they gave her the information about amnio."

David felt physically sick and leaned into the wall. That was why she'd called, to tell him. Why hadn't she called him back? Annie walked over and placed a hand on his back.

"I'm guessing from the look on your face you didn't know."

"No. I got a call the other night..."

"From Kate?"

"Yeah. She didn't leave a message."

Annie rubbed his back like a child. Of everything that could have blindsided him, this was the last thing he expected. He looked down and shook his head. He was going to be a father. David may not have thought about getting married much, until recently, but being a dad was always high on his "important things to do" list. "She has to tell me, doesn't she?"

Annie shrugged. "She should. That would be the right thing to do, but I don't know, Dave. She may not be planning on it."

Jay came into the room after working through the reporters. "So are we ready? I'm freaking starved."

The last thing David wanted to do was go out, but he didn't know what to say. Jay glanced from his friend to his wife and back, waiting for one of them to answer. David straightened up and made a decision to get the hell out of there.

"I'm gonna pass," David said. "I'm not feeling very

good."

Jay's face dropped and he looked at his wife. "What's wrong?"

"Nothing." David slapped him on the shoulder. "I'm going back to the hotel. I'll see you later on."

Jay nodded and David knew Annie would tell him the news. He pulled out his phone and went to the missed call log. Her number was still there. All he had to do was hit send and get his answers. But he closed the menu and decided to wait until he could see her in person.

He stepped out into the cold night air and decided to walk to the hotel. It was only two blocks away and he needed the time to clear his head and think.

What a fucking mess.

Legally, he had parental rights, but he hoped that Kate would come to him on her own. He wanted things to be good between them, even if they weren't together.

KATE SAT ON her bed, surrounded by pregnancy books and literature from the doctor. So much had changed from when she was pregnant with Laura. Worries about mercury in fish and nitrates in cold cuts and microwaves and environmental toxins… she wondered how any babies were born healthy at all. Kate's biggest concern was the alcohol she'd consumed. There'd been the resort on St. Bart's, the night she went to the theater, champagne at the benefit, a glass of wine here and there. The doctor assured her she probably had no reason to worry… she just shouldn't drink anymore now that she knew she was pregnant.

Eleven weeks.

She got pregnant when they were together in California, that wonderful night when Kate felt like a desirable woman for the first time in her life. The night David saved her from momentous despair. Her birthday.

She patted her tummy. "A birthday baby."

Trish bumped open the door with her hip and carried in a steaming mug of tea. "You conceived Junior on your birthday?"

Kate took the tea her sister offered and sipped the hot brew. "Yup."

"I can only imagine what that must have been like for you." Trish made a space on the bed and sat. "Living all those years with Richard and then falling into the arms of a guy like that? Wow."

"I'm trying not to think about it."

"You are a piss poor liar. All you do is think about him."

Kate put her tea on the night stand and faced her sister. "Then I'll get over it."

"That's a lie, too." Trish's voice had grown soft, and had a hint of pity behind the drawl.

Kate looked away and pushed her hair from her face. "I have to get over it."

Trish scooted over and wrapped her sister in a hug. It was the kind of hug meant to comfort, but this one was also for support. Kate needed the support if she was going to do the right thing.

"No, Kate, what you have to do is tell your baby's father what's happened."

Chapter 16

Laura ran around her bedroom, looking for her black platforms while talking to Tracy on the phone.

"He's so nice and polite… shit…" Laura dropped the phone. "Are you still there?"

"Yes," Tracy said. "Has anything you know, like, happened?"

"We've been together for over a month." They knew what the other one was talking about, but how sad that neither one could say it. There hadn't been any sex yet, but the operative word was 'yet'.

"So he's kissed you?"

"Well, duh." She tried to be cool about it, but kissing? *Boy did he kiss her.* His kisses were addicting. Laura didn't know boys could kiss like that. Then it dawned on her that Jack didn't kiss like a boy, Jack kissed like a man.

"*Sor-ry.* I've barely talked to you."

Laura sat on her bed and blew out a breath. "I know. I'm sorry."

"What's wrong?"

"I like him, Trace, and this has disaster written all over it.

He's going to want to sleep with me, and I don't know…"

"You're still a virgin, right?"

"Yeah, although I wish I weren't. It would be easier then."

"Laura, if he has sex with you, he could get arrested."

"Don't exaggerate, Tracy. I'm seventeen; he's not going to get arrested."

"So, you're thinking about it?"

Of course she was. She thought about it all the time. Jack made her body heat up in places Laura didn't know she had. "I have to finish getting ready. He's picking me up in a few minutes."

"Is he going to meet your father?"

"Marie's covering for me. Tonight, one of her friends is having some kind of seminar on Cosmic Meditation, so they went to center their *karmas* or some shit like that."

"Oookaaay. I'll bet your father will love that."

"Who cares? I have to go. Jack just pulled up." Laura glanced out the window and saw the headlights of Jack's Envoy go out. She hung up the phone, spritzed on some perfume and gave a last look in the mirror. Maybe it was time to grow up and have sex. She could do a lot worse than Jack as her first. The phone rang again and Laura picked it up as she left her room. "Tracy, I have to go, he's here."

"Laura, it's Mom."

"Mom! Hi, uhh, I thought you were Tracy."

"Apparently. Who's there?"

"Oh, a friend from school." The doorbell rang. She opened the door and held up one finger to Jack, who nodded when he walked in and closed the door behind him.

"Is it anyone I know?"

"No, I don't think so. Look Mom, can we chat some

other time?"

"Is Dad there?"

Laura rifled through her purse and popped a mint in her mouth. "No, he's out with Marie."

"Laura? You know the rule about dates. One of us has to meet who you are going out with."

Laura walked into the kitchen and let the swinging door close behind her. "That's your rule," she hissed. "When I'm here Dad and Marie treat me like an adult. And... and... they have met him." *Okay. That was a big lie.*

"Laura, I'm just concerned." Her mother's voice was firm, but Laura could hear the worry.

"Don't be. Since I won't be living with you much longer, it's not your problem. Goodbye."

She hung up and tossed the phone on the kitchen counter. Then she looked at it and felt a pang of guilt. Her mom did care about what was going on in her life, and she didn't sound meddling or difficult. Laura wished she could talk to her about this—but if she did, no more Jack.

Laura left the kitchen and found Jack looking at the pictures on the table in the foyer. He smiled when she approached. He was so sweet. Laura figured she could stall sex for a little while, but looking at him, why would she want to?

"Are you ready?" he asked before kissing her hello.

"Yes, sorry. That was my mother."

"I've met your future stepmom, but never your actual parents." He helped her on with her coat and Laura looked up into his big blue eyes.

"I guess you'll meet her eventually. My dad works all the time and my mother and I aren't close. That's why I live with my dad."

"That's too bad." Jack paused as Laura locked the front door and took her hand when she put the keys in her purse. "Why?"

"Why what?"

"Why aren't you and your mother close?"

Pausing, Laura couldn't name one thing. Why *did* she hate her? She opened her mouth to say something, but it wouldn't be the truth, so she stopped before taking the easy way out. "I'd rather not talk about it, if that's okay. It's pretty complicated." He nodded and touched her cheek. Laura saw genuine concern in his eyes and she thought about how nice it would be to be able to talk to him about everything. "Where are we going?"

"The movies? Is there something you want to see?"

Laura smiled, and held his hand tighter. The movie was irrelevant. She wouldn't be watching anyway.

❧

KATE HUNG UP when she heard the dial tone. "Shit."

"What's wrong?" Julie entered the kitchen. She'd been with Kate since Trish left for the airport.

"Laura's going out. I think she had a date."

"A date? On a Sunday? Where the hell are Richard and Morticia?"

"Who knows, obviously not giving a shit."

"Calm down. I know you and Laura have problems, but she is a good kid."

"I know." Kate had to agree Laura tended to do the right thing. She had her father's attitude, but she seemed to have Kate's conscience.

"Why do you think she had a date?" Julie was licking chocolate chip ice cream off a big serving spoon.

"The way she answered the phone. Then she told me to mind my own business." She paced. "I can't believe they're just letting her do whatever the hell she wants."

"Is there anyone you could call?"

"No, I don't... well, maybe her friend Tracy." Kate picked up the phone, held the receiver to her chest and hung it up. "Call about what? I don't even know what to say."

Julie put a glass in the sink, came up next to her, and rubbed Kate's shoulder. "My sister said to me once that being a parent is like hell and heaven at the same time."

"She's right." Kate turned around and folded her arms. "I really, really hate this."

Julie ventured where Kate didn't want to go, into reality. "You're going to have to get used to it, though. If you don't step up the fight, you won't have any say in her life."

Kate had been trying to block out the custody petition, and the anxiety over her new pregnancy was allowing her to do that. Of course, the new baby wouldn't be a secret forever, and since no daddy was in the picture, she was fairly certain Richard would paint her as an unstable and unsuitable influence on Laura.

He would conveniently forget he cheated with Marie and had his own closet full of skeletons. But she wasn't in any position to say anything.

"You know what? Considering how things are going with me, maybe I'm not the best person for her to live with."

"What? Kate, don't say that in public."

"Julie, I'm not in a relationship and I'm pregnant. The baby's father is a playboy, for lack of a better word, ten years younger than me, and not in my life. That doesn't exactly make me a good role model."

"Well, if that's the problem, you need to make him part of your life." Julie took her coat off the hook by the back door and put it on before she wrote something on the blackboard by Kate's phone.

"What's that?" Kate examined the information.

"The Flyers have an open practice tomorrow morning at their facility in New Jersey. If you don't want to be the woman you described to me, go and talk to your child's father."

"I can't."

"No, you *won't*. You've known about the baby for almost a week. I'm with your sister on this one. You don't want to tell him on the phone, fine. But tell him." She picked up her keys and gave Kate a hug.

"I thought you guys would take it easy on the pregnant lady."

Julie grinned. "Why would you think that?"

"I don't know. People always handle me like I'm going to break."

"Everything else that's happened has been out of your control. This isn't."

THE TRAINING COMPLEX in Voorhees, New Jersey, was almost a full hour away from Kate's house, which gave her lots of time to think about what she was going to say to David.

She'd called in the morning to confirm the practice time and, as planned, she was getting there about twenty minutes before it ended. Hopefully she would be able to see him, otherwise, she'd have to screw up her nerve for a second time and try again.

As she walked into the main door of the facility, a flood of memories hit her. It was a new building, but in some ways it was the same as the ice rinks she knew on Long Island and Boston. The smell and feel of the air, which was always a little cooler and drier than normal, had her feeling like she did when she had been five and entered a rink for her first skating lesson. She heard the sounds of skates and sticks hitting pucks and followed it to the rink. There were three coaches on the ice in warm-ups, and the players circled around, passing and shooting one of the hundred pucks on the ice.

At first, it didn't seem like there was any organization to what the players were doing, but in a few minutes she saw a pattern emerge with the way the players were working together, passing and shooting.

David skated forward with two other men—his linemates, she guessed—and they brought the puck toward the two defensemen and the goalie. After some quick work with the puck, and before she could see anything, David let go a shot and he watched as the puck flew past the goalie's left shoulder. He pumped his fist in celebration and rejoined his teammates back at center ice. Even though he'd complained about the workouts and the intensity of the practices, just like she used to, it was obvious he loved what he was doing. The love of the game came from inside.

There were only about twenty people watching practice and Kate settled herself on the back of the bleachers. She was there for about ten minutes when practice started to break up. Some of the players headed off the ice, but David continued to horse around with his friend. They were passing the puck and playing a little two-on-two with a couple of the rookies. Kate had picked up a considerable amount of information about the team in the two months she'd been following. David and his friend Jay had played together for a long time, and the younger players didn't have a chance. David and Jay toyed with them, and she could see him having a ball with kids—especially his own.

He stopped for a moment, breathing heavily, and leaned on his stick. When he glanced up, he froze when he spotted her in the stands. His smile went wide at first, but then he sobered when he realized she was there for a reason and held her gaze. He said something to his friend, who looked in her direction, and as David came toward the stands, she made her way down.

When they met, by the entrance to the ice, she still hadn't come to any decision about what to say to him. Should she blurt it out or break it to him gently? The drawn brows and weak smile said he wasn't sure of what to do either.

He took off his helmet and rubbed his gloved hand on his forehead. Beads of sweat dripped off his face, and never had a big, sweaty, smelly man been so appealing. Kate's entire body reacted. Of course, along with being completely crazy about him, she was terrified, and had no idea what she was going to say. Telling him she loved him was out of the question.

"Hey, this is a surprise," he said. "Bring your skates?"

"Not today." This wasn't going to go well. "I guess I should have called."

"No, it's fine. Are you okay?"

Kate felt herself nod. "I'm fine. I… umm… I need to talk to you about something."

"Okay." He kept trying to get a look at her eyes. "Kate, are you sure you're okay?"

"Mmm hmm. Yes. Should I wait for you?"

"I'll be about twenty minutes. Will you be all right out here?"

"No problem. Don't rush." Kate was grateful for the delay. If she could have, she would have procrastinated for another week.

~

KATE CHECKED HER watch. It had been just about twenty minutes when she heard footsteps. Freshly showered and walking up the bleacher steps, David was in faded jeans, a long sleeved T-shirt, and carried his leather jacket in one hand. Her heart did the little flip it always did when she saw him, then settled into a regular rhythm. Once he settled next to her, he leaned so he could have a look at the pile of papers on her lap.

"What are you doing?"

"Grading papers."

He picked up one of the essays she'd been reading and smiled at all the colorful marks. "Guess this one isn't so good?"

"It needs some work." She took the paper from him and put it in the folder, then slipped it into her bag. "So…"

"Yeah. So…" He put his hands together and moved them back and forth. "What do you want to talk about?"

Kate looked at his face, into his eyes, and saw what everyone said was true. He had a right to know, but how was she supposed to tell him? He had no idea what was coming, that his life was about to change. She just hoped he wouldn't offer to marry her. She didn't need a pity groom, she needed him to man up and be a father to their child.

"Okay, there's no easy way to say this."

He took her hand and held tight. "Just tell me."

The words came out of her mouth so quickly she didn't have time to temper them. "I'm pregnant."

Kate sat and waited for David's reaction, but for what felt like an eternity, he didn't say anything. He stared at her hand and traced circles around her palm with his thumb. It was driving her a little crazy, until he looked up and drew her hands to his lips. He planted a soft kiss on her knuckles and flashed the same gorgeous smile that seduced her in California.

"If it's a girl," he said, "I hope she looks like you."

That did it. All the control, all the practiced words, all the cool consideration she'd given to this moment slipped away with those sweet words. One tear slipped down her cheek, then another, and pretty soon Kate was bawling into David's shirt. She hadn't lost control like this for almost a week, but seeing him, realizing what they were facing, broke her reserve. David let her cry, soothing her as best he could, but Kate felt more overwhelmed at that moment than ever before. She knew if he was to be part of this pregnancy, her family, her friends, people at school would all find out about their affair. It wasn't like she and David were going to be together, even though she wished they could be. When she was honest with herself, Kate wanted that more than anything. Instead, she was a joke—the divorcee who couldn't practice safe sex, the one who tried to trap a younger man, *the cougar*. Richard's attorney would crucify her, she wouldn't be able to face her daughter, and she would more than likely lose her teaching job.

But she was going to deal with those things anyway, so to protect this child, to make sure he, or she, only knew love, Kate made the tough call. Their baby needed a father, and knowing how it felt to be cut out of her own child's life, she wouldn't do that to anyone else.

Kate pulled away and wiped her wet face and runny nose with her sleeve, decorum be damned. She was a wreck, she knew it, and David still stared at her with eyes that were telling her everything would be alright.

He took both her hands in his and gazed deeply into her eyes. "What do you want from me?"

"I don't even know. My doctor said that you should know so the baby's full medical background is clear. My sister and my best friend told me you had rights as the father."

His eyes narrowed and his face looked far more serious. "And what about you?"

Kate's eyes filled again, and her breath hitched. Facing her fear for the first time, she told the truth. "I'm scared to death. I don't want to do this alone, and you're the only other person who could love this baby as much as I do."

She couldn't tell for sure, but it seemed she wasn't the only one fighting tears. David blinked hard and then pulled her close, kissing the top of her head gently. "When's your next doctor's appointment?"

"It's today. I'm having my first screening test."

"Screening test?"

"Since I'm over thirty-five, they do tests to detect possible birth defects."

David's face dropped. Reality struck. This was a real baby

and it could have real problems. She could see this was something he hadn't had time to consider. His hand squeezed hers. "I'm done for the day, if you want me to come with you."

Kate nodded frantically. She hated the idea of going alone. He stood and helped her up, and without any hesitation, she wrapped her arms around his waist and laid her head on his chest. David's arms did just what she hoped—they enveloped her in a protective blanket.

"I should have told you right away. I'm sorry I waited."

"Is that why you called me last week?"

Again she nodded. "I'm sorry."

"It's okay. I knew."

Kate stepped back and glared. He was grinning, but she was floored. "You knew? How?"

He took one of her hands in his and held it tight. "When you were at your doctor's appointment, you signed an autograph." She didn't respond but lowered her eyes and he continued. "Amanda is married to one of my teammates. She was telling the story to some of her friends and I overheard her."

"Oh. Small world."

"Very."

Kate drew a shaky breath and looked at him. "I'm surprised you didn't come to see me."

"I was giving you one more day," he said. "If you didn't tell me, I'd have been at your front door."

Kate laughed. She had pictured his reaction a thousand different ways. Panic, fear, anger—but that wasn't what Kate saw. He wasn't angry; in fact, he looked genuinely happy. Then again, he'd had time to adjust to the idea of being a father. "I'm glad I got to you first."

"Me too." He hadn't let go of her hand yet, and didn't seem like he had any intention of doing so. "I'm going to follow you home." His free hand came to her face and his thumb brushed away the remaining tears. "You can change, or whatever you need to do, and then I'll drive you to your appointment. I just need to stop home and change my shirt."

"I can meet you there. I don't want to put you out."

"You aren't. After the doctor, I'll take you out to dinner. How does that sound?"

Kate felt better than she had in a week. She sniffled and wiped her face again. "It sounds wonderful."

Chapter 17

KATE'S HOUSE WAS a testament to her. It was traditional, classy, and warm. He pulled his truck up the long driveway and parked it next to her Volvo. Not only was the house beautiful, but the area itself was exactly what he'd always wanted for a family home. David didn't like the city, he lived there because it was easy, but Kate's home was more his style.

The house was a good size, but not unwieldy, and there were at least two acres of land. At the end of a dead end street, it was secluded and private. There were Christmas lights strung on the trees and bushes, beautiful wreaths on all the doors, and candles in the windows.

They entered through a door on the side of the house, near the garage. A pergola protected the small stoop, and based on the dormant vines he saw, David imagined in summer it was alive with flowers.

They walked into a small mud room where Kate hung up her vest, then brought him into the kitchen. The walls were a soft yellow and bathed in sunshine. He noticed the entire main level had huge windows.

"This house is awesome," he said. "When was it built?"

Kate grabbed a glass from one of the cherry cabinets and pulled a pitcher of water from the refrigerator. She stopped to think. "1927?"

"It's amazing."

"Thanks. It's too big for me, but I love it too much to leave it." It dawned on her she'd forgotten her manners and made a face. "I'm sorry. Would you like anything?"

"Water's good. Thanks." She poured and handed him a glass, and David continued to take in everything he saw.

On the memo board he saw the information about the practice written, and it made him smile. On the fridge was proof this woman was a mother. There were old drawings made by a child's hand, and at least ten different pictures of the same girl at different ages. Her daughter, no doubt.

"Your daughter is gorgeous. She looks just like you."

Kate smiled. "That's not her most recent picture. Hold on." Kate walked into the den, which was really just an extension of the kitchen, and pulled a framed picture off a sideboard. "This was taken a couple of months ago."

David examined the picture. "Just like you." He could see that made her happy, but a hint of sorrow shadowed her eyes when she took the picture back and ran her hand over the smooth glass before placing it on the counter behind her.

"Thank you." Changing the subject quickly, Kate put her glass in the sink and stuffed her hands in her pockets. "I'm going to change. Make yourself comfortable. There's stuff for sandwiches in the fridge if you're hungry."

"Okay. Want me to make you something?" She looked shocked at the offer, but then David remembered she wasn't used to someone wanting to take care of her—someone like him, who was in love with her and wanted to take care of her like this forever.

Kate bit her lip and looked at him in a way that could only be described as coy. "Would you? I'm starved."

"Sure. Go do whatever you have to do."

"Thank you."

David walked over to where she was standing. She'd taken off her sneakers, so she was at her smallest, and he towered over her. "I'm not a bad guy, you know."

"I know." She dropped her head and stared at the floor.

David rested his hands on her shoulders. "Then why don't you want us to be together?"

Kate looked up, and the saddest look he'd ever seen washed across her pretty face. She looked hopeless, and it pained David to see her so unhappy.

"I just don't know how long I can keep your interest."

There were times understanding came slowly, and other times when it hit like a slap to the face. This was a slap. Kate was afraid he was going to leave. It was clear to him now—if they had any chance, David had to prove he was in this for the long haul, especially since the baby was in the picture. He had to show her he could be a grownup.

He decided he wouldn't make any sweeping statements, and proposing was too predictable, but he'd have to show her he wasn't going to let her down. He'd have to build her trust, and that would take time.

"I suppose I can understand why you feel that way, but I'm not going to let you down."

Kate took his hand, seeming to be comforted by the simple statement. But he could see she still didn't know if David had sticking power. He'd have to show her he did.

AT LEAST HE didn't lie. Kate had to appreciate the fact David didn't try to soothe her with empty promises.

Maybe they could be friends. That wouldn't be bad, would it? They could depend on each other and take care of their child and it would all be good.

Kate looked at herself in the mirror on her dresser. Why couldn't she just admit what she wanted? She wanted to wake up next to David each and every morning for the rest of her life. She wanted them to be a family. Friends may be what they were destined to be, but Kate wanted more. If only she had the nerve.

Pressing play on her iPod, music filled the room. Music always managed to improve her mood. She undressed and was checking her profile. Still no belly, but soon enough she would have one—a big one, if her pregnancy with Laura was any indication. Laura was a big first baby at eight and a half pounds, and Kate wondered about this baby.

An old Motown song blasted out of the speakers, and Kate started dancing around the room in her underwear. She zoned out, forgetting that David was downstairs, fixing her lunch. She nearly jumped out of her skin when she turned around and he was standing in the door, smiling. It was complete humiliation.

"Jeez! You scared the crap out of me!"

He laughed out loud and stepped in the room like he belonged there. He didn't flinch, even though Kate stood before him in her pink polka dot bra and panties. Granted, he'd seen her in less, and that stifled her impulse to grab for something to cover up.

"Don't sneak up on me! I'm… pregnant!"

"I heard that someplace." He stepped closer and all the air left her lungs. "You look fine to me."

"Yeah, well…"

"I made your sandwich. It's downstairs." He was obviously amused, and Kate was wondering how long it would take before her latent insanity sent him running.

Feeling the blush creep into her cheeks, she turned off the music and went into her closet.

"Kate?" he called.

Kate poked her head out of the closet. "What?"

"Don't stop dancing on my account."

"I'm glad you're enjoying yourself." Annoyed, she went back in the closet and found pants and a shirt. When she came out, David was sitting on her bed, looking at one of the pregnancy books. So much for staying annoyed. He looked adorable, with a shock of hair falling across his forehead, and he was so absorbed in the material Kate didn't know if he was aware she was watching. Then he looked up, and smiled his sweetest smile. *Oh crap.* She wanted to crawl into his lap.

"I need to get one of these," he said.

"I don't know how well that will fit in your library." She smiled when she remembered his extraordinary collection. Kate slipped the pink top over her head, and that was when she noticed her rounder figure was causing some wardrobe issues. She tugged the top a few times, trying to cover her breasts, which were popping out of the scooped neck. No matter what she did, nothing helped. She caught David looking and smiling.

"Stop it," she said.

"I didn't say anything!" He was still grinning and staring.

"You didn't have to." She smiled back and then tried to get her head around what was happening with them. This wasn't how she'd expected the day to go.

He flipped pages in one of the books and glanced at different illustrations. "Man, if I went into a bookstore and bought this, people would think I'd gone off the deep end."

She giggled just picturing it. "They have books for expectant dads, too."

"Yeah? After dinner, we'll stop by the bookstore by my house. Is that okay?" He stood and took the book to a chair she had by the window, while she put on her makeup and fixed her hair. It was all very easy. David blended into her life. If he was nervous or felt at all trapped by the pregnancy, he didn't show it.

Kate rose from her dressing table and walked toward him, knowing getting this close to him was asking for trouble. He put the book aside, met her gaze, and then he did the most unexpected thing. One of his hands slipped around her to the small of her back, and the other slipped under her shirt and touched her bare belly. Then slowly, he rested his head against her middle and planted a soft kiss right near her belly button.

Kate almost cried.

It was an intense moment, and probably the most intimate they'd shared. Kate's hand stroked his dark hair, and although no words passed between them, the message was clear. He was there with her by choice, and she'd made the right decision in telling him. It would have been criminal to keep this man from his child. Whatever doubts Kate had about David Burke's commitment to her, she had no doubt he would be a wonderful father.

THE DOCTOR'S VISIT was very routine from a medical perspective. Kate was only supposed to have a couple vials of blood drawn, but when Dr. Emmaunel saw David was there, she made time for a consultation. David had concerns of his own, mostly about what the doctor was going to do to keep Kate and the baby healthy. For Kate, this was totally new. Holding her hand the whole time they were with the doctor, David probably asked a hundred questions. He also did something that cemented his commitment. He made himself her emergency contact. It was a small thing, but if anything went wrong, he'd know first. David didn't hesitate, and it was strangely soothing to know he would drop everything to be with her.

David picked up every pamphlet in the office, especially the ones about prenatal testing. The man was an information junkie, and Kate was certain at some point in the pregnancy he would drive her crazy. But he was so excited and so happy, she just enjoyed it.

David worried she might slip since the temperature had dropped and there were ice patches everywhere, so he left her in the lobby to get his car. If he was worried now, Lord knew how he'd be when she got big.

"Kate? Kate Nicholls?"

Kate turned and stuttered when she saw John Connor, a trustee at St. Andrews and the father of her former student and David's ex. *Crap.* "John!" She actually wondered if she could find a hole to crawl into. A pothole would do. "This is a surprise."

He walked over and gave her a kiss on the cheek. "Well, I

do work here. What about you? Is everything okay?"

His concern was really very genuine, which shouldn't have surprised her because basically, John Connor was a nice man.

"Oh, yes. Fine. Just something I had to take care of."

He smiled at her and Kate knew what was coming next—an invitation. The man had asked her out five times, and she'd turned him down on each occasion. He was pleasant enough, but she just wasn't into his type of flashy, I-have-money lifestyle.

"Do you need a lift?"

"No, my friend went to get the car. It was on the fourth level."

"Oh." An awkward silence fell between them because that's just the way it was. But after a minute, he raised his hand and said, "We should make plans to have dinner sometime."

Just as the words came out of his mouth, David's midnight blue Range Rover roared to a stop at the lobby entrance. "There's my friend."

John nodded. "It was good to see you. I hope—" But his words stopped as David walked around the car and right up to Kate. Blinking hard, Kate wondered why the gods were conspiring against her. Things were finally calming down and this was going to unleash a whole new shit storm.

Not another word was exchanged. John turned quickly and drowned his expensive Ferragamo's in a nice big puddle. He shook his foot unceremoniously and stormed off. The man actually left in a huff.

"Who was that?" David asked while holding her door open.

"You don't know?" Kate climbed in the passenger seat, focused her gaze, and felt her jaw tense. "You're going to love this. That was Dr. John Connor."

David's brows drew together and then his eyes widened in shock. "Chelsea's father?" His words were nothing more than a whisper.

"The one and only."

David closed her door, walked around the front of the car, and got in the driver's seat. "How does he know you?"

It suddenly occurred to Kate he didn't know about her connection to Chelsea. She'd never mentioned it. *No time like the present.* "He's on the Board of Trustees where I teach."

"Oh, shit," he said quietly.

"He's going to tell Chelsea he saw you with me. That should be fun."

They were stopped in rush hour traffic. David leaned on the steering wheel and fixed his eyes on her.

"You know Chelsea?"

"I taught Chelsea."

David was frozen in place. Kate was sure he had something to say, he just couldn't get it out. The blinks and twitches told her he was still alive but, Kate pretty much decided he'd gone into some kind of wakeful coma. Someone laid on their horn, and David realized he was holding up traffic.

"You didn't tell me you were her teacher."

"I tried to block it out. I had her twice."

"She's gonna go crazy."

Kate nodded, although she did think crazy was an understatement. Chelsea was never the most stable young lady while she was in school. Oh, on the surface she was peaches and cream, a real daddy's girl. She was a cheerleader, class officer, and had the headmaster's ear whenever she needed it. With her society connections and influential father on the board, she pretty much got whatever she wanted. That meant if anyone crossed Chelsea, she might be sweet to your face, but behind your back, she was plotting your demise. She had a small, tight circle of friends, but even they didn't cross her. The truth was most kids Kate taught were nice, decent people. Chelsea Connor was not the rule.

Of course, it was possible she'd changed.

But not likely.

LATER, THEY SAT in David's den poring over the books they'd picked up after dinner. He'd bought every pregnancy book he could get his hands on, including a few for expectant fathers. She sat next to him on the big suede sofa, intermittently filling in the pregnancy journal and dozing off. Part of him just wanted to tuck her into his bed upstairs and let her sleep, but the other part of him knew that wouldn't be such a great idea.

The doctor told him the best thing he could do for Kate was keep her relaxed, because pregnant women her age tended to have more anxiety. The issue with the doctor's plan however, was logistics. He didn't live with Kate, and he couldn't see her while she worked. Sure, he'd do his best, but he wasn't really part of her life.

Technically, David was still a free man. He could date if he wanted, go out with his buddies. Kate never would have gotten in touch with him if she wasn't pregnant and scared.

She needed him, but he still wasn't sure she wanted him. That was a problem, because the more time they were together, the more he knew he could never give her up.

"I guess I should go home," she said so quietly he could barely hear.

"Okay." He gently moved her body and stood, immediately seeing the worry clouding her eyes. "Everything is going to work out."

"I hope so."

He came back with her coat and held it as she slipped her arms into the sleeves.

"How much did you weigh when you were born?" she asked, looking over her shoulder.

He chuckled. "I probably shouldn't tell you."

She turned to him, her eyes narrowed. "Why?"

"I was big."

"How big?" she demanded.

"According to my mother I was well over ten pounds and twenty three inches long."

"Holy shit." Kate's voice was nothing but a squeak.

He took her shoulders and guided her toward the door. "You'll manage. You're tough."

"Oh, my God."

"It's going to be fine," he said reassuringly, but the whimper from Kate told him she wasn't so sure she believed him.

FOR THE FIRST time in a week, Kate felt like everything was going to be okay. Telling David had been the right thing to do. Seeing John Connor would bring her job to an end sooner than she expected, but fortunately she had her writing career, and as much as she loved teaching, she didn't need it. Walking into the kitchen, she nearly had a heart attack when she saw Laura standing at the kitchen table.

"Good grief! What is it with people sneaking up on me?!"

"Hey, Mom." Laura was rigid. Her arms were folded and her face was stone cold.

"I didn't expect you to be home. I'm sorry. I would have been here."

"That's okay. I had some stuff to do." With those words, Laura moved just enough for Kate to see everything her daughter had collected on the table.

Kate felt all the feeling go out of her legs as she fought to keep herself from collapsing on the floor. She leaned against the counter and looked away. "What did you do, Laura?"

"I found out the truth about you."

"Really?" Kate looked back and focused on Laura's face. "Why did you feel the need to go through my things?"

Laura glanced away and then put on her best show of arrogance. "I needed to know what you were doing and now I do. You're pregnant?"

Kate took two steps toward her and then stopped. Resting a hand on her stomach, Kate looked right in Laura's eyes. She felt so angry, so violated, that for the first time in her life she could have slapped the child. She didn't, but Kate couldn't ever remember feeling so angry.

"I am pregnant. About twelve weeks, and I'm not unhappy about it."

"That's disgusting."

"Disgusting?" Kate advanced and Laura stepped back. "Weren't you the one who told me to 'get a life'?"

"Who's the father? The sleaze who dropped you off?"

Kate grinned at the irony. If only Laura knew who she was calling a sleaze. Eventually it would come out, and on that day her daughter would gag on her words. "That is none of your fucking business."

Laura's shocked expression was worth the guilt Kate felt about the ferocity of the outburst. Kate rarely cursed aloud and she never raised her voice, but she'd been pushed too far. It wasn't a secret anymore. She and David had spent the evening in the city. But just looking at what Laura had gathered made her furious. She'd been all over the house, but the majority of what she found was in Kate's room. Laura was looking for information and there was no doubt who'd put her up to it.

"Why did you do this?"

Laura didn't answer, looking around for someone to save her.

"Dad put you up to it, didn't he?"

Laura wouldn't make eye contact. In every expression and every movement, Kate could see she was panicked.

"Daddy has a right to know what you're doing!" She sputtered. "He's trying to protect me."

"Protect you? From me?" Kate couldn't decide what to do. She really, really wanted to blow the whistle on Richard and tell Laura what a creep her father was, but she shook her head. "I've done my best to take the high road and never bad-mouth your father, but using you to spy on me is despicable, and that should tell you what kind of person he is. It's wrong, and if you need protecting from anyone, it's him."

Laura turned away and almost looked guilty. Kate could tell she knew what her father asked her to do was wrong, but

Laura always did what her father wanted. Always.

"You won't tell me who was in the SUV?"

"Eventually. Not now." Kate waved her off. "Go to bed. Get out of my sight."

Laura took a final parting shot. "It doesn't matter if you tell me, Dad will find out. He's hired people."

"Is that so?" Kate smiled, because now she knew what he was up to. "Thanks for the information. He must be getting pretty desperate, because he has far more to hide than I do."

Laura dashed from the room without responding, and Kate was fairly sure in about thirty seconds she'd be on the phone with Richard or Marie.

Chapter 18

D AVID HAD KNOWN about the pregnancy for a week, and he thought things between him and Kate would settle down, but she was still running hot and cold. Maybe it was hormones, but the truth was, he didn't really know.

What he needed was a woman's opinion.

His first choice, his sister Rachel, would have to be brought up to speed on the whole Kate situation, and that would take too long. He'd tell her all about it when he saw her in a couple of weeks.

So, he went to see his second choice, Annie, because like his sister, he knew she would tell him the truth. Even if he didn't want to hear it.

Having long passed the formality of a doorbell, he walked into the Hemmings' house through the garage and found Annie feeding the twins lunch. Jay had stayed at practice and was doing some extra conditioning work with the trainer, so that gave David some time to get Annie's take on his love life.

Their kitchen was big, bright and modern. It had clean lines, white cabinets and stainless steel. It was a stark contrast to Kate's traditional, warm décor, but there was a common thread. This was a family home, and just like Kate's house, the kitchen had a place for finger paintings and pictures of the children.

Annie was wiping down the stainless steel island and smiled as he walked in. "Hey, you."

The twins turned in their high chairs and squealed with delight as David tickled them from behind.

"I will never get tired of that sound," he said as he eased onto one of the stools at the counter.

Annie didn't miss a beat and poured him a glass of iced tea.

"Thanks." He took a swallow of his drink and wondered how to start the conversation.

"How's Kate feeling?" Annie dried her hands on a towel and set the twins free. They ran off into their playroom, making motorcycle noises the whole way.

"Good, tired. It's hard to know."

"How are you?" Annie grinned as she sipped her coffee.

"Preoccupied, overwhelmed. I can't stop thinking about her." He folded his arms on the counter and leaned in her direction. "She doesn't trust me."

Annie smirked. "Well, hell, Burke. I don't trust you either." She reached her hand across the island and patted his forearm. "But that doesn't mean she can't love you."

"You think there's a chance?"

"Definitely." Annie walked around and looped her arms around his neck. It was platonic, sisterly, and just what David needed. "She told you about the baby. Came to you on your turf; that was hard for her."

"I know. So she must trust me a little."

"Eh." She slid onto the stool next to him. "You majorly

screwed up. What were you thinking taking Kate out one week and then jumping right back in the saddle with Chelsea?"

"We went out to breakfast. *That's it.* I didn't think."

"You didn't think you'd get caught."

He dropped his head into his arms and tried to block out any thought of Chelsea. "Why doesn't she trust me?"

"I'm guessing it has to do with her age."

His head came up and he saw this was the biggie. "What about it?"

"David, she's insecure. Trust me on this. She thinks that when you see someone younger and prettier you'll be gone."

"That's just stupid." He'd realized he'd made a mistake as soon as the words came out of his mouth and Annie whacked him on the back of the head.

"It's not stupid, it's real. You're the one who told me she's afraid of being left. Well guess what, honey, *you* are a flight risk."

"Because I've dated a lot?"

"Date? You don't date, you window shop."

"Oh, come on. It's not that bad."

"Yeah, it is." She was dead serious.

All the years David played around, he didn't think it would mean anything, but it did. Now that there was someone important to him, his past was biting him in the ass. He had to find a way to make Kate understand he wasn't going anywhere.

He shrugged. "So what do I do?"

"Make her part of your life. Bring her to a game. Take her to a movie. Bring her here and let her meet your friends." Annie snapped her fingers. "Invite her to the New Year's party at the Girards'."

"Really, you think that will help?"

Annie rolled her eyes. "You can't really be this obtuse." She paused before continuing. "Dave, do you think being a hockey wife is easy?"

"I've never thought about it."

She leaned back and folded her arms. "Women like Chelsea are predators. They hunt down athletes like a wolf hunts down its next meal. Players' wives and steady girlfriends are enemies. I've seen posts about me on the Internet that have made me cry. I'm a shrew and the twins aren't really Jay's and I'm bleeding him for his money and he's looking to get out of the marriage... it's endless. They make this stuff up. If Chelsea wanted Jay, it wouldn't matter that we're married, she'd go after him anyway. Women have hit on Jay when I've been sitting with him, just the two of us. They slip him their numbers like I'm not even there. I can't even imagine how it is on the road. Frankly, I don't want to think about it."

David's eyes were locked on Annie. It could get bad on the road. Women were a regular part of the landscape and in the past, David had taken advantage. Jay didn't, but it dawned on him that her husband didn't have to cheat for the groupies to make Annie, and the other wives, nervous and scared.

"It bothers me and I'm in a happy, stable marriage. I know my husband loves me, but sometimes even I need reassurance. Based on what you told me about her, I can understand why Kate's keeping her distance. The poor woman already lived with a lying, cheating husband." Annie rose, walked to the playroom door, and checked on her sons. "You're the one with the bad track record, so you have to prove to her you're worth the risk, that you want someone who's more than a hot body. Because, as you know, unless she's sure of you, she'll bolt the first second she thinks you aren't committed."

Just then Jay crashed through the side door, and before he acknowledged his friend, the barking dog or the kids who came screeching from the other room, he had his arms around his wife and kissed her. Annie was first in his mind, always. "You giving the big dope some help?"

"I'm trying." Annie gave Jay another kiss and then wiggled away. "David, Kate's not the one who should have to change if you want it to work. You have to change. You have to make her feel like she's more important than anyone else."

LAURA SAT SNUGGLED against Jack while they watched a movie. It was perfectly innocent. They'd been seeing each other for over a month, they really got along well, and he wanted to hang out at home. The only problem with the whole scene was that she'd cut school, taken the train to the city, and managed to find her way to his apartment in Washington Square.

"Do you want anything?" he asked.

"No, I'm good." She leaned forward and picked up one of her mother's books off the coffee table. "Have you read this?"

"Ty recommended it. It's really good so far. Have you read any of her books?"

Laura shook her head. This was her mother's first book, and it was published when she was in fifth grade. She flipped it over in her hands, opened the cover and landed on the dedication page. The words made her breath catch.

To Laura,
You are the light in my life...
Past, present, and future.

There was so much she didn't know and it made her angry. At everyone. Jack's hand ran over her shoulder.

"You look like you have something on your mind." He cared about her, he really did.

She looked into his beautiful face and felt her mouth turn up at the corners. "Only you."

He took one of her hands in his. "I wish I could fix whatever is making you so unhappy."

Laura drew a breath, and not knowing what made her do it, started talking. "It's my family. My parents hate each other and my dad's fiancée is constantly pushing me to do things and say things to make my dad happy, and then I hurt my mother. And she never says anything, but, I don't know, I feel bad." Laura laid her head on his chest. "I'm a mess."

"It sounds like a mess, but it's their mess."

"I wish I knew her better, you know." She breathed out.

Laura thought about Mom having a baby and it made her sad she wouldn't be part of it. There was someone her mother cared about and Laura didn't know anything about him. How had this happened?

Jack didn't say anything, but he kept rubbing her back.

"Tell me about your family," she said.

"Not a lot to tell. I have two younger sisters; one is seventeen and one is nineteen. My parents have been together since they were fifteen years old. They run the farm together. We grow wheat and barley."

"That sounds nice."

"It's really a beautiful place. I'd love to take you there in the summer. We could take the horses out." His voice was so soft, so calm. "You can ride forever and not see another person. It's so quiet, you can actually hear yourself think." He paused and smiled at her. "That must sound strange to you."

"No, it sounds amazing."

"It's home, that's all."

"I wish I belonged somewhere like that."

His hand came to her cheek and he tilted her face toward his. "You belong with me."

His voice was a whisper, and after he said it, he leaned in and kissed her gently, brushing his lips over hers, caressing her face. He made her feel like she was everything. Looking square into his eyes, Laura lost herself. He meant what he said, and for once, Laura did feel like she belonged to someone. She belonged to Jack.

He leaned in and kissed her again.

Each time she and Jack spent time together, they made out a little more. The last time, sitting in his truck in front of her house, his hand inched down into her jeans, his fingers pushed inside her a little, and she came in a great explosion in his arms. At first he'd been alarmed by the intensity of her response, but it didn't take him long to figure out she was a virgin.

When Jack looked at her again, the darkness in his eyes put Laura's body on alert. He was so incredibly good looking, she didn't know how she would breathe, much less stay calm enough to make a rational decision. But that was when he kissed her and Laura lost her ability to think.

"What's wrong?" he asked. "You're so tense." She shook her head in response.

She thought about how lucky she was. He was sweet and considerate, and he obviously liked her. His hands gently ran up and down her sides and her mind raced.

Eventually Jack would find out she'd lied to him. Would he still feel this way about her? Would he forgive her? Doubtful. He'd been straight with her and she'd been dishonest with him. He'd respected her feelings and she'd stomped on his. Jack wouldn't want to see her anymore. So Laura had a dilemma. Did she walk away from a hopeless relationship with her virginity intact or give in, let the most wonderful guy on the planet take her to bed and wait until everything came crashing down?

Jack pushed her hair aside and brushed kisses up her neck, behind her ear and down her jaw. The most incredible heat flooded through her, along with a rush to her nervous system. Everything seemed to melt together, muscles and bones, to become soft and pliant under his hands.

His hands did the most magnificent things. How did hands that were so strong touch so gently? She didn't realize when he'd cradled her in his arms and lifted her, didn't realize when he'd lain her on his bed. Laura felt drowsy, hypnotized, and Jack stared at her like she was the most precious gift. That was what it was supposed to be like, a gift.

Jack kissed her and she kissed him back, feeling his weight settle next to her on the bed. Laura knew this was a mistake, but she was willing to make it for Jack.

He took the hemline of her sweater and tugged it off, did the same to his own and undid the button and zipper on his jeans. He moved closer to her, hovering over her, touching her, kissing the swells above her bra.

"I won't do anything you don't want me to do."

Laura trembled when she looked into his eyes and nodded. His hands caressed her, making her skin feel hot. Her own hands traveled over his shoulders and torso, her fingers stopping just above his waistband.

"You can touch me," he whispered, easing her hand into his pants. "It's just part of me."

She gasped when she came in contact with his erection. Laura had never touched a man like that before and she tried to stay calm, and be mature, but it was so—big.

How would it fit inside her? Thinking about the pain, she pulled her hand away. "I've never... I've never..."

"I know, I know. Don't worry." He kept kissing her and easily removed her bra. She sighed when his lips brushed over one nipple. "The first time is about you. I promise." He tugged at her pants and eased them off. Laura was only barely conscious of the fact that she was laying on his bed in nothing but a thong. His hands gripped her hips and his mouth left hot, wet kisses over the plane of her belly, and finally on the inside of each thigh. He slid her thong down her legs and when she tensed, he came up for a kiss.

"Shhh," he said. "I promise, not 'til you say."

She nodded, wanting to trust him, but thinking about how many girls he'd done this with and who else had been in this bed. She wondered if Marie was right. Did she have to sleep with him to keep him? If she did, maybe it wasn't the right thing to do.

"Why me, Laura?"

She tilted her face toward him.

Jack was looking down at her with such sweetness all

reason left Laura's brain. His hand came up and touched her face so tenderly; Laura could only draw in a breath. His question took her by surprise, and put an end to all the questions running through her mind. He knew this was important to her, and he wanted to know what made him different. Just the fact he asked told Laura if she was going to be with a man, it should be Jack.

So Laura told him the truth. "No one has ever mattered enough until you."

He brushed the hair away from her face and kissed her forehead, her nose, and then her mouth. It was hot and hungry and Laura wrapped her arms around his neck and gave into it. He touched her and it made her burn deep inside. She didn't know what he was doing, but the searing combination of pleasure and pain made her cry out.

"Jack... I... I... please, don't." Laura felt the tears roll down her cheeks, the sob choked her and before she knew it he held her in his arms while she cried.

"Shhh. Please, Laura, don't cry. It's okay. We'll stop. We'll stop. I'm sorry."

"I didn't mean to lead you on. I didn't. I don't know what's wrong with me." She cried again and he cradled her head against his chest.

When the tears slowed, he looked into her eyes, touched her face.

"There's nothing wrong with you."

"I should be able to make love with you, I should."

"There's time."

"I'm being such a baby. It shouldn't be a big deal."

"Yes, it should. Laura, don't make love with me because it's what I want, but because it's what you want."

"I do want it, Jack, I do. I just... I don't know. I'm afraid." Laura took a deep breath, trying to find her words, to take hold of one emotion and make sense of it for him. She finally found one, and made sense of it for herself. *Oh, God, I love him.*

"You're afraid of me?" He looked worried and a little hurt.

"I think," she began, "I think I'm afraid of everything." Laura knew she was afraid of how things would change between them, knowing once they crossed the line, they couldn't turn back. She also knew that emotionally, no matter what Marie told her, if they started sleeping together she had a lot more to lose. "But I do want to be with you. I do."

"It'll happen," he said. "We'll find a time that's right and it will."

Gazing at him, at his beautiful face, Laura knew what she wanted. Being with him like this, stealing a few hours, made her feel slutty, like all she was there for was the sex. What she wanted was to fall asleep in his arms, and wake up snuggled next to him. That would be like love.

Jack glanced down and kissed her nose, examined every feature of her face. He was on the brink of telling her something, something important, but he held back.

Laura kept her feelings to herself, because at this point, she couldn't imagine someone as perfect as Jack being in love with her.

Chapter 19

THE THOUGHT OF having a white Christmas made Kate a little giddy. It had been flurrying on and off for days, but tomorrow they were supposed to get real snow, at least six inches.

It made her happy, but then lately, a lot of things made her happy. She and David were learning the ins and outs of dealing with each other. He called her every day just to say hello or to see if she needed anything. They'd gone out a few times when he sensed she was feeling lonely, grabbing a bite to eat at Piccolo's, or wandering around the bookstore near his house. They kept it simple, but David made Kate feel like she mattered. She, in turn, was learning to depend on him.

One day he didn't call, but instead showed up with a Christmas tree lashed to the roof of his truck, a pizza, and three old Christmas movies on DVD. He knew she couldn't get a tree and decorate it on her own, so he took care of it for her. She was really touched that she was on his mind, and he had given up yet another Saturday night out to be with her. They'd decorated the tree, and every time she walked by, she thought about David, on a step ladder, placing and replacing the angel on the top until it was just right. Then when they were done, he built a fire, she made popcorn, and they stayed up until three in the morning watching *It's a Wonderful Life* and the old version of *Miracle on 34th Street*. It was a picture perfect December evening.

Kate walked him to the door and he said his goodnight. But this time, instead of the platonic kiss on the cheek she'd been getting the past two weeks, David folded her in his arms and dropped a bone-melting kiss on her lips. They stood kissing by the open back door, with light snow blowing around them for several minutes until Kate had to come up for air. David looked at her with the most amazing expression on his face. He was trying to tell her something, trying to get her to understand that he was going to be with her no matter what happened.

Kate loved the feel of his arms around her, of his soft lips, his smell... she basically just loved him. Their relationship was changing, quickly, and Kate didn't know if she could stop it, or if she even wanted to. He owned her heart, but she was still uncertain if she owned his. There were signs, but Kate had never been more scared in her life. She was also willing to take the risk.

Tonight David was taking her to dinner in the city. She offered to make them something at the house, but he said he wanted to take her out, so he made reservations at a beautiful Italian restaurant on Rittenhouse Square. She'd had her dress picked out for three days and was imagining how the evening might go. Rittenhouse was stunning at Christmas. The lights made it the most romantic place in the city. Kate realized she was completely charmed, but David wasn't trying to finesse her, and this wasn't one of his big gestures, this was about her.

He was leaving on a short road trip before Christmas, then going to see his sister in Toronto. So this would be their last night together for over a week, and David said he wanted to make it special.

Everything was perfect until she pulled in the driveway and saw Marie's hybrid parked in Richard's old spot. The mudroom door was open and she could only imagine what was going on inside.

Kate forgot about the presents in the trunk of her car and proceeded quietly when she heard the voices from upstairs. Marie and Laura. Not knowing if she should be angry or upset, Kate dropped her bag and walked up the stairs. Laura's bedroom door was open and Marie was standing in the doorway of Kate's room, surveying the scene. "I had no idea your mother was a slob," Marie said.

"She's not usually," Laura called. "Why?"

"The room is a mess. I wonder if her boyfriend is moving in."

"I don't know," Laura answered.

"Why is she hiding him?" Marie turned and ran smack into Kate. "Oh!"

"What's going on?" Kate snarled and folded her arms.

Marie took a step back and leaned against the railing. Kate used to think she was exotic looking, now she couldn't imagine why. Marie's bones protruded from beneath her clothes and her jet black hair fell in a silky sheet to her shoulders. She looked irritable and rigid. "Kate, you startled me."

"Imagine that. You being in my house and all. What the hell are you doing here?"

"Laura's packing," Marie said.

"Packing? For the ski trip?" Kate clarified for her.

"No," Marie began, hesitating a little too much for Kate's comfort. "She'll be staying with us until the custody hearing."

The words hit Kate like a fist in the gut, but she forced herself to recover when she thought about everything that was at stake. *Everything was at stake.* "Says who?"

"Richard thinks it's best." Marie folded her arms and pursed her thin, red lips.

"Is that so? Screw Richard," Kate said in response.

"Really Kate, can't we be civilized?"

"Civilized? You call what you and my husband did civilized?"

"We'd like to have Laura with us and she wants to be there. Richard and I are planning a family and we think—"

"A family? You and Richard? How are you going to do that?"

"I'm a healthy, fertile woman. Many women my age are having children. In fact, I may have recently conceived."

Kate folded her arms and stifled the laugh that so wanted to escape. "He didn't tell you, did he?"

"Tell me what?"

Kate swallowed hard before continuing, knowing full well she was losing the battle, but she was going to take her best shot. "He didn't tell you about his vasectomy."

Marie's eyes widened. "Vasectomy?"

"He got it about thirteen years ago. He didn't want any more children after Laura."

"You're evil," Marie said. "You'd say anything to hurt us."

At that point, Laura was standing in the doorway of her room with a box on her hip. The look on her face could only be described as confused. Laura didn't know what to do.

"And I'm supposed to just give her up?" Kate said, advancing on Marie. "Let you walk out of here with my child?" Kate turned toward Laura, who wouldn't look at either of them.

"Kate, really," Marie said. "She'll be gone in a year and a half. If you truly love her, let her have a real family for a change."

Kate spun at her and hissed, not even recognizing her own voice. "She had a real family until you took it from her."

"Richard and I are her family." A quiet settled over them as soon as Marie said it.

"Is that what you want, Laura?"

Laura couldn't answer. Kate, who didn't think anything could undo her as much as the divorce, found her heart hurting so much she couldn't speak. Never in her life had Kate felt more alone or more isolated. Her daughter didn't say a word, and Kate didn't know what was holding her back.

Laura retreated to her bedroom and left her future stepmother to deliver the final blows. Marie stared at her. "I've been more of a mother to her than you will ever be, Kate. Let her go."

Kate was about to respond, but out of nowhere a twisting pain, a tore through her stomach and lower back making Kate double over. "Oh, God."

"Please, Kate," Marie sniffed. "Must you be so melodramatic?"

Kate couldn't respond and using the wall behind her as a support, she sank to the floor. There was another pain and then warm wetness between her legs. She knew what was happening now, knew how one story was going to end. She was losing the baby. "Oh no," she whispered.

Unaware that Kate was miscarrying, Marie lashed out at her again. "Honestly, you're a disgrace."

Laura came out of her room and saw her mother on the floor and when Kate locked eyes with her daughter, awareness filled Laura's eyes. She knew something was wrong. Her gaze drifted along her mother's body and saw the dark stain growing between her legs. "Call an ambulance," she said quietly.

"She's having a breakdown, she'll deal."

"No," Laura said, pushing past her and dropping to the floor beside her mother, "I think she's losing her baby. Call an ambulance!"

"Baby? She's pregnant? How?"

Kate was in such pain she couldn't think, but she was aware of Laura kneeling next to her.

"Marie! Call a freaking ambulance!" Laura screamed. Marie rolled her eyes and flipped open her cell. Kate heard her whiney voice on the line.

Another pain hit and her eyes started to tear. Laura grabbed her hand. "On my nightstand is a small notebook. My doctor's number is in there, please call her."

"Okay," Laura nodded and touched her mother's arm as another pain hit. "Anyone else I should call?"

Kate shook her head. "The doctor will call David."

As Laura stood to make the call, Kate caught sight of Marie, who was nailing her with a look that could only be described as pure hate. Laura hadn't told them about her pregnancy. She'd kept the secret. And while Kate suddenly had hope that her relationship with her daughter could be saved after all the lies, she worried what Richard might do now that Laura had betrayed him.

THE AMBULANCE RIDE seemed to take forever, even though it didn't. Laura had the doctor on the phone when the paramedics arrived and she told them to bring her mother to the hospital in the city. The driver balked a little, but when Laura proceeded to rip off his head, he did exactly what he was asked to do. He made the twenty-five minute trip in about fifteen.

Marie left as soon as she saw that Laura wasn't going to leave her mother. She didn't see any reason to hang around, so, Laura rode in the ambulance and now was waiting outside the room on the obstetrical floor where her mother was being examined.

Marie's reaction made Laura sick. Her mother was lying on the floor bleeding and all Marie could do was think about herself. While she was waiting for the ambulance, Laura heard Marie on the phone with her Dad. Granted, it was only one side of the conversation, but it sounded like they were talking about Mom being pregnant and that they weren't aware.

And they weren't aware—because Laura didn't say anything. She didn't know what made her keep her mother's secret, but she had, and Dad would be pissed. He never really got mad at her, but somehow Laura knew this would time it would be different.

Glancing down the hallway, she saw the main nurses' station and beyond that she thought she saw one of the nurses from the ER. She was talking with a man who then turned and looked in Laura's direction. He was tall, dressed in black pants and a maroon shirt. Her cell phone buzzed and Laura looked down at the screen. It was her dad. He'd been trying to contact her for an hour. Instead of answering she went back to the game she'd been playing. It was mindless and the only thing she could focus on.

There was so much blood. It seemed like gallons of it, but the doctor told her that Mom was fine now and other than her blood pressure being a little low, she would recover. Still, it was scary. Seeing Mom in so much pain... and what if it was her fault? Hers and Marie's? Mom had gotten so upset... Laura couldn't stand to think that she may have caused her mother to lose the baby. She drew a deep breath and wiped at her eyes. God, her life sucked.

"Laura?"

The voice was deep and she assumed it was another doctor, but when she looked up there stood David Burke. The Flyers' left wing was towering over her... and Laura made the connection: *David*. Her mother's boyfriend was *David Burke!*

"Holy shit," was all that came out of her mouth.

"Hi," he said. "I'm David."

It took Laura a moment to recover and scramble to her feet. "Hi," Laura took his outstretched hand and tried to make some sense of her mother's life. It appeared Laura wasn't the only one with a secret, hockey-playing boyfriend.

"How's she doing?" He stared at the closed door and his face looked... well, he looked miserable, helpless almost.

"I don't know. The doctor hasn't been out." Laura started to choke up.

Everything had changed between her and her mother in a matter of days. It was the weirdest feeling, but Laura knew she'd done the right thing when she didn't tell her dad about Mom's baby. She'd done the right thing helping her tonight.

Over the years, Marie had been a presence. Laura didn't

understand the relationship between her father and his girlfriend until she was in her teens, but by then her Dad had made it clear her mom didn't want her. So while Marie was a little weird, she made a fuss over Laura, and it helped take away the sting of being rejected by her mother. But she hated that she knew about Marie. She hated that her dad had put her in that position.

Recently, though, Laura started thinking about her mom, searching her memory for something that would confirm the things her father had said over the years. There was nothing. The only things that came to mind were good—old memories from when she was a little girl, of a woman who had never been anything but loving and sweet. Her father was the one who was hard.

David reached out and put his hand on her arm, which broke Laura's trance. Just then Dr. Emmanuel came out of Mom's room. "David, good, you're here. We should talk. Laura, you can see your mom."

Laura nodded and watched for a minute as the doctor led David down the hall to a small lounge. Once they disappeared from view, Laura steeled herself, turned toward the door and knocked.

HER BODY FAILED her.

That was the only explanation. The baby died. It was nothing she did, and there was nothing anyone could have done to stop it. She sat in the bed with an IV in one arm, a blood pressure cuff on the other, and a box of tissues in her lap. She sniffed and dabbed her eyes, trying to hold on to her composure until she was home.

Dr. Emmanuel wanted to keep her overnight, but Kate didn't think it was necessary. She'd rather just go home and mourn her baby alone. That's how she was going to end up anyway—alone.

She wiped her eyes again and heard a faint rap at the door. She didn't respond, but the door opened anyway. Laura, looking scared, poked her head in the room. They made eye contact and Kate was shocked at first, then touched. Not only had Laura stayed with her during the miscarriage, she was still there; something kept her there.

"Hey," Kate said. "I didn't think you were still here."

Laura nodded. "I wanted to see how you were."

"I'll be okay." A tear rolled down her cheek and Laura approached and sat at the end of the bed. "Thank you for staying with me."

"I couldn't leave you like that." Laura paused. "I felt so bad, like it was my fault or something."

Kate thought about the argument she and Marie were having when the first pain hit. "It's not your fault. It's not even Marie's fault."

"Are you sure?"

"Absolutely. It happens sometimes."

Laura nodded, and then she offered a weak grin. "I, uh, met David."

Kate was still teary and sniffled, smiling at how Laura must have reacted to meeting him. "Oh."

"He's with your doctor right now. He seemed pretty upset."

"He really wanted the baby," Kate told her.

"He only asked about you."

The way Laura said it made it sound like all David cared about was Kate, but it was the baby that brought them back together. And now the loss would probably split them apart.

Kate saw Laura close her eyes and scratch her head. "This is going to sound really mean, but he's like thirty years old and fifteen kinds of gorgeous. How did you get him?"

Kate laughed, which made it easier to push down the tears. It was good that Laura was asking questions instead of tossing accusations. "It's a long story," she offered. "That started in California on my birthday."

"Wow," Laura said. "That's amazing."

"It's over, but he's been very supportive since I found out I was pregnant." Kate heard her voice crack and she started to tear up. Her heart broke thinking that she not only lost her child; she was probably going to lose David. There was no more baby and no more reason to spend time with her. Her eyes were like a running faucet, with tears leaking out. Laura rubbed her leg, but when David walked in the room, Laura's hand stopped moving and Kate felt herself dissolve.

David didn't hesitate. He rounded the bed, sat on the edge so they were hip to hip, and gathered Kate into his arms. He didn't say anything, he just let her cry. She'd cried like this when she told him she was pregnant, and now again that she lost their baby. She looked up into his face and his hand stroked her cheek.

"Thank God you're alright."

Kate drew a breath to regain her composure and looked at Laura, who sat as the very end of the bed, trying not to pay attention. Eventually she rose and stepped out of the room.

"Shit." Kate watched the door close behind her daughter. They'd broken some new ground today and Kate didn't want

Laura to feel alienated already. Kate moved to get out of bed, even though she knew she shouldn't. "I should talk to her."

"Stop, you need to take it easy," he said. "You started hemorrhaging when you got here, so you aren't moving."

"She stayed with me."

"I know. You might be in much worse shape if she hadn't." He rose from the bed and started after Laura. "I'll get her."

"Marie wanted her to leave and Laura flat out defied her."

David was halfway to the door and he stopped short when he heard that. He faced Kate.

"She was moving out," Kate told him. "But somehow I don't think that's what she wanted."

"From what you told me about your ex, her taking your side won't go over too well."

Kate nodded.

David resumed his walk to the door. "Don't worry."

DAVID LOOKED FOR Laura, checking every waiting area and lounge finally finding her in the hospital lobby trying to get a cell phone signal. The poor girl looked completely lost. This was new ground for everyone. He never meant to encroach on her time with her mom, but she had to get used to him being around.

"Hey," he said. "Why'd you take off?"

"Oh, hi." David noticed she was flustered and her red eyes told him she'd been crying too. Like mother, like daughter. "You were there," she whispered. "Mom didn't need me anymore."

"I don't know about that." He gently took her arm and led her to a couch in the lobby where they both sat. "I can't tell you how grateful I am that you were there when it happened. You may have saved her life."

Laura kept her eyes down and shrugged. "I couldn't just leave her. There was, blood and…" She gulped hard and tears slipped down her cheeks. "So much blood."

He rubbed her back and let her cry. "The miscarriage happened very fast and it got dicey. It was lucky you didn't do as you were told."

"How could Marie think about leaving?" Laura asked. "How could she? She says she's such a freaking humanitarian, but she'd let my mother bleed to death?"

David said nothing as the grip Kate's ex-husband and his mistress had on Laura slipped away. They had completely underestimated that deep down this was Kate's daughter, and nothing could change the strength of her DNA.

"Laura, I'm new to all this with your family, but I think you and your mom are more alike than you think."

Laura nodded and wiped her eyes.

"Come back upstairs so we can figure out what to do."

David stood and helped her up. She blew out a breath, and he was curious if she knew how much her mannerisms were like Kate's.

"So, can I ask you a question?" She was studying his face, watching for a reaction.

David nodded. "Shoot."

"You're in love with my mother, so why aren't you to-gether?"

Damn. She nailed it. They were walking toward the eleva-tor. "Why do you think I'm in love with her?"

"Seriously?" Laura rolled her eyes and smirked. "You think people can't tell?"

Realizing he couldn't deny it, David stopped at the elevator doors, stuffed his hands in his pockets and answered her directly. "She doesn't trust me."

Laura folded her arms now. Great, he was getting the third degree from a teenager. "My mom trusts everyone. That's why my dad was able to screw her over for so long."

David leaned in her direction. "And that's why she doesn't trust me."

The elevator opened and they stepped inside. This girl knew exactly what her father was doing to Kate. Why she'd stood for it was something else. This, however, seemed to be a turning point. For whatever reason, Laura had made a choice; and from what he knew about Richard Nicholls, David doubted he'd be happy about it.

RICHARD WAS SEETHING. He was so pissed he could have killed someone. Never in his life did he think he'd be so angry at Laura. She always did what he wanted. Always.

He'd been at the college all afternoon, and when he returned home he expected to be helping Laura bring the rest of her belongings to her room. Instead, he found Marie in her office typing drivel into her computer, having completely screwed up the move.

Laura was with Kate.

Marie told him about Kate's pregnancy and apparent miscarriage and that unnerved him on another level. He'd always spread the story that he and Kate never had any more children because she'd been sterilized. He never expected to be caught. He never thought Kate would be able to find someone to sleep with her so quickly.

When she'd met him at the lawyer's office, he'd noticed she was different. Kate had always dressed well, but she tended to be conservative. That seemed to be changing. She walked into the lobby at the attorney's wearing a pair of very high heels and a silky, olive green dress that wrapped around her body. It hugged her in some places and flowed out in others and Richard got hard just thinking about her. The tease of cleavage made him speculate about what was going on, and now it made sense. His ex-wife looked perfectly put together, as she always did, but she'd turned up the heat for someone else.

Marie's presence might have jeopardized the one thing Richard held precious, his hold on his daughter. Defying Marie was the first step in the breakdown of his and Laura's relationship. If she questioned Marie, she would question him, and it looked like it was driving her back to her mother.

That was Richard's worst nightmare.

KATE WOKE UP the next morning and struggled to sit up in bed. She had to pee so bad she thought she was going to explode, but the damn IV was still attached to her. No problem, she'd take it with her.

She started to swing her legs to the side of the bed, and that's when she saw them. David was asleep in a chair and Laura had fallen asleep in the other bed in the room. The two people she least expected to be there for her in a crisis were the ones who were still with her. She must have done something right to get this Christmas present.

Kate grabbed hold of the rolling IV stand and put both feet on the floor. As soon as she stood, the entire room spun and her knees buckled under her. She managed to grab on to the bed before she hit the floor, but the racket she made jolted David and Laura awake.

David's arms were supporting her in a split second. Laura leaned across the bed, holding on to the IV that was about to fall over.

"Jeez, Mom! What are you doing?"

"Hang on, I got you." David's voice was soft and reassuring, but as she held on to the sheets, Kate was suddenly terrified. She couldn't stand and go to the bathroom? What was she going to do? What the hell had happened?

David eased her back into the bed and pulled the covers over her. He looked concerned. Scratch that, he looked scared, and that only compounded her fear.

Laura looked at him. "What's wrong with her?"

"I don't know. I'll get a nurse." He looked at her and tapped the bed. "Don't move."

"I have to pee."

"I said I'll get a nurse." He turned to Laura. "Don't let her out of bed."

Laura nodded, and when he left the room she glared at her. "You could have hurt yourself."

"Sorry, I had no idea I couldn't stand."

"You probably got up too fast." Laura reached out and took her mother's hand, which almost sent Kate right into the emotional abyss. She was feeling better, but the hormones had her hanging onto her control by a thread.

"You scared the crap out of me yesterday," Laura told her.

"That makes two of us."

Everything she'd come to expect from Laura had been turned upside down over the last twenty-four hours. Her girl had done things Kate never would have imagined, and the relationship wasn't lost after all. After several minutes had passed and David still hadn't returned, Kate realized Laura was thinking and trying to get her thoughts into words. Her face and body were tense, and Kate was curious about the sudden change in her behavior.

Finally, Laura blurted it out. "I don't want to move to Dad's full time."

Kate took in what she had said and tried to be objective, because as the words swam around in her brain, they made no sense. The day before, she was moving herself out, now she didn't want to leave. "Okay. Why?"

"Do you want me to move?"

"Not at all, but this is quite a change from yesterday."

"It was his idea. I don't want to live with them full time."

Kate examined Laura's face. Something was wrong, and it was deeper than Kate expected.

"What's going on?" This time Kate reached out and took Laura's hand when she saw her face tense. "Tell me."

"Marie is weird. I mean all she and Dad do is have sex."

Kate closed her eyes tight and pursed her lips. "Say again?"

"It's scheduled. Marie has a calendar on the refrigerator. Every other day... sex... sex... sex... she's trying to get pregnant."

"I heard her. Not happening." Kate wondered what the hell was going on in that house. "What about Dad?"

Laura hesitated and found herself having a hard time. "Dad's either sucking up to the new dean or he's following me around. He's too attached to me. It's like, I don't know, he doesn't want me to have a life. The past year, since the divorce, it's gotten really bad."

Kate knew all about the controlling, manipulative man she'd married. But now his devotion to Laura was taking a perverse turn. "What's he doing?"

"He won't let me date. He doesn't want me to drive. He won't let me see my friends. He went through my closet and threw out the clothes he said were inappropriate. He threatens to restrict my cell phone. He won't let me look at colleges. That college book you gave me? He took it and threw it into the fireplace."

"What?" Now Kate was mad as well as concerned. "This can't happen."

"He's scary sometimes." Laura bowed her head and twisted her fingers. "When I was younger it was fine, but now? I go along with everything because I don't know what he'll do if I don't."

Kate was thinking the same thing. This could go south very fast. "He's going to be angry because he'll see your help as siding with me."

"I was afraid of that."

"You aren't going skiing." Kate turned when she heard the door open. "You need to steer clear of him for a while."

Laura nodded and the tension in her face lessened. Kate may not have had fight in her before, but if Richard tried to do to Laura what he'd done to her, he would learn about mothers who protected their children.

In the meantime, she had to calm down. If she became a

crazy lunatic, that wouldn't help anyone.

She patted Laura's arm. "Don't worry."

Laura nodded again and seemed to relax.

David walked in with a nurse who was carrying a bed pan, which made Laura laugh and Kate cringe. He looked at her and shrugged, all the while suppressing the laugh that she could see was building.

Kate shook her head. "I am *so* not using that thing."

The nurse grinned, half expecting the reaction. What she did instead was help Kate up and make sure she didn't stumble again. It seemed like the walk to the bathroom took forever, but after a few steps, Kate felt more stable.

When she got back into bed after a successful trip, only one thing was on her mind. "Can I go home now?"

The nurse, who had just come on her shift, nodded. "Let me check your chart and call your doctor. She'll make the final decision, but probably."

Kate leaned back in the bed. Going home would allow her to recover on her own, and then David could get on with his life. All along, Kate said she didn't want to trap him into being with her, but she couldn't deny she loved having him around. It was silly how she felt, she was too old to fall for someone so fast and so hard. There were times she questioned if her feelings for him were the real thing.

When his hand dropped on her shoulder, she knew in an instant that her feelings were as real as they come. Time would tell about him.

Chapter 20

I T WAS SNOWING.

And not just snowing, it was almost a blizzard, and all Kate wanted to do was get home. Thankfully, Julie had been able to get to the hospital before the driving got dangerous so Kate had something to wear home. Now, with Laura riding shotgun in the Range Rover and Kate wrapped in a blanket in the back seat, they made their way to her house. She assumed David would be comfortable driving in the snow, but even he was taking it slow.

She was so tired. The entire night had been a jumble of feelings, but the overwhelming sense of loss was what was controlling Kate at that moment, with her mind focused on her baby and on David. Her breath hitched, she sniffled, and Laura turned around.

"We're almost home, Mom." Laura reached out touched her hand.

"I know." She closed her eyes and reined in her feelings. The doctor told her the hormones would be all over the place, but Kate hated how out of control she felt. All she had to do was hold it together until David dropped them off, and then she could fall apart.

They finally pulled in her driveway, and before she could even unbuckle her seatbelt, David was opening her door and helping her out. He was as much of a mess as she was, and it broke Kate's heart. He kept his hand on the small of her back and guided her into the house. Laura took the blanket she'd been wrapped in, and David stayed with her as she walked into the kitchen.

Kate turned to him and took his hand. "I'm okay."

"Promise me you'll take it easy." His eyes were dark and sad.

"I promise." Her other hand came up and touched his face. "But you have to go if you have any hope of making your game."

"I feel like I shouldn't leave you."

"David, Laura's here. Go. I'll see when you get back." She said it, but didn't think it would happen. Kate figured this would be the last time he would be this close.

"Okay. I'll call." He turned to Laura. "Make sure she doesn't do too much for a couple of days."

"I'll try." Laura looked at her and knew immediately that Kate was barely holding on.

"You have all the numbers?" he asked again.

Laura nodded. "The doctor, the pharmacy, your cell, your sister, Julie, my aunt… everyone."

Satisfied, David pulled Kate close, wrapping her in his arms. She slipped her arms around his waist and lost herself in the feel of him. This was goodbye. It was possibly the last time he would hold her like this, the last time she would look into his face and see him smile just for her.

"Have a safe trip, and Merry Christmas."

He hugged her again. "Merry Christmas. I'll call you later on."

He glanced at her as he walked away and again before he left through the kitchen door.

When he'd gone, Kate turned wordlessly from Laura and headed upstairs. She had suffered such unfairness in her life—losing her husband, having to fight for her daughter—but this pain she felt was so acute, so overwhelming, she thought it would consume her. She could barely breathe, and the heaviness in her chest told her this was different from anything she'd gone through before. When she sat on her bed, the first gasping breath came, and then the first great sob escaped.

This was heartbreak.

When Richard left, Kate imagined nothing could ever hurt more than that. She was wrong. Richard betrayed her. He left her feeling inadequate and insecure, but it was nothing compared to what she felt at that moment.

She'd lost her baby and she was going to lose David. Her throat tightened and another sob escaped. Kate fell onto her pillows and let go, allowing the sadness to take hold. Both of them were gone. Her baby, and the man she'd fallen in love with. The tears seemed endless and Kate gave in to them. She didn't stop thinking about David, or her lost child, until she felt someone's weight settle on the bed behind her.

Kate turned her head and saw Laura, tears in her own eyes, sitting on the bed. Laura reached out and stroked her mother's hair.

For a long time, Laura stayed with her, doing nothing more than rubbing her back. As much as Kate wanted to be comforted by her daughter, she was thinking about David and it was killing her.

"Mom, come downstairs. We'll eat crap and watch a stupid movie."

She sniffed and grabbed the box of tissues on her night table. Slowly, because she was still tired, she rolled on her back and sat up. Her breathing was shaky, and big, soggy tears rolled down her face. She mopped them up with a wad of tissues and looked at her daughter. "I guess the hormones are making a mess of things."

"Partially, but you know, it's okay to be sad." Laura laid her head on Kate's shoulder. "I'm sad."

"You are?"

Laura nodded. "It would have been cool having a little brother or sister."

"It was never my intention that you be an only child."

Sitting up straight, her daughter looked her straight in the eyes. "I know that now."

"So," Kate asked. "Why didn't you tell them?"

Laura glanced over and let the question hang there for a while. Kate could see she was thinking. When Laura answered, her voice was steady and unapologetic, and a twitch of a smile teased the corner of her mouth. "It was none of their fuckin' business."

Kate let go a watery laugh when she heard Laura repeat her words exactly. "I'm sure they aren't happy they didn't know."

Laura shrugged. "I'm not happy he lied to me."

Kate smiled. "I never thought we'd be having this conversation."

"Me either." Laura reached over the side of the bed and came up with a bag of Double Stuff Oreos. She ripped the bag open, took two of the cookies and passed it to her mother. "But to be honest, it was when you stood up to me that everything changed."

"Why is that?" Kate took a cookie from the package, twisted it open, and licked the cream inside the cookie.

"You fought back. His version wasn't the only thing I heard."

That made Kate think. Should she be fighting?

"I was such a bitch, Mom. I'm sorry." Laura reached out and hugged her mother. "You didn't deserve it."

Kate held her daughter and didn't question the turn of events, didn't try to figure out why things had happened the way they did. Maybe she had to worry less about doing what she thought was the right thing, and needed to trust her instincts. She started questioning that inner voice a long time ago, when Richard made her question everything about who she was, what she did, and what she believed. Maybe trusting her instincts would help her find herself again.

"So tell me about David." Laura grinned at her mother and settled back with the cookies.

Kate breathed deep and felt the tears start to well up again. "I don't know that there's much to tell anymore. He's been amazing since I told him I was pregnant. I don't know what'll happen now."

Laura reached out and rubbed her back. "He cares about you. He really does."

"You think so?"

Laura nodded and leaned her head on Kate's shoulder. "Do you love him?"

Kate thought for a second, thought about all those inner voices, and nodded in response. "I'm a complete goner."

Laura passed the cookies and the two ate in silence for a while. Things wouldn't be easy for them, but Kate felt she and Laura finally had a beginning.

"Did you love Daddy?"

Kate looked down at her. "When I married him, I loved him with all my heart." That was the truth. She did love Richard. He was her world, but he never respected her.

"What happened?"

This was the first time Laura ever asked her about the divorce.

Kate wasn't ready to tell her everything, but she could tell her some. "There were so many things that went wrong, but I guess it all came down to the fact that he never thought I was good enough for him. He never loved me. He wanted to own me."

"You're good enough for David, and I think he loves you."

Kate could only hope. "I guess time will tell. I'm not counting on it, though."

Laura turned and focused her gaze. "Last night, after you fell asleep, I saw how he was. He sat next to your bed, and stroked your hair. He whispered the sweetest things. The guy was wrecked and it was all about you, Mom. He was worried about you." Kate drew a deep breath as Laura continued. "I've never seen anything like it. It was pretty amazing."

A single tear rolled over her cheek, but this time it was her feelings for David that were coming to the surface. What Laura saw, that kind of love, was the fairy tale. It was the love story, and it was all Kate had ever wanted. He was all she wanted. Just thinking about the possibility was too much to hope for. It took a few minutes to compose herself, then she refocused on something trivial, something she could control. Kate tapped the package of Oreos. "These need milk."

"I agree. Kitchen?"

The cookies were nothing, but the change between them was significant and not lost on either one. Kate, however, continued to be moved by Laura's words. "Thank you for telling me."

"You deserve to be happy. Daddy wasn't good to you, and I wasn't either. You deserve better."

And with those words, Laura left the room. Kate, in spite of everything that had happened, felt more hopeful than she had in years.

DAVID SAT IN the dressing room between periods and his mind wasn't on the game. It had taken him two hours to get from Kate's house to his. He picked up his bag and drove to the arena. Tonight's game against the Canadiens was sold out, but there were only a few hundred people in the stands because of the weather. They were winning and he didn't care.

His teammates all knew what had happened. He guessed Jay or Cam told them because he kept getting quiet looks of condolence or pats on the back. No one knew what to say. He was sure half the guys thought he'd gotten lucky. No baby meant he was off the hook with Kate. But David felt anything but lucky. She'd come back to him because of the baby; now that she'd miscarried, he was afraid she'd want him out of her life again. He couldn't let that happen. He had to find some way to let her know how he felt about her.

After the game, they would board a bus to the airport, and hopefully be able to fly to Boston for tomorrow's game against the Bruins. If not, they would be stuck at the airport. All he wanted to do was curl around Kate and get over what had happened. Physically, she had to recover, but it was the emotional piece that was going to hurt long term. And for that, David knew they needed each other.

When he thought about it, David had a hard time processing how he'd changed since he met her. Something made him take that stupid bet in California and approach her. He'd been issued challenges like that before and he'd blown them off... but something made him accept.

Something made her worth the effort.

She'd made him reassess his whole existence, made him understand he didn't have to be the person he was. Kate needed him, too. He'd been poking around on the Internet and found video of her skating when she was just seventeen. She was a younger version of herself. The smile was wide and there was complete joy in every movement. In the late eighties, triple jumps were just becoming part of a ladies skating program, but Kate had mastered them. It was risky, but based on what he read about her, young Katie Adams wasn't happy unless she was taking risks.

David spent enough time around ice rinks to know there were two types of women who skated: those who were graceful and those who were athletic. Watching a graceful skater was like seeing a ballet dancer on ice. Watching an athletic skater was like watching controlled explosions. When she was competing, Kate was both.

He had to help her see the person she used to be was still inside her, because if Kate didn't find her again, David knew he had no chance. She would close herself off to the risk he represented, and that would be it.

David jolted out of his trance when Jack Nelson slapped his shoulder pads. "How's it goin', Padre?"

Truthfully, he didn't know how he was. His brain and his heart felt numb.

"Pretty shitty, man."

Jack nodded and David saw the kid didn't know what to say. Hell, he didn't know what to say either, so he shrugged and then changed the subject. "When are we meeting this girl of yours, Nelly?"

Jack frowned. "Maybe never. She's not answering my calls or my texts."

The kid had only been seeing the girl for a couple of months, but he talked about her all the time and spent as much free time with her as he could. He said she was a college student, but that was the only information David had gotten out of him so far. The other guys were ripping on him about her being imaginary. The thing was, unless she showed up soon, David might believe that himself. "Did you have a fight?"

"No, but I may have pushed her too hard."

It took a second for David to catch his meaning. "Oh…"

Jack made a face. "I like her, but I don't know; she's very naïve, innocent."

It was David's turn to slap his young teammate's back. "Is she worth the effort?"

Jack nodded. "I think so, yeah."

"Then hang on to her. If she makes you happy, don't let her get away." David stood, pulled on his helmet, and picked up his stick. "Come on. Let's go win this for the three hundred people who showed up tonight."

Jack nodded and followed David out of the dressing room.

LAURA HAD NO idea what she was going to do about Jack now that she was going to be staying with her Mom. He'd called her at least ten times that day and left half a dozen voice mails. He texted her asking if she was okay and she didn't answer any of them. She checked the clock. He was on his way to Boston now, and with his games and the holidays, he wouldn't be back in town for a week. The thought just about killed her.

The right thing to do was tell him the truth. That would solve the problem of seeing him, because it would end their relationship. But just thinking about losing him made breathing a little bit harder.

Laura wiped a tear. Pulling her phone out of her pocket, she opened the photo album. There was a picture of the two of them she'd snapped when they'd been out in the city last week. She ran her hand over the image and felt the first tear fall, then another. Pretty soon, she was muffling her cries into her pillow. She didn't want to wake her mother, didn't want to answer questions. But Laura couldn't keep this secret forever, from Jack or anyone else.

Now though, he was still hers. She opened his last text and started a reply. *"Sorry. Family emergency today. All ok now. I miss you. <3"* Laura sent the text, hoping when he arrived in Boston and turned on his phone, he'd smile, just a little, when he thought of her.

KATE TOOK OFF from work on Monday, but felt well enough on Tuesday to go in. It was the last day before the Christmas break, the school looked beautiful and festive, and everyone was a in a good mood. The faculty members had organized their traditional breakfast, and she enjoyed being with her friends and being away from constant thoughts of David and her baby. Only Julie had known she had been pregnant, so no one offered any condolences or sympathy. It was exactly the break Kate needed.

She felt better today. She was still moody; less so, but she assumed work was helping her keep her moods in check. Her body was healing itself, and in some ways, it was sad to think about. In a week or two, there would be nothing left of the child she'd grown to want so much. But like so many things in her life, Kate was learning to live with the disappointment.

The last day before Christmas, she had a tradition with her classes. She pitched her usual lessons to the wind, which wasn't to say she didn't do anything. Kate first set the mood with boxes and boxes of candy canes. She always wore her favorite red sweater, popped a Santa hat on her head, and then, armed with her favorite Christmas picture books; Kate held story time in English class. Her two favorites were *How the Grinch Stole Christmas* and *The Polar Express*. Very different books, but both captured the magic of the season Kate loved so much.

When she'd finished reading both books to her tenth grade literature class, she spent the last few minutes before the bell sucking on a candy cane and talking with the kids about where they were spending their vacations. Some were going skiing, though the venues varied among Vail, Aspen, and the Alps. Other kids were going to warmer climates, like Barbados, Aruba, and Hawaii. A few were staying home and seeing family, and she knew those kids were going to have the best times of all.

The bell rang and she said goodbye to her class, getting hugs from some kids, the usual holiday wishes from others, and not a second look from a few. She smiled. Already she could see which kids would get out of their own heads and which would continue to think the world revolved around them. Stuffing her papers in her portfolio, she made her way down the dark paneled hallway to the faculty room to see if there was anything left to nibble on. Kate knew all the holiday sweets would go right to her hips, but some things were worth the calories, and Julie's butter cookies were on the top of that list.

The faculty room was busy, filled with colleagues and members of the board of trustees, who'd stopped in to celebrate with the teachers and administration. It was one of the brightest rooms in the school, and the large arched windows offered a picture perfect view of the quad. A few students were outside, trying to make a snowman from the fluffy powder that had fallen a few days before. There were conversations going on all around her, Christmas carols playing, and Kate was glad she'd come in today rather than staying home. The camaraderie and the holiday cheer were healing.

But just like the kids, the faculty was a mixed bag. Kate knew who her friends were and who she wouldn't trust for a second. As in most schools, there were dedicated people who wanted to do good work with the students. They were kind, nurturing, and fun. Another group, however, measured a student's worth by the size of their mommy and daddy's bank account. So, it really shouldn't have surprised her when the assistant headmaster, who was also a St. Andrew's graduate, walked into the room with a group of some well-heeled young alums in tow.

They sauntered over to their favorite teachers, and Kate popped one of Julie's perfect cookies into her mouth.

"Some things don't change," said Julie. "One is more pretentious than another."

"Maybe," Kate nodded. "I keep thinking it takes a lot of effort to maintain that kind of façade. They must be exhausted." Picking up another cookie, Kate vowed to exercise after the holidays.

"Merry Christmas, Mrs. Nicholls." Suddenly chilled, Kate turned her head and watched Chelsea Connor walk toward her table. Chelsea had been a presence since she started seeing David, but she never thought she'd be having a conversation with her. "Or are you going by Adams since your husband left you?"

The room went quiet when she spoke, her voice being just loud enough to command everyone's attention, which, Kate figured, was exactly the plan. She was, without a doubt, a beautiful young woman, but knowing the kind of person she was, what she'd pulled with David, Kate knew this was going to be a bumpy ride.

Chelsea's long blonde hair fell over her shoulders like twisted silk. Her eyes, which were ice blue, nailed Kate with a stare that could only be described as hateful. No, this was not a social call; Chelsea was out for blood.

Kate still hadn't spoken. The words caught in her throat.

Not that there wasn't anything she could say; the girl was evil incarnate, same as always, and now she had a reason to make her old teacher one of her targets. The first lob was nothing compared to what was coming. "Daddy told me he saw you at the hospital not too long ago. Is everything okay?"

"Fine. Thank you for asking. What brings you here, Chelsea?" Natural concern about her health had the other teaches exchanging looks, but Kate waved her hand indicating all was well.

"I'm just visiting," Chelsea said. "I haven't stopped by in so long, and I figured I had to see you since we have so much in common."

Her former student had a lethal grin plastered across her face, and Kate knew she was in real trouble. "In common?"

"Based on what I've heard, it seems that we're fucking the same guy."

Kate would say the room went silent, but it didn't. There was a little chatter and a few muffled exclamations, but all Kate could really hear was the sound of her heart pounding in her chest. In her wildest dreams she never, ever expected her life to be spread open like this—but then again, she shouldn't have underestimated Chelsea's willingness to shock people.

"Chelsea, this is not a conversation we are going to have—"

Chelsea cut her off. "We'll have it if I want to have it."

Kate stood up, straight as a needle, while Chelsea relaxed and leaned against a small bookcase, examining her manicure. The girl did not care. She didn't think she had anything to lose, which told Kate this was going to get even uglier.

"You're embarrassing yourself, Chelsea."

"What? Don't want them to know you had an affair with

a much younger pro hockey player?" She leaned over and faked a whisper in the assistant headmaster's ear. "My boyfriend. He dumped me."

Kate pushed up her glasses and pinched the bridge of her nose. "He was going to do that regardless."

Why didn't she stay quiet? Chelsea's eyes turned stormy, her skin flushed.

"You don't know anything!" Chelsea's scream echoed in the room, bouncing off the large windows. "You know nothing. It was going fine until he went to California and met you."

Kate was, at first, stunned at her information. However, it didn't take long to figure it out; it had been from David or his friends, or his friends' wives, or their girlfriends—the information sources were bottomless.

"You need to leave." Kate was still trying to get her to calm down, even though it was pretty much pointless. Every word that came out of Chelsea's mouth made her situation that much worse.

"I'm not leaving. I'm not leaving until everyone in this school knows what a *whore* you are."

She could handle this if she was alone, but even when a phone rang on a nearby table, no one moved. There was a slowing down of time, and everything seemed to hang, the tension in the air, the guilt, the anger and the words. A few more teachers wandered in and they stood quietly, assessing the situation. "Chelsea..."

"You're disgusting. David picked you up in a bar and now you're pregnant? My God, what is wrong with you? He was mine. Not yours, mine. *Mine!*"

The tantrum was too much. Kate snapped. Hormones,

sadness, humiliation, and anger all churned inside her. There was a hissing in her ears—all the years of being put down, told what she could and couldn't do, came out in one massive explosion.

"You don't own him! He made his decision. David knew what he wanted and he wanted me. Not you." Kate advanced and Chelsea took a step back, then another. "What makes you think you have the right to come here and behave this way? This is a school. A *school*." Kate looked around the room at the stone cold faces of her colleagues. "These were your teachers, Chelsea. You're embarrassing yourself, your father, and making everyone uncomfortable because you didn't get your way. This is all about you not getting what you want."

By this time, Julie and the assistant headmaster were at her side, trying to calm her down. Kate rightly assumed that no one had ever spoken to Chelsea that way, and hearing it in front of a room full of teachers and trustees, people who knew her father, made her so angry she shook. When she picked up her purse, she fired one last shot. "You are a pathetic woman, Kate Nicholls. He's going to drop you just like he dropped me. And for the record, no one ever had to pay David to take me to bed."

She turned toward the door and the teachers parted for her like the Red Sea.

"*Pay?*"

Chelsea looked over her shoulder and smirked. "You were part of a bet. I think each guy had to give David a hundred bucks when he got you in bed. Nice windfall for him. I think he should get a bonus though, considering he got you pregnant at the same time."

Kate turned her back and braced herself against one of the

tables before facing Chelsea and uttering her last words. "You need to get out of here. Now."

Chelsea winked and smiled, and her smugness almost had Kate lunging at that perfect face before she strolled out like she was the queen of the world. The assistant headmaster left with her, as did some of the trustees. Yeah. This was bad.

Kate was staring at her hands, fighting back the rage, when Julie approached. "You okay?"

She started to nod, but stopped and shook her head no. "No, not really."

"I'm going to go and find out what they're doing with her. Be right back. Don't worry."

Kate nodded. "Thank you, but I'm beyond worry." Julie nodded and Kate tried to smile.

The teachers started to leave the room, the festive mood having been ruined. A few nodded in support, a few scowled in disgust, and Kate had to face the facts. Most of what Chelsea said was the truth. She had been picked up in a bar, she did sleep with him the same day she met him, and he had gotten her pregnant. Even the revelation that she may have been the subject of a bet didn't upset her. It just confirmed what she knew to be true all along—everything was a game.

Julie came in the room and stood next to her friend. "Headmaster wants to see you."

"Golly, I wonder why?" It wasn't the time for sarcasm, but Kate couldn't help herself.

"I don't even know what to say. I'd run her down with my car if I thought it would help."

A chuckle escaped Kate's lips, because only a truly good friend would volunteer to off the competition. "Damage is done. It's a matter of time, but I'm guessing I'm going to have to resign."

Julie's face tightened. "No. That would be wrong. You're a grown woman, you have a right…"

Kate stopped her, took off her Santa hat, and smoothed her hair. Considering the situation, she spoke more calmly than she could have imagined. "I'm a teacher who just had her private life exposed to the faculty and the very stuffy board of trustees. Headmaster doesn't care about my rights."

They stood quietly for a few moments, looking around the room and thinking about what would happen next.

"So what made you tell her off?" Julie asked.

Kate took a moment to answer, because she wasn't exactly sure what had made her respond in just that way. It wasn't what people had come to expect from her, nor was it the most professional reaction, but she felt more like herself than she had in twenty years.

"I figured if I was going down, I'd take her along for the ride."

"Do you think it'll matter to her?"

"Her father is ruined here. What happens to me is irrelevant. She destroyed his reputation, as well as her own. She didn't think about that." Kate stretched and pressed her hands into the small of her back. "It'll matter to her eventually."

Julie reached out and touched Kate's shoulder. "You okay?"

"I'm sure I'll have a meltdown later, but at this point I've been kicked so many times, I don't even feel it."

Chapter 21

DAVID PULLED INTO his sister's driveway and stared at the house. She and her husband had moved into this place over the summer, and it was more impressive than she described. On the west side of the city, the brick home had huge windows and what looked like a nice bit of land for this area. She'd need the space with her growing family.

Getting out of the car, he opened the back door and removed his bag. The scene was almost too perfect. The snow on the ground was the perfect setting for the house which was decked out with pine garland, lights and wreaths—very much like Kate's house, very much like the house he grew up in.

It was a home.

He thought about Kate the whole way there, on the flight from Montreal to Toronto, and on the drive from the airport. He wondered what she was doing, if she was thinking about him. Part of him wanted to get a flight to Philadelphia and spend the holiday with her, help her through the recovery. But the other part of him knew they needed this time apart to get a hold of their feelings.

As he made his way up the walk, the front door flew open

and his sister Rachel dashed outside. At thirty-eight, she still looked like a pixie to him, with her large green eyes and auburn hair. Flinging herself at him, she clung to his neck. David dropped his duffle and spun his big sister in a circle before setting her on her feet.

"I'd better set you down or the neighbors will talk, eh?"

"God, it's good to see you." Rachel gave his arm a smack. "Why don't you visit more?"

He picked up his bag, looped his arm around her shoulder and walked into the house. "The season's a nightmare, Rach, you know I can't."

"I know." She hugged him again when they were in the foyer. "You look good, Dave… different somehow."

"Different?" He tilted his head and saw her eye him curiously. "How do you mean?"

"I don't know," she said. "Like someone's gotten into your head."

David shrugged, wondering if his feelings for Kate really were that obvious even to people who didn't know about her. "It's quiet. Where is everyone?"

"Dad's taking a nap and Ian took the rug rats to get the pizza." She helped him off with his jacket and hung it in the closet. "The kids are dying to see you."

"Me too, I bet they're big. Did the presents get here?

"Yup, last week," she said.

"How's Dad?"

Rachel raised an eyebrow. "Better since he moved here with us. Mellowing."

"About time. Where am I crashing?" he asked.

"Come on, I'll show you." They climbed the wide staircase and Rachel opened the door to a nicely sized guest room.

"The bath's through that door. There are towels in the closet to your right."

"This is a great house. Big."

"Yeah, this room will only be guest room a little while longer." She patted her belly. "Number four comes in July."

"Really?" He smiled the best he could. "Another one?" He was genuinely happy for his sister, but then thought of his child, the one who never had a chance. He thought about Kate, too.

Rachel must have sensed the change in his mood, and sat on the bed. She didn't say anything, but watched him as he hung up his suit and a few shirts.

"I think it's great," he said. "Are you feeling okay?"

"I'm fine. What about you?" she asked. "Are you ever going to get married and start having little hockey players?"

That hurt. David thought the married and kid thing was settled; now he wasn't so sure. He stopped what he was doing, looked at her, and then gazed at the sweater in his hand. Kate bought the sweater for him; she bought it because she thought he'd like it, no other reason. "There is someone I'm seeing."

Rachel pulled her legs up and wrapped her arms around her knees. "Tell me," she said.

"Her name's Kate. I've only known her for a couple of months, but..." He paused, knowing what he was about to say could send his sister into a tailspin. "She's it. She's the one."

Rachel was quiet, examining his face, searching for her own answers. Finally, she spoke. "I'm happy for you, David. Why didn't you bring her?"

"She had family coming for the holidays, so she couldn't." He stopped, thought, then started again. "But something happened right before I left." Moving toward his sister, he answered the question before she asked. "She was pregnant and she miscarried. She wouldn't have been able to travel regardless."

"Oh, no," Rachel whispered. "Dave, I'm so sorry." She rose and hugged him. He fought the wave of sadness, fought the echoes of Kate's cries in his head.

"How is she?" she asked in a way that only a woman who'd been through the same thing could ask. She'd had three miscarriages before her three successful pregnancies.

"Recovering. She was about fourteen weeks."

"That must have been awful, for both of you."

"Her daughter was with her when it happened. I didn't see her until it was over."

"Her daughter?" Rachel sat again. Waiting.

"She's divorced. Has a seventeen-year-old daughter." Now he knew the questions would come.

"Wow." Rachel pulled her legs onto the bad and settled herself in for a story. "I'm guessing you're going to fill in the blanks. How did you meet her?"

"Our first road trip of the season, we were in California and she was there for a teachers' conference."

"She's a teacher?"

He nodded. "And a writer."

"I like that she has brains." Rachel grinned because David hadn't dated a girl with brains like Kate's since college. "What kind of writing does she do?"

"Hang on." He rummaged through his bag and produced Kate's latest book. "I asked her to sign it for you."

Rachel's eyes grew wide when she looked at the cover. "You're with Katherine Adams?"

"You're the second person who's reacted that way." He smiled. "Surprised?"

"Yeah." Rachel opened the book to the title page and read the inscription. "This is amazing."

"She's older than me and it bothers her." David sat on the bed next to his sister.

"I figured. How much older?"

"She's forty."

Rachel looked at the book jacket photo. "Looks great for forty."

David leaned forward, rested his elbows on his knees and twisted his fingers. "I don't know how this is going to turn out. She doesn't trust me. And now that the baby isn't there to hold us together, I'm worried I'll lose her."

"Why doesn't she trust you?" The question was asked, but he could see she already knew the answer, so he didn't say anything. Rachel snapped her fingers in mock realization. "Let me guess. You didn't call, you were seeing other women, and unlike the desperate *girls* you tend to date, Kate wouldn't put up with your shit."

"That pretty much sums it up."

"I love you so, but you are such an ass."

"I know, and she's hung up about her age."

Rachel shook her head. "It isn't about *her* age. It's about *yours*."

Thinking about it only made it worse. Kate had been right to hold back, because he'd made a pretty big mess of it so far. David rose and walked over to his bag again and pulled a small red box from a zipped compartment. Rachel sat up very straight as he handed her the box. "I bought this for her when I was in New York."

Rachel ran her hand over the top of the box, which he could see she recognized as coming from Cartier's. "Dropped a bundle, eh?"

"I had to fight the urge to spend more. She doesn't like it when I go overboard."

His sister grinned approvingly and opened the box. A little gasp escaped her lips when her eyes saw the necklace for the first time. "Oh my…"

It was magnificent and simple: a pendant of three intertwined bands, each a different shade of gold, hung on a triple gold chain.

"It's called a Trinity necklace. Each color means something—the yellow gold is for friendship, the white for faithfulness, and the pink for love."

The look in his sister's eyes was hard to explain. But it almost seemed like she was proud of him, like he'd gotten it right.

"It's beautiful, David. Simply beautiful." She closed the box and handed it to him.

"I was going to give it to her the night before I went away, but we spent it at the hospital."

"Have you thought this through? You haven't known her long." Rachel tried to play devil's advocate.

But David knew. For once, he was sure.

"I know. I've danced around this since I met her, and it took me a while to realize she's what I need. When I'm with her, I feel like the person I want to be."

It was the first time David had put into words why Kate was important to him. Now he understood himself how much he needed her. How much he loved her.

Rachel hugged him. "She'd have to be crazy not to love

you, little bro."

Wrapping his arms around her he smiled. "Yeah, well, you're prejudiced." He kept hold and squeezed tighter. "I think Mom would have liked her."

Rachel sat back and laid her hand on his cheek, smiling gently. "Maybe you should trade in the necklace for a ring."

"She'd run for the hills." He grinned, thinking about Kate and her nervousness where he was concerned. "I'll give it some time."

Rachel wasn't one for over sentimental displays of emotion, so before it got messy she changed the subject. "Okay, enough gushy stuff. Let's wake up Dad, and set the table."

David rose, happy his sister approved. "I have to make a call first and then I'll be down."

His sister grinned and left him as he pushed the button on his cell and it started dialing.

LAURA, JULIE, AND Kate sat in the den, feasting on Chinese food. There were a dozen cartons and tins open on the table, and they were full beyond belief. Julie was staying over; all three of them were in yoga pants, T-shirts, and soft, white socks, watching *Rudolph the Red-Nosed Reindeer.* Laura leaned back and belched like a three-hundred-pound man, and Kate, after feigning shock, burst out laughing.

"Where did you learn how to do that?"

Laura shrugged. "Once, I did it in front of Marie. She wasn't amused.

"Sounds to me like she needs a sense of humor." Julie took a pull on her beer and burped herself. "Yeah, we're quite the classy bunch."

Kate laughed again, thankful for the distraction Julie and Laura provided. The scene with Chelsea kept playing over and over in her mind. While she'd managed to avoid being fired or having to resign before Christmas, she was going to have to deal with it soon after. No doubt the bombshells Chelsea dropped were being fed through the school gossip mill. Pretty soon everyone would know what happened.

Kate had opted for wine instead of beer, and the Italian white was going down like fruit juice. She wasn't drunk, was she? It seemed to her she had to cut David loose simply for the sake of her liver. And her pride.

Since he came into her life, it had been one disaster after another. Kate had been out of high school for twenty-two years, and she was still dealing with mean girl crap. Chelsea managed to get off some killer shots, too. From the first line about fucking the same guy to the last one about the bet, Kate had never felt quite so humiliated. Meanwhile, David sat oblivious at his sister's house in Canada.

But there was a bright spot. Through it all, her daughter had stayed with her.

That was worth a thousand humiliations. Kate patted Laura's knee. The phone rang, startling them, and the caller ID flashed on the TV screen. Kate groaned when she saw the number was David's. "Someone else has to answer. After what happened today, I don't know if I've had enough wine yet to talk to him. I've got to get my head around this bet thing."

Kate looked around and Laura held up the hand holding a glass of fizzy beverage. "Don't look at me. Ginger Ale."

Julie grabbed the handset. "Psshht. Losers. I'm plenty drunk enough. *Hello?*"

〜

DAVID WAS CAUGHT by surprise for a second. The person on the other end didn't sound like Kate, but he couldn't be sure. "Kate?"

"It's Julie. Kate's, ahhh, Kate's lying down."

"Oh. Is she okay?" He knew she'd gone to work that day, and he was worried she was doing too much too soon.

"She's peachy. A little tired after being humiliated by your ex-girlfriend, though."

David's stomach turned as he heard Julie's words. "Excuse me?"

"The lovely Chelsea visited her alma mater today. She stopped in to see Kate, and in front of her colleagues, the administration, and some alumni, told them all about you."

"Shit." He could hear Julie's voice tensing.

He thought the crap Chelsea had pulled in the past had been bad, but this was worse than anything she'd ever done to him, a new low. It would hurt Kate and hurt him at the same time.

"Imagine, being called disgusting in front of your colleagues and superiors. Then there was the indignity of finding out she was part of a bet between you and your teammates!"

"Oh, Jesus." His words came out on a breath.

David didn't hate people. It was pointless and a waste of energy, but right then he hated Chelsea Connor. Her anger and jealousy had caused her to lash out, and now Kate knew about the bet. The challenge he accepted and technically won. If Kate didn't doubt his sincerity before, she did now, and he was fucked.

"Let me talk to her, Julie."

"No."

"I need to talk to her. *Please.*"

"Look, this day has moved to the top of the shit scale. Give her some space."

"Julie, wait... shit... let me..." He heard the click and nothing but dead air. He stared at the phone and finally the fury broke through. "Fuck me!" he yelled.

He almost punched the wall, but pulled back before he did serious damage to his hand and the wall. Chelsea Connor was toxic and there was nothing she wouldn't do to get even.

Rachel raced into the room, furious at him. "What's gotten into you? I have small children here."

David sat on the bed with his head in his hands. He felt his body shake with rage. "Sorry."

His sister crouched before him and took his hands, forcing him to face her. "What happened? Is Kate okay?"

"I just called to check on her. She won't talk to me."

"What happened?" She squeezed his hands, but David just couldn't tell her.

It was his doing—accepting the bet was a bad move, as was getting involved with someone like Chelsea in the first place. He was getting everything he deserved, but Kate? Kate deserved none of this.

KATE COULDN'T SLEEP. The scene with Chelsea from earlier in the day ran through her head over and over like a nightmare on endless loop. But she did feel sorry for Chelsea, which surprised her, since she didn't think she could feel sorry for anyone but herself.

When she found out she was pregnant, she worried that people would see her as a joke, the predatory woman looking for the younger man. But it wasn't like that at all. The pregnancy didn't make her a laughingstock; she'd been that all along.

Sniffling quietly in the dark, while Laura and Julie slept in the rooms adjacent to hers, Kate's mind wouldn't shut off. The guest room Julie occupied was going to be the nursery, and that made her think of David. God, she wished he was here. As upset as Kate was, she wanted him there. She wanted him to hold her. Then she wanted to slap him right upside that hard head of his.

A bet. He approached her on a bet, which he won because she slept with him right out of the gate.

"Slut," she said to herself. "Way to be easy."

Rising, Kate paced in a circle before taking the flight of stairs to her office. Her stomach churned and she knew there were some antacids in her desk. Sitting down and pulling open the top drawer, she flipped open the top of the Tums bottle and shook two into her hand. That was when she picked up her cell phone.

When the screen lit up, she saw four missed calls and six text messages, all from David. Her stomach objected again, but she went through the texts.

The texts were predictable—the apology, the plea, the attempt to explain. But it was the last one, the one that went past the "please call me", that made her stop and think.

You can't do this to us. I'm crazy about you. Don't let my stupid mistake wreck everything. Please. I'm sorry.

She stared at what he wrote. Thought about it. Let the idea take hold. His words were desperate. The text was angry.

It meant something. He used the word *us.*

Kate drew in a breath and looked at the message again. Maybe, this was different. Maybe she did matter to him.

Kate thought about it for a minute, thought about the fun they had, how much they cared about each other. She thought about David's behavior when she was in the hospital, how attentive he was, and how sad. And then there were all the things Laura told her.

It was something so basic and logical Kate wondered why she hadn't thought about it before. For someone so smart, she'd been pretty dumb. Why was David still around if she was only about a bet?

Something warm wiggled in Kate's heart, something small that wanted to believe in David and what they had together. Now all she had to do was be brave enough to try.

Chapter 22

I T WAS A beautiful Christmas morning, but Richard came in from the slopes in a foul mood. He'd expected to have some time with his daughter during the holiday, away from his work and away from the pull of her mother, but Marie's screwup ruined his plans.

His fiancée was becoming more and more of a problem. She was making decisions about Laura's education, her relationships, and her clothing. That was *his* job. He was the one who would make the decisions. If he wouldn't let Laura's natural mother be involved in her life, why would Marie think *she* would have any real role in the relationship? She was there for show.

He couldn't stand the fact that he may have lost his daughter. Without warning, she'd decided to stay with her mother for the holidays. They'd obviously connected when Kate had her miscarriage. If only they'd have gotten out of there five minutes sooner. Kate would have missed them and perhaps would have been alone when she lost her kid, doing him the courtesy of bleeding out. Goddamn bitch. She couldn't even die for him.

"Richard?" Marie called. "Darling? Are you waiting for me?"

He cringed. She wanted him to do her, again. It was all she thought about, especially now that she found out Kate had gotten pregnant when she hadn't been able to.

Marie questioned him about Kate's sterility, and he explained it away with some lie. Marie was so gullible, the lies didn't even have to make sense and she believed them. She'd believe anything.

Richard never thought through the consequences of letting his marriage to Kate fail. Inititally, it seemed like Marie would be good for his career. She was a fellow academic, ran in literary circles, and was a published novelist. Granted, both women were writers, but that was where the similarity ended. Aside from her success as an author, Kate had an Ivy League education and breeding, which trumped Marie's bohemian upbringing and academic resumé. He didn't really notice the effect until the holiday season kicked into gear. Two people he considered friends were having their annual holiday parties, and he wasn't invited to either. Finally, he understood the problem. Marie become more social with his friends over the summer and had behaved as she always did: she talked about herself. His friends and their wives, who always loved Kate, didn't like Marie. Or, more sobering, they didn't like him without Kate.

He sat on the edge of the bed and fell backwards when he heard Marie coming up the stairs. He had to think of a plan to get away from her. The more he thought about it, there was nothing remotely appealing about spending the rest of his life with her.

"Look at you! Waiting for me, my love?"

"Not really. I pulled my back on that last run."

He looked up at her face and thought he saw a resemblance to a nasty nun he'd had in grade school. Sister Annunciata. That witch should be guarding the gates of hell by now. He took another look at Marie, with her pursed lips and her bony face, and he realized he was the one in hell.

As she crawled on the bed next to him, Richard's mind flashed back to Kate. His beautiful ex-wife, who was now sleeping with someone else and had Laura at home with her. Richard thought he was so smart, but everything had backfired.

"If your back hurts, I guess I can take care of you this time, just lie still," Marie said flatly. She started to work off his sweater and undo his pants. Richard draped his arm over his eyes and tried to forget about what he'd done to himself.

As Christmases went, it was one of the better ones. Kate had been through hell over the past year, but if she could have one gift, having Laura there with her parents and Trish's family was worth all the heartache. After a crazy Christmas Eve that almost stranded the southern contingent in Atlanta, they stayed up late singing Christmas carols around the piano and baking cookies.

She and Laura still had a long way to go, and Kate was going suggest seeing a counselor to help them over the rough spots. Richard had done damage to both of them, and they needed to heal—together and separately. She wouldn't try to take custody completely, he was her father, but she had to let Laura find her way on her own terms.

As Kate set the ham on the table for dinner, she thought this was as near perfect a moment as they come. Yes, things could be better, but they could also be much worse. For the first time since her husband left, Kate felt like she'd be okay. Her sister and her husband were there with their children. Her parents, still in love after fifty years of marriage, held hands, and Laura hovered protectively, making sure she didn't do too much.

Making one last trip to the kitchen, Trish and Kate stopped and glanced back into the dining room where everyone they cared about was sitting around the table. *Well, almost everyone.*

Kate was missing David in the worst way. It had been two days since Chelsea dropped her bombshell. Two days since Kate found out about the bet.

And there had been two days of texts and voice mails from David begging her to forgive him.

"I like the table better without Richard. More elbow room," Trish joked as she picked up the warm applesauce. But just like numerous distractions the day before, Kate had drifted off and her sister noticed. "Feeling okay?"

"Yeah, sorry." Kate was taking the rolls off the baking tray and dropping them into a basket lined with a crisp linen napkin. "It's been a tough go."

"It's going to get tougher. Getting over him isn't going to be easy." Trish popped a piece of ham from the cutting board into her mouth. "I can't believe he made a bet about sleeping with you."

"I know. I just wish I could shake the feeling that I'm not getting the whole story, you know?"

Trish pressed her hip into the counter. "What do you

mean?"

"The bet thing. I don't know what happened. This is the first I've heard of it. Nothing adds up. And he's sorry. He must have apologized a hundred times by now." She stopped and leveled her eyes at her sister. "He kept coming back for me, Trish. He won the bet, but he kept coming back for me anyway."

Trish considered what she said. "True enough."

"I'm taking everything this unstable, vicious girl said as gospel. Given how I feel about David, shouldn't I listen to what he has to say?"

Taking the basket of rolls from Kate, Trish raised her eyebrows. "Welcome back."

"What do you mean, *welcome back*?"

Shaking her head and smiling, Trish explained, "Let me make the corny analogy as best I can… giving David another chance is like the first time you attempted a triple in competition. There was a good chance you would land on your ass and crawl off the ice humiliated, but the possibility existed that you would stick the jump and win the whole damn thing. I think you said, 'I won't know unless I try.'"

Laura walked into the kitchen right as Kate was going to respond. "What's holding you two up? Everyone is hungry."

Kate bit her lip and looked at Trish, who raised an eyebrow. "I think you know you have to jump, Katie."

Kate handed the pitcher of mulled cider to Laura, then made a beeline to her third floor office. "Start without me. I need to make a call."

STANDING IN THE kitchen on Christmas Day, David felt detached from the activity around him. The kids had pounced at six-thirty in the morning, dragged him downstairs, and now it was barely two o'clock and he felt like he'd been hit by a train. His sister was preparing the turkey for dinner, her husband was cleaning up the remains of some culinary adventure, and his nieces were playing with the new Barbie house he'd given them. Brandon was curled up next to the Christmas tree, asleep in a pile of wrapping paper, exhausted from all the activity. David should have been enjoying the time with his family, but he couldn't think of anything but Kate and how she wouldn't speak to him.

He let out a breath and his sister looked up, almost annoyed he was so distracted. He couldn't blame her. This was supposed to be family time and his mind wasn't in Toronto. When he felt a hand on his shoulder, David turned and saw his father, their coats in hand, motioning toward the front door.

"I need some air," Thomas Burke said. "Come with me."

David hesitated, but stood because he wasn't one to deny his dad's request. It was a gorgeous day—cold, but sunny and crisp. They walked down Rachel's street in silence. His dad waved to neighbors coming back from church or family visits, and looked at the sky with the discerning eye of a man who'd learned to understand the weather. His father had spent years working as a fisherman in Vancouver before meeting David's mother and settling in Alberta. Their footsteps on the sandy pavement were different, one a definite crunch-crunch, the other a slow steady shuffle. They turned into a public park and continued their walk around the man-made lake. When his father finally spoke, his words cut through the cold air like a knife.

"I think your mother would be happy I'm here with Rachel. Eh? What do you think, Dave?"

"I think she'd be relieved you were eating right for a change."

The older man laughed. "That's the truth. She always hounded me about that."

"She wanted you to take care of yourself."

"Too bad she didn't do the same for herself, eh?"

David looked down. Remembering the progression of his mother's cancer was difficult. It was only in the end they learned she'd known about the lump in her breast for over a year before seeking treatment. By then, it was too late. Surgery, chemotherapy, radiation, nothing helped.

"If I'd known, if she'd told me, I'd have taken her to someone. But she didn't think about herself; she only thought about me and you and your sister. Hell, the damn dog got to the vet for a cut paw before your mother got to a hospital."

"I know." David remembered the dog and the time he cut his paw on a piece of broken glass. "Why are we talking about this?"

"Because women are never easy and they're never predictable." Thomas stopped and sat on a bench. "This girl of yours—what's her name?"

"Kate. But she's not mine."

"But you want her to be yours? Is that why you seem like you're a thousand miles from here?"

David sat straight against the back of the bench. "She's been through hell, a lot of it because of me. Maybe she's had enough and I should just leave her alone." His father didn't say anything, keeping his eyes focused on the lake in front of them. "I miss her, though…"

"You love her the same way I loved your mother."

David's head shot up. His father's eyes, no longer focused on the lake, were warm and understanding, just like they'd been when he was a small boy. "I know we've had our problems, son, but I understand better than you think. It hurts way down deep, doesn't it? Like your insides are on fire."

David nodded. "I can't shake it."

"Don't try. When you love a woman like that it never goes away, but it does sound to me that you have some work ahead."

"I don't know what to do."

Thomas found an acorn on the bench that he tossed toward the lake. "If I remember, you did pretty well at that big university you went to. You're a smart man, David. Too smart to give up on something this important."

David hesitated, was going to speak, but stopped himself.

"Fight for her."

"But she said—"

His father waved his hand and cut him off. "I don't care what she said. You never do what a woman says, you do what she wants. The two aren't necessarily the same."

"How can you tell?" Now David was totally confused.

His father shrugged. "Beats me. Sometimes you get lucky. You've got a no brainer here. You love her, make her understand that. She wants you to walk through fire for her. Do it."

David threw his head back and looked at the cover of leafless trees. "I'm scared I'm going to screw it up worse than it is."

The older man laughed and slapped his shoulder. "Fear is part of it. If you aren't scared shitless, what's the point?"

His father stood.

Looking up, David felt small again. "Thanks, Dad."

Nodding, his dad began the walk back toward Rachel's house and David followed.

Walking through the front door was a treat for the senses. The kids were playing, Christmas music was on the stereo, and the house smelled like a mix of pine and good food. He felt better, and he'd never expected a walk with his dad to make him feel better. They'd been at odds for so long, it seemed to become habit. But David was older, and his father had mellowed. Things between them had changed.

He wanted this—the house, the kids, the chaos. The phone rang and blended in with all the noise. He heard his brother-in-law, Ian, speaking to someone. Just as David was about to sit on the floor to put together one of Brandon's toys, Ian waved him over.

"Phone is for you."

"Me?" He couldn't imagine who would call his sister's house directly.

Ian's mouth turned up at the corner. "It's Kate."

SHE HEARD ALL the noise in the background and wished she'd just left a message on his voice mail. No, she had to break out the list he gave her and call his sister's house. Brilliant, just brilliant.

She'd heard another phone and David's voice on the line. "I've got it, Ian. Thanks.

There was a click and a second of silence. "Kate?"

"Hi," she said. "Merry Christmas."

"Merry Christmas."

Now what? What should she say? Her heart was pounding and blood was rushing through her head. *Don't mess up, Kate, don't mess up now.*

"I'm glad you called," he said. "But I thought you didn't want to talk to me."

"I didn't think I did. But, um…" She drew a huge breath. *Here goes, big jump.* "I'm sorry I didn't talk to you the other night. What happened with Chelsea? It wasn't your fault, and I shouldn't have blamed you. And I should have answered your texts, but I had to think and… and… I miss you, David. I miss you."

She thought she heard a sigh of relief creep through the phone. "You shouldn't be apologizing for anything. This is all on me. All of it. I should have told you everything."

"It's okay."

"No, it's not. But I'll be home tomorrow, and we can sort it all out. God, Kate, I'm so sorry."

"When is your flight? I can pick you up."

"Flight comes in at five, but I have a car service coming."

Disappointed, she nodded and squeezed her eyes shut. "Oh, okay."

"I can be to your house by seven. Will that work?"

"That's perfect," she whispered. She couldn't wait to see him, but it seemed only fair to warn him about the crowd. "My family's here, including my parents."

"I'd love to meet them."

"Really?" Kate felt such relief, such happiness, that the worry and sadness of the last few days seemed very far away.

"Yeah. I'm so glad you called."

Kate felt her eyes burn, as her feelings for him broke the surface. She'd promised herself she was never going to fall like this again, but she had, she was all in, and she didn't care. Maybe it wouldn't last, but Kate was tired of being afraid of everything. Fear had never been an option, and it wouldn't be anymore.

"David, I…" There was so much to say, she didn't know where to start. So she let the first thing that came into her head come out. "I don't want to fight this anymore."

"Thank God."

Kate laughed softly. The words they'd exchanged had offered them a place to start and had given her a priceless gift.

"I left everyone at the dinner table," Kate said. "I should go."

"You won't be sorry about this, I promise you that."

"I know. Merry Christmas, David."

"Merry Christmas, babe. I'll be there soon."

After hanging up the phone, Kate leaned back in her desk chair. She could see out the big window in her office to the pond at the edge of her yard. Her heart felt lighter, hopeful. In the chair that had been the location of so much of her crying over the past year, Kate spun herself around and smiled.

WHEN SHE TOOK her place at the dining room table, Trish's husband, Greg, was serving ham. He stopped for a split second and over the top of his glasses, his eyes smiled. Kate was happy and he could see that. Trish, who was sitting to

Kate's left, leaned in.

"Well?" she asked.

"Stuck the landing."

Trish grabbed her hand under the table and gave it a gentle squeeze before returning her attention to the dinner; Kate, however, found herself wishing the dining room chairs could spin.

Chapter 23

RICHARD PARKED THE Mercedes in the driveway behind Kate's car and knew he was going to have company to deal with, specifically Kate's family—the family that wanted his head on a platter. He didn't consider he'd have to deal with them. He'd come to see Laura and try to finesse Kate a little, maybe mend some fences. He'd cut his ski vacation short and told Marie exactly where he was going.

She wasn't happy and wanted to come with him, feeling she had as much right to see Laura as he did. That lasted about thirty seconds. Their plan to move Laura out completely backfired because of her screw-up, and he was going to limit their contact as much as possible.

He thought about going in the side door, like he always did when he lived there, but decided to honor the formality of their situation and made his way around the front of the house to the porch. He braced himself and rang the bell.

He heard very rapid footsteps that he guessed were Kate's. She started speaking as she pulled on the door.

"You're early! I'm so happy to see—"

She stopped talking as soon as she saw him standing there

and her face which had been excited, dropped.

"Richard. What are you doing here?"

"Merry Christmas, Kate. I was hoping to visit Laura, and you, of course, especially since you're happy to see me." He smiled, hoping it would ease the tension in her stance, but she didn't budge.

"Happy to see you? No. You're supposed to be skiing in Vermont."

"We came home early. I missed Laura, and I wanted to see how you were doing. You gave everyone a scare."

"Is that so?" Kate leaned against the door jamb, and her expression was anything but welcoming. She looked gorgeous, though. She was wearing a soft pink sweater with a plunging neckline and her breasts swelled when she folded her arms. He told himself it was because of the cold, but she was also taking a defensive stance. The sexy cleavage was a nice side effect.

It was still civil until he heard Trish's shrill voice come from the far side of the foyer. "I knew I smelled something." Trish approached and stood next to her sister. They were a formidable pair, to say the least. "How are you, Richard?"

"Always a pleasure, Trish. Turn anyone to stone today?" He shifted his position and folded his hands in front of him.

Kate rolled her eyes as the two of them readied for another jab. "Richard, this isn't a good time."

"Ladies, I understand you may not care for me. However, I would like to see Laura. It'll be a short visit."

It was then that he noticed Kate's eyes locked on the headlights coming up the driveway. The large SUV parked, and a soft smile teased her lips. Richard hadn't seen the bloom that came into her cheeks since she was eighteen.

The temperature went up by degrees. Kate kept her wits

about herself enough to look at Trish and ask her to get Laura from her room.

She barely acknowledged Richard as the occupant of the truck emerged. "Visit with her in the library," was the last thing she said to him.

Richard watched his ex-wife walk past him, off the stoop, and down the walk. She stopped, wrapped her arms around her, this time to ward off the chill, and waited. The look on her face was pure adoration. It made Richard sick, because she'd never looked at him that way.

As the man moved toward her, Richard thought he looked familiar. He was big, dark-haired, and young. Approaching Kate, he placed a bag, which looked to be filled with gifts, on the walk. Then he reached for her and Kate walked into his arms.

It was enough. Richard didn't need to see anymore.

THIS WAS HOME. Kate slipped her arms under his coat and held him tight, feeling his strong back and laying her face on his hard chest. At the same time, David's arms came around her and his lips pressed gently into her temple.

The worry, the anxiety, the sadness all slipped away when he was with her. She was safe with David. All her doubts were gone, and all that was left was faith. Faith in him, faith in herself.

"I missed you," she whispered.

"I missed you, too. I felt like the world collapsed when you wouldn't talk to me." David tilted her face toward his and dropped a kiss on her lips. "I am so sorry for everything."

"It doesn't matter anymore."

"Yes it does. We'll fix it." He kissed her again, and again. More kisses. "I love you. Only you."

Kate held him tighter and reveled in the secure feeling of his arms. David loved her. This was right. Nothing had ever felt so right.

Coming back to reality, he led her into the house, out of the cold. She took his coat and watched his face grow serious when he saw Laura and her father in the library.

"Richard?" he asked. "Why is he here?"

"They came back early from their ski trip. He stopped over to see her." She saw the disapproval on David's face. "She's still his daughter. I know he wasn't expected, but I can't say no."

He nodded, and then took her hand and brought it to his lips. "It's more than he deserves."

"I know, but I won't do to him what he did to me. Laura's upset enough."

"She doesn't look happy," he said.

"I know, but she'll forgive him. Eventually."

"You're amazing." David grinned. "So, time to meet the parents?"

"And the sister, brother-in-law, niece, and nephew."

"Ouch. I didn't bring body armor."

"You'll be okay." Kate smoothed his sweater and picked a small thread off his shoulder. "My mother can be a little uptight sometimes."

"Okay."

"My dad should go easy on you since you both went to B-C."

"I'll take what I can get." He smiled and leaned in for one

last kiss. Then another, before catching her eyes with his.

"Thank you for doing this." Her hand came up and stroked his face, leaving no doubt of how she felt. Whatever happened in the past, whatever she believed about him was gone now, replaced with the feeling coming from deep within him. She had his heart. It was hers, and at that moment, everything seemed possible. "They're going to love you. Maybe not right away, but they will."

He laughed. "Let's do this."

RICHARD WAS IN the uncomfortable position of trying to have a conversation with his daughter. Laura was more guarded than ever before, and not the least bit interested anything he had to say. He tried to keep it light, asking her about the holidays, when he made the mistake of asking a question about Kate's caveman.

"So what do you know about Mom's guy?"

"Fishing for information, Daddy?" Laura folded her arms defensively.

"No, just curious. He looks familiar."

"He plays for the Flyers.

Richard leaned forward, more jealous than ever. "Excuse me?"

"It's David Burke."

Richard slumped back in the wing back chair he'd been sitting in, stunned into silence. That changed things. He had many assets, but Richard, at nearly fifty years old, was not going to be able to compete with a pro athlete. "How in the world... that's who got her pregnant?"

Laura looked away and bit her lower lip. She was shutting down, and cutting off his information pipeline. He'd deal with that, somehow, but it was her distance that most concerned him. At first she didn't want to see him at all, telling Trish to send him away. But he had to give Kate's sister credit. She got Laura to talk to him. His goal was to get her to agree to come and stay with him for a few days.

Their relationship had imploded, and he didn't know if he was ever going to get her back completely. He wanted to think he would, but she was defensive and very protective of her mother. He'd made the mistake of underestimating not only his ex-wife, but his daughter.

Laura was his world. Regaining her trust was the most important thing, but he didn't know how he was going to do it.

KATE'S FAMILY WAS gathered in the great room, watching a movie on TV. The tree sparkled in the corner and he remembered the night they'd decorated it. David held onto the memory to fend off the nerves balling in his stomach. He was as scared as he'd ever been. He knew how important these people were to her, and he wanted them to accept him.

All heads turned when he stepped in the room with her. Time seemed to stop; no one moved, no one seemed to breathe.

Finally, Kate's father rose and approached him. He was a strong, solid man, maybe five-ten, and completely confident. A retired judge, he carried himself with the dignity of someone who didn't need to worry about first impressions.

"Katherine, please introduce me to your young man."

Kate smiled like a sixteen-year-old girl, making David think she'd been through the ritual countless times. He straightened himself. These were her people, the ones who mattered to her, so David wanted to make a good impression. "Daddy, may I introduce David Burke; David, my father, Jonathan Adams."

They shook hands as Kate's father sized him up. David knew he had one chance to get in good with Dad, so he took everything Kate told him about her father and used it.

"Judge Adams, it's a pleasure. You're B-C class of '56, correct?"

The smile that crossed her father's face was exactly what he was going for. Common ground. Common ground broke down a lot of barriers. Pleasantries exchanged, David looked around at everyone else. It should be easier now. At least David thought so, until he looked at Kate's mother.

She was sitting across the room in a large leather club chair. The woman was attractive, really just an older version of Kate. Her arms and legs were crossed and her foot was moving up and down frantically, but it was her face, a combination of disgust and concern that put David on alert. Nope, her mom didn't like him at all. *Great.*

David looked at Kate, who'd noticed the same thing. She took a quick glance at her mother and then back at him. This wasn't going to go well. Kate introduced him to her sister and brother-in-law, her niece and nephew. Fine, maybe a little suspect, but nothing like the chill coming off Mom. Kate walked him over to her mother and slipped her hand into his.

"David, my mother, Melinda Adams."

"Mrs. Adams, it's nice to meet you." He offered his hand

and she didn't budge.

She kept her arms folded, looked at his outstretched hand, and drilled him with eyes so full of anger that David almost took a step back.

The final slap came when she rose and walked away without saying a word.

David exhaled audibly. "Wow."

Kate turned to him. "I'm sorry about that. I don't know what's gotten into her."

David shrugged, not able to respond, but Kate's niece shed some light on the subject. "Grandma doesn't think you're good for Aunt Kate. She thinks you're a player."

Everyone turned in her direction and Trish cocked her head to one side, not quite believing what she heard. "Your *grandmother* called David a player?"

Alex ignored her mother's question. "I Googled you," she said to David. "You're not exactly model boyfriend material."

"Alexandra?" Trish began, "What did you tell your grandmother?"

"Nothing, she does know how to use the internet and she *can* read." Alex rose, annoyed, and went to the stairs. "I'll go talk to Grandma."

The air was tense, and Kate decided to let her mother sit and stew for now.

Laying a hand on David's arm, she smiled. "I'm going to make coffee."

Trish followed. "I'll help you."

That left David with Kate's father, the former judge, her brother-in-law, the congressman, and her nephew, the med school student. Were there no plumbers in this family? Jeez.

Jonathan snorted. "Coffee, great. The way Melinda's

going to go at me, I'm going to need something stronger than coffee."

Greg Reed laughed and looked at David. "Melinda can be a bit overprotective," he drawled. "I was going to pick up something to enhance our coffee, but I forgot. I'm regretting it."

David laughed. "I brought a twenty-one-year-old Glenlivet with me. Will that help?"

Greg slapped him on the back as David made his way to the other end of the sofa, and Jonathan nodded approval.

"I knew I liked you." Jonathan paused. "I hope you'll forgive my wife."

Greg continued for him. "Adores her girls, and who can blame her?"

"Not me," David said. "But she looked at me like I was Jack the Ripper."

Greg sat back and rubbed the five o'clock shadow on his chin. "Did Kate tell you about her marriage?"

"Some. Her ex sounds like a first class pri…" He censored himself. "First class jerk. Domineering, controlling." David was painfully aware that Richard was two rooms away.

"Abusive," Greg added. The word hit David like a stick to the head. "He'd hit her from time to time, enough to make her afraid, to get her to buckle under. Words were his preferred weapon."

"I'd kick his ass if I could get him alone for five minutes," David growled, feeling violence overtake his reason.

"Trish almost did. She caught him on one of his tirades. I swear she was looking for a sharp object. The things he said to Kate were horrible. She spent some time in therapy. I can tell you, when he left, the whole family cheered. Kate was terrified about losing Laura, but Richard leaving was the best thing that ever happened to her."

"Why did she stay?" David couldn't understand how Kate would put up with that kind of treatment.

"It's hard to let go of all those years. She adored him once, but mostly she stayed because of Laura. One of Richard's favorite threats was that he would take Laura so far away, Kate would never see her again."

"I can only imagine how that affected her."

Greg nodded. "Staying in Laura's life was all that counted. As long as they were still in the same house, she had a chance. So Kate put up with him a lot longer than she should have."

"Shit," David muttered.

"Now he has Marie doing his dirty work on that front, playing *Mommy*," Jonathan added.

"She doesn't sound too stable," David said. "I can't believe the crap they've been trying to pull with Laura, but it seems things are improving there, too." He looked at Kate's father, who'd gone silent.

It obviously pained him that he couldn't do anything to protect his daughter.

"Nothing surprises me with Richard," Greg said. "He thinks rules are for everyone but him. The guy's a pretentious ass. He affects this Kennedyesque persona, but he couldn't support the family if he wanted to. He's tenured, but he hasn't made full professor, and his research is nothing that's going to rock the scientific world. He treated Kate like she was the handmaid."

"You'd think a guy with a PhD would know better."

"That PhD don't mean he ain't bad." Greg slipped into a

heavy Southern drawl and slipped out just as fast.

"I can understand why everyone is so concerned. Here I am, pro athlete, bad reputation..."

"None of us want Kate to go through that kind of ordeal again, that's all." Greg leaned forward and faced him. "She's been through enough. And as much as she tries to control her emotions, that woman does nothing halfway. I'm resident big brother. I'd have to beat y'all up if you hurt her."

David smiled at Greg, who was a full head shorter and probably fifty pounds lighter. "And you're all worried my intentions aren't honorable?"

"Yes, I suppose so. Are your intentions honorable?"

"She's very important to me. I won't hurt her."

David looked toward the kitchen, where he could see Kate and Trish fussing over the cookies and pastries. The TV was covering their voices, but they were deep in conversation. He'd never hurt her, and neither would anyone else.

"David?" Jonathan was now looking at him, serious and concerned. "That son of a bitch took my Katie from me. She didn't let us help and he destroyed her. She seems more herself, lately. If you have any part in that, I'm grateful."

David didn't know if he was responsible for Kate's 'recovery', but his goal was to make her happy. That was all. He wanted her happy. Alone now in the kitchen, David saw her swaying to the music playing in the background. Then suddenly, she stopped what she was doing, everything about her went rigid, and David saw Richard approach her.

Jonathan stood and Greg went on alert. Kate's whole demeanor changed. Her head dropped, her shoulders sagged. She wouldn't make eye contact with her ex-husband. He was speaking to her, but David couldn't hear what the son of a bitch was saying.

"That's my cue." He rose and, while her father and brother-in-law watched, he walked to her side. It had taken him a while to get here, but this is where he belonged.

~

DAVID'S HAND SETTLED on her back and Kate immediately relaxed. Richard, on the other hand, stiffened.

"Do you need a hand with anything?" David asked.

Looking up into his strong face, she saw why he was there and silently thanked him. David locked Richard in his sights and extended his hand.

"David Burke."

Richard pursed his narrow lips and responded. "Richard Nicholls."

"You're leaving?" David said as he popped a piece of cookie in his mouth. He turned to Kate and smiled, then looked back at Richard.

"I was hoping Laura would come back with me. I haven't seen her in over a week."

"What did Laura say?" Kate asked.

"That she wanted to stay here. She'd come to see us for the New Year."

"Then it's settled," David said. "You have a coat?"

Kate suppressed a laugh. David was being positively obnoxious, and Richard was going to lose his temper—which, she guessed, was what David was going for.

Tilting his head in her direction, she could see Richard was seriously pissed off. "Can't fight your own battles, Kate? You had to sic your pit bull on me?"

David moved toward Richard, quietly, and stood toe-to-toe with him. The contrast was striking. Richard looked small, arrogant, and for once, intimidated. But David, he looked like a man who was protecting someone he loved. He didn't do anything drastic, hadn't made any grand gestures, but he stood with her. That simple act reassured Kate once again.

David didn't address Richard's comment, but motioned toward the kitchen door. Her father and Greg stood by and smiled as her boyfriend escorted her ex-husband out of the house.

RICHARD NICHOLLS WAS easy to hate. He walked slightly ahead of David, toward the sporty little Mercedes, and was pulling on his gloves when he finally spoke.

"If you think you are going to keep me out of Laura's life because you're fucking my ex-wife, you are sorely mistaken." Richard stopped at the car and turned to face him.

He was one arrogant prick—haughty, pretentious, but at the same time, clueless. Stupidly, he wasn't backing down. "I mean, Kate's lovely, I certainly wouldn't mind having at her again. I don't doubt you and she are quite hot and heavy, but it doesn't give you any standing."

The move was so fast Richard couldn't even take a breath. David had him against the hood of the Mercedes, his forearm pressing against Richard's windpipe. His ice-blue eyes bulged, full of terror, and David applied just enough pressure so Richard couldn't make a sound.

When David spoke, his voice was nothing more than a

low growl. "You listen to me, motherfucker. You will stay away from Kate. You don't touch her, or I will beat you to a bloody pulp. As far as Laura is concerned, she knows what you are. She makes the decisions about where she's going to stay. Not you, and not that crazy bitch you live with. Are you getting this?"

Richard nodded, and David was happy they were establishing some boundaries. "You have intimidated Kate for the last time. I'm here now, and if you think you are going to heap the same kind of shit on her now that you have for the past twenty years, I will kick your ass from here to the tundra. Now get in your goddamn car and leave, and before you come back to this house, you ask permission."

Letting go, David heard Richard gasping for air, coughing and wheezing. "You should be arrested."

Before turning to go back in the house, David pointed at him. "Same goes, pal. Now get lost."

⁓

DAVID ENTERED THE house and stopped quickly when he came face-to-face with Kate's mother. Melinda Adams had tears in her eyes and a look on her face that David couldn't read. When she tossed her arms around him, David was caught completely by surprise. The woman wanted his head less than half an hour ago, and now she had him in an affectionate hug.

"Thank you," she choked out. "Thank you for protecting her."

He eased her away but kept his hands on her upper arms. Tears hung at the corners of Mrs. Adams' eyes, and at that moment, he became completely aware of how bad Kate's marriage had been. The face before him was one of an anguished mother, one who didn't want to see her child hurt.

"I'll take care of her. Don't worry," he said softly as she hugged him again. "Don't worry."

TWO HOURS LATER, Kate, her sister, her mother, her daughter, and her niece sat around the kitchen island with glasses of milk, and a tray of brownies that needed to be eaten. They didn't cut the sweet treat, but dug in with forks.

"So, Aunt Kate," Alex said, "How did you manage to land yourself a guy like that?"

Laura snorted, then giggled. "She picked him up in a bar."

Trish and Alex squealed and her mother dropped her head in her hands.

"Hey!" Kate objected. "That's not what happened." She took a sip of her milk. "He picked *me* up in a bar."

"Dear God," her mother said quietly. Everyone laughed. And laughter was always good.

"He's something though," Trish said. "Gorgeous, smart, totally devoted, rich…"

"Protective," Mom said.

"Protective?" Kate repeated, curious about her mother's comment. "Mom?"

Melinda Adams wasn't easily impressed, but something in her mother's voice told her David had managed to do just that. "He and Richard had a little chat outside. I heard the words 'beat you to a bloody pulp', but not much else. Richard didn't say anything because he couldn't breathe."

Kate felt her mouth drop open. "David had him by the throat?"

Mom nodded and took another stab at the brownies. "Had Richard pinned on the hood of that Mercedes you gave him last Christmas. I was trying to figure out where we could hide the body in the event David killed him." Nobody spoke and when Mom looked up she saw everyone's eyes on her. "What? I was just being practical."

Kate stood and gave her mother a hug.

Mom patted her arm and smiled. "He's a keeper, even if he is too young for you." After a moment, her mom's hand gently grazed over the beautiful necklace David had given her before he left. "That pendant is a work of art; it suits you."

The moment between Kate and her mother was quick and quiet, but Kate felt her approval like a warm embrace, and that meant the world to her.

"So, Mom," Laura said, smiling. "I hear you need to get your skates sharpened?"

Kate nodded and thought about the upcoming date night. David had invited the whole family to go skating at Penn's Landing the day after tomorrow. All the people made it less of a date, and more of an outing, but it made her happy. He made her happy. It was shaping up to be a much different Christmas than the one before.

"I can't believe Travis and I are leaving. I've never seen you on the ice, Aunt Kate."

Laura elbowed her cousin. "YouTube."

"I can't remember the last time I was on skates. I'm sure I'm pretty rusty." Kate grimaced as she thought about how many times she might end up on her ass. "I miss it, though."

"You took me skating when I was eight. Me and Tracy. You were beautiful when you skated." Laura smiled and Kate remembered the day. It was a good memory. "You and Dad had a fight after. I remember that, too."

That would make sense. Richard didn't want any part of her old life to touch Laura. Kate thought about it, mentally slapped herself for allowing him to manipulate her, and beamed at her daughter. "You know what? I don't want to talk about him anymore. I'm done with it."

Trish raised her glass of milk in a toast. "To moving on."

Kate clinked her glass against her sister's and took a sip, moving on.

Chapter 24

DAVID WATCHED KATE'S eyes as they pulled up to the ice rink. The outdoor facility was right on the Delaware River, with the Ben Franklin Bridge in the background, and planning a date here was probably the most sentimental thing he could have done. Her parents, sister, and daughter all passed on his invitation, which was nice, but not necessary. So it was only the two of them, and Annie and Jay, who he'd called that afternoon.

When they stopped the car, Kate noticed the sign that said it was closed for a private event and shot him a look.

"You got them to close the rink? Why?"

"If it was too crowded, we'd be worried about stepping on little kids and dodging crazy teenagers."

"We're all alone here?"

"Jay is coming with Annie. I want you to meet them. And Cam said he may come by because he's been dying to meet you since California. But he didn't know if he would make it."

She smiled because she knew they were like his family. He parked and grabbed their skates when they left the car. "I asked Julie to come."

"Really?"

"She can't, but she's going to want to meet you, too."

He smiled. He was glad Julie was willing to give him another chance. Especially since she blamed him for Kate's run-in with Chelsea.

"Thank you for getting my skates sharpened," she said.

He'd gotten the equipment manager to do it for him. It wasn't a big deal, but he liked doing things for her, liked making her life easier. It had been ten days since the miscarriage, and physically she was almost fully recovered. But, over the past couple of days there were times he could see she was thinking about the baby. He'd catch her daydreaming and touching her stomach. It made him feel guilty because he hadn't been there to help her heal. The grief hit him as he thought how beautiful she would have been carrying their child. Maybe someday it would happen for them. But right now, he was happy to have her in his life.

Kate didn't want to talk about what Chelsea had done, but Laura filled him in before she went to her stay with her dad. Even though he couldn't control his ex, he felt like he was responsible somehow. David was happy to hear that Kate had told the bitch where to go, and had gotten a restraining order, but it shouldn't have been something she had to deal with at all. Someday he'd tell Chelsea what he thought of her, and what he had to say would make Kate's words seem tame in comparison.

He glanced over at her and took in what he saw. She didn't ever wear a lot of makeup, and tonight she had her hair long and loose. A soft white headband kept her ears warm and her hair out of her face. She wore a white sweater, a pink jacket, and black skating pants. It always amazed him how she could wear the simplest, most basic things, and look more beautiful than women half her age who were decked out in the fanciest clothes. When she finished lacing up her skates, Kate looked up, leaned in, and kissed him gently on the lips. That was when the whole 'inner beauty' thing made sense to him.

A Christmas melody was playing over the loud speaker, and Kate smiled as she stepped onto the ice. It was flurrying, and she glided like she'd never been off skates. He stood by the boards, watching her skate alone in the rink. The first movements were basic—forwards and backwards, easy, graceful turns, almost like she was floating across the frozen surface.

Annie and Jay came up beside him, skates in hand, and took in the scene. The tempo of the music changed as Kate picked up speed, throwing in little twizzles and turns. He knew she wouldn't be doing anything like the jumps that almost got her to the Olympics, but from what he could see, the years hadn't affected her skills all that much.

She did land an elementary jump and based on her smile, she was pretty proud of herself.

"Wow," Annie said. "She's incredible. I'm going to look like a spaz out there with you three."

Jay smiled. "That's why we bring you along. You're fun to watch." His smile dropped away when his wife punched him in the shoulder.

Carol of the Bells started to play, and Kate skated to the music in perfect time. Her moves were fast, sharp, and dynamic. David could see every step, every spin, came straight from her heart. Against the dark sky, with the lights of the bridge in the background, he was genuinely moved. He'd seen skaters before, girls who practiced until their feet bled, and none had her inborn grace or ability. This wasn't just a sport to her; it wasn't just something to win. It was her soul, and now she had it back. When the song ended, she came to where he was standing and threw her arms around him.

"Thank you for this. It's amazing." Kate stood on her toes and kissed him. Seeing her so happy was all the thanks he needed.

"Come here for a second." He led her to the side of the rink and introduced her to his friends as Jay was pushing Annie onto the ice.

"Don't be a baby, Annie," Jay said. "Nice to meet you, Kate. Don't mind her."

"I'm going to fall!" Annie clung to the side of the rink and her eyes pleaded with Kate for help.

Just as Kate extended a hand, David pulled her away and held her hand as they skated around the ice.

"David, we should help her."

"She always starts out this way and gets going pretty quickly. Don't worry."

Jay called out to him across the rink. "Padre? Wanna bet on how many times she lands on her ass?"

David smirked and shook his head. Poor Annie. If he didn't know that they would be wrapped around each other and cooing like teenagers in a few minutes, he'd feel bad. Kate was the one who sobered him up.

"Do you guys bet on *everything*?" When he looked down at her, Kate's eyes were narrow and she was glaring.

"Damn, I thought I'd dodged that bullet." There was a smile tugging at her lips, so he knew he wasn't really in trouble, but he did have to explain. "The answer is probably yes. We do. And I'm not sorry I took that bet involving you."

"What was the bet? I mean, I know what Chelsea said, but tell me the truth. You had to get me to say yes to dinner or a drink?"

"No, I had to get you into bed. Which, I did." He smiled because the shock on her face was priceless, but he knew it was time to tell her the whole story. "Everyone assumed that something happened between us because I was out all night, but I never said anything. On our next road trip, I paid up and took everyone out for a very expensive steak dinner and drinks."

"Really? You didn't have to lie."

"I didn't. But after we'd been together and I realized how much I liked you, I just felt…" He hesitated, and squeezed her hand.

"What?"

"What happened between us was private. It wasn't anyone else's business."

Taking advantage of the waltz, David turned and faced her, sweeping her into a slow dance on the ice.

"Thank you for that," she whispered.

"Don't thank me. You make me a better man, Kate. I should be thanking you." His mouth grazed over her cheek and Kate's breath shuddered, almost like she was going to cry.

But then she seemed to regain her control and gazed into his eyes. "I should be furious, but the truth is I wouldn't be this happy without that stupid bet. So I don't care why you approached me, I'm just glad you did." She reached up and stroked his cheek. "I love you, David."

Those words were magic. For the first time in his life, he

knew what it felt like to be lost to someone. He kissed her again, softly, slowly, and held her close as they moved through the cold air. Kate looked up and smiled. "This song," she said. "Do you remember?"

He grinned at the memory. "Santa Monica. It was playing at that bar on the beach we walked past."

David remembered everything about that night; because it was the first moment his heart started beating for someone else.

ANNIE HAD CAUGHT her stride; she and Jay held hands and circled the rink while Kate and David danced. He took the opportunity to give her a little twirl and impress the people who'd stopped as they walked by the rink to watch them skate. Not content to keep it simple, she arched her back and lifted one of her legs into a graceful extension.

"Show off," he whispered. He propelled them along while she balanced on one skate. Two people pointed, one of them taking pictures with a cell phone, and he figured he and Jay might have been recognized. David didn't care.

Kate noticed too. "I'm surprised you didn't find a rink that was more private. We have a bit of an audience."

"Whatever. I hope the pictures that one guy took end up on the front page of the newspaper."

Kate smiled, closed her eyes, and laid her head on his chest, trusting him to guide her around the ice.

She loved him. David thought about all the women he'd dated, including Chelsea, who supposedly wanted to marry him. No one had ever said the words to him. No one was willing to take the chance until Kate.

The music changed to something upbeat and quick. Kate wiggled away from him, and skating backwards, issued the challenge. "Think you can catch me, Burke?"

He kicked up his speed when she zipped away and knew his long stride alone would overtake her, but she was weaving in and out. He slowed simply so he could watch her move.

Sadness always hung in the background with Kate. She'd put on her best face, but as David got to know her, he could see the shadow behind her eyes. However, now, with her arms extended over her head, Kate looked like she was praying to the winter goddess. The ice, the snow, and the cold awakened her sleeping spirit. David caught her, spun her around, and in her eyes all he saw was joy.

LAURA HATED THAT she'd gone right back to lying to her mom, but she didn't see any other way if she was going to spend the night with Jack. She said she wanted to try to make things better with Dad. That wasn't a complete lie. She hated all the crap her father pulled, but he did love her, and that had to count for something, right? Her mom didn't like that she came back here, but she understood. At least Mom understood.

Her father had promised not to pump her for information about Mom, and she guessed after the conversation David had with him, Dad would be on his best behavior. She'd been a Flyers fan for as long as she could remember and she'd rarely seen David fight; but when he did, his opponent left the game bloody. There was no way her tweed-wearing, Pilates-toned father was going to match up against one of the NHL's biggest forwards. Mom had nothing to worry about.

And Mom was so happy. Since she'd decided to let her guard down, everything with David had fallen into place. He'd hit it off with the whole family, and Laura had to admit she really liked him. He treated her with respect and he expected the same from her.

Right before David left her house the other night, he'd found her fiddling at the piano in the library. The family was still in the den, but her father had done a pretty good job of making her feel detached from all of them. Even though Mom, her grandparents, and Aunt Trish and Uncle Greg kept trying to get her to interact, she felt guilty for all the years she treated them so badly. Especially Aunt Trish, she'd been horrible to her.

David found her on the verge of tears while she was thinking about her family and Jack. He surprised her when he put the little gift bag on the bench next to her and smiled. He'd gotten her a gift. She felt her face flush when she pulled the little blue box from Tiffany's out of the tissue paper. In the box was the prettiest necklace she'd ever seen. It was a perfect, square sapphire, her birthstone, hanging from a delicate white gold chain. It was beautiful, and she still smiled when she saw it hanging around her neck.

She'd told her dad if he wanted to see her, she wanted to spend the night at Tracy's on New Year's Eve, not go to some dumb party at one of their friend's houses. He agreed, without too much thought. She guessed he figured it was an easy compromise. After they left, Jack was going to pick her up, they would go to a party with his friends, and then she would spend the night with him.

It had been a long week. She and Jack had only talked a few times, and hadn't seen each other at all because she was with her mother. She'd been happy during the week at Mom's, and she faced so many of Dad's lies straight on, but God, she missed Jack. The day after tomorrow would come soon enough, and everything would be better, for a little while at least.

Dad and Marie were out to dinner. He said they had some things to discuss that they didn't think Laura needed to hear. Things had definitely gone south with them since Mom's miscarriage. Marie was probably questioning Dad about why she wasn't getting pregnant, and Dad was still probably pissed at the way Marie handled everything.

She had one fucked up family. Dad was busy all the time trying to resurrect his latest research project and Marie was trying to write a book. Apparently she was struggling with the first two pages because they had to be "just right" before she moved forward. Mom had gotten on a roll one day with her writing and came out of her office with fifty new pages written. She said it needed some work, but she couldn't fix a blank page. She was amazingly disciplined, and Marie was an amazing mess.

Laura liked books and would read pretty much anything she could get her hands on. She didn't pay attention to labels, because she knew what she liked. According to her father, Marie's books were art; but after sitting down one day and attempting to read one, she knew they were crap. Laura had read really good literary fiction, and Marie's book wasn't even close. When she picked up one of her mother's novels the other night, Laura was up until three in the morning reading—it was awesome.

The sound of a car door closing brought her back, and she looked outside to see Jack coming up the driveway. Her heart flipped over when she saw him. She raced down the stairs, flung the door open, and jumped into his arms as he stepped on the porch.

Laura clung to him, her arms wrapped around his neck. He grabbed her around the waist, lifted her, and kicked the door shut with his foot as he carried her into the house. He didn't put her down, but kissed her thoroughly before tilting his head back and looking into her eyes.

Jack smiled. "I guess you're happy to see me."

Laura held him close, it was all she wanted right then. Their whole relationship was based on lies, but the only time she felt safe was when she was with him. But he must have sensed something, because he pulled back and set her down. She held on, not wanting to let go, loving how he felt against her.

"What's wrong?" Taking her hands, he led her into the living room and held her when she snuggled next to him.

"Nothing. I missed you."

"Are you sure? Worried about staying with me?"

She shook her head. "No, that's the only thing I'm not worried about."

"Where are your folks?"

"Out. Probably discussing whether or not they're going to stay together."

"I think you should ditch your crazy family and live with me." He rubbed her arm and kissed the top of her head.

Laura felt a weight crush down on her chest. He wanted her, he really did, and pretty soon he would hate her. A tear ran down her cheek and she wished she had someone to talk to about this, but there was no one.

Jack hugged her when he saw her tears. He must have thought she was the crazy one, always so emotional. She tried to be happier, but she was so worried about what was going to happen when everyone found out.

"I didn't mean to upset you." He kissed her forehead and kept hold of her. "You know," he said, glancing at the piano, "you promised to play for me."

Laura nodded. "I did."

"Will you now?"

At least it would distract her. She wiped her eyes and went to the piano. Jack moved and sat on the end of the couch closest to her and waited. Laura decided on Canon in D, her favorite piece. She was preparing a variation for a recital, so it was something she'd want him to hear, something she was proud of.

The first notes filled the room and her mind went blank. She played her heart out for him and for herself, losing herself in the music. The arrangement she played was exhausting and when she was done nearly five minutes after first touching the keys, she was perspiring. Looking to her right, Jack sat stunned.

"Christ almighty," he whispered. "That was amazing."

"Thank you. I've been working on that piece for a while."

Jack fell into silence. He looked at her, then at his hands, then back at her. Something in his movements told her he had something to say.

"I don't understand." He shook his head and walked to the fireplace. He was truly confused and Laura didn't know why.

"What don't you understand?" She stood and took a step toward him, afraid to go any closer.

"I had no idea. I—" Jack came to her, his long stride covering the space between them effortlessly. He took her hands and his eyes examined them like they were precious objects. "Why the hell do you want to be with a farm boy like me?"

The warmth spread through her, something sure and steady, something real. Even standing on her tiptoes, she could barely touch her lips to his. Jack dipped his head and received her soft kiss. This was it, she could tell him, so at least when it all fell apart he'd know what she felt. Time to jump, as her mother would say.

"I want to be with you because," Laura swallowed and looked into his eyes, "Because I love you."

There was no response at first. Jack stood there, still holding her hands, still examining her eyes, her face. Slowly, he exhaled. She hadn't realized he was holding his breath, but then she saw a smile and relief.

His hands came to her face, he cupped her cheeks in his hands, and touched his forehead to hers. "I love you, too. The last two weeks have been hell without you."

Laura felt her eyes fill with tears, which spilled over onto her cheeks. "This wasn't supposed to happen."

Gently, his fingers wiped her tears. "I know, you weren't supposed to happen to me now, either." He kissed her cheek. "Please don't cry, Laura."

That didn't help, she just cried harder. He held her close and tried to calm her down, not understanding why she was so sad. "Jack, promise me something?"

"Anything."

"Promise me you will always remember that I love you, no matter what happens."

"I promise," he whispered. "I promise."

Chapter 25

KATE WALKED INTO David's bedroom and dropped her purse on the chair. He brought her small bag into the room and put it next to her purse, then hung her dress in the closet. The room was the same as the last time she was in it, but so much had happened since. He came up behind her, slipped his arms around her, kissed her neck, and she wished she could make love with him.

Unfortunately, the doctor wanted her to wait one more week, and then she said everything should be just about back to normal. Unfortunately, waiting was killing her; she could only imagine what it was doing to him.

"You need to stop torturing yourself."

"I know." He groaned and turned her in his arms. "When you're ready."

Her arms instinctively looped around his neck and dragged him into a messy kiss. "So what are the plans for tonight?"

"Let's see." He sat on the bed and pulled her onto his lap. "Jay and Annie are coming here first for drinks. Then we have reservations at seven-thirty at Dante's, and after that, it's up to you. There is a party going on that one of my teammates is throwing at his house, or we could come back here and ring in the New Year on our own. I have champagne in the fridge."

"Your friend's having a party? Do you want to go?"

"If you want to go."

He had to learn this relationship was a two-way street. "David, that's not what I asked you. Do *you* want to go?"

He hesitated and then answered. "Yes. For two reasons."

"Listening." Kate loved how he tried to make everything about her, but that had to stop or he'd start resenting her.

"First, I want you to meet my friends. I want to show you off." She couldn't help the smile that pulled across her face. "And the other reason has to do with the rookie who's my roommate."

"Jack Nelson, right?"

"Yeah. He's gotten involved with some girl. She's a student at Penn, but she lives with her parents and it's not a good situation. Nothing sounds right."

"You want to check her out, make sure she's treating him okay?" Kate rested her head on his shoulder.

"I guess." David thought for a minute and realized he sounded like an old woman and ran a hand over his face. "He's so naïve. He jumped right to the NHL after his third year at University of North Dakota. He's just twenty-one, and grew up on a farm in a small town with a population of like two hundred."

"So says the boy from the middle of nowhere." Kate felt she had the right to tease. Most of her life, the furthest she'd ever lived from a city was about forty miles.

"Maybe so, but I left the 'middle of nowhere' and went to

school in Boston. Grand Forks, North Dakota, isn't exactly a big city."

"I get your point." Lacing her fingers with his, Kate drew his hands to her lips. "Then we'll go. For both reasons."

"You don't mind?"

"No. It matters to you, so it matters to me. And honestly, now you have me curious."

"He is totally in love with this girl, Kate. He said she's the most amazing person he's ever met."

"And that worries you because?"

"He came from a town of two hundred. His experience with people is fairly limited."

Each day she learned something else about David. Today was that his instincts to protect people ran deep. He obviously saw Jack as a younger brother, and felt a responsibility to him as the team captain and as a friend. Kate wasn't going to let her own nerves about meeting his friends keep him from helping Jack.

She figured Jay and Annie were going to the party as well. Which would be good, so at least she would have someone to talk to, but if not, she'd manage. Kate really liked Annie. She was a no-nonsense person without an ounce of pretense in her body.

Married to a millionaire, Annie kept her job as a nurse. Kate remembered her from the night she miscarried. Annie was on duty in the ER and was the first one to Kate's side. She never said anything about knowing who she was or about her situation; she was a cool professional with a very gentle touch.

Her husband, well, the worst Kate could say about Jay was that he was rough around the edges. He cursed, he cracked inappropriate jokes, but the man was totally and completely in love with his wife. That fact allowed Kate to forgive any of his other transgressions. It would be an interesting evening.

David left her to take a shower and Kate started to get ready herself. She took her makeup into the outer part of the bathroom and set it on the counter. This room was just like the rest of the house: strong, masculine, and totally beautiful. Caramel-colored marble topped heavy wood cabinetry. Door knobs and drawer pulls, all antiqued brass. It was a room, a house actually, that was done in complex layers. Like David, a person would look at this house and see something beautiful. But also like him, a person had to look at the details—what was hidden beneath the outer finish to see something, or someone, truly exceptional.

Her whole life, Kate had tended to see what was on the surface, passing judgment or making decisions based on her first impression. She was impulsive, she knew that, and it was the thing that got her into the most trouble. It was the trait that put her in a bad marriage and what almost kept her from David. He wasn't a stereotype and he wasn't a cliché. And it had taken her a long time to figure that out.

Kate's eye was drawn to the corner of the countertop. In a small crystal glass was a pink toothbrush, and around the neck of the toothbrush was a small, satin bow. She picked it up and saw a note in the glass. All it said was, *'This stays here.'* She smiled.

It was symbolic—the first step to junking up his bathroom. The water stopped running in the shower and soon after he was standing behind her. A handsome, muscular, wet, nearly-naked man was watching her put on her makeup.

Damn. Life was good.

"There's an empty drawer on your right if you want to put that away," he said.

Kate smiled and met his eyes in the mirror. He rubbed a towel over his face to remove the remaining shaving cream and a grin tugged at his mouth.

"I saw the toothbrush. Thank you."

He kissed the top of her head. Using another towel to dry his hair, David tossed it in a basket in the corner when he was done. "Just so you know, no one has left so much as a lipstick in this house."

Sliding the wand back into her mascara, Kate placed it on the counter and turned to face him. She rested her hands on his chest and looked into his strong face. It was a beautiful face. One that belied the job he did or the persona he assumed.

For months they'd danced around what they wanted from each other. But it all came down to the fact they needed each other to be whole. The years between them didn't matter, their pasts didn't matter—all that mattered was on that day in California, the fates intervened, the stars aligned, and the split soul had found its other half.

His hand grazed over her back, just above the waistband of her yoga pants. He nudged up the cami she wore, gave her body a good once over in the mirror and eventually his eyes settled on her little tattoo. "I saw that the night you were here. Or at least I thought I did."

"Like it?" She bit her lip and loved that whenever he touched her, she wanted him. Pure and simple.

His fingers brushed the small pink flower with the lightest touch. "It's beautiful. When did you get it? You didn't have it in California."

"Remember when I chaperoned that trip to your game?"

"When I made a fool out of myself trying to get you to go out with me again? Yeah."

"Right before that."

"What made you get a tattoo?"

His hands were still caressing her skin and making her more than a little crazy. The grin on his face told her he knew what he was doing to her, and she couldn't do anything about it, she couldn't have him, not for another week.

Grasping his hand so she didn't lose her mind, Kate answered, even though he was laughing. "I was pissed at Laura and Richard. Pissed at you."

"So you ran off to a tattoo parlor?" he said over a laugh.

"I do crazy things when I get upset or stressed."

"God, you're going to be so much fun." Still damp from his shower, David pulled on a pair of boxer briefs. Then he took hold of her and started backing her into the bedroom, nipping at her neck as he did.

"David, please, you know we can't."

"I know. I just want to make out."

Giggles escaped. "Really?"

"C'mon Katie," he teased. "Make out with me."

His arms locked around her waist and his breath caressed her skin. Lowering her to the bed, his kisses were sweet and gentle. Kate lost her mind every time his lips touched hers.

She wondered if David set out to drive her crazy. His lips brushed over hers and finally settled into a soft rhythm, gently nipping and tugging. His tongue tasted her, plunging into her mouth while his body covered hers. She could feel his arousal, and each time she did, the thought that this man wanted her, was a true miracle. Her hands couldn't resist touching him. His muscles were taut, his skin smooth, and his hair, which was still damp, tickled her, making her her breath catch. When he drew a sharp breath, as her hand trailed over his hip, Kate knew he'd reached his threshold and the choice was to stop or finish.

David knew they had to stop. The crook of his arm proved a good place to settle in and Kate enjoyed the safe, secure feeling she had when she was with him. Then she felt him move and watched as he grabbed something off the night table. He brought it over his head and stopped in front of her face.

In his hand was a small red box from Cartier's.

Kate didn't know if breathing was going to be part of this scenario or not, but she thought it would be good to try and take in some air.

Sitting up, she took the box. Swallowing hard, Kate faced him. "What did you do?"

He grinned and sat up. "Not what you're thinking. It's not a ring, so calm down."

"I mean, I don't mean that, I wouldn't... I..."

"I know. Just open it."

Taking a breath, she opened the little red clamshell. Nestled on dark velvet was a pair of earrings that matched the pendant he gave her for Christmas. Three intertwined bands, each a different color of gold. However, unlike her necklace, the earrings had fire. Set in the white gold band was a channel of diamonds. "Oh, David..."

The earrings were so beautiful, Kate couldn't speak. What made them perfect wasn't the flash factor, it was the unique quality. It was also that he thought about her; he always thought about her. "I don't know what to say. I love them."

He smiled when she kissed him. "That'll do."

"They'll look beautiful with my dress."

"Speaking of your dress, we should get ready. Jay and Annie will be here in less than half an hour."

Kate kissed him again. "Stop buying me presents," she whispered.

He stood and winked at her. "Not a chance."

JACK ARRIVED AT Laura's house and once again saw only one car was in the driveway. There was no Mercedes, which meant she was probably alone.

He was anxious. He wanted everything to be perfect for her. But there was no denying the past month had been torture. He loved her, but if he didn't have sex soon, he'd explode. He hadn't gone this long without sex since he was seventeen, but since he'd started seeing Laura, he hadn't been with anyone else.

In the beginning, he could have kept going out, seen other girls, but once he'd spent time with Laura, kissed her and tasted her, he was done. He'd brought her home after their first date and the good night kiss lasted for half an hour.

He had to be careful with her and make sure she wouldn't get scared off. When she'd been at his apartment a couple of weeks before, he couldn't believe her body. It was amazing, soft and curvy, and just thinking about her got him hot.

Tonight she'd meet his friends, and after that he'd take her home and get her in bed. Then things would be better.

Laura came out of the house as he was walking up the

front stoop. He kissed her first, loving her sweet and the way she responded to him, pressing against him, letting her tongue drift in his mouth. The look she gave him let him know she wanted the same thing he did. He took her bag and put it in the back seat.

∽

LAURA GOT INTO the truck and folded her arms against the cold. "Will there be many people at the party?"

"A good amount. The guys I really want you to meet won't be there, but I guess you'll meet them another time."

He was talking about David and Jay. She already knew they weren't going, which was why she agreed to go to the party at all. If she'd said no, they still could have gone to his apartment for the night, but she wanted to meet his friends and was glad Mom told her about their plans ahead of time.

He looked so gorgeous her heart almost stopped. They were still sitting in the car in front of her house, and he turned to her and handed her a wrapped box. "I never gave you this. Merry Christmas, kind of."

She giggled and took .he box from him. "You didn't have to buy me anything."

"I wanted to. I hope you like it."

She opened the box and gasped at the necklace. A diamond heart pendant. It was beautiful—and, she was sure, very expensive.

"Jack, thank you. I love it." She unbuttoned her coat and took it from the box. She had started to put on the necklace David gave her and stopped, because she felt guilty because of all the lies she was telling. It turned out to be a perfect decision. "I want to wear it. Will you help me put it on?"

He maneuvered himself so he could get behind her, took the necklace and Laura picked up her hair. After he'd fastened the clasp he planted a kiss just beneath her ear. Jack looked at the pendant and smiled.

"It looks perfect on you, babe."

Laura leaned forward and kissed him. "Thank you."

DAVID SMILED WHEN he looked in the rearview mirror and saw Annie and Kate getting along like old friends. The four of them spent the better part of dinner laughing and telling stories. She blended with his friends, and into his life, so easily it seemed she was meant to be there all along. Jay smiled himself, until he heard his name and realized he was being talked about in the third person.

"Hey, hey," he turned. "I'm right here, ladies."

The girls giggled and David made a mental note to himself. It seemed that while Kate could handle wine, if hard liquor was thrown into the mix, the story changed. It didn't seem like a lot, but thinking about it, she'd consumed quite a bit—a martini at his house, another at the restaurant, two glasses of wine at dinner, and one after dinner drink. She had a pretty good buzz going. It surprised him, because she drank a whole bottle the day she met him in California, and he didn't see the silliness he was seeing now.

The drive from downtown across the river to New Jersey had taken about forty-five minutes. David pulled up in front of their destination in Mullica Hill. Kate looked out the rear window of the Rover at the monstrosity his friends called a house.

"Oh, my God," Kate said, staring at the structure of white concrete. She was pretty much speechless because from a certain angle, the turret that made up the eastern side of the house looked like a giant hard-on.

"What is it?" Kate was really examining the building, not quite sure if it was real or if they were playing an elaborate joke on her.

"That," Annie said in her best French accent, "is Chateau Girard. Or as I like to call it, Moby Dick."

"They live here? I mean, this is such a lovely area, they let that be built here?" Kate tilted her head as she stood on the walk in front of the house. "It looks like... people live in it?

Annie laughed. "Sebastien and Brandy designed it together."

"*Brandy?*" Kate asked.

David saw her writer brain going. No doubt someone in her next book was getting named Brandy, and it wouldn't be a good thing.

She looked at David and squeezed her eyes shut. "Please tell me about Brandy before I go in there and say the wrong thing. I'm sure she's perfectly nice, but..."

"Brandy and Bas, that's what we call Sebastien, got together a couple of years ago, I think. Jay, do you remember?" David looked at his friend.

"Two or three years ago. He met her at a bar one night. They hooked up, end of story."

"Pssht. They don't know anything." Annie took Kate aside. "Brandy went to a fancy college, worked in a boutique on Rittenhouse for about ten minutes. Knows a good number of the guys on the team intimately."

Jay made a face at his wife. "I was going to leave some of that out, but fine. She *dated* different guys on the team until she and Bas found each other. Don't judge, Annie. That's not fair."

"She found him," Annie snapped. "As soon as they were engaged he bought all her clothes, bought her a new car. For God's sake, she upsized her engagement ring three times."

Kate was stunned and looked at David.

She didn't know what to think about the gossip, about the Girards, about any of it. "This is going to be an interesting night."

"The Girards are hosting the party, and a lot of nice people will be there. And Brandy may be a flake, but she is nice. However, there's a small group that you'll probably want to avoid. Our goal is to meet Nelly's girlfriend."

Jay snapped his fingers. "That's right, he's bringing the mystery date." David felt Jay pat him on the back. "He's going to need our sage advice, Padre. He's got a big night ahead of him, our little guy."

Annie slapped Jay. "Leave him alone. He doesn't need the whole team telling him how to take this girl to bed."

"Why would the whole team know this?" Kate asked.

David could see she was appalled, probably because she was the topic of a similar conversation once upon a time.

David wrapped his arm around her shoulder when they got to the front door. "Jack wasn't exactly discreet. It got around."

"That poor girl," Kate said. "She's walking in here totally unaware that her sex life has been discussed?"

Jay waved his hand. "Oh, no sex life to discuss. She's a virgin."

Shock crossed Kate's face, and all David could do was shake his head. Yeah, he was going to hear about this later.

DAVID RANG THE doorbell, which was a series of discordant chimes, and Kate wished she'd just gotten David to stay in. Nerves balled in her stomach as she listened to the clickty-clack of high heels from inside the house.

Annie leaned in. "Just a warning. Her voice…"

But it was too late. The door flew open and the sound that emerged was like nails on a blackboard with a helium chaser. "Hi! Oh. My. God. I am soooo glad you could come."

The four of them stepped into the giant house, and Kate felt like she'd walked into a sterile white box. The house was open on the inside, like a great atrium. Wrought iron stairs went from level to level and railings surrounded the open walkways, off of which there were numerous rooms. She guessed the couple had no children because everything was pristine.

She looked at Brandy Girard and took in the whole package. She was ultra-thin, artificially blonde, and artificially tanned. Her blue eyes twinkled happily, but there was definitely an edge to what Kate saw. She knew Brandy's type—she'd taught them for years—they were all about appearances. Kate guessed she was being carefully assessed. The overly bright smile was the final piece. Kate wondered if Brandy Girard's teeth would have looked normal size if her face wasn't so drawn. Kate understood some women were naturally thin, but Brandy looked like she was starving. Diamonds hung from her ears, another was around her neck, and Kate got a glimpse of her massive ring. Words to describe Brandy? Superficial, entitled, and, she guessed, really, really hungry.

David made the introduction and Brandy lunged forward, grabbing Kate's hand with both of hers. "It is such a pleasure to have you here, Kate. I can't believe you came to our party."

David helped her off with her coat and Kate put on her best smile. "Thank you so much for having us. What an interesting home you have."

"Oh, thank you." Brandy hadn't stopped smiling yet. And her voice, it was more than the shrill quality, a sing-songy cadence that was almost childlike. "It's our dream house. We worked with a wonderful German architect. It was important to us to have something truly unique."

"You certainly succeeded there." *It was the ugliest thing she'd ever seen.*

Kate was vaguely aware that she was introduced to Bas Girard, who seemed like a nice man, but Brandy was a fascinating study. She was wearing pencil thin jeans, impossibly high, studded, Louboutin peep-toe pumps, and a ruffled silk halter top. Everything was high-end, and if she had any boobs to speak of Kate might have thought she was a walking, talking Barbie doll.

"I just love your dress," Brandy said as she reached out and touched Kate's shoulder. "Is that a silk and wool blend?"

Kate looked down at her dress. A very simple, sleeveless design with bit of flounce just above her knee, it was a dark, rich brown that shimmered a bit in the light. She didn't remember if it was silk and wool, it might have been.

Kate shrugged. "I don't remember."

"And your shoes are gorgeous. Manolos?"

Kate looked at her feet. "Ah, no, actually, but they are great knock-offs, aren't they?"

Brandy recoiled a little at the term "knock-off". Wondering if the girl would ask about her undies, Kate could at least tell her that tonight she was wearing La Perla.

People were milling around, and she didn't like the kind of attention she was attracting. The men were checking her out, but the women were guarded and she could almost understand it. In this world of gorgeous men and big money, newcomers were definitely on probation. Kate stepped into the sunken living room and let her eyes take in the crowd. Her own fame didn't make her immune to the scrutiny. She'd have to prove herself. What she found odd about the whole situation was that it was the single women, the ones who weren't with one of the players, who were the most suspicious. *And angry*. Wow, did they look pissed.

He must have seen them, too, because suddenly David had his hand protectively on her back, and she felt steadier knowing he wouldn't leave her side until she relaxed.

She saw Amanda Blauvelt, who'd definitely started to bloom since they'd met at the obstetrician's office a few weeks earlier. Kate was a little jealous as she saw Amanda's husband hand her something to drink and gently place his hand on her growing belly. It was a sweet gesture, one his young wife returned with a kiss on his cheek. Okay, she liked Amanda Blauvelt, and she liked her better when Amanda looked in her direction and smiled.

Her eyes returned to Brandy and her equally thin pack of bottle-blondes, and she saw them looking at Amanda and sneering. Kate had taught high school long enough to spot the mean girls a mile away. She flashed a look at David and smiled.

"Be right back." He shook his head, knowing Kate was walking right into the middle of the fray, but that he didn't try to stop her. She'd been the wife of a rising academic, so cocktail parties like this were nothing. She glided over to the group of young women, who were still watching Amanda with her husband. "This is quite a party, Brandy."

"Oh, thank you! You're so sweet." Brandy flashed her best toothy smile and Kate reciprocated.

She introduced Kate to the group and they engaged her in some simple conversation. She tried to find some common ground, but they weren't giving her too much of their consideration. Kate discovered that the women she was standing with weren't connected to anyone other than Brandy.

Finally, one of them looked back at Amanda. "I wonder how long it will be before Mark gets tired of that fat cow and steps out on her."

Kate felt herself flush, but kept her temper in check. She glanced over at the couple who were obviously in love. "I don't think so, he looks devoted."

One of the girls rolled her eyes. "I would be disgusted with myself if I was that fat."

"She's pregnant, she's not fat." *Wow. Did women actually talk this way about other women?*

"Same thing." Changing the subject, because they could see Kate didn't get it, Jack Nelson was the next topic. "So Nelly should be here with his new girl soon. I wish I'd known he was looking, I'd do him if he needed someone."

"Apparently she's some geek who goes to Penn."

"Maybe he likes her," Kate said. The looks went from

impatient to annoyed, and finally, one of them answered.

"Look, Kate," the girl said her name with a lovely snarl. "You obviously need to be brought up to speed on all this, but I can tell you even the man you're with will throw you over in a heartbeat if he gets bored or you don't give him what he wants. He's done it before."

A friend of Chelsea's, perhaps, and it forced Kate to ask a question even though she already knew the answer. "If you have such a low opinion of all these men, why are you so interested in them?"

They looked at her, their little plastic heads turning in unison. They didn't say it, but all their eyes were saying, "Well, duh."

It was the money, the prestige, the power factor of being with a pro athlete. These men were special, and unlike a successful businessman, much harder to come by.

That was it, Kate walked away and back to David. He took her hand in his, kissed it, and grinned. "They're the worst of it. Two of those women are close friends with Chelsea."

"I figured." Kate was sure Chelsea could have been on the guest list, and she was almost sad she wasn't there. It would have been a lot of fun to soul kiss David at midnight with her watching.

The doorbell rang, and Kate saw a very handsome young man walk in. Annie came over. "Jack's here. Moment of truth."

Kate watched the door as eagerly as Jay and David. She felt a kinship with the girl, considering both of them had been thoroughly discussed. What she didn't expect was for Annie to gasp, and for David to take her hand when the girl turned around. The lovely brunette who walked in with Jack was her baby.

"Oh, my God," Kate whispered. "Oh, my God."

Chapter 26

LAURA WAS FINE at the party for the first ten seconds. It took her that long to check out the crowd and see her mother staring back at her. She was standing with David, who was practically holding her up, and another woman who had her hand on Mom's arm. This was the worst nightmare she'd ever had.

Laura sucked in and suddenly found herself gasping for air. She couldn't breathe. She tried to stay calm, but she knew what was happening. No air was going in; her lungs were closing off.

She hadn't had an asthma attack in over two years, and the sudden tightness was terrifying. The only up side of it was she might die and she wouldn't have to face everyone she'd lied to.

It was like trying to breathe underwater with a hundred pounds on her chest. It hurt, and Laura grabbed her chest and dropped to her knees.

Jack fell with her, his face terrified. "What's wrong? Jesus, what is it?"

She couldn't speak, couldn't tell him. In a split second she heard a commotion. David dragged Jack off the floor and Mom was right next to her, along with the woman that Laura now recognized as a nurse from the hospital.

"Give me her purse," Mom snapped.

She heard a shaking sound, voices. Laura started to feel dizzy and tears ran down her cheeks, but then her inhaler was in her mouth and Mom told her what was happening before releasing the medicine for her to breathe in. "Breathe, Laura." Mom's hand rubbed her back. "Take it easy. Breathe. Another puff."

The medicine started to take effect and the pain lessened. She could breathe again, but she was still gasping involuntarily and wheezing. Mom handed her the inhaler and she took another puff herself. Slowly her breathing steadied. She could see again, and looking up, she saw all the people surrounding her, gawking.

Dying would have been less embarrassing.

JACK DROPPED TO his knees, taking Kate's place next to Laura, and pulled her into his arms. Kate shuddered to think of what was going to happen over the next couple of hours. Laura had just been caught lying to pretty much everyone. This was going to get ugly.

Kate put her arms around David's waist, leaned into him for support, and fought the urge to cry.

"Are you alright?" he asked.

Kate nodded and looked at Brandy, who was standing there with a strained smile and her sky blue eyes darting all over the place. "Thank goodness you knew what to do. How did you know she had asthma?"

Kate looked at Laura, who was still being held by Jack. Her daughter's eyes were pleading, begging her not to say anything.

Kate shifted her gaze to David, then to Annie, and to Laura one more time, before she finally answered Brandy. "My daughter has asthma. I recognized it."

Laura turned her face into Jack's bicep and closed her eyes.

"She'll need to go home, though," Kate said.

Jack helped her up and kept his arm firmly around her. It was protective, no one was getting near her without his say so. Kate could see the love between them and it made her heart break. This was going to be very bad for both of them. The crowd started to disperse, but there were lots of looks and questions.

Jay walked over, both hands in his pockets, looked at Jack and Laura, and blew out a breath. "This is your girl? She's pretty." He looked back at Kate and scratched his head. "Yeah."

Jack nodded and stroked Laura's cheek with his finger. "I'll take you back to your Dad's."

David moved next to Jack, but focused his attention on Laura. She was exhausted and he could see it as plainly as she could. When Kate finally regrouped, she walked forward and took David's hand. Jack was so grateful he could barely form a coherent sentence.

"Thank you," he mumbled to Kate. "Thank you."

Kate acknowledged Jack, but focused her attention on Laura. "We need to get you home."

Laura nodded, but wouldn't step away from her guy. He

held her closer and now looked at Kate suspiciously, rather than with gratitude. "I'll take her home."

Laura's eyes were sad and tired. Kate's hand gently touched the diamond heart that hung around her neck and then she looked at Jack. Poor, confused Jack. Her words were barely above a whisper as she told him what was going to happen. "No. I'm her mother, and she's coming home with me."

If his reaction could have been measured, she still wouldn't have seen anything. His face was like stone, completely without emotion.

"You can follow us there, and once she's settled some, you can talk." Kate was trying to be calm. Jack had just had the shock of his life, and he didn't even have the whole story yet.

When she thought about it, neither did Kate.

He nodded dumbly, too stunned to argue, kissed Laura's head, and then let her go to Kate. David reappeared with her coat, and he kept Laura steady as Kate helped her bundle up against the cold air. She wrapped her own scarf around Laura, who was painfully underdressed.

Annie and Jay were also following.

Brandy reappeared, jumpy and nervous. "Hey, so sorry you can't stay. Gosh, I hope you feel better, honey."

David patted Brandy's shoulder. "We'll take care of her."

"Okay, bye then." She waved goodbye like a five-year-old, moving only her fingers. That was the last image Kate had of Brandy Girard. It was enough.

AT THE HOUSE, David gathered some glasses and the

remainder of the scotch he brought with him a few nights ago. There was three quarters of a bottle left, more than enough to dull the ache. God knew he needed one, and Nelly definitely would. Jay had probably let him know he'd been on the verge of taking a seventeen-year-old to bed, so alcohol was definitely on the menu.

He didn't know what to feel. Kate was being Kate, handling everything calmly, but he fully expected her to fall apart later. He'd really grown to care about Laura. In the short time he'd known her, they'd learned to understand each other, but he had no idea what would make her pull something like this. Jack was a wreck. The kid was stupid in love with Laura, and that wasn't going to go away because he couldn't have her.

"Is that scotch?" Annie said, walking into the room.

David nodded and poured one for each of them. They clinked glasses and took a sip. "How's Laura?"

"Better. Kate had a nebulizer and the medicine. Her lungs are settling down. The cold, along with the stress of seeing you and Kate, must have triggered the attack. She's sick about Jack."

"Have you heard from Jay?"

"Uh huh. Almost here. The poor kid's a mess." Jay had followed him to the city and Annie ended up riding in the car with David, Kate, and Laura. They'd dropped Jack's car at his apartment since no one thought he should drive.

"Jay told him?"

Annie made a face. "Are you kidding? Of course he did. You don't think Jay is going to miss a chance to humiliate the 'rook', do you?"

"True." David took another drink, imagining what was going on between Laura and Kate.

He looked out the kitchen window and saw lights in the driveway. He put down his glass and walked to the side door in time to see Jack and Jay get out of the Jag. Jay looked like a man who had an attack of conscience and Jack looked like he'd had the shit kicked out of him.

Nelly walked into the house and saw all the pictures on the fridge, a recent report card, information about college visits—proof that he'd been dating a high school girl. Jay got him to take off his coat and their young teammate took the drink David offered him, downing it in one gulp.

"That's not going to solve anything," Annie said.

"It'll make me forget. Fill it up, Padre."

David poured two fingers of scotch in the glass and watched his Jack drown his pain.

"She lied to me. Everything she said was a lie."

Jay swirled the amber liquid in his glass. "Get used to it, buddy." He downed his own drink and motioned for David to fill it up. "Happy Fucking New Year."

Jack had wandered into the den and examined the shelves of pictures. It was Laura's life story, and he was finally seeing the truth of who she was. All David could think was that it was lucky they decided to go the party or right now Jack would probably have her in bed. If that had happened, he didn't know if his friend could have lived with himself.

David watched him sit in one of the big club chairs and drop his head in his hands. Taking a seat adjacent to him on the couch, David handed him another scotch and turned on Sports Center.

"Drink that one slowly."

Jack nodded. "You must think I'm a total shit."

David looked at him. "No. I think you were a stupid ass.

You can't tell your shit to just anyone."

Jay came and sat with them. "But, it's kind of a tradition, your rookie year isn't officially over until some chick fucks with your head. You're lucky she didn't take a picture and send your junk all over social media."

"I thought I was in love with her."

David downed the rest of his drink. "You are in love with her, but you've got to get over it."

❧

KATE POKED HER head in Laura's room and saw her daughter curled up on the bed. Her hair was damp at the ends from the long hot shower Kate had insisted she take, and her body still shuddered now and again from the leftover tears. Her poor little girl, so misguided, but so very much in love. What the hell had happened?

Nudging the door open with her elbow, she entered, setting the small tray on the desk. Laura turned at the sound, wiping her eyes, and sitting up when she saw Kate.

"Hi," Kate said. "Annie made you a snack since you didn't get to eat."

"Thanks," Laura said, sniffing and rubbing her hand under her nose. She wore an oversized nightshirt and a pair of soft, worn-in white socks. "What's on the tray?"

"Juice and an English muffin."

"Sounds good." Laura took the glass Kate offered and the plate with the muffin. Kate sat on the edge of the bed and gently rubbed Laura's back.

"Are you feeling better?" Kate was talking about her breathing, but got a totally different answer.

"I didn't mean to lie. It just kind of happened. And now..." Laura's breath hitched and she leaned in. "Now he hates me."

"I don't think he hates you." Based on what she saw, Jack's feelings were pretty clear. When Laura collapsed at the party, he was frantic. The boy was madly in love with her, and that was going to make this all the harder. "And believe me; this will be tough on him, too."

"I know. I know." Tears filled Laura's eyes and she rubbed the back of her hand across her eyes. Her voice was small, hoarse from the attack and the tears, but what she said next rocked Kate to the core. "I just wanted someone to love me."

The truth of the matter finally surfaced, and Kate's heart wilted under the realization. Her eyes burned. Laura believed no one loved her. The twisted attention Richard paid to her, the affectionate distance Kate bestowed, were not what she wanted or needed. Her daughter needed love, and when she didn't get it at home, she found it someplace else. It was the most heart wrenching and sobering thing she'd ever felt. No more, never again would her daughter feel unwanted or question Kate's devotion. It was time to tell her the truth. Taking Laura's face in her hands, Kate leveled a watery gaze in her direction.

"I love you. I love you more than anything in this world. And I am so..." Tears spilled and Kate sucked in a breath. "I am so sorry." The great sob escaped when she faced how she failed her daughter. "I love you. I have always loved you."

Laura had started crying again, overcome by Kate's words. "Where were you? When I was growing up? Why did you always stay away?"

Closing her eyes, she tried to verbalize the years of abuse. It was hard, but what was harder was that Kate had to face her own cowardice. "Your father threatened... he said he would..." Drawing a deep breath, she finally said it. "He wanted you all to himself, and he would threaten to take you away if I tried to be part of your life. When I disagreed with him, or tried to do more than he considered acceptable, he'd... he'd hit me."

Laura sat back and stared at her.

Kate had just burst her image of the man who raised her, and looking away, she wondered if she made a mistake. "I didn't want to lose you and I had no doubt he'd keep his word, but it killed me watching you grow up without me. I tried to stay involved in some way, but it was hard." She drew a shaky breath and continued. "When you got older, he'd set the tone—you and him on one side and me on the other. I know I was weak and I should have fought against him, but I was scared." She gulped hard. "I was so scared he would take you away and I would never see you again."

"Oh, God," she whispered. "Daddy hit you? *Hit you?*"

Kate nodded, ashamed that she'd never stood up for herself. Laura took her hand and Kate collapsed, and the two of them held each other like never before.

When they moved apart, Laura said, "I didn't even see what he was doing to you. I didn't know."

Kate nodded and touched her face. "This whole thing with Jack could have been tragic. You're lucky he was the man you met that day, but all of us have to take some blame. We didn't pay enough attention to what was going on with you. God, if anything had happened to you..." She stopped, choking back tears when she thought of all the possibilities.

Laura took a sip of the juice, dropped her head, and told Kate a secret that would blow Richard's life apart. "Marie was paying attention. She knew. Not everything. But she knew he was older, and she covered for me with Dad."

The blinding light that flashed behind Kate's eyes must have been anger, because no other emotion would fit the bill. Covered for her? What did that mean? Lied for her was a better description. That crazy lunatic had messed with her daughter for the last time.

"I am going to get her, I swear to God," she mumbled.

Laura didn't respond, taking a bite of her muffin instead.

There was quiet while the room settled and the two of them adjusted to the new stage they were entering. When Laura spoke again, she didn't waste words.

"I was going to spend the night with him," she whispered.

Kate swallowed and made herself stay calm. It was one landmine after another. "I figured. You're ready to give yourself like that?"

"Only to him." Her voice was hoarse, scratchy.

Great. Kate had to be careful here, especially considering her own situation. "That's a big decision, and I'm sure you didn't make it without a lot of thought."

"Yes, I... I wanted to be with him. But now..." Laura started to cry again, the tears rolling gently down her cheeks.

She curled against Kate, much the way she did when she was little and had awakened from a bad dream. Unfortunately, Kate had no pearls of wisdom, nothing wise to tell her daughter. The only thing left to do was for Laura to face her mistake and take responsibility.

Kate passed her a handful of tissues and Laura dried her eyes. "I have to go talk to him now, don't I?"

"Yeah, you do."

Blowing out her breath, Laura rose from the bed. "I don't know how I'm going to do this. How am I going to say good-bye to him?"

Kate helped her up and put her arm around Laura's shoulder. "You know what you have to do. Just remember that I'm here if you need me. I will always be here."

∽

LAURA WALKED SLOWLY down the stairs, through the hall and to the kitchen. She stopped when she saw Annie sitting at the island. She liked Annie; she was smart. It was like she could handle anything, kind of like Mom. Her sad smile told the whole story. She knew this was going to be bad, too. Laura drew as deep a breath as she could and walked into the den.

David stared at her, disappointed, and she felt ashamed. She was just getting to know him and she hated that she might have lost his trust already. Jay Hemmings looked at her like she was evil, just plain evil. And then there was Jack. He was slumped in a chair, staring at the TV.

Laura sniffed in because she wasn't even trying to stop the tears, and Jack finally looked at her. His face was hard and angry, and she knew she deserved everything he was going to throw at her. He left his chair and stood before her. He was so tall, so big, and she looked away, feeling small and almost a little scared.

"We need some privacy."

Laura nodded and even though she wanted to run away, she turned and headed toward the front of the house. She brought him to the library. The dark paneled room had big leather furniture, shelves from floor to ceiling, and her piano. She closed the French doors behind them and stood with her back to the glass, never fully advancing into the room.

Jack was stalking around like an angry animal. His shoulders strained the fibers of his sweater and she could see he was tight, fuming mad, and all of it was directed at her.

"Jack, I'm sorry…"

He spun at her, the rage coming from every part of him. "The last thing I need to hear is your fucking apology."

Laura wasn't prepared for the internal collapse. He hated her. He truly did. Her lip started to quiver and her limbs shook. Everything in her crumbled. She felt the sobs rack her body, painful deep sobs that made her want to die. Behind the fear of being caught in so many lies, Laura had to face the reality that she was going to lose him. This man was everything to her and she was going to lose him. Occasionally, she let a heavy cough clear her lungs, but the air was sticking in her chest now because of sorrow, not her asthma.

"You lied to me. You told me the first lie and then you just kept it up, one after another."

"I lied about my age."

"And where you lived, and about your family, and where you went to school. I don't know you, Laura. I thought I loved you, but I don't know who you are!"

The truth of what he said hurt. He was right. He didn't know anything about her. Everything she'd given him had been half a story.

"You were going to let me take you to bed. I don't do that, Laura, I don't go after high school girls. You were going to make me that guy, and that's not who I am."

"I'm sorry. I am." Giant tears fell and she sucked in ragged breaths. "I'm sorry."

"I know I'm the dumb hick. I went to college to play hockey, otherwise I'd be working on the family farm. The guys bust on me about that every fucking day. But I never thought you—" He sat on the couch and dropped his head in his hands. "I trusted you."

Laura sat on the piano bench and continued to cry. Giant tears plopped onto the keys and all she heard from Jack were deep shaky breaths. This hurt him, too. Laura did this to him and she hated herself for it. That was worse than anything she felt, because for the first time in her life, Laura understood what love was all about. The tears slowed and she started to resign herself to the fact that it was over.

He hadn't ever lied to her, and all she'd done was lie to him, except when she told him she loved him. That was all the truth she had. "I'm sorry, Jack. I never meant for this to happen."

He looked up at her and his eyes were so sad. Laura touched the piano keys and a single note filled the room. It made her heart hurt. She was a single note, now. Not part of anything.

"I guess I do know one thing about you," he said. His voice was hoarse, deep.

"What's that?"

He stood and approached her. "I know about your music."

Laura's eyes met his and she could see he loved her, but she'd broken more than his heart. She broken his trust, and that was far worse. "It's my heart, just like you."

The silence was chilling and lonely. Laura was so tired; all she wanted to do was sleep.

Jack took three steps and he stood before her, tall, strong, and so very handsome. "Goodbye, Laura."

She bit her lip as it trembled. "Goodbye, Jack."

He ran his hand over her hair and then left the room. Watching him go was crushing, and all the pain from the inside was floating to the surface. Not knowing what to do, Laura turned to her piano, and letting her hands run over the wet keys, started to play.

JACK HESITATED WHEN he saw Kate sitting in the kitchen. She'd poured herself a glass of wine and knew she looked like hell. She didn't care. Now it was time to be the mom. Jack had said his piece to Laura, and now it was Kate's turn to talk to him.

He stepped to the big kitchen island and made uneasy eye contact. He was fidgety, taking his hands in and out of his pockets, tapping his fingers. Jay, Annie, and David were watching from the den, but Kate didn't want to be distracted, so she did her best to tune out the noise.

"I'm sorry if you think I was too hard on her... maybe I was." He shuffled his feet like the boy he was.

"You're angry. I understand that."

"Still, I... I know she's hurting, too."

"She is, but that's not what has me upset with you."

"I treated her right," he said. "I was a gentleman."

"No, Jack, you weren't a gentleman."

"Excuse me?"

"I heard what you said to her, that you weren't 'that guy'. You know, the one who went after high school girls. But did you tell her you *are* the guy who discussed taking her to bed with your friends?" Jack's face froze. "That you discussed it with them? Does Laura know you're *that guy?*"

He said nothing.

"What she did was wrong, but that was between you and her. You ruined her reputation, made her a joke."

"I didn't think..."

"Wow, does that sound familiar?" She cut him off and didn't care that he felt the need to explain. "People do stupid things sometimes. She loves you and she's going to be miserable as a result, but everything she did was because she had feelings for you. Right or wrong, that's it." Kate came around the island and faced him.

"What did you tell people? What you were planning? That she was a virgin? It seems a lot of people know about things that should have stayed private."

Jack glanced around, looking for help, but saw he was on his own. "I... I didn't mean for anything to become public knowledge. I didn't mean to hurt her."

"Well you did. She has a lot to answer for, but so do you. Here's something for you to chew on, farm boy—I don't care where you came from, or how much education you have. The reason I would never want you around my daughter is because you don't respect her."

Kate walked out and left Jack with his head hanging—and David, Jay, and Annie with some insight about Kate the Mom. Stopping by the library door, she saw Laura, throwing herself into the music, trying to play away the pain. The room was dimly lit and her beautiful girl was sitting at the black Steinway in the oversized shirt and fuzzy slippers, her face wet and swollen from tears.

Kate didn't flinch when David's arms slipped around her from behind, she simply placed her hands over his and leaned into the strength he gave her. His chin rested in her hair and the two of them watched Laura play.

"You may have Jack sleeping on your couch."

Kate looked over her shoulder and raised an eyebrow.

"I think he's on his third shot since your conversation."

"Whatever. It doesn't matter to me where he sleeps."

"For what it's worth, he feels like shit."

Kate couldn't feel sympathy for him, not when her daughter was going to be punished for both of their mistakes. "How sad for him."

"Kate? That's not fair." David's admonishment was deserved, but she didn't feel sorry for Jack; the only person she felt for was Laura. Yes, it was her own fault, but that didn't mean Kate wouldn't take her pain if she could.

"All she wanted was for someone to love her. I feel like I failed her."

"Don't be too tough on yourself."

"It's hard not to be."

"Are you telling Richard?" David asked.

"Tomorrow. He'll have company in the afternoon. So I'll go in the morning."

"Not going to make a scene?"

"It's tempting, but no. I just want him to know what happened."

David watched Laura plow through the different pieces of music, and Kate could see the awe on his face. He understood Laura and her passion—he was that way when he played hockey, Kate was that way when she skated and when she wrote. Something came from the inside out.

"Does she even know we're here?"

"Probably not."

LAURA WAS STARVING. She made her way through the dark house at four o'clock in the morning for something to quiet her hunger.

She'd peeked into her mother's room before going downstairs. David was there with her. The two of them were nestled together like they'd been with each other for years. David's shoes were at the end of the bed, his watch on the armoire. She'd noticed earlier in the week that some of his clothes were in Mom's closet. It should have been weird, but it wasn't. They were happy together, and for Laura that was the important thing.

She flipped the switch and flooded the big kitchen with light. There had to be something in the house to eat.

The oversized fridge had tons of leftovers from the many family dinners they'd had over the week. There was cake, cheese, all stuff that would make her cough. Examining the many Tupperware containers, she found the last pieces of Aunt Trish's Southern fried chicken. *Awesome.*

She kicked the door shut with her foot, turned around, and faced the hard wall of Jack's chest. *Shit.* No longer wearing the black shirt he wore to go out earlier, he was in a plain white t-shirt and his dress pants. He stared down at her, his eyes still groggy from sleep and, she guessed, too much alcohol. The big question, why he was still here? There had to be a reason, also probably related to alcohol, and she'd get to it, but right now Laura was too busy inhaling what remained of his Armani cologne. He looked in the container and took a sniff.

"That looks good."

And then he took the chicken. *Her chicken.* Not cool. But not having the energy to fight him, she caved. "I'll get plates." Laura fished two plates out of the cupboard and brought them to the island. "What are you doing here?"

"I guess I passed out when I finished the scotch." He was picking little pieces off a nice big drumstick and Laura slapped his hand.

"That's my piece. Stop that."

"Fine." He pulled his hand back and the corner of his mouth tilted up. "What are you doing up?"

"I was hungry and I couldn't sleep."

"I hear ya." He stared at the chicken on his plate and then looked at her.

Laura was drawn to his eyes. As soon as she looked at him, really settled into the deep blue, she saw all the sadness she was feeling reflected right back. But it was when he reached out and touched her face; it was the gentle stroke of his fingers on her cheek that triggered Laura's meltdown. Leaving him where he sat, she went to the sink and leaned in.

Her hand came to her mouth as she tried to stifle the sob breaking from her chest. She was barely holding it together when Jack's hands dropped onto her shoulders and turned her around.

He pulled her to him and closed his arms around her, pressing her head into his broad chest. His hands ran through her hair, and his lips touched the top of her head. Laura reached around him and held tight. Her tears didn't come in great waves like she expected, but softly, sadly.

"This is killing me," he said. "But you know we can't, it doesn't matter what I feel for you. We can't."

"I know." And she did. It would be all wrong, for both of them. She was too young to be part of his life and he was too old to be part of hers. The number of years weren't the issue; it was the timing. Laura swallowed hard, trying to choke down the sobs, but finally failing miserably. "It hurts so much."

"I know. God, do I know." He tried to soothe her, holding her tight.

Laura thought about how this would be the last time he'd hold her like this, the last time she'd feel his arms around her. He pulled back a little and his hand came to her chin, urging her to look at him.

Seeing his face, she could tell he was hurting too. He was as sad and miserable as she was. Laura didn't know which was worse, the pain she felt, or knowing how he felt.

"I love you, Jack, and I'm sorry. I'm sorry for lying. For everything."

"Please don't be sorry you love me, because I'm not sorry I love you. I just wish it could be different."

Her heart felt like it would explode from her chest. There was so much she felt, so much she wanted to say. Then Laura surprised herself and did something she wouldn't have expected she could have done even an hour ago: she kissed him. It was a kiss goodbye, a kiss to tell him what she felt, and Jack responded, pulling her close. His mouth consumed hers; it was as if he was trying to take as much of her as possible before saying goodbye.

Finally, he pulled back, resting his forehead against hers and dragging in a deep breath as he did. "I'll miss you," he whispered.

Someday the timing would be right. Laura knew it wouldn't be any time soon, but someday.

Chapter 27

MARIE BROUGHT CRUDITÉS to the table in the dining room and examined the feast they'd prepared for their New Year's Day guests. She loved to entertain, especially when it made Richard happy. He was arranging the wine cabinet and fussing over small details to make everything perfect. Marie couldn't wait to marry him. She wanted to be his wife and the mother of his child. Things had been rough for the past two weeks, and they'd decided to take a two-month break from trying to conceive. They needed to re-center themselves, refocus on their own relationship after all that trouble with Kate.

As she thought about children, her mind drifted to Laura. It was almost noon and she still wasn't home. Marie tried to call, but her cell phone was off. Jack must have shown her a wonderful time; so wonderful that Laura didn't want to leave him.

Just seconds after she reentered the kitchen, Richard followed and kissed her cheek. "Everything looks brilliant. Thank you. Hopefully this will smooth the way for that professorship."

"You're welcome. It will be everything you deserve, I'm sure."

He nodded. "Have you heard from Laura?"

"No, I'm sure she's sleeping in."

"I'm getting worried."

"Richard, she'll be fine. Don't be so overprotective."

"I'm not overprotective. I'm her father, let's not forget that. I'm allowed to be worried."

"She's a young woman. You have to let her grow up."

"She's only seventeen."

Just then they both heard the backdoor open and Laura stepped through. Marie smiled. She looked wonderful. Tired, but Laura was fresh with new love and knowledge.

"Hi," she said quietly.

"Laura," Marie said, going to her. "Did you have a wonderful time, my love? Was it all you hoped?"

"It was interesting." Laura stepped away from the back door as Kate entered the house. "Mom can fill you in. I have to go upstairs and get a few of my things."

Marie went cold when Kate stepped into her kitchen. This woman was everything she wanted to be and everything she hated at the same time. And now she was fouling their home with her presence.

"Why are you here?" Richard asked, but it was his physical response that made Marie take notice. His eyes surveyed his ex-wife's body, and then he looked behind her. Once he saw her boyfriend wasn't with her, he relaxed. What he didn't seem to notice was that Kate was ready to tear him to shreds.

WHEN RICHARD TOOK an aggressive step toward her, Kate questioned the wisdom of coming here alone. David had offered to come, but Kate knew this was her battle to fight, and she had to do it on her own. Taking a deep breath, Kate realized that for the first time in twenty years, she wasn't intimidated.

"Do you know where Laura was last night?" Kate asked.

"She was out, but why is that your concern?" Richard dismissed her with a wave of his hand.

"Really?" Kate began. He couldn't possibly think this was going to work. That after all that had happened she'd shy away from him. "Are we going to do this again? I'm her mother, and it is my concern."

Marie sniffed. "It's not like she ever bonded with you, Kate. I mean, I've shared more milestones with her than you have."

Kate really didn't care what Marie thought, but she felt the need to clarify. "You may think you're her mother, but I am. I gave birth to her. I would give my life for her. She's my child, and while you two simply play at being parents, I *am* one."

"You're wasting time, Kate. We'll get her back emotionally and we'll gain full custody." Richard said. "I have pictures of you and your fuck buddy."

From the look on her face, it was obvious his crudeness surprised Marie, but not Kate. Kate knew exactly what was happening. Her ex-husband was becoming the vile pig she knew he was. He was reducing her relationship with David to crude basics, when plain as day, the sex calendar was on the refrigerator for all to see.

"Richard, honestly, you have a PhD," Kate said. "Can't

you find a better way to express yourself?"

"You bitch," he murmured. "You come into my house and tell me how to act?" He was clenching his fists and getting angrier by the second. "What kind of shit have you been telling her?"

He really was clueless. "You truly don't have any idea where she was last night, do you?"

"She was with her friends," Richard said. "This is pointless. We're expecting guests…"

Kate didn't give him a chance to finish. "She was with a *man*, Richard."

"What? No she wasn't, she was with…"

"*A man*. A twenty-one-year-old hockey player named Jack Nelson." She looked at Marie. "He's not a student. He plays for the Flyers."

Richard ran a hand through his hair and Marie folded her arms. "And how do *you* know all this, Kate?" she asked. "Did you introduce them?"

"No I didn't. She was at a New Year's party being thrown by a member of the team. Imagine my surprise when I ran into her there."

He gripped the edge of the counter so tightly his fingers turned white, and if Kate wasn't mistaken, based on the color of his face, he'd popped a blood vessel or two. This should get him nicely pissed off.

"Laura started dating him in November. She met him when she cut school one day." Kate decided to drive one of the nails into Marie's coffin. "She was planning on spending the night with him, but of course you didn't know that, did you, Richard?"

"No, I didn't. I can't believe she'd lie to us like this."

"She lied to you." Kate said. "And me, by omission. Marie knew what she was doing, and that she planned to sleep with him."

Richard focused on Marie, his eyes piercing a hole right through her. "You knew all this?"

Marie was cornered, and not the least bit intimidated by Richard. Which was good from one standpoint; Kate wished she'd stood up for herself more. Unfortunately Marie was messing with her daughter's life, and that was not okay. "She confided in me. It was something you wouldn't understand." Marie stuck her nose in the air and Richard almost exploded. Kate was wondering how Marie would react when that happened. It wouldn't be long. Richard was thinking, processing what he heard. His eyes were starting to bulge. Any second now...

"I'm her *father,* you stupid bitch! I don't care what the fuck you thought."

"How dare you speak to me that way?" Marie snapped at him. "Control yourself."

Richard's temper was ready to flare, but something made him hesitate. Maybe it was because Marie wasn't a vulnerable eighteen-year-old coed. Maybe it was because there were witnesses in the house. But Kate couldn't worry about Marie or Richard, she had to keep her focus.

"You both realize this isn't about either of you," she said. "It's about Laura."

"Laura's always been fine until you tried to get involved. You're a pathetic excuse for a mother," Marie hissed from the doorway.

"*I'm* a pathetic excuse for a mother? You didn't know what was going on with her or who she'd been seeing. You allowed her to go out with someone you don't know because why? He was cute? And then what was the garbage you were feeding her about sex, Marie? That she should just go for it? My poor daughter is so confused, she doesn't know what to think."

"She doesn't need you and your archaic views of sex to pollute her thinking. Laura needed someone to trust, and to guide her. I made sure she understood her responsibilities and gave her the comfort she never would have gotten from you."

"What responsibilities?" Kate heard Richard ask.

"I told her about birth control, about protecting herself."

When Kate looked up, Richard looked murderous. "You call that guidance? No one is supposed to touch my baby girl."

"Richard, really," Marie sniffed. "I can't believe you're so naïve."

"If that fucking Neanderthal touched my daughter…"

"Then good for him," Marie shrieked. "I hope he made love to her until she cried."

That was it. He snapped. Richard lunged toward Marie, but stopped just short of grabbing her when Marie's hand shot out in a halting motion.

"Do not even think about getting violent with me. I'll castrate you."

Still spitting mad, Richard reined himself in, stepping back, but the words were still guttural, angry. "You'd better start thinking about how you're going to explain yourself to me."

"Screw you and your ultimatums, Richard. You'd better be prepared to explain yourself to *me* once that bitch is out of our house."

Marie shot a wordless dagger in Kate's direction and stormed out of the room. The woman was one of the most toxic individuals Kate had ever met, but she had had to give Marie credit. She didn't take Richard's shit.

Richard slammed his fist into a wall and spun on Kate. "I'll deal with Laura. You can go."

His words were typical, but his body language showed tension, weakness, and there was no way Kate was backing down or leaving without her daughter. The son of a bitch was done screwing with her.

"Don't you dare dismiss me," Kate said. "Especially considering what's happened with Laura."

"Marie's poor judgment doesn't change the fact that you are an incompetent mother. Laura will be with me full time, very soon; I'll deal with it."

"I'm incompetent? That's funny. Let's review. First, we have a joint agreement. While in your care, Laura's been going out at all hours, several of her teachers have talked to me about her grades falling off, and your daughter, who is still a minor, has been dating a man four years older than her while your fiancée slips condoms into her purse. It's possible the judge might view that as a tad irresponsible as she's reviewing your petition for custody."

"Don't threaten me, Kate. You have no idea what you're doing."

She wasn't scared. For the first time since he'd hit her, she wasn't afraid. That was when Kate could see Richard had nothing. He'd lost his power.

"I know exactly what I'm doing. You aren't getting custody. You aren't turning her against me, and you are not getting another dime. Listen carefully: don't ever underestimate me again."

She left him in the kitchen and walked through the house. It was sparsely decorated and unremarkable. The dining room table was elaborately set, and Kate remembered the party she'd thrown at her house exactly one year earlier. Richard's colleagues and several of the deans attended, as did Marie. Kate didn't know the woman she entertained in her home was sleeping with her husband. *Poor Marie.* Kate thought. Richard was her problem now.

Climbing the stairs, she knocked on the only closed door in the upstairs hall. "Laura, it's Mom."

"Come in."

Kate entered a room that a month ago would have been forbidden. It was decorated very much like her room at Kate's house, with vibrant apple green walls and bold prints on the bed and windows. However, this room lacked certain touches—there were no posters of bands or sports stars. No whiteboard with notes scribbled by her friends. This room, while attractive, was sterile, like the relationships in the house.

"Do you have what you need?"

"I don't know."

"Talk to me." Kate sat on the bed and patted Laura's knee.

"Why do you even want me, Mom? I've hurt you, I've hurt Jack. I've lied to pretty much everyone. I'm so messed up." Laura looked spent, and Kate knew Jack was just part of it.

Two weeks ago Kate had miscarried, Laura learned about her relationship with David, and she found out everything her father had told her amounted to a pack of lies. *Messed up* was certainly understandable. Her poor girl has a lot of healing to do.

"Oh, honey…" Kate reached out and pulled her close, dropping a kiss on her baby's forehead. "Yeah, you screwed up and I hope you learned from it, but I'm your mother and I love you. We'll get through this together."

Laura shrugged lightly, but was quiet while she gathered her thoughts. "You know, you mentioned seeing that counselor. I'm thinking it might be a good idea."

"I'll make a call."

"Did he tell me the truth about anything?" Her voice cracked, but she didn't cry.

"Dad?" Laura nodded, and it took Kate a moment to give her an answer, especially considering Richard's history. "He loves you. That's the truth."

Laura squeezed Kate's hand and they sat quietly until Laura said what she was feeling. "I miss Jack. And Daddy's gonna hurt him."

"Dad doesn't have the guts to hurt him, don't worry."

There was a noise and both Kate and Laura looked up. Richard was standing in the doorway. He had both hands in his pocket and she and her ex-husband locked eyes. He wasn't angry anymore, but confused, maybe even a little humbled. In the twenty-two years she'd known him, *that* was something new.

Looking back at Laura, she saw her poor girl worried about her dad, and mourning her lost love. This was major. "Are you ready?"

Laura nodded and rose to face Richard. Kate watched as her daughter, for the second time in two days, let go of someone she loved. Her relationship with her father was so complicated. If it was going to survive, Laura had to set the boundaries. Kate could see she made her decision. "I'm going to Mom's for now. In a few days we'll talk."

He nodded. "I do love you, sweetheart."

"I know, but you did some really awful things."

"What can I do to make it right? I'll do anything to make you happy."

Laura picked up her tote and walked past him on the way out of her room. "You'll let me get to know my mother. I need her, so give us some space."

Kate had been staring at the floor, but realized she was now in an interesting position. She had the power in the relationship, and the man in the doorway was at a loss. It was really nice when the stars aligned. When Laura was out of earshot, Richard turned to Kate.

"What did you tell her?" he asked.

"Everything. I threw you under the bus." Kate rose and faced him. "She knows what you did to me, and everything you did to her by driving a wedge between us."

He closed his eyes and pressed his fingers to the bridge of his nose. Knowing what that meant, he shook his head and looked at Kate. "What happened with the guy?"

"It was a bad night and it's over, but it never should have happened."

"I should kill him."

"Nothing happened. And quite frankly, considering our age difference when we met, you don't have a leg to stand on."

"That was different."

Kate nodded. "You've got a point. The difference is that Jack is basically a good guy. You knew I was sheltered and naïve, and you took advantage of that."

He started to say something and then stopped. It took Kate a few seconds to realize he was staring at her, rather intently. "What is it?" she asked.

"You've changed."

"Well, I don't have you to knock me down anymore."

"I don't know what to say to that?"

Kate wasn't sure what to say either. This was the most civil he'd been to her since they walked down the aisle. Now he wanted to play nice? Pay her compliments? No, Kate wasn't buying it.

"It amazes me that you can't see what you lost." He didn't look at her, but that didn't stop Kate from saying her piece. "I loved you, Richard. I loved you with all my heart. You reciprocated by abusing me, cheating on me, and trying to steal my child. There is nothing to say. However, you should be prepared. My lawyers will want another conference about custody." He was squirming. Kate discovered she liked making him squirm. "Enjoy your party."

Chapter 28

L AURA CREPT UP the stairs to her mother's office. So much
had happened over the last few days, she couldn't sleep.
She'd lost Jack, had lost all respect for her father, and had lost
respect for herself. Glancing through the door, she saw her
mom, sitting cross legged in her chair, her earbuds in, and her
head bopping around to the tune playing on her iPod.

Her fingers were flying over the keyboard and she knew
Mom was immersed in her work. Laura found her focus
incredible, and figured the words took over her mom's brain
the same way the music overtook hers. Not wanting to
interrupt, she walked downstairs to the den.

Just as she thought, David was crashed on the couch, ice
on his shoulder and his feet up on the ottoman. He looked so
totally at ease in the house, it was like he'd always been there.
She was certain he probably hated her now because of what
had happened with Jack. But she couldn't avoid him. He was
part of Mom's life, part of their lives, and she needed to set
things straight with him.

And she needed his help.

Walking forward, he looked up from his book and smiled

at her. It was tentative, though. Not quite as warm as even a few days ago.

"Hey," she said. "Good book?"

"Eh," he said. "It's a little slow out of the gate." He put the book next to him. "What's up?"

Laura sat down and breathed out. "I was hoping you could help me with something."

His eyebrow went up slightly. "Sure, I guess."

"I wrote this paper for European History and I didn't do too well."

David sat up and moved the ice off his arm. Reaching out, he took the paper she offered. The red *C-* stood out, and he took a minute to scan the first page.

"I can rewrite it," she said. "But, um… would you be willing to read it and give me some suggestions?"

His eyes met hers and he smiled just a little bit. Then he nodded.

"I'd be happy to. Did you talk to your teacher?"

"I did. He said getting another opinion wasn't a bad idea. Mom said you majored in history."

"I did. The French Revolution is pretty complex," he said as he flipped through the paper. "But I can help you. It's one of my favorite subjects."

"Are you sure you don't mind?"

"Are you kidding? I'd love to help." He looked at the first page again. "When is the rewrite due?"

"Like ten days."

"Can I keep this? I'll read it and we can talk about it the day after tomorrow. Is that enough time for you?"

"That's fine." She knew he had a game tomorrow and she wouldn't see him. "Thanks, David. I really appreciate it." And she did. By helping her, she knew he didn't hate her for what happened with Jack.

"No problem, kiddo." He leaned forward, placing the paper on the ottoman. "Something else on your mind?"

Laura had a lot on her mind, but more than likely David knew she was curious about one thing. "Is he okay?"

David blew out a breath. "It's hard to say. He's not talking much, but he's not himself."

"Oh." Laura ran her hand under her nose as she sniffled. "I miss him."

She felt the tears well up and spill onto her cheeks. She didn't even try to stop them. Everything inside her hurt and it didn't matter why it all happened. All Laura knew was that she would never, ever get over him. She was surprised when David reached around her shoulder and pulled her close. Laura gave into the sadness and rested her head on David's chest. Her tears came a little harder. Her breathing was a little shorter.

"You must think I'm a terrible person."

"No." David reached behind him and came back with a box of tissues from the end table. Laura grabbed a handful, mopped her face, and blew her nose while she listened to him. "I think you made a mistake. That happens to everyone. God knows, I've made some big ones."

"But I knew what I was doing. I did it anyway."

"You screwed up, but no one's going to die from this."

Laura nodded and let out a shaky breath. David handed her another tissue. There were points over the last few days that she felt like dying, but she knew he was right. Nothing was fatal. "Thanks."

"No problem."

"Are the guys on the team torturing him?"

David's face tightened. She knew how the guys on the team treated each other. Jack had told her all about the verbal shots, and she could only imagine what they were saying about his high school girlfriend who collapsed at a party.

"He hasn't had an easy time of it," David said. "But I got them to back off a little."

Laura wiped at her eyes again, fully appreciative of what David had done. "That's good."

He dropped his head and examined his hands as he rubbed them together. He was thinking, and Laura had a feeling it was her turn to make him feel better. "My mom is really happy."

He turned his face toward hers. "That's good. My goal is to keep her happy. And you, too." He paused. "You're okay with us being together?"

"At first it was strange, but I don't mind. After what she went through with my father, she deserves to be happy."

"She told you?"

"Everything." Laura bit her lip. "He's seriously pissed off right now. I'm worried about that."

"I figured. That's why I've been here so much."

"I mean, I know a lot has changed, but Mom's dealt with enough shit."

"That's the truth." He looked her right in the eyes and his meaning was clear. "At least now she doesn't have to deal with him alone."

"Nope," Laura said. "She has us."

JACK WAS ON the couch in his apartment playing hockey on X-Box and thinking about Laura. He should be out celebrating their win, but he didn't feel like subjecting himself to the women who would be at the bar, and he was sick of the shit he was getting from the guys. Padre tried to get them to back off, so did Ty, but he was taking abuse at every turn. He fucking hated it and he hated how he couldn't get Laura out of his head.

He'd left her house that morning before she woke up. He couldn't go through another scene like the one they'd had in the kitchen. Holding her, listening to her cry, was hell. But he couldn't let her go. They fell asleep together on the couch in her den. Well, she fell asleep. He stayed awake and held her, remembering how she felt nestled against him, how she smelled, how she sounded when she slept. He lay with her for a couple of hours, intent on imprinting everything about her into his brain. When Jack said this was killing him, he wasn't lying. He loved Laura, he wanted her, and he couldn't have her.

He had a clear memory of hearing the footsteps on the stairs and within seconds, Kate was glaring at him. She turned, walked out, and before he knew it, Padre was driving him home. The rest was a blur. He played the game that night on autopilot, came home, and slept through most of the next day. The last few days had been like that. No effort, he just did what he had to do.

He heard noise screaming from the TV and realized he'd been playing the video game the same way. He didn't care. Suddenly, he heard a pounding at the door and Ty's voice came from the other side.

"Open the door, Nelly. I can't find my key."

Jack walked to the entry way and threw the bolt, but barely stepped back far enough for Ty, who shoved the door and entered cursing. He stormed through the apartment, throwing his coat and knocking a pile of mail off the table. "I've been fucking traded."

Jack wasn't expecting that. "Traded? Where?"

"Long Island. I have to be there tomorrow. Which means I have to pack my shit tonight."

"When did you find out?" Jesus, first Laura, now his best friend. This week was turning out to be a major kick in the ass.

"I'm standing at the bar at The Brick, having a drink with a *goddess,* and my cell rings. It's my agent with the *good* news."

"Holy shit." Jack couldn't help but worry that he might be next. "When did they finish the deal?"

"I dunno, while I was having my best point game of the season? I've fucking killed myself this season."

"At least you're staying in the division."

"Oh, yeah," Ty said. "That's flattering. They don't even care if I'm facing you guys on the ice."

He dropped onto the couch next to Jack and leaned back into the cushions. "I did three years in the AHL after college. I think I've finally made it, and they traded me for fucking draft picks!"

"This sucks, man." Jack grabbed the beer on the table next to him and took a drink.

"Tell me about it." Ty grew quiet because there really wasn't anything left to say, then looked over at him. "You doin' okay?"

It was the first time his friend had asked him anything about what had happened with Laura. He hadn't given him a hard time, but he hadn't asked him anything either.

Jack shrugged. "It sucks. I'm still trying to get my head around it."

"I can't believe she's seventeen."

"I know."

There were a lot of things hanging in the air. This wasn't something he was going to talk about, but it was good to know someone gave a shit.

"I gotta pack." Tyler stood up. "If I don't see you before I leave…" Ty shook Jack's hand and then pulled him into a quick hug. "Take it easy, man."

"You too," Jack said.

His friend walked a few steps and turned around. "Oh, and Nelly? Keep your head up."

Jack nodded and grinned. That was all the warning he was going to get from his friend. When they met up on the ice, if he wasn't careful, Tyler would check him into unconsciousness.

Ty closed himself in his bedroom to pack and make phone calls to his family. Jack grabbed the remote and started flipping channels on the TV. He stopped and reached into his pocket. He stared at his phone and without really thinking about it, pressed the speed dial. Laura picked up on the third ring.

"Hello?" Her voice was scratchy, like she'd been sleeping.

"Did I wake you?"

"Jack?"

"Yeah. Is it okay to call?"

"Umm, I guess. What do you want?"

"I, ah… I needed… Ty was traded."

"Oh, no. Where?"

"To Long Island."

"Isn't his whole family in Connecticut? That's good, right?"

"His mom drives him nuts."

"Okay, so maybe it's not good." Jack didn't laugh, even though she was trying to be cute. She grew quiet and then asked, "Are you alright?"

"I just wanted to talk to you."

"Oh, Jack." Hearing the sadness in her voice, knowing he shouldn't have called, made him feel a little sick.

"I wish it could be different."

"Me too. Are you worried you'll be traded?"

"It's always something I think about, but I should be fine."

"That's good."

He could hear the strain in her voice, and Jack knew this had been a mistake. "I should go. I'm sorry I woke you."

"Okay," she said.

He heard her take a deep breath and then it hitched a little. She was crying. He was such an ass.

He was about to say good-bye when he heard another deep breath on her end. "Jack?"

"Yeah?"

"Please don't call me again."

Damn, she was tough. "Okay," he whispered.

"It's too hard."

"I know. I needed to talk to someone…"

"You have to find someone else to call. I know it's all my fault, but I can't do this." She sniffled. "It hurts."

He paused, not knowing what else to say. Should he tell her he loved her? That he missed her? "Laura?" He didn't say either, because she was gone.

There was no good-bye, no hysteria, the call just ended. Jack stared at his phone, and for a minute he found himself wishing he could trade places with Ty.

Chapter 29

KATE COULDN'T REMEMBER feeling this displaced in a very long time. Even when Richard left, she still had the things familiar to her. Her home, her job. *Her job.*

She'd been teaching English at St. Andrew's for fifteen years. She'd been in the same classroom in Larchmont Hall for the last thirteen years. She was the advisor to the literary magazine and the newspaper. But not anymore.

She'd just been fired.

She was about to leave for the day. She'd planned on going home, taking a shower, and watching David's game, when she'd been called to the conference room and informed she was being dismissed. No notice, no request for a resignation, just goodbye.

The President of Board of Trustees rambled on about moral turpitude and the school's high standards, and how a woman like her, with questionable morals and a life that bordered on scandalous, couldn't be allowed to continue shaping the young minds on the St. Andrew's campus any longer. They'd tried to be understanding about her writing career and her divorce, but her latest escapade with the athlete was the last straw.

The athlete.

Sitting at the desk in her classroom, she looked around. It didn't seem real. Kate heard footsteps racing down the hallway and her instincts were right on when Julie appeared in the doorway.

"I just heard. Are they fucking crazy?"

"They don't think so." Kate walked to the closet and pulled out two shopping bags and a box from the shelf. "I'm a corrupting influence on the students here."

"That's the dumbest thing I've ever heard." Julie paced around the room and watched as Kate started to put things into the bags. "What are you doing?"

"Packing. I've been asked to leave the premises by the end of the day."

"Kate, you can't just fold, you have to fight this."

"With whom? Julie, I was booted by the Board of Trustees. There's no one to appeal to."

"But why? Is it your writing? What?"

"It's because I'm with David."

"What? I don't..." Just then, Julie understood. "Oh, God. This wouldn't have to do with a certain trustee named John Connor?"

Kate nodded. "Actually, I don't think he had anything to do with it. But what happened with Chelsea was the last straw for me."

"I can't believe it. She goes all batshit crazy, and *you* have to deal with the fallout?"

"They can't fire her." And as the reality of what had happened swamped her, Kate found she needed the wall for some support and leaned against it. "I've been here forever, Jules.

What am I going to do?"

"Kate, you don't *need* the job."

"*Need* isn't the issue. I like my job and I'm good at it. I like teaching and the kids. All my friends are here. When everything started to fall apart, this place gave me a reason to get up every day."

Julie walked over and slid an arm around Kate's shoulder. "Now you have David, and Laura. You have an amazing career, and you'll still have your friends."

Kate looked at Julie and had to smile. "I'll have you. Maybe one or two others will keep in touch. I mean, I knew I wouldn't stay forever. But I wasn't ready yet."

"It won't be the same here without you."

Kate pressed her fingers to her temples before getting back to her packing. She found another box, dumped the books it held onto a table, and started filling it with files of teaching materials she'd created over the years. She wasn't about to leave all her hard work for someone else to use. After emptying the file cabinet, they took a break.

"Are you going to call David?"

"He's in Atlanta. He'll call before they fly out. I'll tell him then if he isn't too tired."

Julie looked at the bags and the boxes that were being filled with fifteen years of hard work. "Do you need some help with all this stuff?"

"Yeah, that would be great. Do you want to have dinner with Laura and me? I started some soup in the crockpot before I left this morning. We're going to eat and watch the game later."

"If you promise to tell me all the Richard and Marie gossip."

"I promise, but be prepared. It's a long and strange story."

"I like long and strange. I feel like I've been out of the loop since I took that trip with my sister and then went right to that conference."

Kate turned and stopped what she was doing. John Connor stood in her doorway, looking uncomfortable. He hadn't advocated for her dismissal, but his daughter was the catalyst. It was hard to look at him as she packed up fifteen years of her life.

"Dr. Connor," Kate said. "Can I help you with something?"

"No, uh..." He stepped into the room. "I wanted to see how you were doing."

She paused, fighting to maintain her dignity. "I've been better."

Julie grabbed two bags and walked toward the door, snarling at him as she walked by. "I'll put these in my car." Kate nodded and Julie left.

John circled the room and stopped by a large framed photograph of F. Scott Fitzgerald. "I tried to stop them. They wouldn't listen to me."

She shrugged, pushing an annoying lock of hair behind her ear.

"The gossip mill got going. Once that happened, you became a liability," he said quietly.

"A liability?"

"St. Andrew's has a very serious and staid reputation. You know that. You're a celebrity and now you have a celebrity boyfriend. It's... unseemly... according to the president of the board."

"But I didn't do anything, John. My biggest 'crime', if

you want to call it that, is that I'm dating a younger man. That's my personal life, John. I'm allowed to have a life."

"I know. I tried to talk some sense into them and so did the headmaster. They weren't having it. They're invoking the morality clause in your contract. I'm sorry."

"I heard." It was such bullshit. She was a single woman in a relationship with a single man. She wasn't breaking any laws. "I'm sure Chelsea's not sorry."

John was quiet for a moment, then tilted his head. "Don't be so sure of that. She's been dealing with some *changes* since her visit with you."

"Changes?"

"Yes." This was tough for him, and Kate almost felt bad. Almost. "The restraining order was a good wake-up call, for one. David's attorney also called our attorney. Chelsea knows she crossed the line."

Kate shook her head. It wasn't like any of Chelsea's epiphanies were going to help her.

"I also know that I'm just as responsible. I let her entitled attitude continue unchecked." He took two steps in her direction and stood very straight. "I'm very sorry about everything that's happened. It was inexcusable."

Kate appreciated his honesty. She knew well enough that parenting mistakes were the hardest to admit to. It couldn't have been easy for him to admit he'd raised such a toxic individual. They lapsed into an awkward silence, and he brought a stack of files to the table where she was packing a box.

"She got a job."

Kate's head snapped up. Could she have heard him wrong? "Excuse me?"

"Chelsea. I told her if she didn't get a job, I was going to cut her off."

"Seriously?" Kate was stunned. Completely stunned. "What is she doing?"

"Working for a media relations company. She's enjoying it. It's a lot of administrative work, but they're tapping into everything she knows about trends and such."

"That's good. She's a bright girl; I'm sure she'll do well if she puts her mind to it."

More silence, and then he looked at her with such a lost expression, her heart hurt for him. "When her mother left, I guess I felt I had to make up for everything she didn't have. I made a lot of mistakes."

That was something Kate could relate to. Thinking about her situation with Laura, mistakes and parenting seemed to go hand in hand. "Too bad there's no manual for being a parent. We do our best, I guess."

"Are you happy? Burke is treating you well?"

"Very well. In that regard, I've never been happier."

He grinned and nodded. "I'm glad. You deserve it."

LAURA WAS EXHAUSTED from play rehearsal. She groaned when she noticed her mother wasn't home yet. That meant dinner was hours away. All she wanted was food and some Advil before attacking her homework. It had been two weeks since she lost Jack, and it still hurt so deep, Laura didn't know if it would ever go away.

She told him not to call her. The other night after he found out about Tyler's trade, he needed her and she wanted to help. But talking to him, knowing they weren't going to be together, tore at her heart, and something possessed her to tell him to leave her alone. Why prolong the inevitable? He wasn't hers, he wasn't going to be. She had to cut him off. Laura expected Jack would move on pretty quickly. Wherever they went, girls looked at him. He was gorgeous and famous, and she was nobody. He'd be fine.

Laura couldn't even look at any one else. A really cute guy in her Psych class had been kind of flirting with her, and wanted her to come hang out this weekend, but she said no. She had her recital, her grades needed to come up, and her heart was still in pieces. No boys for her. Not for a while.

Pressing the code on the keypad by the garage, Laura entered the house, dropped her backpack and coat in the laundry room, and jumped when she walked in the kitchen and saw her father at the kitchen table, having a bowl of soup.

"Dad!" She grabbed her heart. "What are you doing here?"

"I was waiting for you. I thought we could have dinner together and try to work out all that 'stuff' that happened on New Year's Day." He stood and took two steps toward her. He looked fine, but she wondered if he hit his head or something. That had to be it. Maybe he had a head injury and that's why he was acting crazy.

"Oh, ah, I don't know," she said. "Aren't you supposed to call first?"

"Honey, I'm concerned about what's going on here with your mother and the hockey player."

"What are you talking about?"

"I don't know if this is a good place for you. I mean, living here, with him here all the time..."

Was he serious?

"Dad, you really shouldn't be here when Mom gets home. She's still getting some mood swings and... you know... *woo hoo.*"

"How is she feeling?" A distinct chill in her father's voice told her he wasn't sincere. He asked because he had to.

"She's better, most days. She and David are pretty serious."

"Yeah, well. I'm only concerned about you, and what being around your mother and her lover is doing to you."

Laura was dumbfounded. "You cheated on her for *ten years.* You abused her, tried every which way to get me to hate her, and told me Marie was more my mother than Mom. Do you actually expect me to buy this crap? You're worried about her doing what? Setting a bad example for me?"

"Laura, I don't want to argue. I have a right to be concerned."

"No, Dad, you really don't."

"You're my baby. You always will be." He smiled sweetly. Laura had no clue who this man was and what he'd done with her father. It was creepy.

"You know what? You'd better go home and call if you have anything to talk to Mom about."

"Maybe if I stop by tomorrow..."

"Do you have a death wish? In case you didn't notice, David doesn't like you and he won't let you near us."

"I'd like to see him try and stop me."

That sounded like her father.

"Dad, he nearly crushed you when you came here after Christmas. I don't think he's worried."

"Laura. I want you to come home with me. I don't want

to lose you." Now he was resorting to guilt. God, she couldn't keep up.

"Go home, Daddy. I'll come over Friday and I'll talk to you then. We can go out to dinner, okay?"

There was noise at the side door, along with two female voices, and Laura knew it was too late.

*

"JULES, DIDN'T I tell you once that the bad days always managed to get worse?" Kate dropped her keys on the counter. "What are you doing here, Richard?"

"I wanted to see you. We need to talk about things. About your situation."

"My situation?" The last thing she wanted to deal with was Richard. Part of her wanted to threaten him with a visit from David; but at her age, she really didn't want to have to resort to that kind of adolescent posturing. She was tempted, though. "I've had a shitty day, and the last thing I need is you in my kitchen. Get out. Don't come back. I'm going to take a bath."

Just as she was about to leave the room, his arm shot out and he grabbed her hand. "Don't you walk away from me. I want to talk to you."

Kate looked at his hand on her arm and for a split second, she felt the old terror. But just as quickly, it left her. Now it was anger—deep and dark, that filled her. This man was not going to terrorize her again.

"Take. Your. Hand. Off. Me."

Her voice was low, quiet, and she could only assume how it sounded to everyone else in the room. If she had a weapon,

Kate had no doubt that she would use it. Stunned by her reaction, Richard froze. His face, his body, everything froze in place. Except for one thing. He moved his hand, which found its way back to his side.

"Sorry," he said. "Can we talk?"

Kate stared at him. "Your lawyer can call mine. We can talk through them. Now leave."

"This is not over, Kate." Richard retrieved his keys from the table.

"You're right," she said. "It's not. But trust me, you're going to wish it was."

DAVID DROPPED HIS bag when he walked into the bedroom. Kate was asleep, curled up on her side, clutching one of his pillows. *His pillows.* He smiled as he thought about how they had become part of each other's lives. How they'd each laid claim to closet space and a certain side of the bed, and it felt just right.

The light on the dresser was on, casting a soft glow over her. Her hair swirled around the pillow like melted chocolate and her breathing was slow and deep. He decided not to wake her. Considering the kind of day she'd had, sleep was the best thing for her.

He undressed and slid into bed beside her. She must have sensed him because her body scooted toward his and she snuggled right in.

"I'm so glad you're home," she whispered.

"I didn't mean to wake you."

"I wasn't really asleep. I've been dozing on and off for the last few hours." She tilted her face toward his and the sadness in her eyes told him everything.

"Bad day, huh?"

"You could say that. I lost my job."

"I heard." He pulled her close and heard her breath catch, but she didn't cry. "I feel like it's my fault."

Her hand came up and touched his face. "It's not."

"But it's because of Chelsea…"

Her fingers trailed across his face and settled on his lips, silencing him. "She's mean and bitter, and she has nothing. I have Laura and I have you. It'll be okay."

Grasping Kate's hand, he kissed it. "I love you."

"I love you, too."

She cuddled in again, and after a few minutes David figured it was safe to ask about what happened with the asshole. "You want to tell me about Richard?"

She sighed. She didn't really want to tell him about her ex, but she would. They told each other everything. "He was here, waiting, when I got home. I managed it."

"Laura said you were pissed."

"She got that right." He nodded and his hand slid over her body and settled on her hip. "I never wanted to draw Laura into the battle, you know? I don't expect her to take sides."

He grinned at her. "But she took yours, didn't she."

Kate giggled and bit her lip. "Yes. It was awesome."

He gave her a squeeze and she must have seen him wince.

Kate picked up her head and looked him in the eyes. "How's your shoulder?"

David groaned. She'd watched the game, and must have seen the hit he took into the boards during the third period.

When they first got together, she freaked every time he got checked. Lately, she'd been handling the physicality of the game better.

"Sore, but not too bad. It's just bruised."

"How many games are you out?"

"Two or three." It was worse than he was letting on, and would probably need surgery in the off season. But after the day she'd had, Kate didn't need to know about it yet.

She gave him a little nudge and wriggled on top of him, planting a kiss on his lips. "Poor baby. I'll have to take care of you."

"Yeah? What do you have in mind?" Homecomings didn't get any better than this. Kate's hands ran up his sides and David saw the mischief in her eyes. Maybe her day wasn't as bad as he thought. It was certainly possible she needed to face down her ex more often. The sexual aggressiveness he was seeing was a nice surprise.

Her fingers ran through his hair, her lips touched his, and raw electricity shot through him. David needed her right now, wanted her more than anything, and his hard-on was proof. The last time they were together was at his house in November, almost two months ago. He'd missed the feel of her, but he'd been waiting for Kate to be ready, both physically and emotionally. Apparently, she was.

His good arm wrapped around her and his hand travelled up and down her spine. "Are you sure?"

She nodded and kissed him again. "I've missed you."

This was real. The kisses she left over his face and across his shoulder released all the tension in his body. How soft she felt, the way she smelled, was familiar and comforting. This was what David wanted for the rest of his life.

Her lips connected with his, and the kiss was so intense he almost went blind from the lust she triggered. Leave it to his girlfriend the writer to get imaginative. Before he could focus again, he felt her mouth leave warm kisses over his neck, chest, and stomach. Finally, when he could see, Kate's eyes met his and he realized what she had in mind. His breathing became more rapid as she worked her way south, teasing him like a seasoned bad girl. Her hands slid inside his boxers, and pushed them down and over his hips, releasing him.

After that, David's mind went blank.

Chapter 30

D AVID'S PHONE RANG as he walked into his kitchen. He'd spent two hours at the orthopedist about his shoulder, and fortunately the news was good. It was badly bruised. No separations, nothing torn. With a little time, and therapy, he should be fine without any surgery. It was a good thing, too, since he hoped he and Kate could get married this summer. He hadn't asked her yet, thinking if it was too soon, but proposing felt right. Dropping his mail on the table, he answered.

"Yeah?"

"Padre?" It was Jack.

"Nelly, how was practice?"

"Dave, I just left the GM's office."

Shit. David knew the tone in Jack's voice. He'd heard it countless times over the years from other teammates, most recently from Tyler Graves, and he braced himself for the news.

"I've been traded."

"Shit," he said aloud. He could only hope it was some-place close. He hated losing Jack as a linemate, but he'd hate losing him as a friend even more. "Where?"

"I can't believe it. I'm going to Vancouver."

"Vancouver?" David let the word ring in his head. Vancouver. Nice city, but three thousand fucking miles away. They barely played the Canucks.

"I have to leave tonight."

"This blows." Having never been traded, David didn't know how he would deal with the sudden upheaval and being thrust into the unknown. A new town, new people, having to find a new home... all of it sounded like a nightmare. But it came with the job. They all knew it, but no one talked about it until it happened.

"I thought things were going good." His voice was lost, confused.

"Jack, it's the game. No one is indispensable. They traded you 'cause you were worth something."

Jack groaned. For a young player, a trade sometimes shook their confidence. The kid was just putting down roots and settling into a system, and boom—he finds out he's only as valuable as the player they can get for him.

"I've got a late flight out tonight. I meet the team in St. Louis for a game the day after tomorrow."

"I don't know what to say. You're going to a good team. A good organization."

"Yeah."

"You packing?"

"Yeah. I've gotta go get my stuff at the arena. I don't know what the hell I'm going to do about my apartment. God, this sucks."

"I can give you a hand if you need it."

"Nah, thanks." There was a pause, a breath. What else

could be said? "I guess I'll talk to you later on."

David hung up and thought about his own situation. He had a lot more to lose than Jack if he should get traded. And while he never really thought about it, Kate not teaching anymore might be a good thing, since her job was one of the things that tied her to the area. With the team possibly in a trading mood, he didn't want to take any chances. Jack's trade had been the wake-up call. He wasn't going to wait for the perfect moment—he was going to talk to Kate about making things permanent.

LAURA WENT TO grab a pen in her bag, and she saw the light flashing on her phone. She was in the library, it was her lunch period, and even though she knew she shouldn't, she took it out and went to her inbox. There were two texts from Tracy, who was sitting across from her at that moment, a text from Dan, the boy in her Psych class, and a notification from the Flyers. She'd been getting team updates for two years, but today's update was about Jack. He'd been traded.

And he was going to Canada.

Laura stared at the message. She'd so completely zoned out, that when Mrs. Gardella, the librarian, finally touched her shoulder, Laura flinched. "Laura, are you alright?"

Laura looked up, unable to speak for a few seconds as she wrapped her head around the news. *Traded.*

"Honey, did you get bad news?"

"Just something about a friend of mine. It's fine. He's not hurt or anything." She looked at Tracy and then back at the librarian. "He's moving."

Tracy's mouth dropped open and Laura locked her phone. "I'll be fine, Mrs. G. I shouldn't have taken out my phone."

"No, but I'm worried about you. You haven't been yourself the last few weeks. Can I help?"

"Thanks. I'll be okay."

"Okay." Mrs. Gardella left them and Tracy leaned across the library table.

"Who's moving?"

Laura drew a shaky breath and dabbed at her eyes again. "Jack's been traded."

Tracy dropped back in her chair and stared. "Where?"

"Vancouver." Laura gulped down the air and glanced toward the desk. Mrs. Gardella was looking up from her work and watching. She had to hold it together. Falling apart in school was not an option. She'd gotten through her parents' divorce without a referral to student services; she wasn't going to be sent there because she broke up with her boyfriend.

"You'll never see him."

"I wasn't going to see him anyway. Maybe it's better." It would certainly be easier if there was no chance they'd see each other. But she knew it was hard for him, and while part of her wanted him to leave, her heart was breaking for him. Jack would be miserable. She wondered if she should send him a text or something. *No*, that was a bad idea.

Sticking her phone in her bag, Laura made a decision. She had to let Jack go. His life was where he was playing, and she still had a lot to do. There was high school, and finding a college... Laura thought she might want to be a doctor. She had to take care of herself, and that meant her heart couldn't be in Vancouver.

Adorable Dan from Psych was walking towards the table and Laura took a deep breath to steady her nerves. Dan smiled, and Laura found it wasn't too hard to smile back.

He was nice, smart, and really cute… and he was here.

FOR DAVID, SAYING goodbye to teammates who'd been traded over the years was the most difficult part of his job. But nothing quite prepared him for saying goodbye to Jack Nelson. He'd become a good friend over the past year, and David often thought if he had a brother, he'd want him to be like Jack.

He figured Laura would be upset when she found out, but she wasn't as bad as he expected. She even had a date on Friday night, and then Sunday, Laura and Kate were hitting the road to do some college visits. He was amazed at the way the two of them slipped into the mother-daughter roles so easily after such a long time of alienation. It was like Laura wanted it so badly that when the opportunity to have her mother back presented itself, she grabbed on with both hands. Kate was just being *Kate*, doing all the things that made him fall in love with her.

David looked out the kitchen window. It was one of those winters—perpetually gray and cold. A light snow had started to fall, and he knew he should leave before the roads got too slick. He had a morning skate and he needed to get some sleep. But he had to talk to her first. He had to lay the groundwork for their lives.

Jack's trade brought the fact home that anything could happen, and he wanted Kate to know that wherever he was, he wanted her with him. No matter where his life in the NHL took him, he wanted to make a family with her, Laura, and hopefully one or two of their own.

The soft padding of her footsteps made him look up. She was wearing a pair of red pajama pants and an old Harvard sweatshirt. The fuzzy slippers made her an irresistible package.

She sat on the couch and he moved, sitting on the otto- man facing her. He took her hands and thought carefully, because David knew these could be the most important words he ever spoke.

"Get any work done?" he asked.

"Some." She shrugged.

"Is she asleep?"

"No, she's on the phone with Dan," she said.

He smiled and shook his head. He wondered how things would go for her with a guy her own age? As he got to know Laura better, David could see she was a lot like her mother, but time would tell. Kate sat on the couch with her legs pulled up, chewing on those gorgeous lips, and every inch of him responded. Yup. A goner for sure.

"We need to talk." They said it together, and both of them smiled.

"You first," she said.

He took a deep breath. "Okay. Jack's trade scared the shit out of me. He was supposed to be the centerpiece of the club for years, and then, boom... he's gone."

"Are you worried that you could be dealt?"

"I'm very well protected, and I signed a long term con- tract last summer, but anything can happen. We need to think about our future, about our life together, as a family."

She didn't say anything, but looked down at their joined

hands.

"Kate, I know I want to marry you. I think I've known it since we had dinner together in California."

She tried to speak, but stopped, nodding at his words.

"I need to know that if I get sent to Phoenix, you'll be there." He paused again, thinking about what he wanted to say. "I know this is your home, but…"

"Shhh," she finally said. "A home is about people, about family. Without you here, this is a house, that's all. If you get traded, I promise you, we'll work it out."

"Like I said, I don't foresee anything happening, but…" He stood, fished around in his pocket and pulled out the small velvet box. Her eyes locked on it as he held it out for her to accept.

"Oh, David." Her breath caught as she took the box from him and opened it. It was a simple ring, a solitary, round diamond set in a diamond encrusted platinum band. Beautiful and perfect. "I can't believe you did this."

Knowing what she meant, he told Kate a truth that was going to shock her a little.

"I bought the ring in November."

"What? *November?* But—"

"After the whole mess with the article in the paper, before we knew you were pregnant, through all my screw-ups, I knew if I got you back I wasn't letting you go again." He took her face in his hands and saw her eyes fill with tears. "I wanted to ask you someplace romantic, make a big show of it, and I remembered that's not what we're about." He brushed away the tear that spilled onto her cheek. "We're about family dinners, nights on the couch, playing in the snow, and flannel pajamas." He tugged on her pants as he watched Kate dissolve. "I love you. I love you with all my heart. Marry me, Kate. Be my home."

She nodded her response and let the tears flow—happy tears, finally. He'd seen her cry too many times for other reasons, but these were good tears.

"Thank you for not giving up on me," she said. Her free hand covered one of his and she kissed him. "Thank you for being stubborn and competitive and for taking that silly bet."

"I'm not religious, but if I were ever going to believe in divine intervention, it was when I saw you in California. It was my lightning strike. I love you more than I ever thought possible." Kate handed him the box and extended her left hand. David took the ring from the box and slipped onto her finger. It fit perfectly.

"I love you, David."

The kiss she pressed to his lips was light. She wrapped her arms around him, holding tight, and David couldn't believe he was this damn lucky.

Chapter 31

D AN MARTIN GAVE Laura the perfect date. He came to the door when he picked her up, met her mom, and paid for everything, from the movie to the ice cream they got afterwards. He even asked before he held her hand in the movies, and Laura had to say when he touched her, she felt warm inside. It wasn't the same burn she felt with Jack, but it was warm and comfortable and safe. Dan was sweet and safe.

She liked talking to him, too. He wanted to be a pilot, and if everything fell into place for him, he would go to Annapolis. He had the grades, he was a star football player, and he was, without a doubt, someone who always did the right thing. Mom called guys like him 'Dudley Do-Right', and that was Dan to a tee.

"So, what colleges are you seeing next week?"

Laura thought for a minute and grinned. It was going to be a great trip. Not only were they seeing colleges, but Mom promised her some shopping in Boston. "Um, Cornell, Boston College, Boston University, Harvard, and Holy Cross."

"Harvard, huh?"

"My mom went to Harvard, so I'm a legacy, but I don't think I'll get in. B-C's my favorite anyway."

"Yeah? They have a great hockey team." Dan said, knowing Laura was a big hockey fan. He didn't know the half of it.

"I know. My mom's fiancée played for them. He and my grandfather both went there."

"That's cool. Is your mom's fiancée nice?"

"Yeah, he's awesome. It was a little weird at first, because he's a lot younger than her, but he's great. He makes her really happy."

"I'm sorry… your mom's a cougar?"

Laura laughed. "Yup, I guess she is."

She saw him smile in the dark of the car, and her heart tripped a little. He was really cute. "So is he around a lot?"

"David? Mmm hmm. When he's not on the road."

"He travels?"

Laura bit her lip. It wasn't a secret, so she didn't know why it was so hard to say, but finally she blurted it out. "Yup. He plays for the Flyers."

A nervous laugh caught in Dan's throat. "Seriously? David who?"

"David Burke." That did it. His mouth opened, no sound came out, and then it closed. She'd stunned him speechless, but now she had an opening. "I don't know if you'd want to go, but he said he could get me tickets to games whenever I wanted. I mean, if you want to hang out with me again."

They'd pulled into her driveway by this point, and Dan threw the car into park. He turned in his seat and laced his fingers with hers. Laura felt the warmth again. She looked into his big hazel eyes and a shock of dark hair fell across his forehead. She liked him. Her feelings wouldn't ever be like the flash fire she had with Jack, but she figured some relationships were meant to be less intense. Quieter. Easy.

"Laura, I'd hang out with you again, even if all we were doing was watching the grass grow."

KATE HEARD THE car pull in the driveway and she peeked out the mud room door, trying to see what was going on with Laura and Dan. He seemed like a really nice kid. He and Laura had been friends for a couple of years, and only recently had the relationship taken a different turn.

The car was dark and she couldn't see anything, but then the interior light went on as the doors opened. Kate ran through the kitchen, slipping on the tile floor, and flung herself on the couch in the family room. The TV was tuned to the local news, and Kate picked up her e-reader and turned it on. Casual. She had to look casual. Laura could not know she was spying on her. Kate giggled. Laura had to know she was curious, and Kate hoped she would be in the mood for a debriefing.

The book wasn't holding her attention because trying to get a look at the side door was more interesting. She saw their silhouettes in the window and strained for a peek. There wasn't much to see, except the outline of Dan's head, dropping down to kiss Laura, and Kate felt the breath ease out of her chest. From the looks of it, he kissed her on the cheek. Based on the way Laura floated in the house, the date had gone well. Really well.

Kate was relieved, because Laura was getting a life that she could manage. One that was right for a seventeen-year-old girl. There would be hard times, overwrought emotions, and there would be stress, but at least they could handle it together. Hopefully, there would be no more secrets.

Laura dropped her bag on the kitchen island and walked into the den. Kate feigned reading, but knew Laura wasn't buying it. She looked up and she saw a soft smile break on her daughter's face.

"Did you have a good time?"

"Yes, we had a really good time. He's very sweet."

"Seems nice. Very old-fashioned."

Laura nodded and sank into the cushions. "He has two older sisters. I have a feeling he's well coached."

Kate laughed. Laura's cynicism was tempered by the fact that she really seemed to enjoy herself. "That's not a bad thing."

"I know." She paused and turned her class ring on her finger. "I invited him to a game. He said yes."

That surprised her, because she didn't think Laura would want to have much to do with hockey after all that had happened. But since Jack had been traded, there was no reason for her to stay away. "I'll tell David, and the two of you can figure out which game works."

Laura nodded and leaned back into the soft leather. "Mom, is it weird that I like Dan?"

Kate had a feeling she knew where this was going, but assuming generally got her in trouble. If the past few months had taught her anything, it was that things weren't necessarily as they seemed. "Why weird?"

"Three weeks ago, I thought I was in love with Jack, but I really like spending time with Dan." Laura was still playing with her ring. "We had so much fun tonight. There were a bunch of people at the movies, and after we talked about school and college…" She paused. "Did I really love him?"

Kate smiled a little. "You're asking the woman who's engaged to a man she met less than six months ago?"

"It's a good question, though. How do you know you really love someone?"

"What you had with Jack may have lasted. I'm not going to dismiss how you felt about him, but you're both young and it got hot pretty fast. Was it mostly physical?"

Laura took a breath. "I didn't think so then, but now… it was the only thing he told his friends about me. That I was hot. And a virgin."

Damn. David had told her how the gossip about Laura and Jack's sex life had snowballed around the dressing room. One guy with a big mouth and a bad attitude got hold of it, and there was no way to contain it after that. "He definitely talked to the wrong people about you, honey, but I think you meant more to him than that."

"I guess. But was it love?"

Kate didn't know if she had a better answer. She and David had a very physical relationship, but there was so much more to it, and she was having a hard time putting it into words. After a minute, she formed a thought. A simple thought. "When you're in love, you don't regret."

"I regret a lot." Her voice was just above a whisper.

"If you'd been truthful with him about yourself, it may have developed differently."

"It wouldn't have developed at all."

"You're probably right." Jack trusted too many people with information about Laura, but Kate had no doubt that if he'd known her daughter's age, he never would have asked her out in the first place.

Laura nodded and rested her head on Kate's shoulder. "I like Dan."

"Good." Kate smiled, happy her daughter was learning about what it meant to be in an honest relationship.

"It's not good." The male voice snapped the quiet, and both Laura and Kate sprang to attention.

"Dad!"

Oh, my God. He wouldn't go away. No matter what she did, Richard wouldn't stop. It was eleven-thirty on a Friday night, and he walked into her house like he still lived there. "Richard, you need to leave."

He came closer and stuck his finger right in Kate's face. "I have heard enough out of you." As he said it he grabbed her arm and hauled her up. "What do you mean letting her date without my permission? And she's not going away to college, so cancel your fucking trip."

Kate remembered this feeling. The fear that went along with his outbursts. But he'd never done this in front of Laura. Never. "Richard, let go of me."

"Dad, please!"

"Shut up! Both of you shut up!" He let go of Kate's arm and made a tight circle around the room. "You stole her from me! She's all that mattered and you stole her."

"Richard, I..."

"SHUT UP!" He was irrational, and all Kate could think was that David was due home any minute, and then they would have a disaster. "I know what's best for her, not you and your boyfriend."

"Richard, calm down."

"Calm down? You're letting my daughter become a whore